Searching the edges of the leaves for some invisible book mark, Rabbi Loew opened the great book from left to right. It groaned and creaked as though complaining about this unaccustomed attention. Kelley saw that its vellum leaves were hand-lettered with Hebrew in black and red, with illuminated boxed capitals at the head of each page. Rabbi Loew turned several pages to reveal an illustration that occupied a full page.

"What a beautiful work," Dr. Dee murmured, leaning forward to examine it.

"Arabic," Loew said. "This book was made in Baghdad in the Ninth century of the Christian era by a secret Kabbalist sect."

Bright reds and greens leapt out from a background of gold leaf and a silvery material that appeared to Kelley's practiced alchemical eye to be some variety of fixed mercury. The illumination depicted the seated figure of a woman. The upper half of her body was humanoid; the lower half divided into two coiling serpent tails. It was highly stylized. Her hair showed an array of eleven vipers raised as though to strike. Her arms were curling arabesques that spiralled in opposite directions. Similar spirals defined her breasts.

"The degenerate sect of Hebrew Gnostics that made this book worshiped this creature as their supreme goddess," Rabbi Loew said.

"Lilith," Dee muttered in a quiet voice, as though fearful of invoking the spirit.

He bent over the image and studied its details with an expression of distaste. A miasma of ancient evil breathed from the vellum page. Suddenly Dee snatched his face back and stared at Loew. The Rabbi nodded.

"If you look at it for more than a few moments, it moves."

about the author

Donald Tyson is a Canadian from Halifax, Nova Scotia. Early in life, he was drawn to science by an intense fascination with astronomy, building a telescope by hand when he was eight. He began university seeking a science degree, but became disillusioned with the aridity and futility of a mechanistic view of the universe, and shifted his major to English. After graduating with honors, he has pursued a writing career.

He now devotes his life to the attainment of a complete gnosis of the art of magic in theory and practice. His purpose is to formulate an accessible system of personal training, composed of East and West, past and present, which will help the individual discover the reason for one's existence and a way to fulfill it.

to write to the author

If you would like to contact the author or would like more information about this book, please write to him in care of Llewellyn Worldwide. We cannot guarantee every letter will be answered, but all will be forwarded. Please write to:

Donald Tyson
c/o Llewellyn Worldwide
P.O. Box 64383, Dept. K743-9
St. Paul, MN 55164-0383 U.S.A.

Please enclose a self-addressed, stamped envelope for reply or $1.00 to cover costs. If outside the U.S.A., please enclose an international postal reply coupon.

An Occult Adventure

the

TORTUOUS

SERPENT

Donald Tyson

1997
Llewellyn Publications
St. Paul, MN 55164-0383
U.S.A.

Cover design: Tom Grewe
Book design & project management: Amy Rost
Editing & layout: Marguerite Krause
Additional editing: Jessica Thoreson, Darwin Holmstrom

FIRST EDITION
First Printing, 1997

Library of Congress Cataloging-in-Publication Data
Tyson, Donald, 1954–
   The tortuous serpent: an occult adventure/Donald Tyson. —1st ed.
      p. cm.
   ISBN 1-56718-743-9
      1. Dee, John, 1527–1608—Fiction. 2. Hermetic philosophers—England—Fiction. 3. Kelley, Edward, 1555–1595—Fiction. 4. Hermetic philosophers—Czech Republic—Fiction. 5. Occultism—Europe—History—16th century—Fiction.   I. Title.
   PR9199.3.T94T67   1997
   813'.54—dc21   97-16774
                                                                CIP

Llewellyn Publications
A division of Llewellyn Worldwide, Ltd.
P.O. Box 64383
St. Paul, MN 55164-0383
U.S.A.

OTHER BOOKS BY THE AUTHOR

The New Magus, 1988

Rune Magic, 1988

The Truth About Ritual Magic, 1989

The Truth About Runes, 1989

How to Make and Use a Magic Mirror,
Llewellyn, 1990; Phoenix Publishing, 1995

Ritual Magic, 1991

The Messenger (fiction), 1993

Tetragrammaton, 1995

New Millennium Magic, 1996

Scrying for Beginners, 1997

EDITOR AND ANNOTATOR

Three Books of Occult Philosophy,
Written by Cornelius Agrippa of Nettesheim, 1993

CARDS AND KITS

Rune Magic Deck, 1988

Power of the Runes Kit, 1989

FORTHCOMING

*Rune Dice Divination: Reading Fortunes, Doing Magic,
& Making Charms* and *Rune Dice* Kit

Enochian Magic for Beginners

WESTERN EUROPE

Circa 1587

------ Dee and Kelley's journey

In that day the Lord with his sore and great and strong sword shall punish Leviathan the Slant Serpent, and Leviathan the Tortuous Serpent; and he shall slay the Dragon that is in the sea.

Isaiah 27:1

Leviathan is the connection and coupling between the two who have the likeness of serpents. Therefore it is doubled: the Slant Serpent corresponding to Samael, and the Tortuous Serpent corresponding to Lilith.

Moses Cordovero,
Pardes Rimmonon

Lilith is called the Tortuous Serpent. She seduces men to go in tortuous ways.

The Bacharach

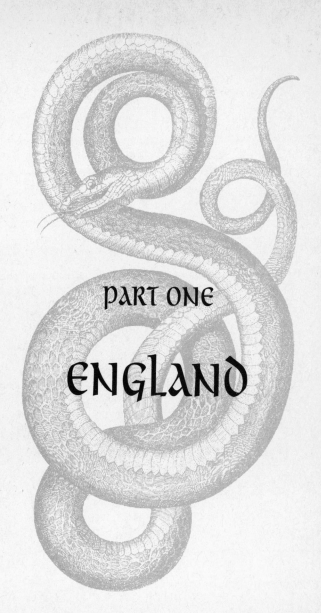

PART ONE

ENGLAND

ONE

The Watcher stirred and expanded itself in the rays of the setting sun. It was incapable of sleep, had never known dreams, but the tedium of long inaction lulled it into a dormant state.

It waited beneath a cleft oak, watching a great timber-frame country house across the meadow that had once served as its lawn. A stone's cast away, reeds nodded to the clucking of waterfowl in the sliding green of the river Thames. A rutted drive, muddy from the recent rains, wound from the door of the house up the gentle slope of the neglected lawn and entered beneath a grove of ancient elms. Down river, on the other side of a hay field, the spire of a small stone church and the wattle chimney tops of the village of Mortlake peeped above a ragged thorn hedge.

A dragonfly darted up from the wildflowers and skimmed past the oak. It stopped in midair and hovered for a moment, then fell to the grass inverted upon its iridescent wings. After several seconds, its legs ceased to twitch.

The steeple bell in the distant church tolled eight. The Watcher perceived and recorded the sound without emotion. Changes of time held no significance. Lacking a body to warm under the sun or shiver beneath the moon, one hour passed like any other, a day like a week, a month like a year. It noted and remembered these divisions of eternity, but they were meaningless apart from the context of its assigned purpose.

With quickening alertness it gathered its diaphanous body more tightly. Brown oak leaves that had fallen the previous autumn rustled uneasily in the tall grass. Several leaves lifted and began a pagan dance on the whirling air. A vortex of translucent shadow formed beside the divided trunk of the oak, its spinning funnel flecked with tiny black sparks that glittered in the slanting solar rays.

Murmured voices and the soft hoof-falls of several horses rippled the dreaming stillness. The sounds emanated out of the mouth of the shadowy woodland tunnel where the drive emerged from under the sheltering canopy of the elms. The black cone of sparks dimmed and faded, and the dried leaves borne up on its turning column of air lost their purpose and slowly drifted back to the lawn.

The Watcher observed the opening beneath the trees with infinite patience. A nameless will with a single function, it had been fully prepared to continue its vigil until the day of judgment, or beyond. As the horses were lit by the slanting golden rays of the dying sun, it extended its array of senses like the delicate strands of an invisible spider web to brush the faces of their riders one by one. Passionlessly, it recognized the well-ordered mind of the man it had been sent to spy upon.

The wait was ended.

TWO

Four weary horses emerged from the shadow of the elms and plodded two abreast along the ruts of the drive, their heads bowed. They had traveled thirty miles since daybreak over some of the worst roads in all of England. Even the appealing specter of hot oats at journey's end failed to perk up their ears.

Their riders were scarcely less tired. They sat hunched in their saddles beneath opened travel cloaks that were caked with a batter of dried mud, road dust, and tree sap.

The tall, slender man with ascetic features and a flowing silver beard who occupied one of the lead mounts was John Dee. A gap in his gray cloak revealed the somber black robe of a scholar. A matching skullcap adorned his head. He raised a pale hand and brushed impatiently at his cheek as though to drive away an insect, then glanced with a keen gray eye at the younger companion who rode beside him.

Edward Kelley stared moodily ahead, lost in his own dark reflections. So sun-browned was his skin that his powerful profile appeared cast from weathered bronze. A shock of jet black hair on his wide brow hung over intense slate blue eyes that darkened to obsidian when they narrowed, as they did now. Premature gray flecked his well-trimmed beard, which was cut short after the Spanish fashion around his square chin. Although he was only thirty-one, he appeared to be a man in his forties. He wore his burgundy cloak thrown back from his broad shoulders. The starched linen ruff at the collar of his black silk doublet bit into his sweating neck.

Behind the men, two ladies rode side-saddle with their cloaks wide against the afternoon heat, their ample skirts and petticoats a cascade of colorful silk and satin across the foam-streaked sides of their horses.

The woman following in the track of the scholar was slightly built, with sable hair, soft brown eyes and a pale complexion. She might have been Dee's daughter. In fact, she was his wife. Jane Dee was the same age as Kelley, a full twenty-eight years younger than her husband.

Her delicate features made a strong contrast with the freckled, turned-up nose and shoulder-length red hair of her companion. Although Kelley's wife, Joanna, was several years younger than Jane, her athletic body gave her a more commanding presence. When she smiled, she drew men like a lodestone. At present, however, she was frowning.

Jane Dee wiped the sweat from her eyebrows with the back of her leather riding glove, unaware that she left a smudge of dust across her forehead. She raised herself in her saddle and peered past her husband with anxious delight. One end of an imposing two-story house emerged from behind a screen of trees, its thatched roof orange in the rays of the setting sun.

"I never dreamed I could be so glad to see dear old Mortlake. It even smells like home."

John Dee turned in his saddle to smile back at his pretty wife.

"That's the mud of the river."

Jane marked his classical features with approval, as she had so often since their wedding day nine years ago. The silver wisps of hair that projected from under the edges of his black velvet skullcap lent him a distinguished aspect, she thought. Her husband was still a handsome man for all his nearly sixty years.

"Listen," she exclaimed with delight. "I can hear the frogs in the reeds."

They rode in silence. The faint peeping carried up from the river over the creak of the saddle leather.

"Damn the frogs," Joanna Kelley grumbled, breaking the spell. "I want to put up my feet and get a drink."

"The last thing you need is a drink." Edward Kelley twisted to scowl back at her. "You had too much wine last night at the inn."

With a defiant toss of her head Joanna sent her curls across her russet cloak in a flaming cascade. Her green eyes glared resentment.

Her husband could be intimidating. A brute of a man with the shoulders of an ox, his blazing temper had caused many another man to regret his hasty words. She had learned early in their relationship that she must never show fear or he would bully her unmercifully. Seldom cruel, and on occasion generous to a fault, he despised weakness.

That was why he held John Dee in such high regard, she reflected. Dee feared nothing but God and the Queen. And everyone feared the Queen.

"If I want a drink, I'll drink," she told Kelley, meeting his smoldering gaze without flinching. "My head hurts and I've got blisters on my bum."

"Wine won't help your bum. As for your head, why do you think it aches? You drink too much."

Joanna held her retort when Dee raised his hand and reined his mount to a halt. The other three followed his example. Dee pointed to the front of the house, which had just come into view as they followed the bend of the drive. Kelley cursed softly under his breath. Jane's brown eyes widened in horror.

Thick pieces of glass from one of the diamond-paned windows on the lower level lay strewn over the open gravel court, twisted bits of leading still attached to their edges. A blackened, sodden pile of books, manuscripts, and scientific instruments rose in a haphazard heap beneath the sill. Scorch marks stained the exposed oak beams and whitewashed mortar panels around the window. From a distance it bore an uncanny resemblance to a black eye set in the immaculate whitewashed facade of the house. Various broken pieces of furniture and household articles lay scattered on the court and across the overgrown lawn.

Kelley and Dee glanced at each other. Understanding passed between them.

"I'll have a look around," Kelley said.

He drew his rapier. Holding the sword with its point up in his right hand, he approached the house and rode slowly around its near end toward the stable in back.

The others crossed the lawn and stopped just short of the brick-bordered rectangle of colored river gravel lest the steel shoes of the horses make a noise on the stones. Joanna Kelley began to dismount, but Dee restrained her with a gesture. They waited tensely until Kelley reappeared on the far side of the house. Kelley sheathed his sword.

"No one in back. The door's still bolted."

Dee dismounted and left his dappled gray mare to tend to itself. It began to crop the tall grass of the lawn contentedly, oblivious to the tension of its master. Dee approached his own front door with caution.

"Collie! Ruth! Is anyone in the house?"

He reached up and rang the brass bell that hung from one of the beams of the overhanging second level. Its clear notes carried mournfully across the river in the gathering twilight. For several moments the frogs fell silent, then resumed their peeping. Dee tried the iron latch. The door opened easily inward. He saw that the heavy side jamb had been splintered by some battering force, and noticed that the surface of the door itself had several deep dents near the latch. On the slates of the hall beyond lay a heavy squared oak beam.

He entered cautiously. After several moments the women dismounted and followed.

Kelley paused in the open doorway and scanned the willows and alders lining the riverbank. His narrowed gaze settled on the cleft trunk of the oak that stood by itself on the lawn, a gnarled sentinel guarding secrets. He stared at it with fixed intensity, watching the last of the solar gilding melt upward from the spring green leaves at its crown.

There was nothing to see—nothing except a shadow that lay close against the base of its massive trunk. With a feeling of unease that tingled the hairs on the back of his neck, he turned into the house and made his was toward the kitchen.

"Why?" Jane Dee asked. "Why would anyone do this?"

She wiped a tear from her dusty cheek and entered the library, where Dee stood surveying the destruction. His features betrayed no emotion. Jane, who understood her husband's moods and knew how much his books meant to him, shivered in sympathetic response to his pain. The blow could not have been greater had he been confronted with the corpse of his eldest son, Arthur, presently safe at boarding school.

The vandals had systematically pulled the manuscripts and the printed books from the shelves that lined the walls of the long low room and torn them to fragments. Not more than one in ten remained in its place. Others lay scattered over the round study table and the writing desk, or heaped upon the floor amid the wreak of Dee's many irreplaceable scientific instruments.

Dee picked up the crushed brass sphere of his terrestrial globe and spent several futile seconds trying to work the mechanism. The central pivot snapped, and the instrument fell to pieces in his hands. It had been fashioned by the great Mercator himself, using the latest maps of the New World and the Japans, which Dee had smuggled to him from agents in Spain, Portugal, and the Low Countries. There was some consolation in the fact that the sea captain Drake had paid to have a copy made, a good copy, though not so good as the original.

"I don't mind the loss of the money," he said, putting his arm around the slender shoulders of his wife. "Even though, God knows, these books cost me the better part of my fortune over the greater span of my life. The tragedy is that some of the manuscripts have never been copied. They can't ever be replaced, Jane, not till the end of time."

"But who would do this, John? To us, who have never hurt a living soul, and have lived as good Christians?"

"The villagers, who else," Joanna Kelley said.

She entered the library carrying in her arms a gray silk gown worked with seed pearls and silver thread. It was rent with long, ragged slashes.

"My best court dress," Jane Dee cried, fingering the ripped fabric in disbelief.

"They didn't even bother to steal it," Joanna told Dee in a dark voice. "That's how much they hate us."

Wailing protests drew their attention to the door of the library. Kelley rounded the edge towing a short, portly man by the back collar of his soiled wool shirt. An equally filthy set of hose covered his bowed legs. The toes of his left foot peeked through one of the larger rents in the stocking. The little man blinked like an owl and tried to writhe away.

"Make him let go, Master Dee, he's hurting my neck. It ain't my fault what happened. I've always been loyal to you."

Dee motioned for Kelley to release him. The red-faced man glared hatred at Kelley.

"Collie, tell us what went on here," Dee said. "Is your wife safe and well?"

"Safe?" Kelley laughed in disbelief. "She's in the kitchen, snoring on the floor beside the dog. She's so drunk, I couldn't wake her up."

Dee scowled at his servant, feeling his patience slipping away.

"Is this true?"

"Well, sir, she may have had a bit with her evening meal. It's only natural, after the shock and all, ain't it? It don't do no harm. She'll be right as rain come morning."

Dee sighed and slowly counted to ten in Greek.

"Just tell us what happened, Collie."

The little man scratched his balding, sunburned scalp and rolled his eyes around the floor, avoiding Dee's gaze.

"I don't rightly know how to explain it, sir. About three days gone by, or was it nearer four days, I don't just recall at the present, this great gang of housebreakers comes in the middle of the night hooting and hollering to wake the sheeted dead. They starts throwing stones and pounding on the doors. Wanted me to let them in. But I said no, sir, since I knowed they was up to no good. But they broke down the door anyways, sir, and come right in. I tried to fight them but there was too many for me. They said they'd burn me with their lit torches. I tried to stop them, Master Dee, truly I tried, but they said they'd kill me if I got in their way, so what could I do? I ask you now, Mistress, what could I do with only myself and my poor wife and one toothless old hound?"

Jane Dee shook her head mutely.

"They was like a pack of wild dogs. They run in here and threw everything out the window. Then they set it on fire. If the rains hadn't come down hard that night the whole house would've burnt to the ground. I couldn't get near to put out the fire. They wouldn't let me."

"You say this was done three days ago?" Dee asked.

"Near enough."

"Then why hasn't the mess been cleaned up?"

Collie opened wide his bloodshot eyes.

"I thought you'd have wanted to see what they did, so you can report it to the Queen. That's the only reason my wife left it this way. I told her you'd have wanted to see it."

"Is that why you both got so drunk you couldn't stand up?" Kelley demanded harshly. "Never mind, don't try to answer. And don't breathe on me, you lout, you smell like a stew."

"Did you see the men who did this?" Dee demanded.

Collie hesitated, then slowly shook his head, sliding his rheumy eyes from side to side.

"It was too dark, sir. Blackest night that ever was. I couldn't see my own hand in front of my face that night."

Dee looked at Kelley, who shook his head slightly. Dee sighed.

"You say you left the house in this wreck for me to see? Very well, I've seen it. Now I want you to clean it up. Find some boards and have this window closed over until

I can hire a glazier to put it right. And get Tom Hobbs and his apprentice to fix the front door."

He held up a hand as Collie started forward.

"No, not now. We're all tired from our journey and need sleep. You can start tomorrow. Right now I want you to unload our travel boxes and bring them into the hall. Then see to our horses. But first, wake up Ruth and get her sober. My wife needs hot water for her bath."

"I'll go," Jane said quietly. "You see to the horses, Collie."

"Thank you, Mistress," he said, touching an invisible forelock.

"I'll help," Joanna Kelley said to Jane. "But if I know Ruth, we'll end up drawing our own water."

The women left for the kitchen. Collie started to bow his way out of the library, then stopped and hit himself on the top of the head with the flat of his hand. He reached into his shirt for a flat leather pouch that hung on a greasy thong around his neck and drew out two folded papers with wax seals.

"These come for you while you was away in Wales, sir. I almost forgot to give them to you, what with your coming home being such a surprise, like."

Dee took the letters and waited for Collie to bow his way out of the library. Then he examined the seals.

"This is from the Queen," he murmured to Kelley as he thumbed the wax in two and unfolded the sheet. He scanned over the familiar sweeping handwriting of Elizabeth.

"She wants me to visit her at Hampton Court at once. She doesn't say why."

Kelley swept a pile of torn manuscripts from the corner of the desk and sat down. He unpinned the silver chain that held his cloak around his neck and let the cloak fall behind him.

"More of her damned political intrigues, most likely. Why does she always involve you in her petty schemes? You'd think you were the only spy in England."

"I'm the only one she knows she can trust," Dee said.

He turned the second letter over with curiosity. The seal, a dark brown wax that was almost black, was not familiar. Impressed in it were three Hebrew letters. He recognized the holy name of Shaddai, the Almighty. Breaking it, he spread out the crackling parchment. His murmur of surprise caused Kelley, who was in the process of pulling off his boots, to look up.

"It's from my old friend Rabbi Loew at Prague."

"The Kabbalist? What does he want with us?"

"Give me a moment—the letter's in cipher."

Dee studied the Hebrew characters silently, a frown of concentration deepening on his pale brow. Loew had used a simple substitution code based upon the Tziruph permutations of the Kabbalah. After puzzling it out, he translated the text of the letter aloud for Kelley.

> To my good friend and honored companion on the path of Truth, John Dee, Doctor of Philosophy at Mortlake, in England, Rabbi Judah Loew ben Bezalel sends greetings.
>
> My friend, I pray that this letter may reach your hand in time to prevent a calamitous event that will have grave consequences for all the nations of the world.
>
> When last you were a visitor at my humble house here in the ghetto of Prague, you will recall that we had occasion to speak of many arcane and secret matters that lie hidden (and should continue to lie hid) from the eyes and notice of common men. In the

course of our talks, which continued until the first rosy glow of morning on several nights, as I remember, I had occasion to show to you a certain book in the Latin tongue (you know the book I mean) that so greatly excited your wonder and interest that at last I was moved by my great love for you, as a fellow seeker after knowledge, to grant it into your hands with the stern injunction that you reveal its existence and show it to no one.

This condition you agreed to most readily. And I am sure (you being a true man, and not a deceiver) that you have honored your word, even though you may not fully have comprehended the reason for this stricture.

My friend, had I known then what since times I have come to learn about that accursed volume, I would rather have cut off my right hand than to have passed it into yours. You know it is an evil book, full of blasphemy and lies and wickedness culled from the primal stirrings of the first sparks and preserved amid the husks and shadows of Assiah. How evil it is, mercifully you do not know, and by the grace of the Lord (blessed be He) you will never learn.

It is enough to say that this book, not by its words but by certain impositions in the very form and pattern of its words, can be made by curious, hellish, and bestial ritual observances to serve as a key to unlock the nether gates of the kingdom of Gehenna. I learned (never mind how the knowledge came to my attention—you know my methods, and they are not to be written down even in a coded letter lest

*they fall into the hands of the enemy, I mean the
Inquisition) of the plan to steal this evil book away
from your possession and use it to open the very
mouths of hell.*

*Those who plan this blasphemous act, so horrible
that my hand trembles as I contemplate it, are those
you have heard whispers about in dark places and
other realms than this material world—they who
call themselves the Sons of Coronzon (which, as you
know, is the true name of that Old Dragon, the
Devil). You need no warnings from me to guard
your back, and your doors, and especially your
dreams, from this dreadful band of blasphemers.
Your own circle of Hermes has pledged itself to their
utter annihilation.*

*Therefore I urge you, my dear friend, to take that
book which I gave into your hands in a moment of
affection with so little thought of the consequences,
and wholly consume it with fire amid all necessary
safeguards and ritual observances of our ancient
art. Do this immediately lest it perchance may find
its way into the service of the Enemy of all
humankind. Believe me when I tell you that the
danger is very great, and comes sooner than later.
May the Lord (blessed by He) bless you and keep you.*

*Written this fourteenth day of May at my house in
the ghetto of Prague, the year of your era one thousand, five hundred and eighty-seven.*

Dee folded the letter and looked around for a place to
set it, then reflectively slid it into the pocket of his
scholar's gown under his cloak.

"What book is the old Jew talking about?" Kelley demanded. "Do I know this book?"

Silently Dee went to the great round reading table and began to remove with care the heaps of documents and torn parchments and fragments of books. After a moment, Kelley moved to help him. When the table was clear, he took from his purse a small iron key and inserted it into a slot in the exact center of the tabletop. A portion of the rich inlaid rosewood lifted to reveal a secret cavity. Dee leaned over to peer within it. The light from the windows was failing fast and the hiding place was full of shadows. He reached in and felt around, then drew out his hand with disappointment.

"As I feared. Empty."

"The book was in the table?"

"I kept my word to Judah," Dee said. "You never saw the book, nor so far as I know did anyone else."

"What was the title of the work?" Kelley asked curiously. If he felt resentment that his friend had kept it secret from him, his dark eyes betrayed no sign.

Dee glanced at the windows, as though afraid the very gathering gloom in the air might have ears.

"It was called in Latin *Liber Lilith*, which in our common tongue is the Book of Lilith."

"Lilith," Kelley repeated softly. "I know this name. She's a night hag of the Jews who strangles babies and pollutes men in their dreams."

"That, and more," Dee agreed. "The Kabbalists such as my friend Judah believe she is the consort of Samael, who is the same as he who is called in the angelic tongue Coronzon. She is queen of Gehenna and presides over all filthy lusts and cancerous growths that flourish unchecked. She is the mother of all demons that work mischief throughout the world."

"I know you for a pious man," Kelley said wonderingly, studying Dee's pale, ascetic features. "What use have you for a book of hellish and unlawful lust? Is everything well with you and Jane in the marriage bed?"

Dee could not prevent a thin smile from stealing onto his lips.

"The day a beautiful young woman like my Jane fails to excite desire in this old frame is the day I wish to enter the grave."

"Why, then? If you've suddenly developed an interest in necromantic arts, you see your teacher standing here before you."

"The Book of Lilith concerns the power of generations by the moon upon the earth, and the making of all things fecund," Dee explained. "I had a notion to use it to increase the fertility of fields and magnify the engenderings of calves and lambs. We've been so occupied with our spirit scryings and the reception of the Enochian magic, and of late with this crack-brained excursion into Wales to look for the tomb of St. Dunstan that you were so keen upon, that I haven't had time to make any trial of the matter."

Kelley gathered in his cloak and draped it over his arm, then pinched up his riding boots between his thumb and finger.

"Do you think this generative art could remove barrenness from the womb of a woman?"

"That is one possible use, though it would be dangerous. Why do you ask?"

"No reason."

Kelley bent over the round table and felt the mouth of the keyhole for scratches.

"This was opened by a man who steals for a living. But how did he know you had the book hidden here?"

Dee shook his head.

"There is no way he could have known. I told no one that I even owned the book. Unless I was spied upon taking it from its place."

"Who would have the leisure to watch your movements with such closeness?" Kelley wondered. "Unless...."

"Collie?" Dee laughed. "Collie doesn't have enough wit to spy on his own wife. Jane tells me that Ruth's been secretly visiting the barn of a farmer across the meadow."

"He knows something he's not telling, of that I'm certain. He said he couldn't recognize the men who broke into the house, but if they were carrying lit torches it would have been as bright as day in here. He couldn't have failed to recognize some of them if they were men from these parts."

"I know," Dee agreed. "He's afraid they'll beat him if he says anything."

"I think I'll have a little talk with Collie," Kelley said. "Perhaps I can jog his memory."

"Don't injure him," Dee muttered absently, sorting through some of the papers on his desk. "Who else could I get to keep this house for us while we're away?"

Kelley grunted noncommittally.

"What are you going to do about the book?" he asked Dee.

"Tonight, nothing. I'm tired and Jane and Joanna are completely exhausted. I mean to take advantage of Jane's bath water before it gets cold. Then I mean to go to sleep in my own bed, a rare luxury in these troubled times. Tomorrow I suppose we must set off down river to Hampton Court. The Queen hates to be kept waiting. If the book has been stolen by a professional thief, I suspect it's far away by this time, maybe even out of England altogether. I don't see how we can trace it."

"Leave that to me," Kelley said. "I'll sniff around and see what trail I can pick up. There aren't many secrets in a small place like Mortlake."

THREE

The door of the ale house banged open. Coarse male laughter spilled out on amber candlelight. Three laborers in rough work clothes staggered through the bright rectangle, supporting each other by the shoulders. They turned in awkward unison, and one of them kicked the door shut. Moonlight painted the edges of their bodies with silver while they lurched and joked together in drunken voices.

One of the workmen separated from his companions and began to stagger along the road that led out of the village, heedless of the barking dogs that marked his passing of each dark cottage. A big man with a belly that protruded over the girdle of his kersey trunk breeches like a sack of flour, he sang to himself in a low tone, his head bent to peer at the rutted track. Every dozen steps he wandered into the shallow ditch that ran beside the road and had to pick himself out and orient himself by the moon.

In this way he progressed about a mile to a stretch of the road that entered under a dense stand of over-reaching trees. Pausing to lick his fat lips, he squinted at the shadows under the trees doubtfully, then took a breath and started forward, singing louder than before.

Under the trees it was as black as a cave. He felt for the ruts of the road with his feet to avoid wandering into the undergrowth on either side. From time to time the canopy of leaves parted to let a ray of moonlight spot the ground like a silver coin.

The workman stopped singing abruptly and stood with his head cocked, holding his breath. From the trees came the sound of a cracking branch, and a low rustling noise.

"Who's there?" the man demanded in a harsh, slurred voice.

A black silhouette only slightly darker than the shadowed mass of foliage behind it moved into the middle of the road a few paces in front of the laborer and barred his path.

"What the devil d'you want?" The drunken man laughed, emboldened by the false courage of the ale. "If you've come to rob me, you're too late. I spent all my brass at Mother Hanna's."

He waited, swaying doubtfully, but the other man made no reply.

"Devil take you," he roared. "I'm going home. Get out of my way."

He lurched forward. With a suddenness that would have bewildered a sober man, he felt himself swept off the road and slammed back against the trunk of a tree. A ray of moonlight fell upon the face of the man who held him pinioned against the rough bark. The eyes of the drunkard widened with recognition.

"I know you. You're Kelley. You work for the witch that lives in the big manor house down on the river."

"And you're Bill Gowdie, one of the drunken louts who looted and burned John Dee's library three days ago," Kelley said, smiling in a way that would have made a sober man shiver with apprehension. "Why did you do that, Bill? Would you like to tell me?"

"Let me go, damn you," Gowdie said, struggling to twist away from Kelley's iron grasp. "Don't...know... what you're talking about!"

Kelley released the laborer's right shoulder long enough to slap him on the side of the head over the ear. Gowdie tried to drive his knee into Kelley's groin, but Kelley was too old a tavern brawler for that trick. He caught the knee on the outside of his massive thigh and butted the drunken man on the bridge of the nose with his forehead. The cartilage of Gowdie's nose made an audible pop as it broke. He began to howl like a whipped dog.

"I don't like drunks, Bill," Kelley said in a low voice. "My father was an ale sot. He used to swill every night and beat my mother with a barrel stave. Every night, until I was fourteen and strong enough to break it over his head. Drunks disgust me, Bill."

"What do you want with me?" Gowdie asked in a whine. "I never done nothing to you. Let me go, Kelley, I don't want no trouble with you."

"Let's have it, Bill. Who put you lads up to it? I know your bunch. You haven't got enough guts amongst the lot of you to have done it on your own. Who paid you?"

"It was Collie put you onto me, wasn't it?" Gowdie said, cursing and spitting blood. "I'll kill that little weasel next time I see him."

Kelley smiled in recollection.

"Collie was only too glad to help identify the mob that broke into his master's house. He told me all your names, Bill. All of them. So if you don't want me to tell my master Dee, who is a close friend of the Queen herself, who you all were, I suggest you tell me what I want to know."

Gowdie's grizzled, blood-stained face sagged. A look of pure terror distorted his eyes.

"Mother of God, don't do that, Kelley, don't do that. The Queen will hang the lot of us."

"I'll think about it, if you promise to stay away from John Dee's house in future, and if you tell me the name of the man who paid you to break in."

Gowdie looked from side to side and licked his lips. Kelley silently tightened his fingers in the loose layer of fat on the man's shoulders.

"It was this Londoner, see?" Gowdie whispered hoarsely. "He come into Mother Hanna's one night when me and the lads was pretty far gone and says he got a silver piece for every man who'll help him burn the Devil's books. We didn't know he meant Dee until he led us up to the house. Anyway, none of us saw the harm in it." He scowled belligerently. "Everyone knows old Dee is a witch. He should've been hung long ago, if you ask me, and would've been except he's got some cursed spell over the Queen."

Kelley slapped him in the head, this time on the other ear.

"I didn't ask you. What was this Londoner doing while you and your friends were looting Dee's private possessions?"

A look of confusion stole like a shadow over the features of the drunken man.

"Doing? I don't know. Same as us, I suppose. I lost sight of him when we started to burn the books."

"You didn't see him carry anything out of the house?"

"No. What should I have seen?"

"Never mind. What was the name of this Londoner?"

"He never said, but...."

"What?"

"One of the men in the ale house recognized him. Said he saw him a month ago at the Rose Theater in Bankside on the stage acting in a play." Gowdie smirked and sniggered in spite of his fear. "He was dressed up like a women named Dido, who was Queen of a place called Carthage."

Kelley regarded the unlovely face of Gowdie with surprise.

"He's an actor?"

"I just said that, didn't I?"

"What's his name?"

"I can't remember."

Kelley shook him so that the back of his head bounced repeatedly off trunk of the tree.

"It was Beecher, I remember now, it was Beecher," Gowdie howled.

Kelley stopped shaking him and considered whether he could extract any more useful information. He decided it was unlikely. This Beecher had obviously used the village men as his dupes, hoping to mask the theft of the book with the destruction of Dee's whole library. Sensing Kelley's change of mood, Gowdie struggled wildly to escape.

"Let me go now, Kelley. You play straight with me and we'll never trouble Dee's house again, I swear it."

With an exclamation of disgust Kelley released him and stepped back. Gowdie swayed and wiped the blood from his swollen nose on his sleeve. Cautiously, he inched his way around Kelley and stumbled down the road. After a few minutes Kelley heard his curses.

"We'll get you for this, Kelley, mark my words," he called from the anonymity of the dark. "We know what you are, you and that witch friend of yours. We don't want your kind in Mortlake. You'll clear out if you know what's good for you. Just clear out."

Kelley barely heard the threats. They diminished with the growing distance as Gowdie put as much space as possible between himself and his attacker. At last there was silence in the wood once more. A mosquito landed on Kelley's neck. After half a minute, he swatted it absently and rolled its blood-swollen body between his fingers.

The trail of the book was cold, but not yet dead. Not as long has he had a name and a place in London where he could pick it up again. Once he had the book, he had no intention of giving it to Dee to destroy. He would use it to make Joanna's womb fruitful so that they could have the child she so desperately wanted. When she was pregnant she would stop drinking. She only did it because she knew how much he hated it, because she felt herself less than a whole woman and resented him because he knew she was barren.

After that, he would let Dee do whatever he liked with the accursed book. But not before.

fOUR

Dee marveled at the pliant strength of his beautiful wife as she moved beneath him in counterpoint to his lovemaking. Although her white thighs were soft as the sheerest silk, they gripped him with a vise-like clasp. He reminded himself that she was only thirty-one years old, still little more than a child from his point of view. Hers was the vitality of youth.

Afterward, they lay side by side in the dark security of their canopy bed, the heavy embroidered curtains creating a private place that was theirs alone. He felt Jane's hip slide across the feather mattress to touch his thigh. Reaching under the covers for her delicate hand, he took it into his own and held it. Even after bearing him four children, her body was still as graceful and as perfect as a Chinese porcelain. Not for the first time, he uttered a silent prayer of thanks for this supreme blessing of his life.

"I thought you would be too tired to make love," he murmured softly.

She giggled.

"Never. Making love with you always renews my vital humors. I feel like getting out of bed and dancing in the moonlight."

"You'll be able to dance your fill at court. You know how the Queen loves to try out the latest French steps."

"Do you think she'll make you throw her into the air and catch her, as she did the last time?"

Dee shuddered.

"Jesu, I hope not. I was terrified I might drop her. As it turned out, I strained my back and couldn't walk for a week."

"I remember," Jane said, laughing. "The Queen was so concerned about your health, she asked after you every day you were in bed."

"I'm not a young man anymore, Jane," he said, releasing her hand to pat the gentle dome of her stomach. "Soon I won't be any use to you."

"For the wisest man in England, you can say foolish things at times," she said in mock anger. She swatted his flaccid penis through his nightshirt. "Do you think I married you for this? I can get one of these anywhere. No, John my dearest love, I married you for this, and this." She touched his head and his heart. "These are riches not to be found in any marketplace, as I know full well and so should you. You've made me a very wealthy woman."

He kissed her tenderly on the lips.

"What in heaven am I going to wear at Hampton Court?" Jane murmured. "They cut my best dress to shreds."

"Surely you have others? I seem to remember taking you to a dressmaker in Brussels only three, or was it four, years ago."

"It was five years ago, and yes, I do have others that are no longer in fashion. They left the old ones alone, the devils. I can probably fit into one of them if I'm laced up tight."

"Jane," he said in mock protest, "Don't tell me you're getting fat?"

"No, not fat." She hesitated. "Just broadening, my love. I'm not a girl anymore."

"You're a child," Dee said, voicing his thought aloud. "And the most beautiful woman in England. It doesn't matter what you wear, it will look beautiful on you."

She shifted restlessly and lay silent for a while. Dee thought she had drifted into sleep, and prepared himself to follow her.

"I still don't understand why, John," she said in puzzlement.

"What? What's that?" Dee forced his mind awake.

"Why do the villagers hate us? You've never hurt a single soul in all your life, and I try to be friendly to everyone at church and on market day."

"There's no understanding evil, Jane. That's part of its nature. If men stopped to think before they did a wicked deed, all the evil would go out of the world. The trouble is, they don't think. Those men who broke into the house didn't know what they were doing or why, they just acted on their baser impulses. They were probably all drunk. Although I do have reason to suspect that there may be more behind the housebreaking than just too much ale."

He summarized the contents of Rabbi Loew's letter, and told her how the book had been removed from its hiding place without damage to the lock.

"The book is almost certainly out of England by now. Had we returned from Wales two days ago, we might have had a chance to trace its whereabouts. I fear I did a foolish thing in taking it from under the wings of Judah's guardian angels. While it was in Prague it was invisible."

"Is it really so dangerous, my love?"

"I don't know," Dee said in a worried tone. "I never found time to make a study of it. Now it's too late. But I doubt if Judah would have written except on a matter of grave concern."

"Why don't you ask Madimi if her Mother knows where the book has gone?"

"I will do so, of course, when Edward and I have an opportunity to erect the table and scry into the stone, but I suspect that whoever took the book has placed it under the same sort of veil that concealed it in Prague. Had I know the book's importance, I would have taken the same measures myself."

He waited for her response. When it failed to come, he realized that she had drifted into sleep at last. Releasing her hand gently, he turned on his side away from her and allowed the flood of worried thoughts he had held off since arriving at Mortlake to fill his mind.

Why did the Queen wish to consult with him? It was surely no small matter. These were dangerous times. Spain was building a great fleet of ships in the port of Cadiz. Rumor said that King Philip planned to use it to launch an invasion of England. Drake and a small fleet of English raiders had managed to set fire to part of the armada and had delayed its completion, but with the vast wealth Spain was raping from the body of the New World behind the project, it was impossible to stop it altogether.

Should he persecute the men who had destroyed his library, or let the matter rest? They deserved to be hung. There was no greater crime than the killing of a book. But a serious attempt to convict the vandals would only stir up more hatred against him. The fools thought he was a witch and a devil worshipper and heaven alone knew what else. He had tried to explain to some of them that he only sought to understand the secrets of nature. It was hopeless. They saw a geometrical drawing and thought it was a seal of black magic. Fools! In their eyes, Greek and Hebrew were Satanic. Anything they didn't understand— which was most of everything, he reflected sourly—they tried to destroy.

And what about *Liber Lilith*? He did not see what he could do, now that the horse was out of the barn, but it galled him to do nothing. In large measure he was responsible due to his carelessness. Dolt! He should have taken greater precautions. Once he determined the business of the Queen, he must write to Judah and ask for more details. He was not completely lacking in resources. The Enochian angels were a potent hierarchy, perhaps even equal to the demons of Coronzon.

Eventually the thoughts swirling in Dee's mind grew less clamorous, and he sank into the soft embrace of sleep. He dreamed that he stood in a small, sunlit meadow that was very like his own front lawn. From behind the bent trunk of a massive oak a little girl nine or ten years of age with long golden hair came skipping and singing toward him. She wore a green dress lined with scarlet and carried a wicker basket of wildflowers. When she saw him, her face broke into a radiant smile.

"Madimi?" Dee said. "Are you Madimi the spirit that my seer Edward Kelley has so often described to me in the crystal showstone?"

"I am, sir. Are you well this morning?"

"Well enough. But I seem to remember that it was night and I lay down in my bed at Mortlake. Is this a dream?"

"It is, sir. My Mother made it. Isn't it pretty? She asked me to give a message to you in response to your question."

"But I asked no question of your Mother, although it was in my mind to do so."

Madimi smiled and began to pick at the petals of a white daisy.

"You forget that time is not for us as it is for you. You asked for information about a book. Whether sooner or later, what matter is this?"

Dee knelt before the figure of the little girl, marveling at her beauty. She reminded him of his own six-year-old daughter, Katherine, who had been left with her two younger brothers at the house of a relative in Wales for schooling. Kate's hair was dark while Madimi's was like spun gold thread, but they both possessed the same air of innocent expectation.

Madimi frowned and rolled her blue eyes heavenward in her effort to remember her message.

"My Mother says to tell you that the book has not yet left England. She says it is somewhere in London."

"Where in London, Madimi? London is a very big place."

Madimi seemed to listen to a voice heard in the distance, but only the hum of bees and the chirps of birds came to Dee's ears.

"She says it has a glamour on it and she can't see it exactly."

"But it is still in England? She is sure of this?"

"She says to tell you that the glamour cannot hold over water, and that were the book to pass from this island by sea, she would learn of it."

"What does she know about the use of the book, Madimi? Can she tell me where its danger lies? How do I fight the forces of Coronzon?"

As Dee uttered the name of the Fallen One, the sky darkened in a moment and a cold wind sprang up. Madimi said something, but the wind and the rustle of the overhanging leaves in the oak concealed her words. Dee called for her to come closer. She shook her head fearfully and dropped her basket of flowers to cover her ears. A whirlwind, made visible by the dead leaves and flower petals it picked up from the grass, swirled around her and lifted the hem of her dress. He stood and reached forward to help her, but when his hand passed into the whirlwind, a bright flash blinded him and fire ran up his arm and through his shoulder to his heart.

Dee woke with a jump, his face covered with a fine mist of sweat. He gasped and drew a shuddering breath into his lungs. It was still night. Jane lay sleeping peacefully at his side. Slowly, he forced his knotted muscles to relax and took several deep breaths. It had been a nightmare, nothing more. The weight of cares on his overtaxed mind had raised bilious humors into his head.

Reaching over to the embroidered bed curtain, he drew the corner aside and peered into the darkness beyond. The moon had set. He could see nothing, and felt a trifle foolish even for troubling to look. No, wait, there was something. A grayness floated upon the air, just barely distinguishable against the deeper gray of the background. What was it? He watched it bob up and down several times as though supported on a thread.

Growing curiosity dispelled sleep. Dee held the curtain aside and slid gently out of bed so as not to disturb Jane. The night draft chilled his flanks beneath the hem of his long linen shirt. He felt the cool floorboards against his bare feet as he took several cautious steps forward in the gloom and reached out his hand. Something brushed past his fingers. He snatched them back as though burned, even though they had suffered no hurt. The gray patch fell out of the air with a soft, fluttering sound.

Fully alert, Dee felt his way to the table and struck a light with flint and tinder by touch. The quickening candle flame revealed his empty bedroom. It seemed unremarkable in every respect, until Dee noticed a curious moving shadow in front of the window. It swirled and turned like a living pillar of black sparks, almost completely invisible against the dark glass. Fascinated, Dee took a step forward and held the candle up to get a better look. The shadow contracted quickly into a turning sphere and seemed to melt through the diamond panes.

Dee opened the latch on the casement with care so as to make no sound and swung the window wide. The night air blew cool against his face and refreshed him. He could see nothing outside except the stars, and the dim outline where their bright glittering points were interrupted by the trees on the horizon. He closed the window and made his way back toward the bed.

Something rustled under his bare foot. He bent and picked it up. By the candle flame he made out a broken seal of brown wax with Hebrew letters impressed upon it. Rabbi Loew's letter.

A chill premonition of approaching menace closed its bony fingers around Dee's heart. With utter conviction he sensed that the theft of the book had irrevocably ceased to be an incident in his past which he could, if he chose, put out of his mind. Tonight's airy visitor had borne it forward into his future. It waited for him in the murk of things to come at some dim crossroad of his life with claws unsheathed and teeth barred, and he had no choice but to walk under its looming shadow.

fIVE

The Italian wrinkled his long nose in disgust as he climbed the narrow stairs to his third floor tenement flat. The atmosphere hung heavy with effluvium from the Thames. It mingled with the stench of raw sewage and rotten vegetables and lingering chimney smoke from greasy cooking fires. The only relief came after a heavy rain—an all too common experience in this foul climate.

London was without doubt the filthiest city in Europe. Unlike towns on the Continent that had grown at a steady, predictable rate and upgraded their municipal services to keep pace, London had expanded like a tumor during the early reign of Elizabeth, overwhelming the modest provisions for water and sewage disposal that had existed in Henry VIII's time.

A plague was inevitable, the Italian thought with a sour smile. As far as he was concerned, it couldn't come soon enough.

He stopped and pressed his back against the rough planks of the wall to allow a fat woman in a white apron and peaked white cap to squeeze past. She carried a copper pot in her burly arms filled with some noxious green liquid that the Italian supposed must be pea soup. He suppressed a shudder.

With extravagant and insincere civility, he doffed his plain blue hat and bowed in greeting. He felt her magpie gaze flick from the gleaming crown of his bald head to his unfashionable naked chin, his scuffed shoes, loose kersey hose, and cheap blue cloak. He had deliberately adopted a mode of dress that would not attract envy. Conscious of the sumptuary laws that prohibited commoners from adorning themselves with silks or gold, he wore no jewelry.

As he lifted his head, he trapped her darting brown berry eyes in his emotionless gaze. His own eyes were so pale a blue that they appeared frosty white in the glow of the hall candle.

"Evening to ye, Master Doppelman," she puffed. "You're about late, ain't ye?"

He smiled at the sound of his absurd pseudonym, as he always did. These English were so stupid.

"Evening, Madam Brodie. I might easily say the same about you."

She nodded up the stair.

"Old Granny Clarke's got the consumption something fierce. Lord knows what'd happen to her without me to look out for her health. I took her up a little soup to build her strength, poor thing."

"You are a charitable woman. As for myself, I was out sketching London Bridge by moonlight."

He opened his folding portable easel and showed her his charcoal drawing of the bridge. She glanced at it indifferently and gave him a lewd wink from the corner of her eye.

"I bet that ain't all ye was lookin' at by moonlight," she said with a dirty laugh.

Repressing the strong urge to throw this repulsive woman down the stairs, he smiled and continued up to his rooms. He could easily have afforded to stay at one of the better inns—better being a relative term in England—

but did not wish to draw attention to himself. It made no difference what this gutter trash thought of his comings and goings, which was why he had selected lodgings on the river.

Tenements similar to the one he had chosen were springing up like mushrooms. Already two had collapsed with great loss of life to the inhabitants. The builders had not bothered to prepare adequate footings in the soft Thames mud. There was an insane rush to build, even with the threat of Spanish invasion looming just beyond the horizon. A mad race, the English. All they cared about was their bearbaiting and their cockfighting and their public theaters.

Bolting the door behind him, he cast off his cloak and dropped his drawing easel with indifference on the bed of the outer chamber of his adjoining rooms. He unlocked the fine new Italian lock he had fitted to the door leading to the inner chamber and slipped inside. Its furnishings consisted of a cupboard, a table, and a chair. The walls, ceiling, floor, even the small window, were painted over with scarlet. When he lit the silver oil lamp on the table from his tinderbox, its flickering flame gave the room the appearance of a raw wound.

The sound of consumptive coughing and the squalling of a colicky infant drifted faintly through the thin walls. Most of the inhabitants of the tenement were asleep. From a stoppered crystal flask ringed with silver the Italian poured a thick black liquid into a shallow silver bowl. It fumed slightly. He bent over the bowl to inhale the leprous scent and felt his testicles creep tighter into his scrotum and his penis begin to stiffen. The smell of power.

Positioning the lamp so that its flame reflected off the inky surface of the liquid into his eyes, he stared abstractly into the bowl and allowed his mind to open the dark corridor between the worlds. His consciousness left his body and slid into the limitless midnight realm beneath the black mirror. Once established there, he sent out a summons along a ray of his will. A turning vortex of glittering black sparks formed before him. This was how he conceived it, though in truth there was no seeing in the black void and no direction before or behind. It simply was.

"What have you learned?" It seemed to the Italian that he spoke, but he knew this to be an illusion.

Slowly a single lidless eye coalesced in the center of the vortex. It regarded the Italian with a mixture of fear and hatred.

He has returned, it reported, its "voice" an echo in the Italian's mind.

"Was he deceived?"

The Watcher laughed soundlessly.

No. Your plan failed. The Jew sent him a letter warning him to guard the book. He opened its hiding place and found it missing.

The Italian accepted this news without emotion. He had expected as much. The ruse had been worth the effort, if only because it had resulted in the destruction of Dee's library.

"Read me this letter."

The Watcher recited the deciphered text of Rabbi Loew's letter word for word.

Tomorrow he goes to Hampton Court. The Queen has summoned him.

Little rodents of worry gnawed the edges of the Italian's thoughts. If Dee succeeded in involving the vast resources of the English throne in a quest to recover the book, it might result in an awkward confrontation at some crucial stage in the work of the brotherhood. It was generally assumed the English sage held some spell over

Elizabeth—how else to explain her constant affection for him? Dee was too powerful a foe to confront directly, and too well-protected on the astral plane. It would be better to turn his interest from the book into some benign channel. Perhaps a distraction would serve. The Italian came to a decision.

"Follow Dee. When his party reaches Hampton Court, kill his wife."

He dismissed the spirit with a mental gesture. Hissing hatred, the eye dissolved into the darkness.

Feeling some trepidation, the Italian reoriented his mind and sent a second ray deep into the bowels below the foundation of the universe, under the roots of a great mountain that straddled the boundary between the earthly realm and the dimension of nightmares. It was not a place to be located on any human map.

He felt a great cavern open all around his awareness. By the white radiance of a single, infinitely remote star that blazed overhead, he saw moisture seeping through thick clumps of moss that clung to the walls of the vault, and a vast dead sea with a small island of black volcanic rock in its center. Unwillingly, he forced his mind to glide toward the island.

The thing that covered most of the surface of the island was not material. In the strict sense of the word it was not even a shape. Nonetheless, he saw it with his cringing mind. It exuded terror. Nothing could venture within its dwelling place and not be overwhelmed with fear. Only long years of unimaginably rigorous mental training enabled the Italian to cling to his precarious sanity.

His awareness hovered like a bird high above the island in the vault of the cavern. From the pulsating sides of the slimy mass, buds formed and ripened with incredible swiftness, then split open with a soft sound and released blind horrors that mewed and groped around the margin of the Mother-thing. They fought each other with savage ferocity and fed endlessly on her excrements.

"What have you learned, my lover?" the thing said caressingly in his mind.

From a great distance away the Italian sensed his desire harden.

"The thief lied. He has the book but wants more money. Tomorrow I will obtain it."

"Bring the key to me."

In his mind he sensed the word "key" but also at the same time the words "talisman" and "spell." The book was all three, and many more things besides. He knew from experience that it was useless to try to explain the alien concepts of solid matter and physical distance to the thing on the island. Once he carried the book to the stronghold of the brotherhood, he and his fraters would work magic to separate the physical shell of the book from the arcanum of the key and send it to her ritually.

"I will, soon."

"Very soon."

She caressed his mind. From an infinite height he felt his physical body ejaculate its seed in fierce pulses. As always, the pleasure was indescribably intense, beyond the experience of ordinary sensation.

The moment she released him, he fled the cavern in horror. He swam upwards through the black sea of his unconscious like a pearl diver, trailing silver bubbles of thought in his wake. With a gasp he broke through the surface of the fluid in the bowl and fitted himself into his body. It was always difficult. Once the soul had been away from its physical case for more than a few moments it expanded and altered, rendering it necessary to compress and reshape it before it could be inserted into its fleshy envelope.

He found himself trembling and covered with cold sweat, as he always did. His warm semen lay wet on his thigh. From elsewhere in the tenement the tortured sound of coughing punctuated the stillness of the night.

He poured the inky liquid from the bowl back into its crystal holder, taking extreme care that the last drop entered the vessel before sealing its mouth with the stopper. On trembling legs he left the red chamber, locked it, and began to undress for bed. His long-waisted doublet and trunk breeches, absurdly padded in the English style, fell carelessly across a chair. He stared for a moment at the pearly glisten on the crease of his thigh before wiping it away with the sleeve of his shirt. The maddening cough persisted, rhythmic and hard, like a nail hammered into a coffin lid.

Blind fury, mingled with shame and self-loathing, welled up inside the Italian's heart. He reached out with his will and located the source of the racking cough. With vicious satisfaction he created an astral noose and drew it tight. The cough changed into a strangled gasp. The darkness fell silent on his ears.

He let the astral noose slip with a tight smile and listened. There was no sound of the crying infant. Presumably its mother had coaxed it into sleep. So much the luckier for the brat, thought the Italian. He would need a full night of rest if he was to obtain the book tomorrow.

SIX

"One night in my own bed," Jane Dee sighed. "Who knows when we'll see Mortlake again?"

She stood beside Joanna Kelley in the stern of the flat-bottomed river barge looking back at the imposing facade of the house through a gap in the willows that lined the edge of the sloping lawn. It was a beautiful June morning. The jade water of the Thames slid like a rippled serpent, and seemed to dream in the warm sunlight. The bare-armed bargemen had little to do except keep their craft in the middle of the stream and let the river carry it along. They stood like twin sentinels with their poles at the ready.

"Why didn't you stay home?" Joanna asked.

"I couldn't. The Queen will expect to see me. If John went to court alone she would think John and I were fighting; or worse, she would take it as a slight. Anyway, John insisted that I come. He said it would be safer."

Joanna Kelley laughed bitterly.

"Edward would like nothing better than to leave me behind so that he could have a fling with some London doxy. I don't intend to let him out of my sight."

"You're wrong about Edward," Jane said. "I've never seen him cast eyes at other women."

"My husband's a crafty bastard. I know him better than you or John. Trust me, he's up to something."

Jane did not try to argue with her friend. It hurt her that Joanna and Edward spent so much of their time bickering over imagined slights and trifles. She had always liked Kelley. He was a dark bear of a man who suffered from severe bouts of melancholy, but she trusted him. Even so, when he fell into one of his towering rages against his wife, Jane always took her part. She wanted Joanna to be as blissfully happy as herself. Perhaps if Joanna had children, Jane reflected, her marriage bed would be more peaceful. But the Kelleys were childless.

They watched until the sooted chimney pots and thatched roof of the house slipped behind a bank of trees, then moved under the canopy in the middle of the barge and sat on their travel trunks. Their husbands continued to converse in low voices in the blunt prow.

Jane tugged at her ruff to loosen it. Knowing it would be a warm day, she had worn a travel dress of white linen. It lacked a farthingale of whalebone at the hips to add stylish volume to her petticoats and skirt, but she was more concerned with comfort than impressing the impassive bargemen. Despite her practical choice, the reflected heat from the water was already causing her to perspire. Thank heaven they would only be on the river for two hours. At least the morning breeze was keeping the flies penned in amongst the reeds near the banks.

Joanna was attired more ornately in a gown of Lincoln green satin embroidered with gold thread and slashed to expose its red velvet lining. Her petticoats were a cascade of white and silver lace beneath the triangular peak of her stomacher. Jane wondered how she could bear such confinement. A glow of fine sweat glistened on the flush of her friend's freckled cheek.

"Barely on the river and I'm starting to get nervous," Joanna said in disgust. "Here, feel my heart, it's beating like a blacksmith's hammer."

She grasped Jane's small white hand and pressed it over her ample left breast. Jane dutifully nodded, although she felt nothing.

"What a fool I am. As if it made any difference what the Queen thinks of me."

"Everyone's nervous the first time they're presented at court," Jane reassured her. "I know the Queen will like you."

"What's she really like?" Joanna asked, glancing at the back of one of the stoic bargemen. "I've heard she's got a fiery temper."

"She's always been good to John and me," Jane said. She forbore to mention the many times as a maid-in-waiting to Lady Howard of Effingham that she had heard Elizabeth curse her unhappy political advisors. Yet what she had told her friend was true. The Queen had never so much as spoken a harsh word to her.

"Be honest with me, Jane." Joanna's wide green eyes searched the face of the other woman. "Will I be out of place? Will the ladies laugh at my dress?"

She was so serious Jane could scarcely resist smiling.

"Don't be silly, Joanna. All kinds of persons come to Hampton Court. No one will expect you to wear the latest thing from France. My gown is so out of fashion I'll look like a grandmother, but I don't care. The Queen pays no notice to the finery of others. You should see Francis Drake when he arrives back from one of his sea voyages with his face sunburned and his doublet smelling of tar, and he's her favorite. It's the French dandies with their silks and lace that she despises." Jane giggled behind her hand. "She calls them little frogs."

This seemed to pacify Joanna. Privately, Jane was worried about the reception of her friend at court. Her country accent was broad, and her manners uncouth. Worst crime of all, she said what was on her mind without snide insults or flattery. The Queen would favor these forthright qualities, but Jane was not so sure about the other ladies of the court. Many were brittle society tarts who lived for the chance to slander those they considered beneath their rank.

Joanna came from Chipping Norton, a small market town a day's journey from Oxford. Her father, Thomas Cooper, owned an inn. Kelley had first met her while studying law at the university, when she was a child of nine. Years later, he spent the summer in a room at her father's inn. The two fell in love. They kept up a written correspondence, and Kelley visited from time to time. Shortly after his arrival at Mortlake, Kelley returned to Chipping Norton and married Joanna, contrary to the wishes of her father, who was against the match because he had to hire a serving wench to take her place at the inn. This much Jane had pieced together from chance remarks made by her husband and Joanna.

Why Kelley had given up the lucrative profession of legal advocate in Lancaster to become an alchemist, Jane Dee did not know, except that it had something to do with a red powder discovered by Kelley while on a walking tour of Wales. He had come to Mortlake five years ago seeking permission from Dee to study Dee's large collection of alchemical texts. It was not uncommon in those years for a dozen strangers to stay at the house and spend their time studying in the library by day and carrying on animated debates with her husband by night. The Queen herself came several times on the Royal Barge or by horse, and the captains Drake and Frobisher were frequent visitors.

Her husband had been searching for months for a skilled seer to assist him in his spiritual experiments. He had succeeded in establishing communication with a group of angels by means of his crystal showstone, but as he confessed to her more than once, he possessed no true talent for seership. When he discovered that Kelley was an extraordinarily gifted spirit medium, he was beside himself with joy. He regarded Kelley as manna sent from heaven, and immediately employed the alchemist at fifty pounds a year as his seer. Kelley readily entered into this arrangement. Jane gathered from odd comments he made that, in the past, he had himself undertaken magical experiments of some kind. His only condition was that Dee help him to uncover the secret of the philosopher's stone.

Her husband had once hinted that Kelley was sought by the authorities in Lancaster on some legal matter, but had never explained further, and Jane had not attempted to learn more. When Kelley brought Joanna to Mortlake to live, the two women became instant friends. Joanna was Jane's first true friend since her marriage to Dee and her departure from the royal court nine years ago.

Jane did not understand precisely what work the two men pursued into the wee hours of the night behind the locked door of Dee's study. She only knew that it concerned a spirit guide named Madimi, whom Dee regarded with such fondness that sometimes Jane thought the spirit was one of their children, and Madimi's mysterious Mother, a being of great wisdom and power that neither her husband nor Kelley had ever seen face to face. Jane understood in a general way that Dee was seeking to use the spirits to forward the expansionist schemes of the Queen, but how he intended to accomplish this she neither knew nor inquired.

Other women might shudder to learn their husbands practiced what were commonly referred to as the black arts. Jane Dee felt no qualms. She believed with complete certainty in her own heart that her beloved was the wisest and best man in all England. It was impossible to imagine that he could be engaged in any ungodly or treasonous activity. That was enough for her.

A wave of nausea swept through her lower body. She pressed her hand over the gentle dome of her belly and waited for it to pass. It left her dizzy. Joanna failed to notice. She continued to chat away, her face turned to the sliding bank of the river. Jane closed her eyes. Cold sweat broke out on her cheeks and brow. She licked salty droplets from her upper lip. The sickness returned, this time with irresistible force.

She stood up hurriedly and lurched to the rail of the barge. Leaning far over so as not to stain her dress, she was violently ill. Her breakfast displayed itself in unlovely colors as it spread over the surface of the water. She felt strong hands at both sides and allowed them to help her back under the canopy.

"Jane, what's wrong?" Her husband held her face between his hands and peered intently into her eyes. Among his many other skills, he was an accomplished physician.

"I don't know, John. It must be the motion of the boat."

The younger bargeman passed her a tin cup of water. She drank a mouthful and spat it out weakly on the deck.

"She's river-sick," Kelley said, an uncharacteristic tone of kindly concern in his deep voice.

"Jane, how can you be river-sick?" Joanna demanded. "The boat isn't even rocking. If it were, I'd be sick myself."

Jane blushed and dropped her gaze.

"I'm fine, now, really. There's no need to make a fuss."

With many flustered words she managed to convince her husband to let her rest. He withdrew with Kelley once more to the open deck in the prow of the barge, but continued to tug at his silver beard and cast worried glances in her direction.

Joanna wet a cloth with cool river water and gently touched it to her friend's flushed face.

"For heaven's sake, Joanna, I'm not an invalid. I just lost my breakfast."

"You have a delicate constitution," Joanna muttered angrily as she wrung the cloth between her strong hands. "I don't know what that fool husband of yours can be thinking, to drag you all over Europe and Wales."

Jane's gaze wandered past the fiery curls of the other woman to the river. At the inside of the bend they had just rounded, beneath the shadow of an overhanging willow, she noticed a dance of movement. Something ruffled the still surface of the water.

"How odd," she said.

Joanna turned her head to follow Jane's gaze.

A spinning funnel of tiny black specks whirled over the mirror surface near the tall grasses. It almost seemed to keep pace with the slow drift of the barge.

"A cloud of midges caught in a whirlwind," Joanna said indifferently, and turned away.

Jane narrowed her eyes against the glare of the sun. It did not look like insects to her. The black specks moved with cohesion, almost as though they were part of a single living organism. She started to call to her husband, but as her lips parted, the spinning inverted cone faded into nothingness.

With puzzlement, she stared for a few moments at the place it had been. Other thoughts intruded themselves into her mind, concerns about Joanna's reception at court, the purpose for which the Queen had summoned John, and that other private matter that she had kept secret from everyone. A short while later when John Dee came under the canopy to check on her condition, Jane forgot to mention the strange black whirlwind.

SEVEN

The Queen stood with her back to the door, hunched over a long table under a mullioned window. The surface of the table was strewn with books and charts. When Dee was announced, she did not bother to raise her head.

"Come in, come in, Master Dee," she said in a gruff, querulous voice. "Have a look at this chart."

Dee moved around to the other side of the table, noting as he did so the austerity of the chamber. It was in the rear of the palace away from the sounds of revelry and the bustle of court life. The walls were lined with books. A writing desk occupied the corner next to the fireplace. Apart from a tall cupboard and several plain wooden chairs, the room was otherwise empty. No hangings adorned the oak panels of the walls. The wooden floor was bare of a carpet. Every feature of the room proclaimed it a place of work.

In sharp contrast to the austere furnishings of the room, the Queen wore a magnificent emerald satin gown with long puffed sleeves, a tightly gathered waist, and hugely flared skirts that swept the floor. Her ornate petticoats were silk. A high ruff of starched white lace framed her broad masculine features and towering red wig, which was woven with seed pearls. Perched incongruously on top of the wig sat a small French hood of damask.

It was plain in the harsh glare of the window that she was no longer a young woman. Even the thick cosmetic layer of white lead on her face could not hide the deep lines around her eyes and painted scarlet lips.

Not for the first time, Dee wondered why the Queen, who cared little for court pomp or adornment in others, wasted so much expense and energy on her personal appearance. He found such peacock displays both vulgar and incomprehensible. As was his usual custom, he had come to the audience dressed in a plain black scholar's robe and skullcap. His sole concession to fashion was a small ruff collar of white lace.

He seldom varied this Spartan attire, which he had first adopted in his Cambridge days. His wife Jane sometimes chided him in a gentle, teasing way on his lack of fashion sense, but thus far he had resisted change. For clothes he cared nothing. His secret vanity was his splendid silver beard, which grew longer with the passage of years as the white hairs on his head became thinner.

"There, look at this," Elizabeth said brusquely. She twisted the parchment on the table and stabbed with her crooked index finger.

Dee studied the parchment for a few moments. It was a crude pen sketch of a coastline. He recognized the Bay of Cadiz. Beside the port of Lisbon a complex series of rectangular boxes had been marked. These were interlaced with arrows to indicate movement.

"I had Francis Drake draw this up the moment he returned from the raid on Lisbon. You know what I'm talking about, I suppose?"

Dee nodded, studying the drawing. On the nineteenth of April Sir Francis Drake had taken a fleet of thirty ships into the Bay of Cadiz, where Philip II, King of Spain, was assembling the largest naval force the world had ever seen. It was not known with certainty what Philip intended to accomplish with this vast armada of ships, but rumors were rife throughout Europe that it was an invasion fleet to be shortly launched against England. Drake had managed to send blazing, unmanned fire ships amongst the anchored fleet. The fire had spread from rigging to rigging of the closely ranked Spanish vessels, resulting in the destruction of many.

"We met a merchant from London on the ship when we were returning to England from the Low Countries," Dee murmured. "He was full of the news of Drake's victory."

"Victory?" Elizabeth snorted. "He called it that, did he?"

Dee looked into the eyes of the Queen with mild surprise.

"What would you call it, Majesty?"

She pushed herself away from the table and began to pace back and forth, wringing her hands in anger.

"A minor skirmish, nothing more. Drake estimates that he was able to destroy some ten thousand tons of Spanish shipping."

"Surely that is a great many ships," Dee said.

She whirled on him, eyes blazing.

"For England, yes, it would be a crippling blow, but not for Spain. Gold flows like a river into Philip's coffers from the New World. He'll merely order the fleet rebuilt. Valiant Drake has bought me a respite, nothing more. A few months, perhaps even as much as a year. Then we're right back were we were in April, facing an invasion."

"Philip may become discouraged and call off the war," Dee suggested.

Elizabeth shook her head. Her yellowed teeth met in an unconscious snarl between her scarlet lips.

"Not that papist devil. He hates me for daring to challenge him on the high seas. For years he's had all the gold of the New World for himself and he's determined to keep it that way. He even begrudged Raleigh's attempt to establish the Roanoke colony on the northern coast. How he must have danced with glee when he heard of its failure."

Dee reached along the table and pulled a map of Europe toward him. He recognized it as one of his own, drawn according to the rules of projection invented by his teacher, the great Flemish cartographer Gerhardus Mercator. The distance between England and Spain seemed so insignificant. Yet the English Channel was one of the most treacherous straits in the world, as many of those who made the perilous crossing could testify to their sorrow.

"If we only knew in advance the date the Spanish fleet will be launched, it might be possible to arrange a little foul weather," Dee suggested.

The Queen set her heavy knuckles on the table and smiled at Dee.

"The thought had also occurred to me. Tell me, friend Dee, how many days would you need to brew up a Channel storm?"

Dee considered the matter under the disquieting eyes of the Queen.

"Weather magic can't be rushed, Your Majesty. Some seasons are more favorable for storms than others. It's possible through the judicious application of the magical art to encourage a change in the weather, but such a change cannot be forced."

"Yes, yes, I know all that," she said with an impatient wave of her hand. "How long?"

"At this time of year, perhaps a week. Perhaps two."

"Damnation, that's too long," she said with disgust. "Philip's army would already be in London by then."

"If only we knew the day of the invasion ahead of time," Dee observed. "I could begin to raise the storm before the fleet departed from the coast of Spain."

"Exactly!" Elizabeth exclaimed, slamming her hand flat on the table. "Why do you think I've been trying to contact you for the last three weeks?"

"Your Majesty?"

She crossed the floor to her desk and took from it a small, oval miniature. Returning to the table, she cast it down in front of Dee. He picked it up and examined the features of the man in the painting.

"What do you know of this man?" she demanded.

A long, sallow face with glittering black eyes and deeply-lined cheeks stared with sardonic mockery from the silver frame. Its pinched nose and immaculately manicured beard spoke of high-born arrogance. It was not the face of a generous man, nor of a man who could be trusted.

"He looks vaguely familiar," Dee murmured, stroking his silver beard thoughtfully. "It seems to me that I met him in Prague some years ago while traveling through Poland and Bohemia in the company of Albert Laski, the palatine of Siradz."

"A Bavarian count named Friedrich Niebuhr, who has attached himself to the court of the Emperor Rudolph at Prague. I believe you know the Emperor from your travels in Bohemia."

"My seer Edward Kelley was closer to Rudolph than I ever was," Dee commented. "Rudolph once employed him to manufacture gold for his treasury."

"With how much success?" the Queen asked with a cynical smile.

"Little," Dee admitted. "When we came into Bohemia, Kelley possessed a small portion of the red powder. This I verily do believe he was able to use to manufacture gold."

"You saw this?" she demanded.

"No. Only the result of the process. Over the course of our stay in Prague the red powder was exhausted. Kelley squandered it making gold to buy trinkets for fawning court lapdogs who pretended to be his friends. He was certain he could create more of the powder using his alchemical arts. When this proved impossible, I persuaded him to return with me to England."

"Is that what you were doing in Wales?" the Queen asked. "Searching for more of this red powder?"

Dee nodded silently. The shrewdness of Elizabeth and her remarkable ability to store away in her mind countless details of those who served her never ceased to amaze him. He had no doubt that if he spoke to her again a year hence she would be able to report almost verbatim their present conversation.

"Where is the alchemist, anyway?" she demanded. "I expected him to accompany you today."

"So he did, Majesty, to Hampton Court at least. He went off on horse earlier this afternoon to see a play at the new Rose Theater in Bankside."

"A play?" The Queen blinked heavy-lidded eyes. "Well, no matter. You can inform him of our doings when next you see him."

She tapped her fingernail against the painted features on the miniature.

"Niebuhr has close ties to the court of Bohemia. His sister, who is married to one of Rudolph's most trusted advisors, is one of Rudolph's lovers. She remains very loyal to her worthless brother, though God knows why.

In return for a sum of gold he has indicated to Captain
Peter Gwyn, my agent in Bohemia, that he can obtain a
document that reveals the projected date for the launch-
ing of the Spanish fleet."

"Forgive me, Majesty," Dee said, "But if that is the
case, why have you summoned me? Surely good Captain
Gwyn can handle this transaction and transmit the information to your agent in Brussels."

"There is a complication. Niebuhr reports to Captain
Gwyn that he will be able to obtain the document, which
is presently in the keeping of one of Emperor Rudolph's
advisors, for only a few hours. Apparently Rudolph's soldiers intercepted a packet of communications from Philip
en route to Pope Sixtus. It was being smuggled through
Bohemia by a Jesuit spy. Niebuhr was able to interrogate
the spy shortly before he died. He says the fools in
Rudolph's court have no idea what the document is
about. It's in an unbreakable cipher code."

Dee's interest quickened.

"No cipher is unbreakable, Majesty."

"I am glad you believe it," she said, smiling. "That is
why I intend to send you and Kelley back to Prague to act
as my confidential agents in this matter.

"But Your Majesty," Dee protested. "I have only this
past month returned from Europe. My poor wife Jane has
barely seen her home at Mortlake these last four years."

"Did I ask you to stay on the Continent all that
time?" the Queen demanded sharply. "Did I order you
to go to Wales?"

Dee bowed his head.

"No, Your Majesty."

She tapped the table with nervous irritation.

"I could arrange to have the document copied, of
course, but key elements of the code might be omitted by

the copyist. No, Master Dee, you must examine and copy the document yourself. It is vital that we discover when the invasion is planned so that we can prepare the weather to meet it."

"As you wish, Majesty," Dee said, bowing his head in resignation. "May I leave my wife here at Hampton Court in your safe-keeping?"

"Why here? Why not at her own house at Mortlake?"

Dee described the sacking of his library, and its covert purpose, and admitted his apprehension that Mortlake was being watched by some airy spirit of darkness. The Queen, whose mind was occupied with affairs of state, paid little heed.

"This evil book you speak of is a matter for your own Order of Hermes and none of my concern," she said. "Though I do question your judgement in carrying it into England."

"In hindsight, so do I, Your Majesty."

She scowled and sniffed.

"Of course, if you think there is danger from this evil brotherhood of Coronzon, you may leave Jane with me. I will watch over her as if she were my own child. I confess that at times I miss her good company in the evenings. As does her former mistress, Lady Howard."

"And may Joanna Kelley remain here as well?"

"Kelley's wife? She is here?"

"I believe she is presently walking with Jane in the garden."

"Take me to her," Elizabeth said grimly. "I want to extend my sympathy to the poor child for having the misfortune to be wed to such a man."

Dee suppressed a smile. The Queen affected an outward dislike of Kelley, but he suspected that she secretly admired the dour alchemist. Kelley was one of the very few men in England not terrified of her. He neither flattered her nor fawned after her good graces. He always spoke his mind. Elizabeth admired truthfulness and courage above all other virtues. Dee reflected that he could boast of the first, but as for the second—though he tried to conceal it, the Queen frightened him more than the Devil himself. He would rather ride into the mouth of hell than risk her anger. Which, if the truth were known, might be exactly where he and Kelley were headed.

EIGHT

Kelley passed the reins of his hired horse to a dust-caked boy who stood in the yard beside the Rose Theater and pressed a farthing into his sweating palm. He was in an ill temper, having ridden hard the dozen or so miles from Hampton Court to Bankside to be in time for the afternoon performance. Even so, he was late. The play had already begun.

He entered through the open doorway under a hanging sign painted with a single red rose in full bloom, its petals expanded in a concentric swirl like a crimson arabesque. The smells of fresh wood and stale, unwashed bodies assaulted his nose. From somewhere deeper inside the playhouse came the measured voices of the actors and the shuffle and occasional laughter of the audience.

A big man with lanky dark hair, a great sack of a belly, and a full rust beard barred his way. He eyed the alchemist without enthusiasm.

"One farthing for the pit, two for the third gallery, three for the second, four for the first," he recited in a bored voice.

"Is there a place on the first gallery near the stage?" Kelley asked.

The porter's scowl became a smile, revealing gaps between his decaying teeth.

"Indeed there is, good sir. And it holds the finest seats in all London, if you don't mind me saying so. Burbage has got nothing to compare with 'em. All the best rank uses 'em. We've screened 'em off from the rabble for the benefit of such gentlemen as yourself. They're a real bargain at six farthings."

Kelley counted the copper coins out from his purse and passed them over without complaint.

"Before you sit, would you want a mug of cool ale to wash the dust out of your throat?" The fat porter indicated a low table to one side of the door with a cask on a rack. "Only a farthing. The finest ale in London, sir."

Without waiting for Kelley to respond, he began to fill a wooden mug with foaming amber fluid from the tap in the head of the cask. Kelley silently laid another coin on the table. He eyed the rim of the mug dubiously. It was not the cleanest of drinking vessels, but his throat was parched from his long ride. He drained it in one go. The ale was warm and thin.

"They tell me you just opened this spring," he said in a conversational tone. "How's business?"

"Couldn't be better, sir," the man said with enthusiasm. "Every day the house is near capacity. The people love the new plays. Can't get enough of 'em."

"I understand you had a play on about Carthage a while back," Kelley said.

The porter's little round eyes lit up.

"The Tragical History of Dido, Queen of Carthage. A real corker, sir. Sorry to hear you missed it."

"The friend who told me about it said that he was especially impressed by the actor who played Dido. What was his name, do you know?"

"That would be Thomas Beecher. A clever fellow, right enough. Very dramatic, the way he waves his arms all about in the death scene and weeps fit to break your heart."

"I hope I get a chance to watch him someday," Kelley said.

"Well now, as to that, you can see him this very day. He's playing the part of Miles, the poor young scholar of Roger Bacon. You can't miss him, sir. He's the one with the blond hair and the pale face."

"What's the name of the play?"

The porter blinked and wrinkled his brow in thought.

"I don't know that it's got a proper name yet. The writer, who's a clever young fellow named Greene, is testing it out this week while he makes some improvements. You'll like it though, sir. It's all about Friar Bacon and his brass head."

A waiting boy led Kelley through the dark interior of the tiring house where the actors prepared their costumes, up a short flight of steps and out through an archway. They emerged onto a covered gallery with seats ranked along the side that overlooked the octagonal pit of the theater, which was open to the blue sky and thronged with entranced spectators.

The crowd stood staring up at the stage, a rectangular platform that thrust out from the decorated front of the tiring house from beneath an overhanging roof painted on its underside with stars to simulate the heavens. The stage roof, intended to keep the actors dry during rains, was supported by two wooden columns that rose from the middle of the stage itself. There were two entrances in the back wall for the actors, and an open balcony over the projecting stage roof.

Kelley gazed about in admiration, marveling at the splendid carvings and gilt plaster ornaments. The three roofed galleries that ran all the way around the pit and stage overflowed with spectators who dangled upon the railings, staring down with rapt intensity at the actors.

All types and classes of humanity were to be found in the audience. He noticed mainly poorer working men and women standing in the pit around the three sides of the projecting stage. Some of the men carried young children on their shoulders. Most of the better dressed spectators occupied the first gallery, which was just slightly above the level of the actors.

The boy indicated a section of chairs with padded leather seats that overlooked the side of the stage. Kelley slid into one of these and found himself almost close enough to the actors to reach over the rail and pluck hairs from their heads as they passed back and forth, had he wished.

They wore archaic costumes from a bygone era. The scene appeared to be a royal audience. An older, dignified actor in an ermine robe and golden crown stood with other lords and ladies watching a debate between a scholar in a black robe and a portly Franciscan friar. Despite his ulterior motive, Kelley found himself interested in what they were saying. It concerned magic.

"Stand to him, Bungay," the king said in a loud, resonate voice. "Charm this Vandermast, and I will use thee as a royal king."

"Wherein darest thou dispute with me?" the scholar challenged the friar in a thick German accent. He was a rough-looking man with a great wart on the side of his nose. He glared in a threatening manner at the friar.

"In what a doctor and a friar can," the other meekly answered.

The German spread his arms to encompass the nobles on the stage.

"Before rich Europe's worthies put thou forth the doubtful question unto Vandermast."

"Let it be this," said the friar. "Whether the spirits of pyromancy or geomancy be most predominant in magic."

An easy question, Kelley thought to himself as he scanned the theater for a slender blond man. The spirits of fire were proud and distant, difficult to summon and, after being called, of little practical use. Conversely, the spirits of the earth came easily and were adept at material matters such as locating hidden treasure.

"I say, of pyromancy," Vandermast declared.

"And I, of geomancy," Friar Bungay responded.

The German magician began to pace back and forth on the very foot of the stage, declaiming at length the virtues of the spirits of fire in blank verse. When he concluded his argument, the assembled nobles on the stage gave the German a polite round of applause, accompanied by boos and hisses from the English groundlings watching from the pit. He retired to the rear of the stage, and Friar Bungay took the fore to defend the uses of the spirits of the earth. A fragment of verse captured Kelley's attention.

> *I tell thee, German, magic haunts the grounds,*
> *And those strange necromantic spells,*
> *That work such shows and wondering in the world,*
> *Are acted by those geomantic spirits*
> *That Hermes called Sons of the Earth.*

The words carried his mind back to another time and place. Ten years ago, when Kelley with his necromantic arts had raised the shade of a dead man out of the ground of Law Church in Lancaster, he had commanded the spirits of the earth, not those of fire, to bring the departed soul before him. He had threatened the trembling shade with punishment from these same earthy demons if it failed to answer his questions.

He still felt an inner pang of resentment after all the intervening years. The rumor of his necromantic experiments resulted in his being hounded out of Lancaster. Once it became whispered abroad that he dabbled in the black arts, his legal practice dried up overnight. No one wanted their deed drawn or their case pleaded by a witch. The fools had even slandered him, accusing him of drawing up false title deeds.

His first impulse had been to remain in Lancaster and fight the accusations of professional misconduct, but after discovering that all the great men of the town stood against him because of his study of magic, he had been forced to flee to Wales. Still, things had a way of working out, he reflected. It was in Wales that he had found the broken ivory box with a portion of the fabled red powder, and this had led him to the house of John Dee.

His attention was drawn to a blond actor who entered through one of the rear doors carrying a silver tray of food. He set it upon a table on the far side of the stage and began to arrange the table. Kelley studied his back and profile. He was a slender man in his twenties with the creamy complexion of a woman.

"What pleasant fellow is this?" one of the regally dressed actors inquired.

"'Tis my lord Doctor Bacon's poor scholar," the king replied.

The blond actor must be Thomas Beecher. Studying him with a narrow gaze, Kelley found it difficult to believe that such an effeminate fop could organize a band of drunken louts into housebreakers. The actor obviously possessed hidden talents, not the least of which was the ability to pick a lock.

Kelley continued to watch him closely as the play progressed. Several times Beecher glanced in Kelley's direction. Although he seemed aware of Kelley's attention, the
actor showed no sign that the intense gaze of the dark
man troubled his conscience. Just the opposite. When a
bit of physical business drew him stage right, he seized the
opportunity to smile at Kelley and wink.

With a shock Kelley realized the actor thought Kelley
was enamored of him. The notion aroused his macabre
sense of humor. The next time Beecher glanced in his
direction, Kelley smiled back and squeezed shut his left
eye. Beecher blushed like a maid. Kelley allowed no sign
of his inner amusement to show on his features.

The play progressed to another scene. Kelley made no
attempt to follow the plot. He waited for Beecher to reap-
pear and wondered how he should proceed with the
actor. It was possible Beecher still had the book, but
unlikely. If the book had been passed into other hands, he
needed the name of its new owner. Should he use threats,
or should he play upon Beecher's misunderstanding?

The scene changed to Friar Bacon's study. Beecher, in
his character of Miles, the young scholar, sat beside a
great demonic head, gilded to resemble brass. Holding a
sword, knife, blunderbuss, and halberd in his lap, he
regarded the head with a timorous expression. A curtain
across one of the entrances at the rear of the stage drew
aside to reveal Friar Bacon, dressed in a nightdress and
nightcap as though prepared for sleep, with a book in one
hand and a lamp in the other.

"Miles, where are you?" asked the friar.

Beecher leapt up as though startled. The weapons
clattered on the stage around his feet and drew laughter
from the audience.

"Here, sir."

"How chance you to tarry so long?"

Beecher snatched up the sword and waved it in the air.

"Think you that the watching of the Brazen Head craves no furniture? I warrant you, sir, I have so armed myself that, if all your devil's come, I will not fear them an inch."

The actor playing Bacon came forward through the entrance and stood far enough down stage that the slanting afternoon sunlight fell upon his head and lit his hair in a golden halo. It was a simple stage trick but effective. Kelley listened with only half an ear while Bacon described the extent of his magical skills and revealed the worthy purpose of the Brazen Head.

> With seven years' tossing nigromantic charms,
> Poring upon dark Hecat's principles,
> I have framed out a monstrous head of brass,
> That, by the enchanting forces of the Devil,
> Shall tell out strange and uncouth aphorisms,
> And girt fair England with a wall of brass.

He stepped back a pace so that the light no longer lit up his face, and bent his back until he resembled a very old man, heavy with weariness and cares. Sympathetic clucks arose from women in the pit. Beecher hurried over to support him by the elbow, but the older actor waved him away with an impatient gesture, and with many portentous warnings about the need for his student to watch the head closely in case it should speak, he made his way off stage, supposedly to bed.

It was a pity such a great magician no longer lived, Kelley reflected. With the threat of Spanish invasion, England stood in sore need of a battlement of brass, or some other defense equally effective. Not even John Dee could work so great a magic as Bacon boasted, yet Dee was the wisest sage in England. It must be true, as they said at the universities, that the powers of mankind were in decline.

With various comical remarks to the audience upon the ugliness of the Head, Beecher gathered up his weapons and settled himself down before the Head to watch it. Twice the Head spoke amid great rumblings from the upper level of the tiring house behind the stage. The first time it voiced the words "Time is." The second time it said "Time was." Beecher in his character of foolish Miles mocked and scorned it.

A thunderous rumble shook the theater, much louder than before. The Head spoke a third time in a wrathful tone.

"Time is past!"

From a plume of sulfurous smoke a green and scaly arm with a hammer clutched in its fist rose up behind the Brazen Head and struck it. The Head split apart into two jagged fragments and the arm disappeared into the stage. The audience gasped. Even Kelley found himself impressed by the stage art in spite of his better judgement.

Beecher dropped his sword and ran to the rear entrance to tear aside the curtain.

"Master, master, up! Hell's broken loose! Your Head speaks; and there's such a thunder and lightning that I warrant all Oxford is up in arms."

Friar Bacon came onto the stage rubbing the sleep from his eyes and supporting his steps with a cane.

"Miles, I come. When spake the Head?"

Beecher looked in surprise around the theater.

"When spake the Head! Did not you say that he should tell strange principles of philosophy? Why, sir, it speaks but two words at a time."

There was an ominous pause. A ripple of laughter ran through the audience.

"Why, villain," Bacon demanded. "Hath it spoken oft?"

"Oft!" Beecher said cheerfully. "Ay, marry, hath it, thrice; but in all those three times it hath uttered but seven words."

Bacon glowered at his young scholar with gathering fury.

"As how?"

"Marry, sir, the first time he said, 'Time is;' then he said 'Time was;' and the third time, with thunder and lightning, as in great choler, he said, 'Time is past.'"

He moved aside, allowing Bacon to see the broken ruin of the Head. Bacon howled in agony.

> *'Tis past indeed! A villain! Time is past!*
> *My life, my fame, my glory, all are past.*
> *Bacon, the turrets of thy hope are ruined down;*
> *Thy seven years' study lieth in the dust!*
> *Thy Brazen Head lies broken through a slave*
> *That watched, and would not when the Head did will.*
> *What said the Head first?*

The younger actor did not respond. All eyes in the theater turned to him. He stood as though transfixed to the stage, staring into the pit, a look of sheer terror on his sheet-white face. The actor playing Bacon waited for several heartbeats, then bent close and whispered into his ear. Still Beecher refused to move. He might have been turned into marble, so motionless and cold did he appear.

Kelley followed the direction of Beecher's gaze. There seemed nothing remarkable about the men and woman who stood looking up at the stage. Some of the tilted faces were coarse and others were refined. Some smiled while others appeared puzzled. The fashions ranged from the poorest peasant clothe to fine silks. Nowhere in all of

Europe was there a greater mixing of ranks and occupa-
tions to be observed than in the pit of an English theater.

One face caught Kelley's roving eye. It stood out by its
lack of emotion. Along with the rest it stared at Beecher,
but there was no amusement, no sympathy, not even
curiosity in its frost blue eyes. It was beardless and hairless,
like an image drawn upon the surface of an egg. The man
the face belonged to stood several inches above the sur-
rounding crowd. He seemed to sense the gaze of the
alchemist upon him and turned his chill white stare into
the gallery.

Sensing something amiss, the audience began to murmur. The actor playing Bacon repeated his last line in a
louder voice.

"What said the Head first?"

Beecher seemed to shake himself out of a trance.

"Even, sir, 'Time is,'" he replied in a quavering voice.

Bacon strode to the front of the stage and began to
pace back and forth with animation. Behind him,
Beecher continued to stare into the pit like a bird hypno-
tized by a serpent.

> *Villain, if thou hadst called Bacon then,*
> *If thou hadst watched, and waked the sleepy friar,*
> *The Brazen Head had uttered aphorisms,*
> *And England had been circled round with brass.*

He whirled upon Beecher and began to beat him with
his cane. Beecher seemed to collect his wits. Once more
adopting the mannerisms of Miles, he covered his head
with his arms and cringed away under the blows to the
other entrance at the back of the stage. Bacon pursued
him with the cane.

Villain, avoid! Get thee from Bacon's sight!
Vagrant, go roam and range about the world,
And perish as a vagabond on Earth!

Having reached the safety of the doorway, Beecher thrust his head back through, drawing a laugh from the audience, which had allowed his brief strange behavior to pass.

"Why, then, sir, you forbid me your service?"

Bacon fairly began to foam at the mouth. He waved his cane threateningly at his unfaithful pupil.

My service, villain, with a fatal curse
That direful plagues and mischief fall on thee!

Beecher shrugged and forced a smile for the audience. Kelley noticed that he continued to glance in fatal fascination at the pit. The alchemist turned to search for the bald man with the icy gaze but failed to locate him amid the milling human press.

Beecher reached around the edge of the stage entrance and snatched a leather-bound book out of one of Bacon's bookcases. He waved it at the audience.

"I'll take but a book in my hand, a wide-sleeved gown on my back, and a crowned cap on my head, and see if I want promotion."

Swiftly he withdrew his head to avoid a carefully timed cut from Bacon's cane. The audience applauded heartily while Bacon continued to curse after him through the opening.

The play progressed. Troubled by Beecher's strange behavior, Kelley no longer attempted to follow the plot. He waited impatiently for Beecher's reappearance, wondering what strange sight in the pit had so disturbed the actor. Perhaps he had seen a familiar face. Yet why should this have such a paralyzing effect?

After several scenes that Kelley found tedious in his impatient state of mind, the Devil appeared in Friar Bacon's study to carry Miles the foolish scholar off to hell in answer to Bacon's curse. When Miles entered, a murmur of surprise rippled through the theater. The role was being played by a different actor.

Kelley damned himself for his complacency. He leapt from his seat and made his way back into the lower level of the tiring house, where the changing rooms of the actors were located. The tiring house was a rat's maze of small cluttered rooms and narrow, unlighted corridors. Following his instinct, he felt his way along a shadowy unpaneled hall and climbed a steep set of stairs.

While his eyes were fixed on the steps in an effort to keep from stumbling, a dark shape hurtled down the stair and bowled him over backwards. The two rolled down the stair together and landed in a heap at its foot. Cursing, Kelley fought to disentangle himself from the man on top of him. He caught the gleam of steel and ducked his head. A knife flashed past his cheek and embedded itself deep in the floor. He heard the thin stiletto blade snap when his assailant tried to wrench it loose from the hard oak, and rolled over just in time to see the naked scalp and dark cloak of the other man disappear out the door at the end of the hallway.

Cursing in a continuous stream, Kelley ran after him. The fat porter with the ruddy beard barred his way.

"What are you doing in here?" he demanded. "These rooms are private."

"The bald man who just ran out. He attacked me."

"Do you think to mock me?" The porter glared. "No one came forth but you."

Kelley tried to push past him. The porter pulled a wooden belaying pin out of his belt and swung at the alchemist. Kelley took the blow on his shoulder and at the same moment hit the porter with his massive fist between the eyes, knocking his head backward against an iron lamp bracket. The porter sagged into a sitting position and remained motionless with his chin upon his chest.

There was no outcry. Apparently the banging had not been noticed. Kelley slipped back toward the stair and picked up the hilt of his attacker's dagger. An ivory seal gleamed from a base of polished ebony. The blade had broken halfway along its length. A drop of blood, still liquid, left a scarlet trail as it slid down the edge of the steel. Kelley judged it was not an English blade—probably Italian, he decided. There was no occasion to examine it further. He slipped the hilt into his pocket and hurried up the stair.

He paused on the small, dark landing and wondered which way to proceed. A low groan decided him. It issued through the crack of a closed door at the far end of the upper hall. The door was not locked, but something hindered it from opening. He pushed harder, and saw the legs of a man lying in a smear of blood. By putting his shoulder to the door he was able to shift the body behind it enough to squeeze through.

Thomas Beecher lay on the floor with his hand pressed to a glistening patch of blood that seeped through his black scholar's costume under his heart. He stared at Kelley with a strange expression of wonder. His blue eyes widened with amazement.

"I'm going to die," he said.

Kelley knelt and lifted Beecher's hand away from the wound to part the actor's clothes. His eyes narrowed.

"Yes."

"Damn him, he didn't have to stab me," Beecher said. "I would have given him the book. I only wanted a little more money, that's all, just a little more to pay for all my trouble."

"You stole a book in Latin from the house of John Dee at Mortlake," Kelley demanded.

Beecher's gaze wandered about the cramped dressing room. He made an effort to focus on Kelley's dark features.

"He paid me twenty pounds. I told him I had to bribe the villagers. I said I wanted another twenty. He refused to pay, so I kept the book. I knew it must be valuable, even though I can't read Latin. He said he would get the money. He lied to me."

"Beecher, what is his name? Where does he live?"

The eyelids of the actor fluttered. He coughed and spat up a thick gob of black blood. It ran slowly down his chin until he wiped it off with his fingers.

"He never said his name. I don't know where he stays in London, but he's foreign. I think he's a devil."

"How do you know he's a foreigner?"

Beecher smiled. He clutched Kelley's arm with surprising strength.

"It was the way he talked. I'm good with accents, see? It's one of my specialties."

"Can you tell me any more about him?"

"His face in the pit." The actor groaned in pain. "A devil's face."

Kelley cursed himself for badgering a delirious and dying man, but he needed to know. He repeated his question.

Beecher seemed to consider. His eyes closed, and for a moment Kelley thought he had fallen unconscious.

"Scar in the corner of his left palm, like a crooked cross," he murmured.

Kelley tried to pry the dying man's fingers away from his arm.

"Don't move," he said in a gentle voice. "I'll get a leech. There may still be time."

Beecher clutched him more fiercely and pulled himself up to a sitting position. He stared passionately into Kelley cold slate eyes.

"I was good tonight, wasn't I?"

"You were good," Kelley agreed.

But Beecher was already dead.

NINE

Joanna drew the goose feathers of the cloth yard arrow to her right cheek and slowly lowered her longbow, sighting across the manicured garden lawn of Hampton Court at a round wickerwork target that stood on a wooden tripod fifty yards away.

"That's right, my lady," the serious young archery instructor said in a thick Welsh accent. "Just as I showed you. Aim at a spot in the air above the bull's-eye and let the string slip from your fingertips."

Joanna gently released the string. The bow sang. She watched with delight as the arrow flew in a shallow arc and buried itself a handbreadth to the left and below the red circle at the center of the target.

"Joanna, that's wonderful," Jane said in admiration. "Where did you ever learn to shoot?"

"I've never pulled a bow in my life," Joanna admitted, smiling.

"I can hardly believe it, my lady." The instructor's sunburned face beamed. "There's women here who've practiced for years who couldn't make that shot."

"Beginner's luck," Joanna said, feeling pleased in spite of herself. "Here, Jane, you try it."

She passed the bow to Jane, who allowed the instructor to lace a protector to her left forearm and fit a leather guard over the palm of her right hand so that the bow-string would not cut her fingers. She pulled the string with difficulty. It was a woman's archery bow not more than five feet in length, but constructed of stiff English yew. The arrow buried itself in the grass thirty feet in front of the target.

"Very respectable for a first try, my lady," the young instructor said politely. "It takes most a while to get the feel of it. Your friend here's a real natural archer."

The sound of hand clapping drew their attention to the garden path that passed behind the archery range. Two court ladies approached, attired in silk walking dresses that flashed in the sunlight with dragonfly colors, their enormous puffed sleeves and wheel farthingales quilted, slashed, jagged, pinched, and laced in the latest French style, their petticoats embroidered with silver and gold.

"Well shot, Jane," said the taller woman with an ironical quirk of her painted lips. "The Queen has no need to fear the Spanish while you're here—provided they plan to tunnel under the Channel like moles."

Joanna Kelley sized the woman up and down and took an instant dislike to her. She was statuesque and slender-necked, with glossy black hair and a long, straight nose that indicated Norman blood in her heritage. Her unblemished skin had the color of fresh milk. She carried a white silk parasol to ensure that it stayed that way.

"Jane, you've put on weight," her companion said with a smile. "How glad I am. You were so skinny, we always worried about your health."

"Joanna, this is Eleanor Champlain and Mary Ellis, two friends I knew while I was living at court," Jane said in introduction. "Eleanor, Mary, this is my dear friend Joanna Kelley."

The two women smiled and bent their knees in the shadow of a curtsy. Mary Ellis snapped open her fan and began to beat it furiously in front of her doll-like face, her blue eyes darting over Joanna's dress.

Both Jane and Joanna had changed from their travel clothes to more formal attire immediately after leaving the river. Jane wore a modest but well-made court gown of pale blue silk with white petticoats, while Joanna had put on her best dress, purchased three years earlier in Europe. It was made from velvet of such a deep red color that it appeared almost purple in the bright sunshine.

"I love what you're wearing," she said to Joanna. "Red is such a bold choice. I used to have a dress just like it three years ago. Do you know I've searched and searched but I can't find a single milliner in London who carries that material anymore. Wherever did you find it?"

"In Dresden," Joanna said, feeling her face begin to burn.

"Well, that explains it," Mary said sweetly.

"You must come to court more regularly, Jane," Eleanor told her. "The Queen often speaks about you."

"I have a husband and children," Jane said, glancing at Joanna. "My first duty is to them."

"But surely your first duty is to your Queen?" Eleanor persisted.

"Not in my view."

"How interesting."

"Kelley, Kelley," Mary murmured, quirking a blond eyebrow at Eleanor. "Where have we heard that name before?"

"You remember, Mary," Eleanor prompted. "John Dee's friend, the one who claims to be able to turn lead into gold."

"Of course," Mary exclaimed. She returned her gaze to Joanna's dress. "I admire your restraint, my dear. With all that gold it must be tempting to buy the latest fashions, but that would be such a vulgar display."

Jane stepped in front of Joanna and smiled sweetly at the two women.

"It's been so good to see you again after all these months. I hope you won't think it rude, but I promised to show Joanna around the grounds of the palace."

"Of course," Eleanor said, her gray eyes gleaming like flint in the sun. "You two run along. Perhaps we'll talk again later."

"Perhaps," Jane said, steering Joanna toward the maze by her elbow.

"Or perhaps I'll wring her scrawny chicken neck," Joanna muttered darkly when the two women were out of earshot.

"Not everyone at court is like that," Jane assured her.

Privately, she wondered. The whole atmosphere seemed somehow more shallow and brittle than she remembered it from the years before her marriage. Had she been like those women, she mused, before coming under the wholesome influence of her husband?

Each time she returned to Hampton Court since her wedding, she found herself enjoying it less and questioning the artificial manners of the courtiers more. It was all show and no substance. Nobody ever actually did anything. They bowed and laughed and whispered behind their hands and waited for the chance to thrust themselves beneath the eye of the Queen. It was like some horrible painted purgatory of lost souls.

Joanna walked quickly ahead of Jane into the tall hedge maze and wandered down several of its turnings before she began to cry silently. Jane caught up with her, put her arm around the shoulders of the taller woman, and guided her over to a bench. She sat without saying anything while Joanna daubed away her tears.

"I know I shouldn't care," Joanna said in a tremulous voice. "But I wanted them to like me."

"Their sort never like anybody unless they can use them to advantage," Jane said. "The Queen is quite different. You'll see."

"I'm not sure I want to meet the Queen anymore." She turned to her friend and stared earnestly into her gentle brown eyes. "I don't belong here, Jane. I'm the daughter of an innkeeper. I've served ale to drunken merchants and changed their beds and emptied their slops. You and John have been too good to me. I've forgotten my place."

"Your place is wherever you happen to be at the time," Jane said with passion.

"Easy for you to say." There was veiled bitterness in Joanna's voice. "You come from a noble family. Your father was Sir Henry Fromond, the great hero of the Irish rebellion."

"Who died without a penny and deep in debt," Jane said. "When John married me I was living at Hampton Court on the charity of Lady Howard of Effingham. My dowry consisted of nothing but a chest full of unpaid bills. John told me then that it didn't matter to him how much money I had, and it never has."

"Money's one thing and blood's another," Joanna said. "Both Edward and I were born commoners. Had he been knighted by the Queen it might be different."

Jane smiled with secret mischief.

"What?" Joanna asked.

"When I was a girl at court there was a story told that Eleanor Champlain had been sired by her father's stableman."

Joanna's green eyes widened. Jane nodded.

"So much for noble blood."

The sound of a conversation drifted from the garden through the dense wall of the maze. Jane recognized the voices of Eleanor and Mary, and realized they must be walking past the maze along the path. Their voices were surprisingly clear, as though they had been raised deliberately for the purpose of being overheard.

"Did you see that dress?" Mary said with a brittle laugh. "Who but a common tart would wear whore's red to meet the Queen? Doesn't she know that the Queen hates red?"

"No wonder she could shoot a bow," Eleanor agreed. "She probably hunts rabbits for the table. She has the arms of a fishwife."

Joanna stood angrily but Jane shook her head and put her finger to her lips, drawing her friend back down on the bench.

"Poor Jane," Eleanor said, her lips dripping with pathos. "I felt so sorry for her. Forced to wear that old rag. That what comes from living in the wilderness with that crazed witch of a husband. You'd never know it, but she was actually pretty once, in a common sort of way."

"Did you see how fat she's grown?" Mary asked. "When a woman lets herself go like that it's a sure sign that she's unhappy."

"I know what you mean. God knows what that ancient sorcerer makes her do at night. I've heard that he consorts with demons."

"That's why he employs the alchemist," Mary interjected. "They raise demons together. Dee knows the alchemist won't betray him because Kelley was driven out of Lancaster or some such place for necromancy."

"How horrible. I wonder that the Queen doesn't have both of them hanged."

"I think she would, were it not for her fondness for Jane. No one could wheedle her like Jane. I've heard they even slept in the same bed."

"I don't doubt it, my dear. Jane always was a bit of a witch herself. No wonder she married the sorcerer."

The voices faded gradually as the two women walked away from the edge of the maze. On the other side of the hedge wall, Joanna stared at Jane Dee and fumed.

"The things she said about you. I'll kill her."

Jane shook her head. Privately she was shocked at the venomous spite in Eleanor's words, but she did not wish to arouse Joanna's anger. Once ignited, it burned like a heath fire and was difficult to extinguish.

"It serves us well to know exactly what they think. They can never deceive us."

"Now you sound just like your husband," Joanna muttered. "His ways are too meek and forgiving for my taste."

"His ways are wise."

"To call you fat," Joanna fumed. "Just because you're forced to wear an old dress that you've outgrown."

"But I am fat," Jane said in a reasonable tone.

"Nonsense. You're no more fat that I am."

Jane took her friend's hand between her own and met her frank gaze.

"Joanna, can you keep a secret?"

"Of course," the redhead said, a faint frown shadowing her freckled features.

"I don't want John to know yet, but I'm with child again."

Joanna stared into Jane's eyes, then studied her belly.

"That's why you were sick on the journey down river," she said with comprehension.

Jane nodded.

"I've been certain about it for several months. I didn't want to trouble John until it became necessary. He has so many cares already, and he worries needlessly. When I was in labor with little Michael I almost bled to death."

Joanna nodded. A vivid image stirred in her memory of Jane lying on a mattress with her legs spread apart, a pool of bright crimson between her blood-stained thighs.

"John's been observing the cycle of the moon and taking precautions to prevent conception. He wants more children, but he worries about my health."

"His precautions weren't very effective."

"They would have been, had I applied them."

Joanna regarded her friend silently for several moments. Jane nodded. A smile played across Joanna's lips. Jane seldom defied her husband. It was a refreshing change of habit.

"He's not a fool," she observed. "He'll figure it out for himself if you wait much longer."

"I'll tell him before that happens. I want to be quite sure I won't miscarry before raising his hope. He's hasn't spoken, but I know he's worried that if we don't have another child soon, he'll be too old to impregnate me. But he's been hesitant to try."

"There's life in the old goat yet," Joanna murmured, looking away. Jane thought she detected a trace of envy in the tone of the other woman. She squeezed her hand.

"I wanted you to be happy for us."

"That I am." Joanna forced a smile. "It's just that Edward so much wants a son, and I can't give him one.

Every time I see a nurse with a babe at her breast I feel a pang here." She touched her heart.

"How can you be so certain that you're barren?"

"What other explanation is there?"

"Have you ever thought that it might be Edward?"

Joanna laughed and shook her head.

"He's too strong, too virile. It can't be him. So it must be me." Tears gleamed at the corners of her eyes. She blinked them away. "I feel as though I've failed him, Jane. The one thing he wants of me I can't give him."

"You're still young, the both of you," Jane soothed. "There's plenty of time."

Joanna jumped up and pulled Jane to her feet.

"Enough sad talk. Come on, I'll race you to the center of the labyrinth."

She darted off without waiting for Jane's reply. Jane smiled in a bemused way at her quick change of mood. Moving at a sedate walk, she trailed her right hand in the prickly leaves of the hedge wall and traced the twisting and bending course of the maze. She had walked the same path many times in her youth. The trick was to never lose touch with the right wall and you could not fail to reach the center.

As she expected, Joanna was nowhere to be seen when she emerged into the central clearing beneath the shade of a holly tree. The square was deserted. Bright chirps of nesting songbirds issued from somewhere within the hedge wall. Overhead, scattered clouds hung motionless against the blue sky. Jane stood and breathed the flower scents. The walk-lined quadrangle with its stone benches and decorative sundial possessed a magical virtue that always made her feel happy and safe.

To pass the time, she left the cool shade and wandered over to study the ornate sundial on its fluted marble column. Its engraved brass face had weathered to an attractive dull green. The pointer inclined toward six of the clock. She had not realized it was so late in the afternoon.

A shadow fell across the dial. Jane looked up at the sky and was surprised to see the blazing golden orb of the sun. Suddenly she felt cold, as though wrapped in a clammy sea mist. The world darkened around her. A swarm of angry black mites began to dance before her face. Crying out, she stumbled back, beating at them with her hands, but to no effect. Her fingers passed through them as though they were not really there.

The shadow dust thickened over her nose and mouth. With quickening terror she discovered that she could not breathe. Tiny pricks from a thousand invisible needles probed throughout her entire body. Her fingers and toes began to tingle. A numbing paralysis gripped her limbs and froze her as motionless as the white stone pillar beside her.

When Joanna entered the grassy clearing at the center of the hedge maze, a strange and horrifying sight snatched the smile of triumph from her lips. Jane stood like a statue encased in a swirling column of glittering black specks. Her mouth gaped and her rolling eyes silently implored Joanna for help. The shadowy mantle appeared almost to make love to her, so intimate was its clinging caress.

Indifferent to her own safety, Joanna ran toward her friend. Before she had taken three steps, the black column abruptly stopped its rotation and seemed to withdraw itself from Jane. It hung motionless for a moment as if frozen in thought. All at once it darted up into the blue sky and hung there in the form of a spinning funnel. Released from its embrace, Jane collapsed onto the grass.

As Joanna knelt at her side, the black whirlwind expanded upon the air and dissolved without a trace.

"What happened?" Jane gasped.

Joanna supported her head on a gentle palm.

"Something attacked you. It was like a black cloud."

"I remember," Jane said, struggling to sit up. "It was inside me. It strangled me so that I couldn't breathe. I felt it touch my baby. Then it left me."

"Is the baby all right?" Joanna asked in alarm.

"I think so." Jane pressed her belly gingerly. "It didn't hurt. It seemed to be probing my womb."

"We better get out of here before it comes back."

Joanna helped Jane to her feet and caught her as she started to fall. Jane was still too weak to stand alone. Joanna put her strong arm around the waist of the smaller woman and wrapped Jane's arm over her shoulder.

"Damn, this is going to take forever," Joanna muttered to herself as she left the center of the maze.

Jane extended her free left hand and touched the left wall of the walk.

"I know the way. I'll guide us."

Following Jane's directions, Joanna traversed the maddeningly convoluted path of the maze. It seemed to take an eternity, but under Jane's guidance they made no false turnings. They were able to emerge through the exterior entrance in far less time than it had taken Joanna to find the center.

A group of ladies and courtiers approached across the garden lawn from the palace. Joanna recognized the wide-sleeved black scholar's robe and black skullcap of John Dee. He walked at the side of a large woman in a spreading green dress and a huge lace ruff who strode across the lawn like a man. The ladies in waiting and courtiers clustered in her wake like workers and drones around a queen bee.

"That's Elizabeth," Jane said weakly in answer to her friend's unvoiced question. "Quick, help me stand straight, Joanna. I don't want John to think I'm sick."

The request came too late. John Dee was already running across the lawn ahead of the rest with long strides. His keen gray eyes never left the pale face of his wife as he caught her up by her free arm and embraced her.

"Jane, what's wrong? Are you ill?"

"She was attacked," Joanna said.

As the Queen approached, she described the events that had transpired in the maze.

"It was like that thing we saw on the river," Jane said. She drew several deep breathed and seemed to regain much of her lost strength. Dee released her.

"What did you see on the river?" he demanded with alarm.

"It was like a whirlwind of black dust, or smoke. It followed our barge down from Mortlake."

Dee's face became grave.

"I wish you had told me about this earlier. You should never have been left unattended."

"What is this strange intruder?" the Queen demanded, staring from Dee to Jane. "Can my guard capture it?"

"I fear not, Majesty," Dee told her. "It is an airy spirit, sent by those who sacked my library to spy upon me."

Elizabeth sniffed with dissatisfaction.

"As you say, Master Dee. You know best in matters that concern the black arts. Am I or my good ladies in danger, do you think?"

"I think not, Majesty. It was sent to watch me and my friends. When we depart it will depart with us."

Elizabeth looked at Joanna with an appraising eye.

"Who is this fine young woman?"

"Joanna Kelley, Your Majesty," Joanna said with a deep curtsy, blushing so furiously that she felt the heat in her ears.

"Kelley's wife," The Queen said. "You're a fit match for him, by the look of you. I warrant you've got a temper with that flaming hair. I don't suppose you're thinking of having it cut?"

"No, Your Majesty," Joanna said in surprise, glancing at Dee and Jane.

"Pity," the Queen said. "It would make a splendid wig."

"I could have it cut if it would please Your Majesty."

"Don't be silly, girl. It looks far more becoming on you than it ever would on me."

The Queen drew Dee aside to talk with him privately.

"Your wife is ill," she said. "I'll send for my physicians."

"I'm sure it will pass, Majesty. Spiritual attacks sometimes disorder the vital humors for a short while. The effect is similar to that of being struck by lightning."

"While you are away in Europe I'll post a guard at her door day and night, I promise you. Nothing will hurt her."

Dee shook his head with regret, a troubled expression on his long face.

"I can't risk leaving her in England. I thought we had abandoned this dark watcher at Mortlake, but now that I know it can follow us, I don't dare allow Jane or Joanna to walk unprotected. They must come with Kelley and me to Bohemia. I see no other safe course."

TEN

W hat do you make of this?" Kelley laid the hilt of the broken dagger on the round table before the seated John Dee.

Since returning from London he had spoken barely a word. Such periods of moodiness were not uncommon for Kelley. Dee had not asked his reasons for leaving Hampton Court. When he described to Kelley the attack on Jane, the dark man had been visibly angered. His affection for Jane went deeper than he ever admitted, even to himself.

It was late evening. Jane rested in bed across the corridor from Dee's temporary study at the palace, and Joanna sat watching over her.

Dee picked up the dagger gingerly and examined the ivory inlay as he might a sleeping scorpion. Its polished ebony hilt gleamed in the flickering glow from a single candle in the center of the table.

"A serpent climbing the naked blade of a sword. This is the emblem of the Sons of Coronzon. Where did you get it?"

With a few terse words Kelley described the events at the Rose Theater.

Dee frowned in annoyance.

"Why didn't you tell me about your interrogation of Bill Gowdie? I would have gone with you to the Rose."

"I didn't know if there was any truth in his story. Anyway, you had your audience with the Queen and there was no time to waste."

"You realize it may have been your pursuit of the book that inspired this attack upon Jane?"

Kelley nodded. A dark shadow of remorse passed over his brooding features as he stared into the candle flame.

Dee allowed his face to soften. He took a long breath.

"You're not to blame, Edward. I should have realized the Sons would try to strike at me through Jane, where my emotions are most vulnerable. But I thought the Watcher had been left behind at Mortlake. Old age has made me careless."

"What exactly is this Watcher?"

"A spirit of the ethereal regions, able to span vast distances and carry communications back to its masters. It is relatively harmless in its airy state. To injure living things it must take on a body of matter, at least partially. The more matter it assumes to itself, the stronger it grows."

"Can it be destroyed?"

Dee stroked his silver beard thoughtfully.

"Perhaps. Were it to become completely corporeal it might be killed with the sword. But in its airy state it is indestructible. The most I can do is ward it off with occult barriers of protection."

Kelley slid into the chair across the table from Dee and toyed with the broken dagger.

"Who exactly are these Sons of Coronzon? I noted Loew's reference to them in his letter, but since you chose not to discuss them I let the matter pass."

"There was no need for you to know of them. Knowledge is dangerous. They are a secret brotherhood of black magicians dedicated to the task of bringing about the aeon of Coronzon upon the earth."

"Him-That-Is-Fallen," Kelley murmured. "The Death Dragon."

Dee nodded. "I first became aware of the existence of the Sons while still a student at Cambridge." He smiled grimly. "One of the Sons attempted to recruit me into their brotherhood. When he saw that I was an unsuitable candidate, he tried to kill me. He was unsuccessful, as you see, but the Sons have never ceased to make the attempt, when the opportunity presents itself. That is why I was moved to establish the Order of Hermes."

"This is a night for truth telling," Kelley said, eyeing his friend with admiration. "I've long known that you were the head of a Hermetic fraternity. Why have you shut me out all these years?"

"The Sons were dormant, so the Order was dormant also. We exist solely to oppose Coronzon and his instruments. That is the chain that binds us together. When first you came to my house seeking knowledge of alchemical secrets, I had grave doubts about your motives. You yourself have admitted to dabbling in necromancy and other black arts. Since that time I have come to know you as a good man, so all may at last be revealed."

"Will you make me a member of your Order?"

"Are you sure you want to join? You should know that it's a delayed death sentence from the Sons of Coronzon to be connected with the Order of Hermes. They will never cease trying to kill you."

"They have already tried, and failed," Kelley said. His expression darkened. "More than this, they tried to kill Jane. For that reason alone I'm their sworn enemy."

Dee arose and took down from one of the bookcases a worn quarto edition of the Genevan Bible. He laid this upon the table. Kelley solemnly placed his left hand over its leather cover.

"Do you, Edward Kelley, swear in my presence and in the sight of God that from this day forward you will do all in your power to frustrate and overthrow the forces of Coronzon in whatsoever manner or form they may arise, prosecuting this enterprise single-mindedly even unto the day of your death?"

"I do swear."

"Do you furthermore swear never to reveal the existence of this Order, not even under the extremity of torture and the threat of execution, except to new initiates of tested and proven worth, or in times of dire need, should such need ever arise, to your own wife and family?"

"I swear it."

"Do you accept that by breaking these oaths, you consign your immortal soul to eternal damnation?"

"I do."

"Before God and his angels I declare you to be a member of the Order of Hermes."

He took a small square of paper from the drawer of the nearby writing desk and with his quill pen inscribed it with a symbol, then slid the paper across the table to Kelley.

"This is the sign of our Order, by which you may be known and may know other brothers and sisters."

"I recognize this glyph," Kelley said, studying it. "This is your own hieroglyphic monad, about which you wrote a book in Latin some twenty odd years ago."

"It was a mistake to have the book published," Dee admitted. "Too many friends of Coronzon came to know about our Order. I was seduced by my own pride in having solved great mysteries, and wished to proclaim my wisdom abroad for the help of other true seekers of the art. I repent of it now."

"You said sisters. Do you admit women into your Order?"

Dee nodded.

"Is Jane—?"

"No. I saw no reason to endanger her life further by making her a member. She knows of its existence, of course."

Kelley lit the corner of the paper in the candle flame and watched it burn down to his fingers before dropping it on the broad base of the brass candlestick. His thoughts danced like the reflected flame in the dark orbs of his eyes.

"I begin to see why the Queen uses you so often in her intrigues. It must be convenient for her to have a secret society at her beck and call on the Continent."

"The Order is never used for political ends," Dee said. "It has a sacred purpose that transcends political borders. I serve the Queen in my own capacity. I serve God through the Order."

Doubt was evident in Kelley's features, but he said nothing. His personal intent was to obtain the Book of Lilith and kill the man who had tried to kill him. The other uses of the Order, be they few or many, did not interest him.

Dee replaced the Bible on the shelf and bolted the door of the study. He dragged his travel trunk over to the table with some difficulty.

"Thus far the Adversary has broken into my home, stolen my property, spied upon us, and abused my wife," he said, unlocking the trunk with a small key that hung on a thread around his neck. "I say it's time we did a little spying of our own."

"Agreed."

Dee removed the candle from the tabletop and set it upon the corner of the writing desk. From his trunk he took a plain white linen cloth, which he spread over the table. In the center of this he set a thick wax seal nine inches in diameter that was inscribed on both surfaces with occult symbols and lettering.

Kelley recognized the Sigillum Aemeth, a pentacle of immense potency that the Enochian angels had revealed to him not long after he entered Dee's employ as a scryer. He averted his eyes from the sacred instrument out of respect until Dee covered it under a cloth of iridescent silk.

On top of the wax pentacle Dee put a red satin cushion with four crosses in its corners. He positioned a silver candlestick on each side of the cushion and pressed white candles into their sockets, then lit the wicks with the flame from the candle already burning on the writing desk.

With careful reverence he removed from the trunk a spherical globe of pale rose quartz that was about the size and shape of an orange. This was one of the scrying stones he and Kelley had often used in the past to make contact with the Enochian angels, who had delivered to Dee so many arcane secrets of magic. Dee placed this in the center of the satin cushion.

"Do you mean to keep a record of this night's work?" Kelley muttered.

Dee shook his head.

"One day my diaries may fall into the hands of the Inquisition. That is why I take such care to alter the names and dates, as you yourself know. This present work is too secret to set down with pen and ink."

He proceeded to erect a magic circle about the table while Kelley sat staring into the shining depths of the

stone. At last assured that they would not be interrupted
by mortal or spiritual intruders, Dee sat opposite his seer
and waited. It was always the same. Neither man knew at
the beginning if the Enochian angels would answer their
summons. The angels were independent beings who
came when it suited their own purposes.

Dee often wondered in idle moments whether the
angels served them, or they served the angels. It was the
archangel Michael who had commanded Kelley to take a
wife shortly after Kelley's arrival at Mortlake. The
alchemist had protested bitterly, declaring that he needed
to remain celibate during the practice of his art, but the
angels had refused to yield. The angels had also commanded Dee and Kelley to leave England with their wives
some four years ago, and had predicted dire consequences
should they fail to obey. This not even the Queen knew.

Over the past four years they had transmitted through
Kelley an elaborate system of magic composed of a series
of evocations in a strange angelic language and a complex
table of letters and sigils. This system Dee had dutifully
recorded in his diaries, but he had yet to fathom its mysteries. Only his immense erudition and knowledge of
ciphers had allowed him to make any sense at all of the
obscure communications, which were delivered by means
of a series of bewilderingly complex magic squares.

"Anything?" Dee inquired.

"Nothing," Kelley said with disgust. "The stone
remains dark."

Dee stood and delivered a formal Latin invocation to
the angels of his own composing. This had often been
effective in the past when the spirits were slow to respond.
It proved its worth again this night. The crystal began to
glow with a soft radiance.

"I see the curtain," Kelley murmured, his chin sunk
upon his chest as he stared into the stone. "Now it

parts. Someone comes forth as if from a great distance. It is Madimi."

"Welcome, Madimi," Dee said. "I trust both you and your Mother are well."

"'Welcome father,'" Kelley said, echoing the words of the spirit from the depths of the crystal.

"Why do you call me father, Madimi?" Dee asked.

"'Have you not in the past thought of me as a daughter?'"

"I have," Dee admitted.

"'So I am disposed to think of you as a father.'"

"I am honored, Madimi."

"'Have you at last joined the forces of light?'" Kelley frowned and glanced at Dee. "This was spoken to me."

"She means your joining the Order of Hermes," Dee said.

"I have always served God and opposed the Devil," Kelley said into the crystal. "Now she is laughing. I do not like her manner. She mocks me. She says, 'The book will not serve you.'"

"Where is the book, Madimi? Can you see it?"

"'No, but my Mother can. She says to tell you that it has been carried across the sea this very night.'"

"The book has left England," Dee said to Kelley. "We are too late."

"Can you show me the ship?" Kelley demanded.

"'It is a Flemish flyboat called the *Emmanuel*. The dark man stands on its deck looking to the north. He carries the book in his pocket. He has conjured a favorable wind to speed his voyage.'"

"I see it now," Kelley said. "Everything is very dark. Only a single lantern burns on the bow. There is a man standing at the rail. I can't make out his face. He's in shadow. The wind blows strong. The crests of the waves are white in the moonlight."

"Madimi, what can you tell us of the thing that attacked my wife?" Dee inquired.

"The ship is covered with a mist," Kelley said. "The mist parts. Madimi appears as before, but this time she is older, more like a maid of eighteen years."

"Why have you aged?" Kelley asked the vision in the stone.

"She says, 'Because I have to speak of more serious matters.'"

"What is the nature of the fiend that follows us?" Dee asked again.

"'It is a mindless thing,' she says. 'It is an abomination shaped from the foul, yeasty humors of the tomb to hunt and slay the enemies of she who is the shadow of my Mother.'"

"What is the name of this shadow?"

Kelley cocked his ear and listened, then shook his head in disgust.

"She is afraid to speak the name."

"Was the spirit that pursues us sent by the Sons of Coronzon, as we suspect?" Dee asked.

"'Yes.'"

"Do they have the book?"

"'Yes.'"

"Do you know where they are taking it?"

"'That is a variable matter of the future.'" Kelley looked at Dee with one eyebrow cocked. "What does she mean?"

"Perhaps that the Sons have not yet decided where to take the book."

"Will you watch and tell us where they take it?" Kelley demanded of the spirit in the crystal. He listened, and shook his head in disgust. "She says once the book returns to the land it will lie hidden under a spell of glamour that her Mother cannot penetrate."

"Madimi, can you tell me the condition of my friend Rabbi Loew at Prague? I have great concern over his safety."

"'He is well. He walks abroad through the streets of the ghetto thinking about you this very minute. In his pocket he carries a letter addressed to you.'"

"What does the letter say?"

"The stone has gone cloudy again," Kelley said.

"No matter," Dee muttered. "We'll talk to Loew when we reach Bohemia."

For many minutes Kelley remained motionless, silently staring into the crystal. Dee was about to end the scrying session when at last he spoke.

"The clouds grow black. They roil and churn. A little space between them like the bottom of a maelstrom opens. I see an image of black cliffs and blasted sand. Something approaches. It is monstrous thing like a great bloody serpent with many legs and heads. Upon its back rides a woman. She is naked. Her eyes are insolent, like the eyes of a harlot. She smiles at me and beckons.

"Now she is become your wife, Jane. Her face twists in agony. She holds onto her belly, which grows fat and round all in an instant. Something issues from between her parted thighs that is like a great, black worm. She picks up the black thing and holds it to her left breast. It sucks. Now it splits open. Out comes a green serpent that twines itself lovingly all about her body. She stiffens and begins to struggle against the serpent. It strangles her and swallows her. Now it splits open like an overripe plum.

"A woman arises from it on the back of the dragon. She is dark of face and beautiful, but terrible of aspect with a huge swollen belly. A star blazes on her brow. From between her thighs flows a river of dark, monstrous shapes. They copulate with each other and give rise to still more monsters. Their excrements cover over the whole face of the world. Now she looks my way as though she sees me. She sneers with scorn. She points at me."

A jagged bolt of blue flame crackled from the crystal and struck Kelley in the forehead. He fell over backward, overturning his chair, and lay staring up at the ceiling as though dead. A smell like heated metal filled the chamber.

Dee grabbed a black cloth out of his trunk and draped it over the crystal. He inscribed the five Hebrew letters of the name Yeheshuah in the air and gingerly dropped the crystal into the trunk, taking care not to touch its surface. Only after closing the lid of the trunk did he hurry around the table to examine Kelley.

The seer drew a racking breath and sat up. Fine droplets of sweat glistened on his face. He blinked in a dazed manner and looked around as if he had never seen the chamber before. Slowly, intelligence seeped back into his dark eyes. He pushed himself to his feet and shook off Dee's solicitous hands.

"You told me once that nothing could penetrate your circle of protection," he said accusingly.

Dee shrugged his slender shoulders.

"I was wrong."

"What the devil was that she-hag? My head feels as though it's been hit by a hammer."

For answer, Dee went to the bookshelf and took down the Bible. He turned to the end and read: "And upon her forehead was a name written, Mystery, Babylon the Great, the Mother of Harlots and Abominations of the Earth."

Dee shut the book. He and Kelley regarded one another solemnly without speaking.

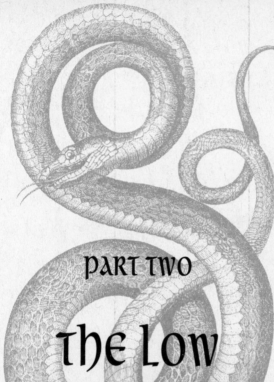

PART TWO

THE LOW COUNTRIES

ELEVEN

The Italian sat in a high-backed chair of ornately carved black walnut and stared at his own dark reflections. No other furniture occupied the midnight floor of the strange, eleven-sided chamber. Its windowless walls were sheathed in polished slabs of obsidian glass, so cunningly joined that the seams were invisible in the flickering flames from the eleven lamps set in iron brackets at the angles of the walls. Even the door was covered in obsidian and invisible when closed. The arched ceiling, like the floor, glittered with polished black granite.

The chamber lay hundreds of feet beneath a stone fortress, deep in the heart of a great mountain, yet the impression on the senses was one of limitless space. This illusion was so powerful that members of the brotherhood entering the room for the first time fell to their knees and covered their eyes. The sole touch of color came from an eleven-cornered, interlocking pentacle inlaid on the floor with red semiprecious stone. It seemed to float in a starless night on a sea of darkness, ringing the chair at its center with a circle of blood that matched the scarlet of the Italian's hooded robe.

Staring fixedly at his dim image in the obsidian mirror that formed the wall opposite his chair, he allowed his mind to abstract itself from his flesh, and propelled it

101

along a ray of will, westward beyond the boundary of the physical plane. This required less effort than it had in London. The catacombs beneath the fortress had been erected on the borderline that divides the world of matter from the world of spirit. Those who sought to follow its winding passages often found themselves crossing into the astral plane between one step and the next.

This was his first communication with the Watcher since his hurried flight from England. It had been essential to get the book safely to the sanctuary of Coronzon in the shortest possible time. Flying like the wind across sea and land, he had driven himself at a pace far beyond the endurance of most men. He had not slept forty hours in the last ten days. Beneath his rigid shell of self-control his corrupt heart lusted with impatience to learn the reaction of John Dee to the murder of his cherished wife.

Spurred by its master's heightened power, which was multiplied in the obsidian mirrors, the black whirlwind began to coalesce as soon as he sent forth a mental summons. He stared into the center of the swirling vortex of sparks with his astral perception until its lidless eye formed.

"Did you kill Jane Dee as I commanded?" he asked impatiently.

The dimensionless void filled with an aura of mingled apology and regret. It reached the awareness of the Italian as an odor that was sickly sweet, like decaying flowers.

At first the Italian failed to comprehend the meaning of the scent message. It had never occurred to him that the spirit might fail to carry out his command. When the truth finally crept into his awareness, his curses erupted through the void in exploding balls of astral fire. The Watcher calmly endured its master's colorful display of fury.

"Why does the bitch still live?"

You commanded that I slay one. There were two.

The Italian puzzled over this cryptic mental statement for several moments.

"Jane Dee is pregnant?" he demanded.

The assent of the Watcher communicated itself.

She carries a man-child.

"Fool! What does that matter? You should have killed them both."

You said to slay one. There were two, the vortex repeated with the logic of the idiot.

The Italian suppressed his anger, knowing that its display would serve no purpose. The mind of this class of elemental, insofar as it could be called a mind, was completely literal, akin to that of a young child. It could scarcely be expected to take the initiative.

"Where is John Dee and his gravid bitch presently?"

They take a ship across the Channel.

"Good. You have the opportunity to redeem yourself in my sight." The Italian sucked the black pit of his malice with renewed enjoyment. "Fly to them. Raise a tempest and sink their ship before it makes landfall."

The vortex paused in its turning, then resumed its motion. Again, the faint odor of regret wafted through the astral darkness.

The newly growing soul in the woman's womb has no stain of sin. It is difficult to slay such innocence.

The Italian exerted the lever of his will. He felt the distant reflection of red needles of agony as they stabbed into the eye in the whirlwind. It resisted, but the will of the Italian was too powerful.

I will kill them all, my master.

Satisfied that he had reasserted his authority, the Italian allowed the red needles to withdraw themselves. He began to sever the astral contact, then realized the Watcher wanted to say something more.

"Yes, what is it?"

You have the book, it sighed in his mind.

"What about the book?" The Italian was not accustomed to interrogations by his astral servants.

When the book is opened, you will give me a body.

He stared into the unwinking red eye with astonished amusement, too surprised for the moment even to be angry. Never before had a spirit of this class expressed personal desire.

"When the book is opened, we shall see," he said.

You will give me a body.

The astral space was pervaded with the mingled scent of urgency, need, and something more, a new odor the Italian had never smelled before—threat. He frowned mentally. Jagged bolts of lightning crashed across the void in sympathetic response.

"When the book is opened and She comes forth, She will decide what to give you. Go now. Fulfill your function. Report to me when you have wrecked the ship."

The red eye in the vortex stared at him for several moments. Whatever thoughts or emotions lay behind it were unreadable. Slowly it dissolved into a swirling cloud of glittering black points. These faded like ice crystals under a hot sun and vanished.

TWELVE

John Dee studied the towering gray clouds massed along the northwestern horizon of the sea with growing alarm. Already it was blowing near a gale. The skilled English crew of the little boyer *Bridget* found themselves pressed to the limit managing its strained linen sails. He heard the wind singing in the rigging and the rattle of the spray as it washed over the rail like pellets of hail. The deck dipped and surged under his feet. Had he not held firmly to the creaking mainmast, he would have fallen.

"You shouldn't be up here, sir," warned a seaman with a red bandanna around his head and a dark socket where his left eye had once resided. "It's dangerous."

Dee thanked the man for his well-meaning concern, but made no attempt to return below deck.

Having performed what he considered his Christian duty, the seaman forgot about Dee and went on with his business. He squinted through his single eye at the lowering northern horizon and shook his head. There was enough to worry about without wasting time on foolish passengers.

Kelley worked his way along the storm lines and lurched against Dee as he grabbed for the mast.

"How are they?" Dee found it necessary to raise his voice over the howl of the wind.

"Jane's fine, as usual. The sea never bothers her. Joanna's sick as a dog. She keeps begging Jane to cut her throat and put her out of her misery."

"She may not have much longer to suffer."

Kelley followed Dee's gaze to the horizon.

"Jesu Christos," he said. "We're finished."

Like some vast gray mountain, the line of storm clouds towered over the sails of the ship and blotted out the blue sky. In an instant it became dark as night. The wind doubled in fury. One of the foresails tore down its middle with a terrible ripping sound and began to lash the mast and the rigging. Barefoot seamen swarmed up the dancing ropes to gather in its tatters. A blast sent the boyer over onto its starboard side so that the crests of the waves covered its rail.

The entire voyage across the Channel had been beset with obstacles. After leaving Hampton Court they had traveled down the Thames by barge to London. A wherry had conveyed them to Greenwich, where they 'had refreshed themselves at the house of Dee's friend, the potter Goodman Fern. The ferry boat had been late from Gravesend to carry them to their ship, which lay at anchor some seven miles beyond Gravesend in the mouth of the Thames. They had not reached it until the small hours of the morning. For three days they had waited for a favorable wind. Joanna had retired seasick to the Kelley's small cabin on the first night and had not set foot on deck since.

Finally the English captain of the *Bridget* had grown tired of waiting on the weather and had sailed into choppy seas, beating his way with great difficulty out the estuary of the river and battling the wind north across the Channel. Even though the little Flemish-built boyer ran close to the wind, she made almost no headway. She was heavily laden with a cargo of tin and copper billets from the mines of Cornwall, which greatly hindered her excellent sailing qualities.

The perverse, contrary wind drove the ship toward a section of the Dutch coast unfamiliar to the captain of the *Bridget*. He did not dare attempt a landing, but was able to work his way back out to sea against the main brunt of the blast, and by a combination of skill and luck managed to avoid the treacherous sand bars along the shore. As a consequence, for more than a week the ship was gradually driven south, away from its destination of Rotterdam, which in ordinary weather would have been reached in three or four days.

"This storm is unnatural," Kelley shouted in Dee's ear. "There's sorcery behind it."

Dee nodded. He thought it ironic that he, who hoped to defend England against the Spanish fleet by raising a tempest in the Channel, should himself fall prey to the same device. He knew from experience that weather magic of this magnitude was slow in the making and equally slow in the breaking. Even so, be began to chant in the sonorous Enochian tongue, calling upon the angel Adire, ruler of the airy element in the northern quarter of the world, to calm the wind by the authority of the holy names of the Watchtower of the North.

"O you angel of God, Adire, flowing with truth and goodness, who rule in the northern part of the world; O you Adire, bright angel that liveth in the air of the north and hath vision of all its diverse qualities; O you Adire, faithful to God and the ministers of our Creator: I, John Dee, in the name of the same our Creator and God, humbly supplicate you through these holy names of God, Rezioner and Narzfem...."

As he concluded the invocation and inscribed the last of three crosses upon the air toward the north with his right hand, lightning struck the top of the mainmast with a blinding flash and a simultaneous crack of thunder. The upper shaft of the mast exploded and scattered deadly splinters several feet in length over the deck. One of the larger shards transfixed a seaman as he bent to pull a rope. He dropped to the deck like a slab of beef, dead before his head struck the planks. His shipmates continued to heave the line. They were battling for their lives and had no leisure for sentiment.

"Look!" Kelley shouted to Dee. "The mast is on fire!"

The lightning had ignited the splintered end of the mast. As Dee watched, it burned like a torch in the driving wind and showered a plume of sparks over the side. Suddenly the dark window of the sky opened and torrents of rain poured out of the firmament, extinguishing the mast in an instant.

"There's something up there," Kelley said, pointing. "Do you see it?"

Dee squinted against the driving rain that blurred his vision. Lightning crackled and lit the clouds. He saw nothing but the flapping sails and the stark outline of the spars. He shook his head.

"It's there, clinging to the mainmast," Kelley insisted. "Some kind of demon. It must be causing the tempest. I have to drive it off before it sinks the ship."

Before Dee could respond, Kelley leapt into the rain-soaked rigging and began to climb.

"Edward!" Dee shouted.

He released the mast and staggered after the alchemist. Kelley was already high overhead and out of hearing. Faintly Dee heard his name. He looked back to the elevated cabins in the rear of the ship and saw Jane clinging to the edge of the door. So steeply was the deck inclined, she had to hold on to keep from sliding down to the starboard rail, which rode half in and half out of the water. As he watched her, a wave rolled up the deck and swirled around her sodden skirts.

Dee glanced up at Kelley and realized he could never follow the alchemist through the rigging. With an uncharacteristic curse he pushed himself away from the base of the mast and caught a storm line, then hauled himself hand over hand toward his wife, praying the fates would be kind and a wave would not sweep her into the sea before he reached her.

"Get down, Jane, get down! You'll be washed overboard."

The wind tore his words out of his mouth and carried them away. He saw her lips move but heard nothing above the roar of the tempest. It seemed to take an eternity to reach her. He threw himself across the inclined deck and knocked her into the open doorway just as a great wall of gray water swept completely across the ship. Its power broke on the sturdy work of the rear cabins. Although much water poured through the opening and ran down the stairs to the deck below, Dee was able to shield Jane with his body and cling to the frame of the doorway. He pulled the door shut and latched it against the wind.

"Jane, are you mad? You might have been killed."

An anguished expression distorted her face.

"It's Joanna. She stopped breathing."

He raced through the dark chaos of the ship with Jane following close at his heels. A swinging lantern offered some illumination in the cabin itself. The wet floor was littered with furniture and possessions that rolled back and forth with each surge of the waves. Joanna lay sprawled across her bunk, her damp red hair draped across the footboard like a tangle of seaweed, her night-dress twisted around her bare thighs. Dee observed that her lips were blue and her face as pale as wax.

"She's choking," he said. "Jane, help me lift her."

While his wife supported Joanna's shoulders, Dee pried open her jaw and reached into her mouth to pull her tongue forward. He saw that her throat was clogged with vomit. Quickly he laid her across the bed on her stomach and pressed forcefully against her lower back, driving the remaining air in her lungs out through her throat and nose. A spurt of vomit jetted onto the sea-washed floor of the cabin. Still she did not take a breath.

Dee sat on the bed and turned her over across his knees. Her head rested on his thigh. Drawing a deep breath, he sealed her nose, put his lips to her open mouth and blew air into her lungs. Her chest rose. He was grat-ified to see that when he took his mouth away, her chest fell. At least the air passage was now open. He continued to blow breath into her lungs for several minutes while Jane called her name and chaffed her hand.

Suddenly Joanna jerked and coughed. Dee tilted her head to the side. Vomit mixed with spittle trickled from her mouth. She drew a shuddering gasp. He sat her up gently and held her while she breathed, her entire body racked with the effort.

"Get her some water, Jane."

Jane hurried to empty water from a hanging bottle into a tin cup and held it to her friend's trembling lips. Joanna took a sip and turned her head to spit the foulness from her mouth. Then she drank greedily.

"What did you do to her?" Jane asked her husband wonderingly.

"I breathed vital humors into her lungs to stimulate her paralyzed spirit. It's a technique mentioned in a medical tract by the Arab Alkindi. I never thought to have occasion to test its worth."

Joanna tried to speak. Her voice was husky, barely above a whisper. Dee and Jane bent their heads close to hear.

"I had a dream. A nightmare—some hellish thing sat on my chest and started to choke me."

"Hush, Joanna, rest now," Jane said, stroking her damp forehead. "You're safe now."

Dee drew his wife to the doorway of the cabin so that Joanna would not overhear their murmured conversation. He held her in his arms and braced his knee against the side of the door frame to keep from falling.

"It may not have been merely a dream," he said. "Watch her closely. Stay beside her at all times. I don't want either of you left alone."

Jane met his comforting gaze with a worried expression.

"John, what are we going to do? You see how sick she is. If we don't reach land soon, I'm afraid she'll die."

"I know," Dee agreed. "We must hope she'll regain some of her strength when this storm abates."

They both listened. The howl of the wind and the lash of the waves mocked their hopes and battened on their fears, growing ever stronger. Jane did not need to voice the thought in her mind. Her husband read it in her anguished eyes. If the storm did not let up soon, they would all perish together.

THIRTEEN

Reluctantly, the Italian turned his thoughts downward into the dead sea that lay like a fen beneath the foundation of the world. It was the final repository of each wicked act and every evil thought, the dark pool where all secret horrors lay drowned. Suicides and murders formed its wellspring. Rage warmed its waters, hatred kept them bitter. The Italian viewed it as the reservoir for his grandiose ambitions and the fountain of his perverse desires. Yet the obscene Mother-thing that ruled this dark kingdom terrified him.

It was impossible to prepare for these meetings. She manifested to his awareness in a bewildering variety of forms that were shaped and defined by his thoughts and feelings, and by her own capricious and unpredictable moods.

He became conscious that the black mirror of the chthonian sea hung overhead, reflecting in its depths the frosty glitter of the ever-present solitary star. In the vast rocky valley below, pale blind creatures squirmed and slithered and undulated over each other, fighting to reach and attach themselves to a bloated white hill covered with innumerable swollen breasts that had eyes instead of nipples. She watched his approach with her devouring gaze.

Disorientation threatened to tear out his mind at its roots. The sea and valley spun lazily around and inverted their places, and he realized with shock that he hovered in the vast darkness close under the roof of the measureless cavern of nightmare. Monstrous grubs swarmed over its moist black surface, clinging to the rock, and lent it a parody of life. They looked very much like maggots seething in the putrid abdominal cavity of a corpse.

"You have the key," the Mother-thing demanded. The thought-words "talisman" and "incantation" and "charm" echoed in his mind.

"It is safe within the fortress," he said. "Even now my fraters begin the work of its unfolding."

A wave of satisfaction undulated across her pendulous bulk.

"I sense danger. The Sacred Scribe still lives."

This was the she-thing's name for Dee. The Italian did not understand its significance, but accepted it as a label.

"Not much longer. I've sent my servant to raise a storm against him."

"Why did you allow him upon the waters?"

He found himself explaining the failure of the Watcher to execute his earlier command. Before he could finish, an icy ray of fury stabbed into his mind. From a vast distance he felt an echoing agony in his groin, as though a nail transfixed his testicles. His concentration wavered. He sensed himself slipping back upward through the darkness toward his incarnate vessel and fought dizzily to sustain his awareness within the vault of the cavern.

"Fool! Why did you not tell me the mate of the Sacred Scribe was gravid?"

"I only learned of it today," he gasped, battling to remain conscious.

The agony relented an iota.

"She must not be harmed. Bring her to me."

Terror shivered through the Italian.

"It may already be too late to turn the storm...."

He screamed silently as the nail twisted in his scrotum.

"If she dies, you die," the Mother-thing promised. Her pallid breasts dripped blood from the nipples of their eyes. "Instruct your demon."

Struggling frantically to compose his mind, the Italian endeavored to send a ray of will westward. The distance was great, the intervening aether unsettled by thunderheads. He made a feathery flicker of contact with the Watcher and commanded it to cease intensifying the storm and withdraw from the ship. As the Italian well knew, not even the Watcher could make the tempest cease. Once raised, it must run its course regardless of the consequences.

He sensed confusion in the simplistic mind of the spirit and cursed the weakness of his will. For an instant he saw through the eyes of the Watcher and knew profound relief. The ship still floated above the waves, although it leaned far to starboard on the very brink of foundering, the top of its mainmast gone and its sails in tatters. Whether the Watcher had understood his order was not clear, but the Italian could not afford the luxury of uncertainty.

"She lives," he gasped in his astral voice.

The pain in his testicles relented and gradually dwindled to a dull ache.

"Guard her life. Allow her to come to me. She is the gateway foretold in prophecy. She is the mother of the aeon. If she dies...."

The Italian fled her dreadful weeping eyes and entered his physical shell still screaming.

FOURTEEN

While Dee was in the process of breathing life into the unconscious Joanna, her husband clung with his left arm to the highest spar on the mainmast and confronted a creature out of nightmare.

In the driving rain and darkness it was no more than a hulking shadow, but when the lightning flashed he saw that it was humanoid. Fine white fur or feathers covered its muscular legs. Its naked feet ended in great curved black talons similar to those of a hawk. With these it gripped the spar while it slashed at the ropes supporting it with its clawed hands. Membranous pink wings that were also fledged on the back with white feathers stretched down the sides of its body from its wrists to its ankles. Its head was birdlike, save for large pink ears that spread themselves on ribs of bone like two sails in the wind.

Kelley shouted a curse. The demon ignored him. It continued its destructive attack on the tough hemp ropes with single-minded glee. Kelley drew his rapier and pulled himself to a sitting position on the rain-slick spar, his back to the mast. Heart pounding, he inched his way outward, relying on the flapping remains of the sail that pressed against the toe of his boot to hold his precarious balance. The sky was a wall of darkness, the sea a black pit. The deck of the ship became visible only when the lightning crashed. He might almost have been alone in the universe with the demon.

He extended his upper body and cut at the monster with his sword. The keen curved tip of the rapier passed through its torso as if through water. The demon stared at him with gleaming black eyes and hissed in derision through its hooked beak. It hopped back two steps, then resumed its clawing at the rigging. Kelley realized that if the rope broke before he reached the creature, he would have nothing against which to balance his body. He would certainly fall. Grimly he pushed himself farther out on the spar.

He remembered what Dee had said about the airy Watcher at Mortlake. To do physical harm, a spirit must take on physical form, and then it might be slain with cold steel. Why, then, had his blade passed through the body of the demon? He studied it as he inched nearer and noticed that its taloned fingers were darker than the rest of its body, which had a misty quality.

Taking deliberate aim, he directed his sword cut at its nearer left hand and had the satisfaction of seeing two razor-tipped fingers fall into the darkness. The demon shrieked its pain and fury. The sound chilled Kelley's blood. Tightening his legs around the spar, he managed to cut off the entire right hand of the creature when it reached out to rend him. Black ichor spurted from the stump of its sinewy wrist.

It clutched the stump beneath its opposite armpit and glared at Kelley with such a look of concentrated malignant hatred that the alchemist felt it strike him as a physical force. He wavered, but managed to keep his balance and retain his sword at the same time. The demon stared at the shining ribbon of steel extended before its face. With a hiss of contempt it knocked the blade from Kelley's fingers as if from the grasp of a child. Kelley saw it flash once in the silver rain before it vanished into darkness.

The demon hopped forward and reached out with its remaining claw. Kelley read his death in its soulless black eyes and prepared to fling himself into its embrace. If he could close his hands around its throat, he might be able to take it with him beneath the waves.

For no reason apparent to the alchemist, the spirit hesitated and stood perched on the spar motionless, its head cocked as though listening to an inner voice. It glared at Kelley, its black eyes wrestling with his blazing gaze. The rain-washed, snarling bronze face of the man, teeth barred and nostrils flared, was scarcely distinguishable from the countenance of the demon. Kelley sensed the mingled regret and rage in its heart. It body became darker and seemed to grow indistinct. Suddenly it dissolved into a whirling vortex of grainy shadows and spun away on the wind like some satanic pinwheel.

Taking infinite care, Kelley began to inch blindly backward. His arms and legs trembled with fatigue. He knew full well the flying thing might choose to circle in the wind and attack him from the back, but as there was nothing he could do to defend himself, he concentrated on reaching the mast without falling.

A hand clutched his left shoulder. Kelley felt his heart skip, then resume its frantic beating. The weathered fingers were human. Other hands dragged him back to safety. The crew of the boyer had seen him from the deck in the lightning flashes, and two of them had risked their own lives to help him. With gratitude he allowed the skillful seamen to guide him to the rope ladder and support him on the way down.

"What were you doing up there?" the younger of the two seamen, barely more than a boy, shouted into his ear.

"Didn't you see it?" Kelley demanded, staring with wild black eyes from the one to the other.

"All I saw was a madman battling the wind with his sword," the grizzled older seaman said.

Kelley shook them off and searched in vain around the deck for Dee. He made his way below to his cabin, where he found Dee and Jane sitting on the bed on either side of a pale and visibly shaken Joanna. She trembled violently despite the blanket around her shoulders. When Kelley came in, she glanced up without enthusiasm. He knelt on one knee and captured her icy hands between his own.

"I'm all right," she rasped, her throat burned raw from the acid of her vomit.

Dee explained to Kelley what had taken place since they parted on the deck. In his concern over Joanna's welfare the alchemist forgot his own encounter with the aerial demon. He tried to embrace his wife, but she seemed embarrassed by her weakness. She refused to meet his eyes, and kept pushing him aside, until at last he gave up and allowed Jane to hold her. Joanna laid her head wearily on her friend's shoulder and closed her bloodshot eyes.

Dee rose from the bed and drew Kelley outside the cabin into the corridor.

"If we survive this storm we must reach port soon," he murmured. "The sickness is killing her."

"She always gets seasick on the Channel," Kelley said. "But never like this."

"She's never been in such foul weather for so many days," Dee observed. "Some men don't recover from seasickness. It just gets worse the longer they're away from land."

Jane appeared in the doorway of the cabin.

"She's asleep," she whispered. "I elevated her head. She seems to be breathing easier."

"The acid from her stomach has burned her lungs," Dee told Kelley. "It will take days for her to recover. You must watch her closely."

Kelley nodded, a worried expression drawing down the corners of his thin lips.

"Listen," Jane said.

They stood listening to the rhythmic creak of the ship and the howl of the wind.

"I think it's dying down a little," she continued.

"She's right," Kelley agreed. He noticed that the heaving motion of the deck was marginally less pronounced.

Leaving Jane to watch over the sleeping Joanna, the men returned to the open deck. The waves no longer washed over the rail, and the rain had almost ceased. In the north the sky was lighter, foreshadowing a break in the clouds. Kelley glanced up at the mainmast. It was occupied by several toiling forms, but all of them were human. He related to Dee his encounter with the demon.

"Why it flew away when it did mystifies me," he concluded. "It might have killed me at its leisure."

"Perhaps it thought the gale would do the task," Dee suggested. "This storm was more than natural. The Sons of Coronzon seek to bar us from the Continent."

"If not for the foresight of our captain in keeping us well away from shore, we would have been wrecked. We may still be," Kelley added.

Dee studied the eastern horizon and shook his head. "I don't think so. My invocation to the Enochian angels has done its work."

No land was in view. This was a good sign in their present battered condition. It gave the crew time to rig fresh sails and pump the water out of the hold. The sight of land, so devoutly wished for on some occasions by mariners, under other circumstances was a curse. So it was with all things in life, Dee reflected.

"I'll be damned," Kelley murmured.

He made his way across the rolling deck to the starboard rail, where his rapier stood embedded through the oak, its bare tip projecting a handbreadth out the underside. He worked it back and forth with care until it was loose enough to worry out of the tough wood.

"Good Damascus steel," he muttered with a grin to Dee, who peered wonderingly up at the mast.

The dark clouds rolled across the sky and vanished below the southern horizon. The waves continued high, but their crests were no longer white with anger. A gull appeared, its wings golden in the slanting afternoon sunlight. The wind gradually changed and began to blow steadily from the west. So swiftly could the sea change from killer to lover. The *Bridget* tacked east and sailed past the coast of Flanders and into the islands that lay off the Netherlands. By twilight they reached the estuary of Antwerp.

FIFTEEN

The *Bridget* anchored in the estuary of the river Scheldt to carry out emergency repairs on the damage from the storm before attempting to limp on to Rotterdam. The Spanish governor of Antwerp would not allow the ship to tie up to the quay or unload its cargo of tin and copper bars. However, when informed of the grave condition of Joanna Kelley, he agreed to permit Dee's small party to come ashore. At sunset a flat-bottomed rowboat conveyed Dee, Kelley, and their wives, along with their travel cases, from the *Bridget* to the docks of Antwerp.

It had been Dee's original intention to sail directly to Rotterdam, then take the first available ship up the Frisian coast to the German town of Hamburg, and from there proceed by barge up the Elbe river to Bohemia. In view of Joanna's illness this course was clearly impossible, even were he able to persuade some ship's Catholic captain to accept English passengers. He decided the safest plan was to remain in Antwerp for a week or so at the house of his old friend William Silvius, the printer, until Joanna recovered her strength, then set out overland to the Dutch port of Amsterdam. From there he stood a good chance of finding a coastal trading vessel that would carry them to the mouth of the Elbe.

They clustered together on the dock while a sullen porter loaded their trunks onto a two-wheeled cart. The waterfront presented a desolate aspect. Only a scattering of ships occupied the numerous berths. Most of the cargo cranes stood forlornly empty. The few seamen and fish-wives hurrying past cast them suspicious glances when they heard their English accents.

Kelley surveyed the many burned-out roofs and boarded windows that disfigured the skyline of the town like some creeping disease. Lit red by the rays of the setting sun, the houses presented a ghastly aspect. The tall spire of the cathedral rose against the golden clouds like a blood-stained sword.

"A cheerful place for a hanging," he observed to Dee.

Dee nodded sadly.

"It is completely changed from when I dwelt here in 1562. In those days Antwerp was the trading capital of all Europe. As many as five hundred ships landed their cargo at these docks in a single day. On every street there were foreign merchants from England and Holland and Germany engaged in buying and selling. It was a prosperous, happy town."

"Whatever changed it?" Jane wondered.

She supported Joanna by the arm and watched the actions of the porter closely to see that he did not damage their luggage. Both women had put on simple travel dresses of gray cloth that lacked the large farthingales so much the fashion in England.

"The Spanish Fury," Dee murmured darkly. "That's what the locals call the massacre of 1576. Spanish troops put eight hundred houses to the torch and murdered more than six thousand citizens before sating their blood lust."

"That was more than a decade ago," Kelley observed. "Why hasn't the town been rebuilt?"

"Antwerp has no money. Two years ago Alessandro Farnese, the Duke of Parma, captured the town with Spanish troops and ordered all Protestant residents into exile. Most of the wealthiest merchants were Protestants."

"What a foolish thing to do," Jane said.

"Perhaps," Dee told her. "But it endeared him to the Catholic population, which had long looked with envy upon their rich Protestant neighbors."

"Your friend Silvius is a Protestant, isn't he?" Kelley asked.

Dee nodded.

"How is it he escaped exile?"

Dee smiled bleakly at the suspicion in Kelley's tone.

"Silvius is no collaborator. He's a pragmatist. At the time of the expulsion, some Protestants were permitted to stay if they paid exorbitant bribes to the Spanish and swore to abide by the forms of the Catholic faith. In this way they were able to hold on to their property."

"A heavy price," Kelley muttered. "Property for honor."

"Indeed. Most would not pay it."

With the porter following, Dee led his little group to the house of William Silvius. He rang the brass bell outside the door of the imposing two-story brick building with trepidation. He had received several letters from Silvius over the past year, but had not seen his old friend for more than a decade. He was not even certain the printer still resided within the town.

Candlelight from the opening door outlined a stout little man. The fringe of fine blond hair around the back of his bald head and his bushy mustache seemed to give him a halo of spun gold. He squinted suspiciously at Dee and Kelley. His pale blue eyes widened in recognition.

"John Dee!" he cried with delight. "Is it really you? It is! Come in, come in."

He embraced Dee like a lost brother and lifted him over the threshold, gesturing for the others to follow with a smile of delight beaming from his face. Jane helped Joanna into the sitting room while Kelley indicated for the porter to deposit the trunks in the front hall.

"Take off your cloaks. Sit by the fire, my friend," Silvius said, pressing Dee into a comfortable chair before the glowing hearth. "Gretta, we have visitors. Bring something to drink and set the table."

His wife appeared around the edge of the door and surveyed her unannounced guests nervously. Strange visitors in the night were unpopular in Antwerp during these trying occupation years. Citizens lived in terror of the knock of the Inquisition.

She smiled with apple cheeks when she recognized Dee and ran to embrace him, babbling effusive words of greeting in her native German. Dee answered her in the same tongue.

"Speak English, or French, so that I can understand you," Silvius protested in good humor.

"I scold him why he stay away so long," Gretta said to her husband, smiling. "And tell him I beat him if he do it again."

Dee introduced Kelley, who was just entering from the hall, and then presented Jane and Joanna to Gretta. She immediately inquired about Joanna's health, and stood sympathetically wringing her plump hands in her apron while Jane narrated the adventures of the voyage from England, supplemented by occasional remarks from Dee.

"I never go on the water," she said, shaking the pointed white cap on her tightly braided head. "I tell William, I never go on the water so long as I live."

"Sure, you can stay a week," Silvius said expansively after Dee explained their situation. "Stay a month. Stay a year if you like."

A kitchen maid entered with a decanter of port on a silver tray. Silvius filled small crystal glasses and pressed one into every hand. He raised his own glass.

"I drink the health and long life of my best friend in the world, John Dee."

They drank gratefully, warmed in their hearts more by the gracious hospitality of their host than by the excellent port wine.

Kelley touched his lips to the wine, then set his glass upon the mantelpiece. He glanced with disapproval at his wife as she drained her glass, but reflected that in this case the wine would probably do her more good than harm. Since coming off the ship she appeared stronger. Her naturally robust constitution was reasserting itself.

Joanna sensed the dark gaze of her husband upon her and cast him a look of defiance. Only Jane noticed this private exchange.

Gretta excused herself from the sitting room to oversee the laying of the table and the preparations for supper. Silvius filled the inclined cone of a white clay pipe with his ink-stained fingers and used fire tongs to remove an ember from the fireplace to ignite the tobacco. He threw one fat leg over the corner of a desk and sat puffing with contentment.

"When did you take up this strange new custom?" Dee asked, watching the plumes of blue smoke rise from between his friend's pouting lips.

"This smoking? Many years ago. You mean to say you don't have it in England?"

"Walter Raleigh brought news of the custom to the Queen only last year," Kelley said.

"The Spanish have been doing it for decades," Silvius informed him.

Dee shook his head in wonder.

"Extraordinary. Doesn't the smoke burn your throat?"

"Not at all." Silvius extended the pipe to Dee. "Would you care to try it, my friend?"

Dee waved the offer aside.

"Perhaps tomorrow. I've had too many novel experiences today."

"I'll try it," Kelley said.

He accepted the pipe, and after studying both ends, put the hollow tube in his mouth and sucked a deep lungful of smoke. Silvius rescued the pipe from his hand as he doubled over with a hacking cough and blindly felt his way into a chair. Joanna laughed.

"It takes getting accustomed to," Silvius said placidly.

"I'm glad to see that you're so well, William," Dee told him. "How have you survived the occupation?"

Silvius took the pipe from his lips and spat into the open hearth. He glanced meaningfully at Dee, then gathered up a stack of printed papers from the surface of the writing desk. He passed them silently to Dee, who studied them and shared them with Kelley and the two women.

They were galley proofs for a book in Latin. Dee recognized the text as Erasmus's *In Praise Of Folly*. Many sections of print had been struck out with diagonal pen strokes in black ink. On a number of the proof sheets a large X obliterated the entire text.

"I publish what the Church tells me to publish, or I publish nothing," Silvius said bitterly.

"It's worse than I believed," Dee said. "I'm sorry for you, William."

Silvius shrugged his round shoulders and forced a smile.

"The Censor is a superstitious Jesuit priest. A complete fool, but he has absolute power. One act of defiance and he will take away my license and confiscate my presses."

"Why do you stay?" Kelley demanded. "Why not move to Germany or England?"

"I would not be permitted to take my presses out of the province. My little wealth would be seized, my house auctioned away. If I left Antwerp it would be with empty pockets. Gretta is too good a woman for me to put her through such hardship. So I stay and do what the Jesuit fools tells me. It's not like the old days. I could never bring out a book like John's *Monas Hieroglyphica* as I did twenty years ago."

"How terrible," Jane said with feeling. "I don't think I ever truly realized before how much freedom we enjoy in England in comparison with the nations under Spanish domination."

"That is why the Spanish Armada must not be allowed to succeed," Dee said.

Silvius put his blunt finger to his lips and looked at the closed door of the sitting room.

"I trust my servants," he said softly. "But it is not a good thing to trust too much."

A hearty supper was made on the remains of a reheated leg of lamb, freshly boiled potatoes, and what tender green shoots the spring harvest of the garden offered, along with plenty of bread, cheese, and wine. Joanna drank two glasses for every one of the other diners, but managed to contain it so well that only the watchful Kelley and the sympathetic Jane noticed. When the meal ended, Gretta escorted Jane and Joanna upstairs to show them their rooms and have a private chat. Silvius released the servants for the night, and the men retired to the sitting room.

Silvius bent his gleaming round head close to Dee.

"Is he of our number?" he murmured, glancing at Kelley.

Dee nodded.

The printer tore a scrap of paper from a page on his desk and drew on it with his pen. Blotting the scrap, he passed it to Kelley. The alchemist turned it over and recognized the hieroglyphic monad.

"Greetings, Brother Kelley," Silvius said, grasping the hand of the alchemist in a curiously stylized grip.

With a glance of surprise at Dee, Kelley returned the handclasp.

"Greetings to you also, Brother," he muttered, dropping the slip of paper into the fire.

"I didn't want any talk of secret matters with the women present," Silvius said. "It's dangerous to know too much. The Inquisition is expert in the arts of torture."

He unlocked a drawer of the desk and took from it a letter. With quickening interest Dee recognized the brown wax seal.

"The angels must have guided you here," the printer said, handing the letter to Dee. "I was told to forward this to you by the next ship, but I never dreamed that I would be able to give it to you personally."

"Another letter from Judah," Dee said to Kelley.

He cracked the holy seal with his thumb and unfolded the leaf of parchment. After deciphering its coded Hebrew script, he translated the text aloud into English.

To Doctor John Dee, late a scholar of Cambridge and privy advisor to the Sovereign Queen Elizabeth of England, presently of Mortlake near London, his friend Rab. Judah Loew ben Bezalel sends greetings.

My friend, it is imperative that you come to Prague at your earliest convenience. I have obtained new information concerning the certain book that formed the subject of my last letter to you, which by the grace of the Holy One (blessed be He) you have received and understood. I know now that the book was stolen from your house, and have learned more about its awful power since last I wrote. Most important of all, I anticipate the place where it is being carried.

It is an evil thing, far more dangerous than I ever dreamed possible. A thousand times a day I condemn myself for my foolishness, that I did not consign it to the flames the instant it fell into my hands, but as you know, it is against the custom of my people to burn books. If only I had known then what I know now (never mind by what agency). That accursed tome is a sleeping serpent whose poison will corrupt the very heart of the world. The fools who have stolen it mean to awaken its power. They have no notion of the dreadful forces they play with, but mistakenly believe they can be controlled! When they finally understand the truth, as I have, it will be too late for all of us.

Were it possible I would come to England, but it is not convenient at this time for me to leave my house unprotected, since I have reason to suspect that it is under constant watch. Also, as you know, it is difficult, if not impossible, for a Jew to travel freely in Europe during these troubled times. Therefore I must implore that you hasten to me, since I cannot come to you, and believe me when I assure you that the matter is of pressing consequence to the stability of this whole earthly realm. I cannot be more plain in a letter, but when you are with me I will reveal all.

Written by me this ninth day of June, in the common year one thousand, five hundred and eighty-seven, at my house in the ghetto of Prague.

Dee folded the letter and dropped it into the fireplace. He watched it burn and stirred its ashes with the iron poker.

"What is this book Judah writes about?" Silvius asked.

"I begin to suspect that it is much more than a mere book," Dee muttered darkly.

He told Silvius all that had taken place in the duration between their return to Mortlake from Wales and the present day. Kelley supplied details of what had occurred in London.

"If you had a key to a precious treasure that you did not wish others to destroy, what would you do?" Dee asked.

"Hide it," the printer said.

"Suppose you were afraid that if you concealed it too deeply, those you intended it for would never find it?"

Silvius puffed thoughtfully on his pipe.

"I suppose I would conceal it among common things, where it would remain available but not be recognized."

"The Book of Lilith is such a key," Dee said. "Though what it opens, or how, I do not pretend to guess."

"I begin to see," said the printer, nodding. "This explains many strange happenings in Europe over the past several months."

"What do you mean?" Kelley demanded.

"There has been great turbulence on the astral plane. Spirits rushing every which way on secret errands. And strange men have been observed searching the libraries for occult books and manuscripts. Something has stirred up the Sons of Coronzon like a nest of angry wasps. It must be this book. It can't be anything else."

"Why didn't you write to advise me of this activity?" Dee asked.

Silvius shrugged.

"What could I write? That something was going on, but I didn't know what it was? For weeks I've been trying to learn more so that I would have something to report. Now you know as much as I."

"And you as much as we," Kelley added. "But Rabbi Loew must know something more. Why don't we try to contact him through the crystal?"

Dee shook his head with regret.

"The spirits could never penetrate the circle of protection around his house. It's an astral fortress, though it looks ordinary enough on the material plane. We'll just have to wait until we reach Prague."

There was little more to be said. After a few idle remarks Silvius set a wire spark screen across the mouth of the fireplace and the three men retired to their rooms upstairs to discover whether or not their wives had waited for them.

In the dark and silent study the glow of the dying embers on the hearth was barely visible. Something moved in the back of the fireplace. A tiny flake of black ash no larger than the head of a pin began to dance upon the warm air. Soon it was joined by another, and another, then many other fragments, until the entire cavity of the fireplace swirled with minute black specks. These began to reassemble themselves with inhuman precision into a rectangular black sheet. Before the assembly was complete the large patches of ash that had been pieced together swirled into a column as though caught in a miniature whirlwind and rose silently up the chimney.

SIXTEEN

Dee held the tapered end of his beard flat against the front of his robe and stuck his head through the window of the jogging coach to look back. The town of Antwerp was no more than a gray smudge between earth and heaven. Only the tall spire of the cathedral remained distinguishable above the southwestern horizon. It reared up into the cloudless blue sky like the censorious finger of God.

Idly, Dee watched the scenery slide past the rocking window. The land between Antwerp and Amsterdam was for the most part flat and low-lying, crossed by streams and occasionally interrupted by bodies of stagnant water. Where the road was well-maintained near the towns, it had been built above the level of the marshy ground, but in less traveled boggy sections its spine-jarring surface consisted of half-rotted tree trunks laid close together. When the fitful breezes died, insects, stirred up from the marsh on either side of the road by the thunder of the wheels, rose in dense clouds and became a torment.

The roofed coach held the heat like a bread oven, even with all the window flaps raised. Dee envied Kelley, who had wisely chosen to ride on top on the open rear bench. Dee sat facing forward on the right, his slender shoulder wedged against the wall of the coach by an incredibly fat

Dutch merchant and his equally large wife. They chattered unceasingly to each other in their native language and seemed oblivious to the other passengers. Jane Dee sat across from her husband, and beside her, Joanna, who despite her susceptibility to seasickness did not mind the rocking and jouncing of the coach in the least.

The only other passenger was a young man of about twenty years with wavy blond hair and a pale complexion, who sat to the right of Joanna. Beyond the initial perfunctory greetings he had made no attempt to talk, but had opened a book and begun to read almost as soon as the coach lurched into motion. Studying him, Dee noted his long, straight nose and high cheekbones, which suggested Norman blood. He wore a dark blue doublet and hose of conservative cut but fashioned from the finest materials. This, coupled with the large garnet pin in his soft velvet hat, suggested that he belonged to a prosperous family.

Joanna peered in curiosity at his book. Now that her stomach had ceased to revolve she found herself increasingly able to take an interest in the world.

"What strange writing," she said. "Can you really read it?"

The young man glanced at her and smiled. He turned the book and held it out for the others to see.

"It's Greek," he said in a cultured voice with only a trace of French accent. "And yes, I can read it, though I confess that understanding it is quite another matter."

Dee addressed him in Greek. After a moment of hesitation the young man responded in the same language.

"What did you say?" Joanna demanded, looking from one to the other with amazement.

"I asked our fellow traveler the title of the book he was reading," Dee told her with a smile.

"It is a work on ethics by Aristotle," the young man explained. "Allow me to introduce myself. My name is Paul Normand. I am a scholar traveling to the University of Wittenburg to study philosophy and mathematics."

Dee introduced himself and his party and said they were destined for Bohemia. The Dutch couple continued to talk to each other as though alone in the coach.

"Where's Wittenburg?" Joanna asked Jane.

"I believe it's on the Elbe," she said, looking at her husband for confirmation. "Is that right, John?"

Dee nodded.

"It seems that we follow the same route," he said to Normand. "Do you intend to take ship from Amsterdam or continue overland?"

"Ship, most definitely," the young man answered. "Sea travel is so much easier."

This elicited an involuntary protest from Joanna, who then found it necessary to explain some of their adventures on the voyage across the Channel.

"I've been told that the sailing along the northern coast is much less rigorous than the Channel crossing," Normand said. "The Frisian Islands break the force of storms."

"I hope you're right."

"Forgive me for asking," Dee said, "But I would expect a scholar of France to attend the University of Paris. What takes you so far afield as Germany?"

The handsome face of the young man darkened.

"I am a Huguenot. I would not be admitted at Paris."

Dee nodded with sympathy. The on-going persecution of the Protestant French Huguenots at the hands of the king of France and the Inquisition was a scandal throughout northern Europe. Their lands had been seized, their faithful servants and retainers tortured and murdered, and they themselves put to the flames in great burnings where sometimes hundreds perished in a single day.

"My father is in prison awaiting trial. There is nothing I can do to save him. I was lucky to escape from France myself. Thank God my mother is dead."

He looked sadly at Joanna with pale blue eyes. Impulsively, she took his hand and squeezed it. Their hands lingered together a moment before parting.

"Perhaps we can take ship from Amsterdam together," Dee offered.

"I would be honored," Normand said with a slight bow of his head. "I did not expect to find kindred spirits on so lonely a pilgrimage."

The coach made excellent speed on the first leg of its journey from Antwerp to Breda. At the provincial border it was stopped by Spanish soldiers. The letter of passage secured by William Silvius for Dee and Kelley from the Spanish governor of Antwerp was examined and returned with barely a glance. The Huguenot's papers were inspected more critically. The Spanish captain of the guard asked Normand to get down from the coach and accompany him to the small log hut at the roadside that served as his barracks.

After ten minutes Dee began to worry. He hated to see the young Frenchman stopped so close to freedom.

"Can't you do something?" Joanna said, staring past Jane at the closed door of the hut. Her anxiety increased by the minute.

"About what?" Kelley demanded through the open window on the opposite side of the coach. He had climbed down from the rear bench to stretch his legs.

Dee told him about Normand. Kelley shrugged.

"I feel sorry for him, but it's none of our affair."

Joanna wheeled on him.

"How can you be so heartless? Haven't you got any human feelings at all? You're like a piece of flint."

Kelley blinked at his wife's impassioned face with surprise.

"Why are you so upset? You only met this Frenchman a few hours ago."

"He's a human being. He—oh, never mind," she said angrily, turning away from him.

At that moment Normand stepped out through the door of the hut. He turned and removed his hat to solemnly bow at the Spanish captain, who returned the salute. Wordlessly, he climbed back into the coach.

"What happened?" Joanna demanded.

"He is a Catholic, but not a fanatic," Normand said with a slight smile. "For three pieces of Spanish gold he was able to forget his suspicions about my letter of passage."

"You were fortunate, sirrah," Kelley said through the window, staring with little affection at the smooth good looks of the Frenchman. "My wife was very worried about you."

Normand flashed even, white teeth at Joanna.

"She is a gracious woman."

Kelley glanced at Dee, who raised a silver eyebrow.

"Would you care to ride inside for a while, Edward? I don't mind trading places until we come to Breda."

Scowling, Kelley met the smoldering green glare of his wife.

"Thanks, John, but no. I believe I'll be more comfortable on top."

The ride from the border to the small Dutch hamlet of Breda was uneventful. Several times Dee thrust his head through the window to look back. He was searching for any sign of an anomalous dark whirlwind amid the swirling dust from the road.

He saw no trace of this mysterious spirit, but did notice two riders following along behind the coach at the extreme limit of visibility. They could only be seen when the coach reached the end of a long stretch of straight road. Then they occasionally came into view for several moments just before the coach rounded the next bend.

Dee dismissed the riders from his thoughts. It was a busy road. No doubt they hung back to avoid the dust from the wheels of the coach. He was more concerned about Jane. To his familiar eye she looked paler than usual. He noticed that she pressed her left hand over the pit of her stomach when she thought he was looking elsewhere, as though she did not want him to perceive her discomfort.

Courageous woman, he thought to himself. She is sickened with the motion of the coach but doesn't want to worry me. It was so often the fate of those who traveled badly to be compelled to travel much.

He made the mistake of inquiring in Dutch the profession of the fat Hollander seated beside him during an uncharacteristic lull in his conversation with his wife, then had to endure an hour-long lecture on the craft of leather-making. Resigning himself, he listened with half an ear and a fixed smile on his thin, ascetic lips. He would have preferred the conversation of the Huguenot, but Joanna Kelley held the full attention of the young scholar. They were discussing some question in Aristotle.

"Why must good be stronger than evil?" Joanna demanded, her emerald eyes sparkling as she challenged the condescending smile of the Frenchman.

"Good is from God and evil from Satan," he said. "No derivative quality can be greater than its source. Since the Devil is weaker than Christ, evil must be weaker than good."

"But we see evil triumph every day. How can it defeat good if good is stronger? Shouldn't good always be victorious?"

"So it is, in an ultimate sense."

"Why is it that wickedness goes unpunished?"

"Punishment may be delayed in this world, but in such cases theologians assure us that it must follow in the next. That is the function of hell."

Joanna shook her head in puzzlement.

"I'm still confused, Monsieur."

He smiled winningly, his eyes roaming over her red curls and freckled shoulder where it showed bare at the wide neck of her loose white travel dress.

"Tell me what troubles you. I'll be your teacher."

"Very well. Will you grant me that God is stronger than Satan?"

He laughed.

"Of course. To do otherwise would be the rankest heresy."

"And the power of God is omnipotent, is it not?"

He nodded, smiling indulgently.

"And God's power extends over every part of His creation. Isn't that so, also?"

Again he nodded.

"And will you grant that God is all goodness and intends only good for the world?"

Normand nodded, the smile slipping from his lips, replaced by a slight frown of concentration as he thought about what she was saying.

"Then given all these truths, how is it that evil exists in our world?"

"Evil stems from the sinfulness of Eve and the disobedience of Adam," he said. "When they were cast from the Garden they carried the seeds of evil with them into the world."

"Granted," Joanna said, conceding his point. "But where did the evil come from?"

"I don't understand," Normand said, gazing at her frank green eyes with awakening respect.

"If God is all good, and God created all things, then all things must be completely good," she said. "This being so, how could Adam sin? Or for that matter, how could Satan be evil, if he was a creation of God?"

He laughed shortly, gazed for a moment out the window at the tall grasses that slid past the coach, and seemed a little discomforted.

"You argue like a Jesuit," he said. "Where on earth did you learn such logic?"

Joanna smiled.

"My husband and his companion are learned men. I have often listened to their discourse."

"Anyone might listen to the talk of sages, but few are those who can profit."

"Will you not answer my question? I confess it's a matter that has puzzled me greatly from time to time."

Normand thought for a moment.

"The answer must be free will," he said at last. "Man was created all good by God, but he was made with the capacity to choose freely between good and evil. In choosing to eat the apple, Adam allowed evil to enter into his soul by choosing the evil course."

"That I understand," Joanna said. "What I don't understand is, where did the evil that entered Adam come from? It must have been created. And all things were created by God. But surely it is not correct to say that God created evil, for then we must say that he intended evil to fall upon the head of Adam, else why create it in the first place?"

Normand shook his golden head with amazement.

"My lady, I confess that you have confounded me. I've never found occasion to consider the matter in this light."

Joanna tried unsuccessfully to conceal her pleasure at this compliment. Even if the young Huguenot was merely flattering her, the experience was agreeable.

"Surely the answer must be that God created evil as a temptation for man," Jane Dee interjected quietly. "As a test of man's obedience and correct use of his free will. But God always hoped that man would choose the good, even though his free will allowed him to select the evil."

"I think you have it, my lady," Normand said. He gazed wonderingly from Jane to Joanna. "Never before have I met such oracles of wisdom in long skirts. Are all English women as learned as you?"

"Only those whose husbands are the wisest scholars in Europe," Jane said, smiling with affection at Dee, who was at that moment gaining deep insight into the art of removing foul smells from mildewed horsehides.

Joanna puzzled silently over Jane's solution to the problem of evil for several minutes.

"But if evil is the test of man's goodness," she said to Normand, "Why create man with free will in the first place? Why not simply make him good in the beginning? Then God would have no need to test him."

Normand confessed his ignorance of the matter, and Jane could offer no further insights. Joanna was forced to mull the problem over in her own mind with dissatisfaction.

Philosophy was poor nourishment for the brain, she reflected. Every question was a hunger, and the satisfaction of one only raised another in its place. A philosopher was like a toothless old hound who futilely attempted to extract the marrow from a beef bone. Inwardly, she gave thanks that the profession was not open to women, who were free to devote their energies to more useful pursuits.

SEVENTEEN

The coach arrived in the small Dutch town of Breda just after sunset. All the passengers chose to stay overnight at the sign of the Lamb, an easy decision to make since the Lamb was Breda's only hostelry.

The innkeeper, a cadaverous man whose narrow face was adorned by a great beak of a nose, wore an expression of perpetual disapproval. A raggled black beard that smelled of rancid butter only served to accentuate the thinning hair on the top of his skull. When Dee politely pointed out to him that the fee he charged for two modest rooms on the second floor was double the usual rate, he replied in solemn tones that Dee and his party were free to take themselves elsewhere.

"Is there anywhere else in this filthy sty of a town for travelers to board?" Kelley demanded.

The innkeeper looked at the blackened beams of the ceiling of the common room and seemed to consider.

"No."

Dee held up a hand to stifle Kelley's retort and silently counted from his purse the required pieces of silver while the innkeeper sucked on the corner of his dirty beard.

The Dutch merchant and his wife took the largest room on the ground floor. The merchant did not even flinch when a price was demanded. Either he was very rich, or well-accustomed to the casual robbery of his countrymen. Normand settled on a small garret on the third floor under the steeply-pitched roof of the inn.

After bathing and changing into more formal attire, they gathered in the dining hall and made a greasy supper on scraps of boiled ham, onions, and potatoes, accompanied by coarse brown bread with cheese and a thin port wine. The cheese was excellent. Jane found herself eating large blocks of it to cut the grease of the meat, which her stomach threatened to reject.

"You must be tired, Jane," Dee murmured into her ear. "Why don't you go up to our room and lie down? I'm sure everyone will understand."

"I feel much stronger now," she said brightly. "I think I was only a little hungry."

Dee noted with approval that she was eating large portions of the bread and cheese. She had been looking plumpish over the past several weeks, a change he approved of, since he had always regarded her as too thin for robust health. Even so, her complexion appeared unnaturally pale. Were it not for the increase in her weight he would suspect the onset of leprosy of the bone or some other wasting disease. However, he knew from his medical studies that these diseases were always accompanied by a loss of fat from the body.

On the other side of the large table, Joanna ate and drank liberally, ignoring Kelley's frown. To spite him, she began to flirt with Normand, who sat to her left.

"Tell me, Monsieur Normand, is it true what they say about French women?"

"What exactly do they say?" he inquired with a polite smile, glancing past her at her husband.

She tossed back her flaming hair and leaned toward him. The heat of the wine made her expansive.

"They say that French women are more passionate than English women," she murmured.

"Nonsense. In my experience it is only that English women are more restrained."

"Have you had much?" she asked, her eyes sparkling with a mixture of spirits and mischief.

He blinked at her.

"Pardon?"

"Experience. Have you had much experience?"

Normand blushed. Joanna noted with delight that the tips of his ears turned from white to bright red. She laughed.

"Not very much," he admitted. "My studies occupy most of my time."

"Then you're not really qualified to make a judgement on the question, are you?"

"No, I suppose not," he said with mild discomfort. He might have added more, but Kelley's slate eyes darted across to lock with his like the predatory gaze of a hawk.

Joanna reached for the half-emptied bottle of port. Before her fingers closed on its neck it was snatched away by Kelley's blunt, dark hand.

"Give it to me," she hissed through clenched teeth.

"You've had too much already," he said flatly.

In fury she grabbed the bottle and tore it out of his hand, slopping some of the port from the open top in the process.

"I'll decide when I've had enough," she said in a loud voice.

The other guests at the table stopped eating to glance at her with surprise. After a few moments when nothing more was said, they returned their attention to their plates, and the general buzz of conversation resumed its former level.

Kelley glared at his wife. He knew that the only way to prevent her from drinking more would be to drag her kicking and screaming from the dining hall and lock her in their room. The thought of this public scene sickened him. He looked across the table and found the sympathetic eyes of Jane Dee upon him. They communicated understanding like a gentle caress and cooled the fury blazing in his heart.

Joanna saw the defeat in his face and smiled with triumph. Deliberately, she overfilled her glass so that some of the wine slopped onto the table. She drained it in a single draught.

"You disgust me," he said. Without another word he left the dining hall.

A wave of pain washed over her face. She suppressed it and angrily poured herself a second glass, then smiled at Normand. He returned the smile more winningly now that Kelley was out of the room.

"Your husband is a very intolerant man," he murmured.

"He's a fool," she said bitterly. "Just because his father was a drunkard, he thinks that everyone who likes a glass is going to turn into some sort of raving monster."

"In France, we drink wine rather than water. Babies are given wine in place of their mother's milk."

"Very sensible." She laughed. "I bet those tykes can hold their port."

He laughed in appreciation of her wit, all the while studying her closely with his pale blue eyes.

"Forgive me if I'm wrong, Joanna, but you seem to be a woman who is unhappy."

The wine caused sentimental tears to well quickly into her eyes. She blinked them away.

"It's true, Monsieur."

He touched the back of her hand.

"Please, call me Paul."

"You're very perceptive, Paul, and also very kind."

"Perhaps you only need someone you can tell your troubles to. I would be happy to listen anytime you feel like talking, day or night."

Their eyes met. He filled her empty glass from the bottle before his own plate.

The supper ended informally, with individuals and couples leaving the table to wander into the drinking hall or common sitting room. Joanna rose and headed for the latter, which was less noisy, with a bottle and glass in her hands. Normand accompanied her.

John Dee leaned close to Jane.

"Go with Joanna and take care of her. I don't trust this Frenchman."

He went to search for Kelley while Jane followed her friend into the sitting room. At her appearance Normand scowled an instant before concealing his annoyance beneath a mask of social geniality.

Joanna beckoned when she noticed her friend standing in the doorway.

"Over here, Jane."

Jane drew up a chair opposite the bench where Joanna and Normand sat, their knees almost touching. She composed her skirts and wondered how she could persuade Joanna to retire upstairs to her bedroom.

"Paul was just telling me all about the Huguenots." Her words were blurred. "Do you know that in the last ten years those damned papists have murdered over fifty thousand men, women, and children?"

"Horrible," Jane said. "Surely it can't be so many."

"Those are the best estimates, Madame," Normand said. "The killing began in Paris on St. Bartholomew's

Day ten years ago and has not ceased to this day. The Catholics wish to exterminate us to a man."

"Why would the people of France do such things?" Jane wondered.

Normand shrugged philosophically.

"Many reasons. Our leader, Henry of Navarre, opposes the occupation of Flanders by Spain. The King and that whore Catherine de' Medici fear our growing political power. But I believe the true reason is that the people are afraid to learn that the way they have worshiped God all their lives is a lie."

"I'll never be able to comprehend such intolerance," Jane said quietly.

"They're evil," Joanna said. "All evil. Who can understand evil? You can't. It never makes any sense."

The words spoken by Dee on the night of their return to Mortlake, while he and Jane lay together in their bed, returned to Jane's mind. It seemed so long ago.

"We have good hope that soon Henry of Navarre will become king of France. When that happens I will be able to return home. All the Huguenots will return then."

"Huguenot. That's a strange word," Jane said, merely to make harmless conversation.

"It is a term of derision, but we bear it with pride. It was given to us by the papists in memory of the ghost of King Hugo, near whose castle our early leaders met. They were forced to walk abroad only at night, like the shades of the dead."

"Persecution is something we do understand," Joanna said, patting Normand on the knee. "Don't we, Jane? The English commoners hate us because they say we practice sorcery."

"Sorcery? How interesting." Normand glanced at Jane. "I've always been fascinated by the black arts, though of course I have very little understanding of them."

"You should talk to John Dee," Joanna told him. "Greatest magician in all of Europe, or so my black-hearted husband says, and he should know, shouldn't he, Jane?" She drank deeply from her glass.

Normand looked at Jane.

"Is this true? I would be honored to speak with your husband."

"My husband is a philosopher and a mathematician," Jane said evenly. "To the common people of England his work has the appearance of magic."

"Then he doesn't practice the black arts," Normand said with disappointment.

Jane shook her head.

"What of Madimi?" Joanna said to her.

"Madimi?" Normand gazed from one to the other.

"The niece of my husband," Jane said. "She has a gift of second sight."

"Niece." Joanna chuckled. "Is that what he calls her?"

It was impossible to catch Joanna's eye or kick her without being observed by the watchful Frenchman. Jane could only try to change the subject.

"Your leader must be a courageous man."

"So they say."

"Have you never met him yourself?"

"I've not had that honor," Normand said. A shadow passed over his face, and his fingers unconsciously tightened. "But I would very much welcome it."

"Anyone who hates the Spanish is a friend of mine," Joanna said. Her eyelids drooped with fatigue. She fought to keep them open.

"Do you hate the Spanish, Monsieur Normand?"

The Huguenot hesitated.

"Not really," he said, meeting Jane's probing gaze. "In my experience all men are very much alike under the skin. Hate is a wasteful emotion."

"You're a lover, not at hater," Joanna said, giggling.

"I'm amazed that you were able to escape from France," Jane observed mildly.

"Amazed? Why so, Madame?"

"Surely all of northern France and Flanders is overrun with agents of the Inquisition and Spanish soldiers. No one can move without letters of travel."

"Necessity can be a powerful motivator," he said. "But I am curious about your own reasons."

"How do you mean?"

"You said it yourself, Madame. Flanders is filled with Spaniards. The agents of the Inquisition are everywhere. What can have possessed an English philosopher and courtier to carry his beautiful young wife into such danger?"

Jane saw that he enjoyed this kind of verbal fencing, and realized that she would extract no information from this man beyond what she had already obtained.

"You forget the storm, Monsieur. We never intended to land in Flanders."

"Even so, in these dangerous times long journeys cannot be undertaken lightly. You husband must have compelling business in Bohemia."

"If that were the case, it would be our business and not yours, sirrah," she said coldly.

Normand blinked, realizing that he had gone too far in his familiarity.

"Of course, forgive me, I intended no offense."

"Where no offense is intended, none can be given," she said.

Joanna looked from one to the other with blurred concentration. "Don't be so formal, Jane. Paul is only trying to be friendly."

"I can see that."

When she did not say anything for several minutes, Normand stood and stretched.

"If you ladies will excuse me, I am tired from the long ride and intend to make an early night."

"Don't go, Paul," Joanna said. "I feel like talking."

He glanced at Jane, then flashed Joanna his boyish smile.

"We will talk tomorrow in the coach. But for now, *au revoir*."

With a deep bow, he left the sitting room and mounted the stairs. Jane followed the sound of his boots on the treads until it mingled with the general murmur of the drinkers in the ale hall.

After some flustered protests, Joanna allowed her friend to guide her up the stairs and into her room. Kelley was not there. If Joanna noticed the absence of her husband, she chose not to mention it. Jane helped her to undress and put her to bed, then retired to her own room across the corridor, where her husband sat reading by the feeble glow of a solitary oil lamp.

"Where is Edward?"

He looked up.

"I assumed he would have returned by this time. He said he was going out for a walk."

She sat on her husband's knee and draped her arms around his neck. They kissed.

"I'm worried about Edward and Joanna. They're drifting apart."

Dee frowned.

"We mustn't let that happen. Edward's work is too valuable to risk disrupting it over a silly domestic squabble."

She jumped up and stared at him, hands on her hips.

"John! How can you be so unfeeling? Edward's your best friend. Surely his happiness is more important than your work."

Dee hesitated, then nodded sheepishly.

"You're right to chastise me. Sometimes I become so wrapped up in my work that I lose sight of everything else. Edward has been a true friend these past five years, and I do value his happiness more than his utility. Only sometimes I forget."

She leaned down to kiss him.

"I'll always be here to remind you."

"Sweet Jane. Is it any wonder that I love you?"

As they prepared for bed, Jane narrated the conversation with Normand in the sitting room.

"Your suspicions were justified," she finished. "I'm sure he wanted Joanna alone so that he could question her about your work and your reasons for going to Bohemia."

"Perhaps he's only a curious young man enamored of Joanna," Dee suggested. "She is quite attractive."

"No, I'm sure he some sort of spy."

"How can you be so certain?"

Jane's brown eyes sparkled with excitement.

"He was very clever, but his own words betrayed him. He referred to you as a courtier."

Dee stroked his silver beard thoughtfully.

"No one mentioned your connection to the Queen," Jane continued. "I'm sure of it. How would he know you were attached to the English court unless he was sent to spy on us?"

"How indeed?" Dee murmured.

EIGHTEEN

Racing clouds obscured the moon. In the darkness the rutted dirt road that ran past the sign of the Lamb was indistinguishable from the coarse plots of grass that grew in front of the shops and houses on either side. No lights burned in the windows of the inn. It was well after midnight.

The door opened with a soft creak of dry hinges. A pale ghost glow from a narrow slot in a hooded lantern outlined the figure of a man in a long cloak. He held the lantern up to show the step, then covered it and closed the door of the inn by touch. With slow caution he made his way around the side of the timber-frame structure and down the narrow alley that separated it from the stable. Every few moments he opened his lantern just long enough to reveal the ground directly in front of his feet.

Weeds and wild shrubs choked the yard behind the stable. In one corner a small mountain of garbage exhaled decay into the cool night air. A dilapidated storage shed, its roof sagging and the planks of its sides bleached to dull gray, occupied the rear.

He made his way to the center of the yard and drew the hood quickly off his lantern three times. Then he waited, listening to the rustle of the grass. There was no response. He was about to leave the yard when a soft hiss

151

drew his attention. He opened the front of the lantern. Its yellow ray fell upon an arm beckoning around the corner of the shed. With stealthy steps he picked his way over the rough ground and went behind.

The pallid glow of the candle in the lantern revealed two human figures. The man with the lantern raised it on the end of his arm until its light illuminated their brutal, emotionless faces. They were dark of skin, both lean and weathered with ragged, unkempt beards. Broad hats shadowed their eyes.

"Now show us your face," the shorter of the two men hissed in gutter Spanish. The scar from an old knife slash twisted his lower lip.

The man in the long cloak turned the front of the lantern so that it lit up his handsome features and wavy blond hair.

"You are Normand?" the other demanded in a whisper.

Normand nodded.

"We were told in Antwerp to follow the coach and wait here for your orders."

"I have reasón to believe the man we watch is an English spy," Normand said in cultured Spanish. "He must be killed."

"Tonight?" asked the shorter Spaniard.

"Impossible. There are too many witnesses in the inn."

"When?"

"Tomorrow night. I will arrange a delay with the coach. With luck it will make your task easier. If not, you must do the best you can."

"How will we know to find this English?" the tall man demanded.

Normand considered for a moment.

"I will put a cross in white chalk upon his door. After he is asleep, enter his room and slit his throat."

"We know our job," the shorter man grumbled.

A twig cracked. In the silence it was like the report of a musket. Normand dropped the hood over his lantern and peered cautiously around the edge of the shed at the back yard of the inn. He heard the rear door of the inn open. The dim glow of a candle burning in the hall outlined a man entering. The door clicked shut.

"Nothing," he said, returning to his silent companions. "Some servant at the inn using the outhouse."

"We were told we would be paid in advance," the short man murmured. It was not said in a threatening tone, but menace lurked under the surface of the words.

"When the work is done," Normand said.

"Now," said the taller man.

Normand caught the gleam of steel in the flickering lantern glow.

"Very well." He counted out ten silver pieces from his purse and gave five to each man.

They bent close to the light to examine the money.

"There is another matter," Normand said. "I want you to kill the companion of the English, the man named Kelley."

The two stared at him with suspicion.

"We were told only that we might have to kill this Dee. Nothing was said about a Kelley."

"Well I'm saying it now," Normand hissed with impatience. "Kelley is Dee's confidant. They share the same secrets. Kill them both."

The assassins withdrew under a tree to hold a whispered debate. Normand cursed inwardly at their stupidity. They returned in silence and stood side by side in front of the lantern. He expected them to demand more money.

"We will do as you ask on one condition," said the short man.

Normand exhaled between his teeth. It was unfortunate, but he needed these fools.

"What is the condition?"

The two Spaniards dropped to their knees and removed their broad-brimmed hats.

"Give us your blessing, Father."

He murmured the Latin blessing and made the sign of the cross in the air before the kneeling assassins. This seemed to reassure them. He felt the tension leave the air, and knew they would fulfill their purpose.

"Go now. You must not be seen near the inn."

The short man with the twisted lip shivered and looked behind him. He stared at his companion.

"Did you feel that?"

"I felt nothing," the other said without curiosity.

"It was like a cold hand on my shoulder."

"You imagine things. Let's go."

The assassins melted into the dark wood, tracing their path back the way they had come by touch. They were well accustomed to moving through the darkness without a light. It was a skill demanded by their profession.

Normand returned to the alley between the inn and the stable. He opened the unlocked side door of the stable and entered, shutting it behind him. He was inside for almost half an hour. Once, the neighing of a horse broke the stillness. A dog began to bark somewhere down the road. After a few minutes when nothing else was heard, it stopped.

The Frenchman left the stable and carefully closed the door, then made his way back into the dark front hall of the inn. He was returning the wooden bolt to its locking bracket when he sensed movement behind him. He whirled with a drawn dagger in his right hand.

The glow from the lantern on the floor lit the brooding figure of Edward Kelley, who stood with arms crossed on his broad chest, regarding Normand impassively.

"You're up late," he said, his voice a low rumble.

Normand struggled to regain his mental balance.

"I might say the same about you, Monsieur."

"Let me see your knife."

The priest considered. This was a poor place for a murder. The sound of a struggle was sure to arouse the sleeping residents of the inn. On the other hand, Kelley might not be in a reasonable frame of mind. With a mental shrug, he turned the dagger in his hand and passed it to the Englishman hilt first. Let it be God's will.

Kelley examined the handle of the dagger by the light of the lantern. If he was disappointed, he showed no sign. He passed the knife back to Normand, who returned it to its sheath.

"An excellent blade. But not the one I'm looking for."

"What are you doing here?" Normand demanded. It was easy to simulate the rush of righteous anger. "Have you been following me?"

"No. I was out walking to clear my head. When I returned a while ago I went to your room, meaning to have a few words with you about my wife, but your bed was empty. I reasoned you had gone out and waited for you."

"Where I go is my affair, Monsieur," Normand snapped.

He give silent thanks that Kelley had not observed his meeting with the Spaniards. It would have complicated matters. Apparently it was Kelley he had seen returning to the inn by the unbolted back door, which was left open so that the servants of the inn could use the outhouse.

"You can go to hell for all I care," Kelley said in a dangerous tone. "Just keep away from my wife."

"I was not aware that you disliked my polite respects to her," Normand said smoothly.

Kelley took a step forward. His dark bulk loomed over the Frenchman like the prow of a ship. Normand instinctively touched the hilt of his dagger. He wondered if it was worth the risk to kill this boor of an English. No, he reflected, it might disrupt the travel plans of John Dee.

"Well now you know," Kelley said softly.

"I cannot very well avoid your wife if we ride in the same coach."

"Tomorrow you'll ride on top. I'll sit beside Joanna."

"Is that an order, Monsieur?" Normand asked softly.

"You'll either do it, or you'll be searching in the dust for your broken teeth."

"I have no wish to fight you."

Kelley grinned.

"That shows the difference between us, sirrah," he said. "For I very much wish to fight you."

Normand shrugged. He edged his way around the immovable Englishman.

"It is a matter of small concern. I will of course respect your wishes regarding your charming wife. Now, if you don't mind, I am tired and intend to go to bed."

He started up the steps, half-expecting the mad English to stop him. Kelley made no attempt to follow. Normand felt his moody, smoldering gaze burning into his back until he turned the corner of the upper landing, but did not give Kelley the satisfaction of a backward look.

After a few minutes Kelley picked up the abandoned lantern and opened its window of bullseye glass to blow out the candle. He set it back on the floor beside the door and stood in the darkness, thinking.

"You're not one of the Sons of Coronzon," he murmured to himself. "So who the devil are you?"

NINETEEN

The coach departed Breda shortly after daybreak. Normand expressed a desire to ride outside, since the day promised to be so fine. Kelley chose to sit inside between his wife and Jane Dee.

Joanna felt keen disappointment. She thought about riding on top next to Normand but knew Kelley would object. It was considered undignified for ladies to travel outside a coach. The wind played tricks with their skirts. Joanna thought this custom foolish, but did not feel determined enough this morning to set a new fashion.

She was not in the best of health. Her head throbbed like a beating drum, and the bright light from the blue sky hurt her eyes. She slouched down in her seat with her hand pressed to her forehead and responded to Jane's polite remarks with short groans, wishing mightily that she had allowed Kelley to keep her away from the second bottle of port at supper.

The distance between Breda and the next stopping place on their journey, the small hamlet of Leerdam, was less than they had traveled the previous day, but the road was poorly maintained and the rivers Maas and Waal, offshoots of the Rhine, crossed it. The owner of the Lamb had informed Dee with a sorrowful expression that the ferryboats were often unreliable, and were constantly breaking down.

They reached the Maas late in the morning and endured a delay of only thirty minutes while the flat-bottomed barge unloaded and loaded its passengers and cargo on the opposite bank of the river. The crossing was uneventful. Dee occupied himself with a study of the mechanism that drove the ferry. A thick hemp hawser across the river kept the large boat from drifting down stream in the sluggish current. It passed through iron loops on the side of the barge and around a large wooden pulley that was driven by a tired-looking pony who walked in a circular track on the deck.

He overhead the driver remark to Kelley that one of the lead horses appeared to be coming up lame, but thought little about it until they were approaching the crossing point on the Waal. The driver halted the coach in the middle of the road and got down to make a serious examination of the horses.

"What's the matter?" Dee called through the window in Dutch.

Muttering to himself, the driver ignored him. Dee got out of the coach, followed by Kelley and the other passengers, who welcomed the opportunity to stretch their legs. The fat wife of the merchant waddled into the bushes to answer the call of nature. Normand set his boot on the rear wheel of the coach and jumped down to the road.

"Why have we stopped?" he asked Dee.

Dee regarded the Frenchman keenly for several moments.

"Something appears to be wrong with some of the horses."

"How can that be?" Normand said with a puzzled expression. "They were all fine this morning."

"The ways of providence are mysterious," Dee murmured. He wandered over to the sweating driver, who struggled to free a knot from the harness of one of the horses.

Normand made his way around the rear of the coach to where Joanna stood stretching her arms over her head. The sunlight made a glorious amber halo in her loose, windblown hair. Wise in the ways of travel, she wore the same open-necked white peasant dress she had worn the previous day. What it lacked in style it gained in comfort.

She smiled brightly when their eyes met, welcoming the opportunity to talk with him. In the rush of departure they had barely exchanged a dozen words.

"You must be tired of riding on top," she suggested. "I'm sure my husband would be glad to exchange seats with you."

The Frenchman shook his head.

"Please don't trouble him on my account. I enjoy the fresh air."

"You must think ill of me," Joanna murmured, dropping her eyes. "I'm afraid I drank too much at supper last night."

"Nonsense, you were perfectly charming," Normand said. "There is nothing more attractive than a beautiful woman of strong appetites."

He glanced around. They stood in plain sight, but for the moment the attention of the others focused elsewhere. Screening the action with his body, he took her hand and pressed something into her palm. With a meaningful gaze he left her and walked to the other side of the coach.

Joanna felt the sharp corners of a folded piece of paper. She glanced down into her hand but saw her husband approach from the corner of her eye. Nervously, she slid the paper into the sleeve of her dress, which gathered tightly at her wrist.

"What did that damned Frenchman have to say?" Kelley muttered, glancing through the windows of the coach at Normand, who paced up and down on the opposite side of the road.

"He remarked on the weather," she told him. She felt a blush of warmth on her cheeks, as she always did when she lied. Kelley did not seem to notice.

"I don't want you talking to him."

"I'll talk to whoever I please!"

"You're my wife. You should respect my wishes."

Joanna laughed in his face.

At last Dee managed to corner the harried driver, a gray-haired Hollander in a leather vest who possessed the arms of a blacksmith. He was cursing softly to himself in Dutch.

"My lead horse has gone lame," he snapped in his native tongue at Dee's question. "He can hardly walk. Must have stepped on a piece of glass. Odd thing about it is that two other horses are limping as well. We'll be lucky to make Leerdam by sunset."

With the help of his hired boy he unhitched the ailing horse and tied it to the back of the coach. At greatly reduced speed they managed to reach the ferry landing on the Waal. This was not so well run as the previous ferry. They waited two hours while the barge remained tied on the opposite bank. Sounding the bell brought no response. The ferry operator was a surly little man who scowled silently at the furious driver when at last he managed to work his barge across the river. The driver's insults rolled off his hunched shoulders. He was accustomed to abuse from irate passengers.

"The fortunes of travel," Dee remarked to Kelley when once again they were moving along the road on the far side of the river.

"I'm not so certain," Kelley said.

He described his encounter with Normand the previous night.

"He had more than enough time to lame the horses, had he wished to do so."

Joanna made a derisive sound.

"Why would Paul want to lame the horses on his own coach? It's absurd."

"Keep your voice down," Kelley said harshly.

He knew from his own experience that the noise of the wheels masked ordinary conversation in the coach from those riding on top, but Joanna had spoken in a combative tone.

"Why?" she mocked. "So Monsieur Normand won't know what a fool I have for a husband?"

"You're too trusting, Joanna," Jane said. "Last night I'm certain Normand was trying to obtain information about our purposes in Bohemia."

"There is something not quite right about him," Dee added. "No Huguenot of noble birth could travel unchallenged through northern France and across Flanders."

Joanna looked at the three of them in disbelief.

"You're all mad. You see spies everywhere. Paul is just a charming young man on his way to university."

"Believe that if you wish," Kelley told her. "But watch your tongue in his company."

"What could I say?" Joanna retorted. "You haven't yet told me why we're going to Bohemia. How can I betray what I don't even know?"

"You know more than you think," Dee said.

He glanced at the Dutch merchant. As usual, the man was engaged in a heartfelt conversation with his equally attentive wife, and paid no attention to the other passengers in the coach. Dee was fairly sure neither of them spoke a word of English, but when conducting political espionage it was impossible to be too careful.

"I know why you don't want me to speak to him," Joanna grumbled at Kelley. "You're jealous. It's the first time in months that a handsome young man has paid attention to me."

"Haven't I every right to be jealous, the way you've been flaunting yourself at him?"

Joanna crossed her arms over her ample breasts and stared sullenly out the window.

Looking at her profile, Kelley thought to himself how pretty she was when she frowned. Her full lips pouted outward, and little wrinkles formed on the freckled slopes of her turned-up nose. It reminded him of the first time he had ever seen her, a mere child scowling in anger at her father while tending bar in her father's small inn.

Unfortunately, he had enjoyed increasingly frequent opportunities to appreciate this aspect of his wife's beauty over the past few months. In some intangible way he felt her slipping from him more quickly the harder he tried to hold onto her, like sand sifting between the fingers of his clenched fist. It both frustrated and saddened him. His opinion counted for nothing anymore. Sometimes he thought she deliberately set out to provoke him.

Joanna glanced past her husband at Jane Dee as though peering around the edge of a stone.

"I suppose you know why we're going to Bohemia?" she asked.

Jane looked at Dee, then nodded to Joanna.

"Of course you do. You husband trusts you well enough to confide in you."

"How can I trust you when you get in your cups every second night and flirt with strange men?" Kelley demanded.

Joanna turned her face back to the window and ignored him. He immediately regretted his words, but reflected that perhaps they had been unavoidable. Joanna knew just what to say to infuriate him, and of late seemed to take perverse delight in doing so in the company of others.

The progress of the coach became increasingly slow. Three of the horses were lame to some degree. By late afternoon they were still many miles from Leerdam. The driver sent his boy running ahead. The boy returned breathless in an hour. The driver stopped the coach to inform them that he had obtained lodging for them at a farmhouse about three miles outside of Leerdam. He said that he would ride through the night to the village to obtain fresh horses and return with them by early morning to continue the journey. None of his passengers were overjoyed by this news, but under the circumstances it seemed the most reasonable compromise.

The farmhouse was a large two-story timber-frame cottage with a thatched roof. The hospitable Dutch farmer and his wife were delighted at the prospect of earning a windfall so unexpectedly. They turned over their entire upper floor to their guests. The rooms were small, with low, sloped ceilings of thatch, but clean and comfortable. The Dutch merchant was given the farmer's own bedroom. Dee and Jane got the unoccupied guest room. Kelley and Joanna were placed in the children's room with its three separate single beds. They made no complaint over this arrangement, since they had stopped talking to each other in any case. Normand was assigned the cramped servant room at the end of the narrow upper hall. He accepted it philosophically.

The first opportunity Joanna had to be alone came after supper, when she went upstairs to change out of her travel dress and put on her nightgown. She saw by the light of a single candle that the farmer's wife had laid out a tin basin of cold water and a cloth for washing. At least the cloth was clean.

She took off her dress and, with a nervous glance at the closed door, unfolded Normand's note. It read in English:

> *I must speak with you tonight. Come to my chamber when your husband is asleep.*

With trembling fingers she touched one corner of the paper to the flame of the candle on the low dressing table and watched it curl into black ash.

Despite many opportunities in the past, she had never cuckolded her husband. She felt flattered by Normand's attention. The handsome Frenchman wanted her even though she was at least six years older, well past the first flush of youth. Temptation pulled strongly at her heart.

She sat at the table, naked to the waist before her travel mirror, brushing her flowing red hair with long strokes. The mirror had become her cruelest critic in the past year. It callously proclaimed the dark shadows under her eyes, the tiny lines at the corners of he mouth, the beginning of a sag under her chin. Even her breasts were not so erect has they had been in her youth. The pale pink nipples crinkled in the cool air, a startling contrast of color with the flaming locks that cascaded over her milk white shoulders.

As she worked the brush through her hair, she wrestled with her conscience. She knew Edward went whoring from time to time—or at least, she suspected as much, she corrected herself. There had never been actual proof. But even if true, was it reason enough to betray his trust? In so many ways he was a good husband. He fought for her honor, cared for her when she was sick, provided a roof over her head and food for their table. If only she could bear his child, their marriage might follow its natural evolution. Surely Edward could grow to love her as the mother of his son, even though he had not loved her on their wedding night.

She went through the familiar ritual of tying up her hair for the night with deft, automatic motions. Kelley entered as she was slipping into her linen nightgown. He undressed without speaking and washed his naked body with the same basin and cloth she had used. Joanna studied the rippling muscles of his hairy shoulders and thighs. Although he was not a particularly tall man, his powerful body always reminded her of a caged beast that might burst forth into explosive motion at any moment. It frightened and attracted her simultaneously.

She wondered if he would suggest pushing two of the small moveable beds together. They were simple boxes of wood filled with mattresses formed of straw inside a cloth bag. Somehow she could not quite bring herself to suggest it, not after his harsh words in the coach. He seemed lost in thought. A slight frown on his brooding face, he pulled on the loose linen trunk breeches that he favored for sleepwear during the warmer months and tied the string at his waist.

"Best if we go to bed early," he muttered without looking at her. "Tomorrow's journey will be longer than usual."

He blew out the candle. She heard the rustle of straw as he lay down on his cot, and felt her way to her own bed by the pale light of the moon. Without discussion they had managed to select beds on opposite sides of the room, leaving the center cot empty.

Joanna lay listening to her husband's breaths and the beat of her own heart. Her mind refused to come to any firm decision. One moment she told herself to ignore the note. The next moment she plotted how to ease herself out of the room without waking Kelley. She heard his breathing deepen into the familiar soft snore that indicated sleep. They had been traveling for so many days, both of them found it a simple matter to fall asleep in minutes in a strange bed.

Still she lay upon her back, her body rigid, her hands clenched into fists at her sides. Confusion and doubt roared through the corridors of her mind. The very thought of the danger excited her. She pictured Normand lying naked in his bed, waiting for her touch, his pale blue eyes open in the darkness.

As the stillness deepened, she found herself able to distinguish the sounds of the night. The mournful hoot of an owl through the open window, the rustle of leaves in the high branches of the trees, the creak of settling timber, the faint squeak of a bat somewhere in the thatch of the roof overhead. Once she thought she heard a brush from outside in the hall. She held her breath but the sound was not repeated.

Heart fluttering like the beating wings of a trapped bird, she eased the quilt off her legs and sat up by careful increments so that the straw beneath her would not rustle. All her attention focused on the sound of her husband's snores. She pushed herself slowly to her bare feet and moved with hesitant steps toward the door. Still she had no clear idea of what she intended to do. Her body seemed to move of its own volition, while her paralyzed mind refused to halt it.

The effort to open the door soundlessly on its dry wooden hinges consumed ten minutes. It was even darker in the hall than it had been in the moonlit room, but Joanna remembered the position of Normand's door and made her way toward it, trailing the tips of her fingers over the wall.

The door was unlocked, as she knew it would be. Before her nerve failed her completely, she opened it with a reckless disregard for the noise it made and stepped inside, pulling it shut behind her. By the dim light of the moon she saw a shadow move from the bed toward her.

Suddenly he was kissing her.

TWENTY

The two assassins tied their horses to a hedgerow in the field behind the farmhouse. They spent the hours of early evening examining the various ways of entry. There was no dog, which made their task easier. It was possible to enter a house with a sleeping dog, but the slightest misstep brought disaster.

"The back door won't be locked," the tall man said in his broken peasant Spanish.

"If it is, the window over that shed is open," his companion observed.

"They'll be upstairs in the bedrooms," the tall man continued as though he had not heard. "I want a clean, quick job. Cover the mouth and put your blade in the heart. Don't cut the throat—it's noisy."

"Who are you to give orders," the shorter man said bitterly. "I know my work."

"Cover the mouth, stab through the heart," his companion repeated without emotion. "If the wives are in the rooms we'll take them together at the same time."

"I won't kill a woman," said the short man.

"I'll kill the women, if need be. Just be sure you do your part clean. Remember what happened in Lisbon."

"I've told you not to throw that in my face. It wasn't my doing."

"All I know is, the job went wrong and somebody made a mistake," the tall man murmured.

They sat beneath a spreading elm in the field behind the round barn, hidden in the deep shadow cast on the grass by the high-flying moon. The grass felt soft and cool, the night air mild. It would have been an easy matter to fall asleep. The whisper of their conversation kept their minds occupied. It was necessary to wait until all the lights had been out for some time to ensure that everyone inside the house lay deep in sleep. Periodically one or the other made a wide circle around the house looking for the glow of candles or movement.

"They're asleep. They must be," the shorter man grumbled, returning from one of these inspections.

"We'll wait another half hour," his companion said complacently.

"I say we do the job now and get back to Antwerp."

"Only a fool runs when he has time to walk."

The Watcher listened to their whispered argument without interest. It recorded the words in its memory in case its master ever asked for an accounting of the night, but impatience was an incomprehensible emotion. It acted when it was time to act, never before. Now, something in its mindless intellect told it the time had come.

Neither Spaniard noticed the silently turning whirlwind, shadow against shadow, as it focused itself into a slender column. From the moist night air it gathered vapors and concentrated them into a human form. It reveled in the increased ease with which it was able to take on a physical body. The astral gate was already being pried open by the distant Sons of Coronzon. Soon, very soon, it would be possible to assume a body and keep it alive, to take on the stability of matter and think and plan and dream, to experience the pleasures of the flesh directly.

This thought was the closest thing to lust the Watcher was capable of feeling.

The taller assassin grabbed the shoulder of his companion with an iron grip and stared into the silver night. Something moved over the field, coming toward them. As it drew closer it appeared to become more solid. He blinked, scarcely able to believe his eyes. It was a naked woman. She walked casually across the grass, as though on a stroll through a park. Her silver body moved with unearthly grace, like that of a cat. About her shoulders, long black hair lifted on the night breeze and undulated with a life of its own.

The Spaniards were struck speechless. The shorter man jumped to his feet and drew his dagger. The woman continued to approach, her dark eyes fixed on the tall man with wordless promise. He pushed himself slowly to his feet. His initial alarm at being discovered began to change to something else. What was life, after all, but the willingness to take advantage of circumstance?

"Who are you?" the short man demanded in a harsh whisper.

She walked past him without turning her head and opened her arms to embrace his wondering companion. He stepped back, then stood like a statue while she put her arms around his neck and pressed her body against his. The bone of her hip ground into his increasing hard erection.

"This one wants to play," the tall man said with a low laugh. He began to caress her smooth back and buttocks while she writhed against him.

"Who is she? Where did she come from?" the short man wondered.

"Who cares?"

His meaning was plain. After they were finished with the woman they would have to dispose of her in any case.

She would be able to identify them and place them at the scene of the murder.

The short Spaniard began to feel his arousal quicken as he watched her twisting bottom.

"You like me, too?" he asked, trying to attract her attention.

He spilled silver coins from his purse into his palm and held them out to her.

"Maybe you would like some money to buy something pretty?"

Since he had no intention of allowing her to leave the field alive, he could afford to be generous with his offer. He displayed all five of the silver pieces given to him by Normand the night before.

The woman ignored him. She slid slowly down the swaying body of the tall man and parted his cloak. She began to tug at the fastenings of his breeches. He twined his fingers into her long hair, so strangely damp, and tilted his head to stare at the moon from under the broad brim of his hat. When her lips closed over the tip of his standing penis he felt lightning strike through his limbs to his toes and fingertips.

"Santa Maria," he breathed.

The Watcher engulfed his yard and drew it deep into her throat, then abruptly exhaled with inhuman force, driving the compressed vapors of her artificial body through the Spaniard's urethra and into his bloodstream. In an instant all his arteries filled with a froth of boiling bubbles. His lungs hemorrhaged, his racing heart swelled and burst apart and the major vessels in his brain exploded. He had time to feel only a brief moment of the most intense, burning agony that he had ever experienced. He shrieked, the sound driven involuntarily from his bursting lungs with unnatural force. No normal man could make such a sound. Its pitch was higher than that of a woman.

She released him. He fell on his face, already dead, blood seeping from every orifice of his body. Slowly she turned to face his companion, who stood paralyzed with a terror that was beyond fear. It took away every thought, every power of action. He could not even collapse onto the grass. From one hand the silver coins slid softly into the night. From the other his dagger slipped between nerveless fingers.

Somehow, drawing on a well of primal survival instinct that lay many levels deeper than volition, he turned and took a running step. She leapt onto his back like a leopard and brought him down by twining her legs around his. He fought to push her away, screaming mindlessly at the sheer horror of it, but her strength was many times that of a human being. She turned him over and pressed her red lips to his shrieking mouth. Sucking in his vital spirit, she consumed it with relish, then exhaled. His lungs exploded an instant before his brain, allowing him a brief moment to savor the pain. A black curtain of oblivion descend over his soul.

The Watcher stood with inhuman ease, as though lifted up on currents of wind. It surveyed the corpses with expressionless eyes. It felt no satisfaction, no regret, as it recorded the scene for the possible future reference of its master. Without a backward look, it walked from under the elm into the open field. It began to exhale steaming white vapor from all its pores. This turned dark and swirled around its melting human shape. Before it had taken a dozen steps it had become a turning vortex of black sparks that were almost invisible in the moonlight. A moment more, and even this expanded into the night without a trace.

TWENTY-ONE

Joanna surrendered for a moment to the heady intoxication of Normand's kiss before reluctantly pushing against his naked, hairless chest.

"I can't," she breathed into his ear.

"But you came," he whispered, kissing her bare neck.

"Only to tell you that it's impossible. I must be loyal to my husband."

"That pig?" His words dripped with contempt. "Don't be absurd."

"This isn't right," she said, twisting away. "I'm sorry, Paul."

She slid her back along the wall toward the door. He stopped her with insistent hands.

"Wait, Joanna. You must stay. We can talk if you wish, only talk. Don't leave me alone tonight. I've been dreaming about you."

He forced her hand down to his groin. She felt the heat radiating from his erection and snatched her fingers back as though burned.

"This was a mistake," she whispered.

Suddenly she realized with utter clarity that the words were true. It had been a mistake even to consider the liaison. She felt for the wooden latch of the door in the darkness but failed to find it. All the while he pressed her to the wall and showered her face with kisses. She smelled the scent of rose water in his hair, and beneath its sweetness the more earthy odor of his sweat. His clean-shaven chin felt so strange against her cheeks.

Again she tried to force him away, but he resisted with determination, twisting his hand on her wrist so that the skin burned.

"You can't go back to your room tonight. Believe me, Joanna, it's your own good I'm thinking about. Stay with me."

She began to struggle in earnest, matching her athletic body against his maleness. He pleaded with her under his breath, cursed in French, and slapped her cheek.

The bedroom door burst open and banged to a stop against the opposite side of the wall. Joanna sensed more than saw a hulking figure enter. She felt herself torn away from Normand's grasp. In the dim moonlight she saw the dull gleam of a ribbon-thin curving blade. The breath caught in her throat.

"Edward, no!" she cried.

Normand danced back with surprising nimbleness through the murk and drew something from the clothing that hung on a rack beside the head of the bed.

"Would you kill an unarmed man?" he said.

"Get your sword." The words grated between Kelley's teeth.

"I'm a scholar. I carry no sword."

The shadow that was Normand took a step toward them. She saw a flash of steel in his hand.

"Edward, he has a knife."

Kelley swept her back out of harm's way with his left arm as easily as he might have thrown aside a doll. Normand started forward again. Kelley swung high his rapier to deliver a killing cut. Its double-edged tip caught in the thatch of the sloping roof. In the confined space its long blade was more of a hindrance than an asset. Both men realized this at the same moment. With a triumphant curse, Normand stepped inside the arc of the sword.

A scream cut the night, so high-pitched that it was impossible to tell whether it issued from a male or female throat. Both men froze motionless. It was followed by another shriek in a different voice.

"Sweet Jesu, what was that?" Joanna said weakly. She felt her knees tremble and reached for the wall to support herself.

Kelley grabbed her wrist and forced her roughly out the door behind him. He backed up with his rapier held in a defensive position, eyes fixed on the shadow outline of Normand. The Frenchman made no attempt to follow.

"This isn't finished," Kelley told him.

Normand slammed his door shut in the face of the alchemist.

The doors of the other bedrooms spilled flickering candlelight into the hall as their bewildered occupants came forth to inquire about the terrible shrieks. Kelley heard stirrings on the lower level as well.

"Go to Jane and stay with her," he hissed. "Bolt the door."

He pushed Joanna toward the open door of Dee's bedroom. Dee came forth in his nightshirt and sleeping cap with a candle in his hand. Jane peered nervously past his shoulder. When she saw Joanna she opened her arms and the two women embraced. Jane drew her friend into the room.

Dee observed the drawn sword in Kelley's hand without comment.

"It came from outside," Kelley said. "The back of the house, I think."

Ignoring the terrified babbling of the Dutch merchant, they made their way down the steep stair. The entire household was in an uproar. The farmer's wife tried vainly to comfort her weeping daughter while bouncing an infant on her knee. The farmer examined the firing mechanism of a rusted blunderbuss in the light of a storm lantern held up by his white-faced elder son.

"Has anyone gone outside?" Dee asked in Dutch.

The farmer shook his head, a look of dread elongating his features, which distorted strangely in the flickering lantern light.

Kelley led the party of four men out the back door, closely followed by Dee, who exchanged his candle for the more reliable lantern of the youth. This was just as well, since the first strong breeze blew the candle out. The waxing moon provided enough light to guide their steps past the round barn to the shadow of a spreading elm. On the grass lay what looked like two disordered piles of old rags.

Kelley approached the tree with caution, his keen eyes darting into the black and silver shadows that lay alongside the barn and adjoining chicken coop. With his bare toe he turned over the nearest body. The head of the corpse lolled on its neck to reveal a sinister, brutal face distorted by terror in its death mask. The dead man's trunk breeches were bunched around his ankles and his privates bared. Black liquid oozed from the tip of his flaccid penis. More of the same seeped from his bulging eyes, his gaping mouth, his nose, even his ears. Kelley realized with a rolling sensation of nausea that it was blood.

Dee bent to examine the other man with clinical detachment. He was in a similar condition, save that he remained fully dressed.

"Massive internal hemorrhage," Dee murmured. "I've never seen anything similar. Their hearts must have exploded within their chests."

"What were they doing here?" the farmer asked in bewildered Dutch. "They look like Spaniards."

"Indeed they do," Kelley said to Dee in English.

"Why is this one half-naked?" the farmer wondered aloud. "Was he relieving himself, do you think?"

"That seems the simplest explanation," Dee told him in his own language. "We should drag them into your barn and cover them. We can't leave them here for the rest of the night—animals may get at them."

Regaining some of his composure, the farmer numbly agreed. He and his son dragged the corpses into the barn and left them on the earthen floor, covered with straw. Dee and Kelley examined the ground in the vicinity of the elm but found nothing except a dagger and a scattering of silver coins. The dagger was a murderous instrument of Spanish design, its blade browned so that it would not show a reflection.

"The tool of a professional assassin," Dee murmured.

"Whatever killed them gave no warning," Kelley observed. "Could it have been poison?"

"There's no sign they were eating or drinking. Anyway, I've never seen a poison that could do that to a man."

He spoke with more than common knowledge. A number of years before, at the behest of Queen Elizabeth, who worried about assassination at the hands of the papists, he had conducted an extensive series of practical experiments on animals using all known types of poison. He was as near an expert on the subject as lived outside of Italy, where poison was both an ancient tradition and a high art.

"It's as if their lungs and their hearts ruptured from the inside under intense pressure." He shook his head, baffled. "It's more than natural."

"The spirit that dogs our steps," Kelley murmured, casting his gaze around at the darkness. The mild night breeze felt chill against his naked back.

"But why these two?" Dee wondered.

While Dee searched the yard with the lantern, Kelley returned into the house to make certain the women were safe. Pacifying the frightened Dutch merchant and his wife as well as he could with his poor command of that language, he lit a candle in a brass holder from one burning in the sweating hands of the merchant. He had not forgotten about Normand. As he climbed the stairs, his anger at the smooth-cheeked Frenchman returned.

He went first to Dee's door. It was shut. He heard the soft murmur of Jane Dee's voice as he tried the latch, and was gratified to find that Joanna had possessed the good sense to shoot the bolt.

"Who is it?" Jane asked.

"It's me. Don't come out yet. Leave the door locked."

With a frown he noticed for the first time a small white cross on the planks of the door, no larger than his thumb, just below eye level. He brushed at it and it fell away as dust. Chalk, he realized. The door to Normand's room was closed. He examined the doors one by one and found a similar cross on his own. The other doors were unmarked.

Returning to Normand's door, Kelley took a fresh grip on the hilt of his rapier and used it to depress the door latch.

"I told you our business wasn't finished, sirrah," he said, kicking the door inward with his bare foot. It banged loudly against the wall.

He thrust the candle forward and stepped inside. The room was empty. Normand had vanished.

PART THREE

PRAGUE

TWENTY-TWO

John Dee led his small party across the cobblestones of the market place in the old city of Prague, which surrounded the tower and chapel of St. Lawrence and the adjoining town hall. Opposite the town hall stood the ancient Tyn church. The market place possessed an indefinable air of dignity and stability. It was the preferred concourse for the many intellectuals who studied or taught at Prague University and the recently founded College of Jesuits. It was one of the great public squares of Europe.

After this airy, sunlit plaza, to pass under the stone arch of the open gate into the cramped, stinking streets of the ghetto was like stepping between worlds. Jane had been to Prague before with her husband, but this was her first experience of the Jews' Quarter. She stared around in shocked wonder at the squalor, her senses assaulted by the smell of rotting cabbage and urine, the sight of strange letters painted on signs, the unfamiliar sound of Yiddish, and the suspicious faces of the inhabitants.

The ghetto of Prague was the most ancient in Europe. Established in the tenth century as part of the original town, which then occupied only the right bank of the Moldau River, it became segregated from the rest of the community by gates and a wall in 1235, when King Wenceslaus I constructed fortifications around the old city.

Since that time the Jewish population had grown but the available building area had not. The streets were narrow, the sanitation poor, and the houses piled one on top of another so that they seemed to lean over the streets and gasp for air. Even the headstones in the Jewish cemetery tilted and jumbled grave on grave, respect for the dead forced to accommodate the harsh reality of ghetto life.

"Why does the ghetto have its own gates?" Jane asked.

"The Jews are locked inside at night, all day Sunday and during Christian holidays," Dee explained. "They're let out into the old city six days a week to conduct business in the Jew's Market."

"That's terrible," she said. "They're penned up like animals."

"Would you rather have them overrun the city with their filthy smells?" Kelley asked, staring with distaste at the swarm of flies over the fish on a street-vendor's cart.

"I'd rather they were free to come and go like anyone else," Jane told him quietly.

"It's for their own safety," Joanna said. "The papists would murder them."

"That's probably true, unfortunately," Dee agreed. "When the Protestant uprising was crushed here forty years ago, any chance for greater tolerance for the Jews died with it."

He led them around a corner into a street that was wider and less squalid than the others. The houses along both sides, though modest enough, had the appearance of prosperity. They touched each other on the sides and their plain, painted doors opened directly onto the cobblestone street. Most were three or four stories high and very narrow to take greatest advantage of their small lots.

Dee stopped before a house framed with square oak beams. The spaces between the beams were filled with red brick. Small round windows of grayish glass diamonds peered like eyes from either side of the door. Each of the three stories of the house projected farther out than the one below. Looking up, Jane judged it would be possible to step across the street from its roof to the roof opposite. The projecting stories created the curious impression that the house would fall over at any minute. On the green door was a small brass nameplate incised with Hebrew letters.

Dee worked the heavy brass knocker above the nameplate. Echoes reverberated inside the house. After what seemed an uncommonly long time, the door was opened by a young man in a black hat with a brim. He had long curling hair, a full beard, and liquid brown eyes. He regarded the four gentiles with an expression of polite surprise.

"Is Rabbi Loew at home?" Dee asked in English.

"Do you have an appointment with the Maharal?"

"In a manner of speaking. The Rabbi asked me to visit in his last letter."

"Do you have the letter?"

"No," Dee said, suppressing impatience. "It never occurred to me that I might need it."

The young man blinked thoughtfully, then shrugged.

"The Maharal is a very busy man. Most people who call have appointments. I don't know if he will see you."

"Why don't you ask him, instead of standing here wasting our time," Kelley said.

The young man looked at him with a mild expression for several moments, then opened the door and stepped aside.

"Please wait here. I will speak with the Maharal."

There were chairs in the dark entrance hall. Jane and Joanna sat gratefully.

"What a handsome man," Joanna said in a low voice to Jane. "At least, he would be if he cut his hair and trimmed his beard."

"I wonder if he's Rabbi Loew's son," Jane said.

"Do rabbis have children?"

"Of course."

"I thought they were celibate, like priests."

"Jews don't believe in celibacy."

"Why did he call Rabbi Loew 'the Maharal'?" Joanna asked.

"John told me it's a title of respect formed from letters in the Hebrew words 'Our Teacher the Master Rabbi Loew,'" Jane explained.

"He must be some kind of religious leader, then."

"More like a saint, I believe. But John says he has great moral authority within the ghetto."

Dee drew Kelley aside out of the hearing of the women.

"I know your feelings about Jews," he said, lips close to Kelley's ear. "Judah Loew is my friend. While you're in my company I won't permit him to be insulted."

Kelley smiled sourly.

"It's true that I have no great love for the tribe. That doesn't mean I go out of my way to insult them."

"I've never understood your dislike of these people," Dee murmured. "It's not Christian charity."

"They're parasites," Kelley said. "They move from place to place, profit where they can, risk as little as they must, and give loyalty to no man or nation."

"I can't speak for all of them, but Judah is the most godly man I've ever met. I'm proud to call him a friend."

Kelley said nothing.

The young man in the hat returned. He appeared embarrassed.

"The Rabbi will see you," he said, gesturing for them to follow.

They made their way up a flight of dark stairs. Midway on the stairs Jane shivered and clutched at the banister.

"What was that?" she asked.

Joanna drew in her breath as she passed Jane and hurried up the next few steps. Dee felt it then, a chill that passed through his body.

"An occult barrier. Keep going, Jane, it's no danger to us."

Jane recovered once she had passed the invisible wall. To Kelley's mediumistic perceptions it appeared to hang across the stair like a faintly glowing curtain. He passed through it as though walking through a veil of mist and felt it draw the heat from the surface of his skin.

"There are many such wards and guardians in this house," Dee told them. "Pay them no notice."

The young Jew gave no sign that he had heard the discussion. He led them down an elegant paneled corridor to a door at the rear of the house that was padded in red leather studded with brass nails.

Kelley saw dark shadows on either side of the door. They moved as though alive, twining and changing their shapes like endless columns of black smoke. No one else commented upon them. Looking at the faces of Jane and his wife, he realized they could not see the amorphous sentinels. Just as well, he thought.

Their escort opened the padded door and stood to one side with his head bowed. They filed into a spacious library with a high-beamed ceiling and tall windows that let in slanting streams of sunlight. The walls were covered with books. Jane, who was well-accustomed to her husband's large library, was astonished by their number. Midway up the wall, a narrow walkway with a railing ran around the perimeter of the room. This was reached by means of a spiral staircase in one corner. The railing and staircase glowed with the rich color of polished cherrywood.

Behind an enormous desk sat a gray-haired Jew reading a parchment scroll through two round glass lenses that perched on the bridge of his thick nose in a frame of ivory. His hair hung down on either side of his shoulders from beneath his brimmed hat, and his equally gray beard spread across his chest. He appeared very old, due to the innumerable lines and creases in his leathery face, but this was an illusion. Dee had once mentioned to Jane that Loew was only two years older than himself.

The young man withdrew from the library and closed the door without announcing them. They waited while Loew finished reading. As he read, he rocked back and forth in his chair and his heavy lips moved soundlessly. Without haste he rolled up the scroll and kissed it before putting it to one side. Taking off his reading lenses, he rose from his chair with a broad smile and walked stiffly around the desk.

"John, I'm so relieved you could come to Prague. The situation I wrote to you about grows more serious with each passing hour. And you've brought you lovely wife and your assistant, I see."

Dee introduced Jane and Joanna to Loew. Jane extended her hand. The Rabbi smiled and shook his head.

"I am very sorry, my dear, but I am not permitted to touch you."

Slightly embarrassed, Jane blushed and stepped back.

Loew noticed Joanna eyeing the glass lenses in his hand and held them up for her to see.

"They are called spectacles," he told her. "I got them from an Arab trader to help with my reading."

"This is my seer and good friend, Edward Kelley," Dee said, gesturing for Kelley to come forward.

Kelley approached with hesitation, his eyes fixed on the air around Loew's head. It shimmered and glowed for a distance of several inches away from the hair of the rabbi and above his hat in the shape of a nebulous white halo. This was the first time Kelley had ever seen a halo around a living human being. It frightened and subdued him.

Loew stood within touching distance of the alchemist and stared with his clear gray gaze into the darker eyes of Kelley as though searching for something. Kelley felt the hairs as the back of his neck lift. The old Jew seemed to look directly into his heart.

"It's all right, my friend," Loew said, nodding at Kelley with a compassionate expression. "It's not your fault. You don't yet know any better."

Kelley dropped his eyes and turned away.

"Please, come and sit down. Tell me about your journey."

Loew motioned them with his arms to the other side of the library, where a settee and several chairs were arranged around a fireplace. No fire burned on the hearth, the weather being quite warm. He seated himself in one of the chairs across from the two women, who chose the settee, and he listened with attention while Dee related some of the events of their travels, supplemented by remarks from Jane and Joanna. Kelley remained silent.

"So you had no more trouble after you reached Amsterdam?"

"None at all," Joanna said, smiling. "After that we left all our bad luck behind us."

"The voyage along the northern coast was aided by fine weather and favorable winds," Jane said. "The trip up river from Hamburg was scenic but uneventful."

"That is the best sort of travel, scenic but uneventful," Loew said. He seemed amused by her choice of words.

The young Jew who had opened the front door appeared with a tray of small glasses. He placed this on a table beside the settee and filled the glasses from a decanter of dark red sherry, then handed one glass to each person, including the rabbi himself.

"This is my son-in-law, Rabbi Yitzhaq Katz. He attends to the needs of my household and acts as my secretary. I don't believe you know him, John—he was away from Prague at the time of your last visit."

Rabbi Katz smiled and nodded to each of them in turn before withdrawing from the library.

Loew continued to question them about the journey. He was especially interested in hearing details concerning the incident in the maze at Hampton Court, and in the condition of the two dead man at the farmhouse in the Netherlands. Neither Kelley nor his wife spoke about Normand's attraction to Joanna, but the Rabbi seemed to understand more than was conveyed in words.

"This Huguenot, you say he vanished immediately after the horrible deaths of the two men?"

"Within the hour," Dee said. "When we returned from examining the corpses, he was gone."

"Curious," Loew murmured.

They chatted about inconsequential matters for a while longer. Loew asked Dee where they were staying while in Prague.

"We haven't decided on an inn as yet," Dee told him. "We came straight to your house after leaving the river."

"Then you must be my guests here in my house." Loew waved his hand impatiently to stifle their protests. "Nonsense, I have many rooms going to waste. I insist that you be my guests."

"Perhaps it would be wise," Dee said, meeting his eye.

Loew glanced from Dee to Kelley and nodded seriously.

"I thought so. I will send Yitzhaq for your trunks. Where did you leave them?"

Dee described the inn near the river where they had deposited their luggage for safe-keeping. Loew called his son-in-law from the door of the library.

"Our guests will be staying with us. Please introduce these two gracious ladies to my wife and ask her to take care of their needs. Then send someone to pick up their trunks."

He repeated Dee's directions. Jane stood and glanced uncertainly at her husband. Dee nodded to reassure her.

"Go with Rabbi Katz," Loew said, smiling at Joanna. "We will see each other again when we break bread."

He waited until the library door shut, then turned to the men with a grave expression on his lined face.

"Now we can get down to business. Quickly, tell me everything you know about the movements of the book."

Dee described the theft of *Liber Lilith* from Mortlake, then let Kelley narrate the events at the Rose Theater.

"I am sorry to hear about the destruction of your library," Loew said, shaking his head. "A great tragedy."

"The spirits told us the book was on the Continent," Kelley said. "Do you know where it was taken?"

"It is here in Bohemia, that much is certain. Exactly where I have been unable to learn. The Sons of Coronzon have surrounded it with many veils, and are keeping it inside their stronghold, which is somewhere in the mountains east of Prague."

"Can you lead us to this stronghold?"

Loew regarded Kelley with a curious expression and shook his head.

"For years we have tried to discover its exact location. We failed—the fortress is well-concealed. Forgive me for asking, but your interest in the book seems greater than I would have expected."

"I want to see it destroyed, the same as you do," Kelley told him with a belligerent edge in his tone.

The Rabbi raised his bushy gray eyebrows. He turned to Dee.

"You know that you were followed here?"

"We saw no one," Dee told him.

"Not by a human being. A spirit. Probably the same that was set to watch you at your house in England. The one that killed the Spaniards."

"You think they were killed by this Watcher?"

"Very likely."

"What exactly is the nature of this monster?" Kelley demanded. "The thing I fought in the rigging of the *Bridget* looked to be half bird and half man."

"Its shape means nothing. It is a creature of the airy wastes, a thing of the desert places between the worlds. Only a tiny portion of its being projects into our reality. It puts on forms as we do clothing, to serve its momentary purposes. It is nothing more than a hunger, a great whirling emptiness."

"I understand why it was sent to attack the ship, if indeed it was the same spirit," Dee said. "Its masters wanted us turned back or sent to the bottom of the Channel. But why reveal itself to Jane at Hampton Court, and then withdraw without harming her?"

"Who knows?" Loew said with a shrug. "My guess is that it was sent to kill her, but withdrew in confusion when it discovered she is with child."

Dee stared at him as though struck by invisible lightning. He glanced at Kelley, who shook his head to show that he knew nothing of the matter.

"What on earth makes you think Jane is pregnant?"

"You mean you didn't know?" Loew said with surprise. "I'm sorry, my friend, but I thought she had told you. It's so obvious."

"Not to me," Dee said.

Then he remembered the increasing plumpness of his wife, and her sickness on the barge coming down the Thames, and wondered how he could have been so blind. He had assumed, wrongly it appeared, that his birth control measures would be effective. His surprise began to give way to a growing pleasure. Another child. That would make five, all by Jane over the last eight years. His first wife, Katherine, had been infertile. His second wife, Anne, had died after only a few months of marriage. He wondered if it would be a girl or a boy.

"A boy, I think," Loew said absently, although Dee had not spoken.

"Why would the Watcher care whether or not Jane is with child?" Kelley asked.

"All spirits of the wastes are the children of Lilith. She is the Great Mother of abortions. The fetus in the womb and the newborn infant fall under her power. She uses this authority capriciously, sometimes to kill, sometimes to comfort. Who can say why she chose to protect the child? Tomorrow she may decide to kill it."

"I'd like Jane to stay within the walls of this house until the danger is over," Dee told him. "Even if it means waiting here until after the birth of the child."

"Of course, my friend, I understand."

"I have another reason for coming to Bohemia besides the pleasure of seeing you again."

"I suspected as much when you spoke of the murdered Spaniards."

Dee described his political errand on behalf of Queen Elizabeth. Loew was fascinated to hear the details of Drake's attack on the Spanish fleet at Cadiz, the news of which had only recently reached Prague. Dee went on to tell him of the cipher document and the manner in which it was to be obtained.

Kelley was privately shocked at the trust Dee seemed to place in the Jew, but said nothing. The cipher was not his business. He was more interested in the book.

"The Queen's agent, Peter Gwyn, is presently in Prague," Loew observed to Dee. "I saw him yesterday while out walking in the market place."

"I'll meet with him tomorrow," Dee said. "The sooner I complete the Queen's errand, the sooner we can concentrate on finding the book."

"What is the mysterious power of this book?" Kelley demanded impatiently. "Why is it so important?"

Loew nodded to himself and seemed to come to a decision.

"It's time I told you the whole truth. You should have the choice to withdraw and go back to England, if you wish."

"You know we would never do that," Dee said.

"Don't be so quick to decide until you know what you are facing."

"Is the book that dangerous?" Kelley asked.

Loew regarded the alchemist seriously.

"My friend, I would be lying to you if I said that I believe any one of us here in this room will come through this ordeal alive."

TWENTY-THREE

Rabbi Katz escorted Jane and Joanna into a small parlor in the rear of the house.

"Wait here, please," he said. "Madame Loew will be with you shortly."

It was a clean, pleasant room with a lived-in atmosphere. An Oriental rug covered the highly polished floor. The panels of the walls were painted with pastoral scenes of flowers and trees. Lace curtains softened the brightness streaming through the window and cast a pattern of small sunspots like scattered beads across the embroidered settee and gilded French chairs. A small harpsichord stood against the wall in the corner. There was no trace of ostentation about the room, but all of the furnishings were new and of the finest quality.

Jane went to the window and drew aside the lace curtain to look out.

"Joanna, come and look," she said.

Her friend joined her at the window. Behind the house a small walled garden bloomed with bright flowers, an unexpected oasis of green in a desert of squalor.

"It's so pretty," Joanna observed.

"Thank you. It is a pastime of mine."

They turned. A tall woman with olive skin and black hair streaked with gray stood in the open doorway with her hand on the brass doorknob. A smaller young woman stepped into the room and smiled a timid greeting. Both were dressed in black with white lace upon their heads. By contrast, the pale blue of Jane's conservatively cut dress and the light green of Joanna's flaring skirts seemed a riot of color.

"I am Miriam, the wife of the Maharal," the older woman said. She stepped forward with a regal air, her back straight as a pillar, and offered her hand to Jane. "This is my daughter, Esther. Welcome to my house."

Jane took her hand warmly and introduced herself and Joanna. They seated themselves. Miriam Loew occupied a chair at the head of the room positioned to allow easy conversation with all the other places. Jane and Joanna sat together on the settee, and the nervous Esther sat opposite them with her lustrous dark eyes downcast, wringing her hands.

"I'm glad you noticed my garden," Miriam said. "The Maharal is so busy all the time, I don't think he knows it's even there."

"It's wonderful," Joanna said. "I never imagined there could be anything so pretty…." She stopped and blushed.

"In the ghetto?" Miriam finished for her. She did not appear offended. "You would be surprised at the many treasures that lie hidden behind these walls. My people have lived here for five centuries. We've had time to make this our own place."

"I didn't mean, I just thought…." Joanna cast an imploring glance at Jane.

"This is all new to us," Jane said. "We've never been inside the gates before."

"I understand. You gentiles think we all live like rats in the ghetto. But my husband is a very important man. It is necessary for him to keep up appearances. We receive many visitors from across Europe, some even from Africa and Asia."

Detecting the note of pride in Miriam's voice when she spoke of her husband, Jane decided to pursue this line of conversation.

"They all come to meet with your husband? He must be vary famous and wise."

"He is the Maharal," Miriam said simply.

"Was it your husband who met us at the door?" Joanna asked the silent Esther in an effort to draw her out.

She nodded with a shy smile.

"He's very handsome."

"Yes," she murmured in a heavy accent. "He is a very good man."

"My daughter's English is not good," Miriam said. "We do not have many occasions to practice."

"No, it's fine," Joanna said to Esther with encouragement. "I can understand every word you say."

"Thank you."

Poor child, Joanna thought. She's afraid to even open her mouth with her dragon of a mother in the room.

"John once tried to explain to me your husband's position in your community, but I'm not sure I really understood," Jane said brightly to Miriam. "Is he an elected leader or is his authority honorary?"

"We have no leaders as such," Miriam explained. "For political purposes, in dealing with the gentiles and maintaining internal order, there is an elected council. Those who violate holy law are tried before a rabbinical court and punished according to our code of justice. My husband is the Ab Bet Din, what you would call the chief justice, of our court. But these are offices imposed upon us by circumstance. Strictly speaking, all Jews are equal."

Jane thought of the filth and squalor in the narrow streets outside the house, the infants screaming with hunger in the gutter and the smell of open sewers.

"My husband is what you might call a holy man. He teaches the mysteries of our faith to his chosen disciples, one of whom is my son-in-law, Rabbi Katz. He is respected throughout the ghetto. When there is difficulty in dealing with the outside world, Jews seek out the Maharal for guidance."

"Is such trouble common?" Jane asked.

The other woman frowned and pursed her lips in thought. This caused a sunburst of fine wrinkles to appear around her mouth.

"There has been friction between Jew and gentile for centuries. Since the Jesuits built their university at Prague thirty years ago, it has been growing steadily worse. There is a priest named Thaddeus who is determined to drive us from the ghetto so that the Church can seize our wealth. The council called upon my husband to fight the lies of this priest."

"How can he do that?" Jane wondered.

The ardor that shone from Miriam's eyes when speaking about Loew was replaced by reserve.

"You must ask him. I am only his wife. He does not discuss his work with me."

A maid entered with steaming black coffee. Miriam drew her close and whispered in her ear. After the maid left, she occupied herself by filling the small china cups and passing them to her guests and her daughter. Jane tasted the coffee curiously. The flavor was pleasant but very strong. She was glad she had added cream and honey.

"I've ordered my maid to fill my bath for you," Miriam said to Jane and Joanna. "You must be hot from your voyage up the river. Rabbi Katz has sent a boy to fetch your trunks from the inn."

"I'm looking forward to seeing the sights of Prague," Joanna said to Esther as she sipped her steaming coffee. "Perhaps you could go with me and keep me from getting lost."

"I'd like that very much," Esther said.

"Esther, you know that's impossible," Miriam injected. "It's far too dangerous in old Prague for a woman to walk without a male escort."

"I'll be with her," Joanna said brightly. "I'll keep her safe. Jane will tell you that I can handle myself around men."

"That's true," Jane said. "Joanna's not afraid of anything."

"I'm sure," Miriam said coolly. "However, it would still be too dangerous for my daughter. She is a Jew, remember."

"I thought you left the ghetto frequently," Joanna argued.

"The men go to the Jew's Market because they must. Even then, they risk attack from mobs. Women never go out for pleasure."

"But, Mother, there hasn't been a beating for weeks. I'm sure I would be safe with Joanna," Esther protested in a pitiful voice.

"I've said it's too dangerous," Miriam snapped. "Must you force me to repeat myself?"

"No, Mother," Esther said, dropping her eyes.

Joanna glanced at Jane, who shook her head imperceptibly. The last thing they needed was to become embroiled in a domestic dispute with their hosts. Joanna seemed to understand. The redhead suppressed her anger and forced a faint smile onto her lips.

"We can go on some other visit, when the situation is not so dangerous."

Esther nodded without looking at her. The silence lengthened. Joanna shifted in her seat, the rustle of her petticoats loud in the sudden stillness. Jane tried desperately to think of something to say, but the awkward moment had left her mind blank.

"Why don't you play something for our guests, Esther?" Miriam said at last with a false brightness.

"I don't feel like playing."

"Nonsense, of course you do." She turned to Jane. "Esther is a wonderful musician. When she was a little girl she took lessons every afternoon for an hour."

Reluctantly, Esther set aside her coffee and went to the harpsichord. She began to play and sing a German folk song from memory. As she sang, her nervousness and embarrassment melted away from her. Jane, who was well-accustomed in her youth to attending performances by German and Italian musicians before Queen Elizabeth, decided that she had never heard so sweet a voice.

"That was wonderful, Esther," Joanna said, clapping her hands when the dark-eyed girl finished. "Wasn't she wonderful, Jane?"

Jane agreed with enthusiasm. Esther endured their praise with a blush, but it was clear that she enjoyed their flattery. Jane reflected that the poor girl probably never played before her mother without having to suffer through a critique of her style afterwards. She reminded Jane of a delicate flower wilting because it did not get the sunshine it needed to grow. What a tragedy that Esther's husband had chosen to remain in Loew's house as his disciple. It meant that she could never escape the smothering love of her mother.

The maid returned to announce that the bath was ready. This came as a relief to everyone.

"I'll go with our guests in case they need anything," Esther said as Jane and Joanna were leaving the parlor. She slipped through the door behind them before the disapproval in her mother's eyes could frame itself into words.

They ascended the main stair to the third level. The bath was located in its own little room at the end of the hall. It was a wonder to the Englishwomen, who were accustomed to washing themselves in wooden tubs barely large enough to sit in. It stood on its own legs, its tall, curved sides formed from sheets of riveted copper. Jane felt momentary pity for the kitchen staff, who had been forced to fill its deep basin with buckets carried up two flights of stairs from the lower level of the house. But the seduction of the steaming, rose-scented water was too great for these guilty thoughts to overcome her delight at the luxurious prospect of soaking all her limbs at the same time.

"You go first," she said to Joanna in a spirit of noble sacrifice.

"No, you," Joanna said. "You're not as dirty as I am, Jane. You know I always sweat more than you do."

The truth of this observation somewhat placated Jane's conscience. Without another word she stripped off her dress and underclothes. Released from the constriction of her stomacher, the dome of her lower belly was unmistakable.

"You're with child," Esther said with surprise. "When are you due?"

"About five months," Jane murmured.

She slid with a sigh into the steaming bath water, and was delighted to discover that it covered her up to her shoulders. The maid, who stood beside the tub like a silent sentinel to ensure that she did not slip, handed her

a large sea sponge. Jane drew the sponge from shoulder
to shoulder under her chin and reflected that when they
returned to Mortlake she would being up the subject of a
copper bath to John. He was by nature so ascetic that he
never even thought of creature comforts unless she suggested them first.

"I'm sorry you won't be able to come walking with
me through the city," Joanna said to Esther.

"I am, too."

"Do you always do what your mother tells you to do?"
Esther smiled sadly.

"Yes, I suppose I do."

"It must get lonely for you in this house with only
your mother to talk to," Joanna said with sympathy.

"I have my books and my music. Anyway, I talk with my
husband all the time." She glanced at the maid and lowered
her voice. "Yitzhaq tells me all about his studies with the
Maharal and the happenings in the city. I'm not supposed
to know about such matters because I'm a woman, but
Yitzhaq is a kind man. He tells me everything."

"Is it really so dangerous for Jews on the other side of
the gates?"

"How can I know?" Esther said with a fatalistic shrug.
"There have been incidents. Men have been beaten and
robbed for no reason. We all live in a constant state of
fear. I will tell you a story to show how it is. One time
many years ago there was a fire in the ghetto. The rabbis
were so certain the men from the city intended to loot
their houses, they barricaded the gates from the inside.
The Christians who came to help fight the fire couldn't
get in. Half the ghetto burned to the ground before we
Jews were able to put the fire out by ourselves. That is
how frightened we are."

"But if you've been here five hundred years, you have as much right to live here as any other people," Joanna said with righteous anger.

"I believe you," Esther told her with a smile. "Go convince the Jesuits."

They left Jane splashing happily in the bath water and went down the hall to look at Esther's tapestry, which she had been working on since the day of her marriage more than two years ago. It was set up in a wooden frame in an empty room. On the way Joanna stopped before a door with a heavy hasp of iron that was locked from the outside.

"What's in here?" she asked, rapping on the planks of the door. "The family treasure?"

Esther caught her wrist and put her finger to her lips. Sadness and compassion mingled in her brown eyes. She bent her head to the door and listened. Puzzled, Joanna also listened with stilled breath. A faint scuffing noise came from the other side of the door. Joanna heard the shuffle of slow steps dragging across the floor.

"We must go," Esther whispered.

She pulled Joanna away from the door by the elbow with an affectionate backward glance.

"Who's in there?" Joanna asked.

"One who is beloved by God," Esther told her.

Despite Joanna's intense curiosity, she could not induce Esther to say another word about the inhabitant of the locked room.

TWENTY-FOUR

Rabbi Loew led Dee and Kelley up the spiral staircase in the corner of the library. From the floor of the library the stair had seemed to terminate in a shadow on the beamed ceiling, but now that he stood upon the stair itself Kelley saw that it continued upward through an opening—a curious illusion. Presumably this opening led to the garret of the old house, he thought.

When they continued to climb for several minutes, circling the central pillar of the staircase more than a dozen times, unease crept into the heart of the alchemist. By his estimate they must be well above the slates of the steeply-pitched roof. This was impossible in the world he knew.

Loew stepped off a landing on the stair into a moderately-sized chamber with a low ceiling. Dee followed him. Kelley glanced upward in wonder before going after his companions. The spiral stairway continued into darkness with no sign of an ending. Light from a small, square window cast a dim illumination throughout the room. Kelley saw that its walls were lined from floor to ceiling with shelves of books. A round table and several plain wooden chairs composed its spartan furnishings.

The rabbi paced back and forth stiffly across the open floor and flexed his legs.

"Forgive me for being so slow," he explained with a rueful smile. "My knees aren't what they once were. I'm afraid I'm growing old."

"Nonsense," Dee told him. "You're only two years older than me, and I'm expecting a new baby boy."

Loew laughed.

"I'll tell Miriam what you said. She can start redecorating the nursery."

There was something indefinably strange and otherworldly about the books. Their dusty, faded leather spines, lettered in obscure and forgotten tongues, exuded hoary age and vast, timeless power. Even their smell was alien. Without reading the titles Kelley knew they were occult texts. This must be Loew's magical library.

He wandered around the room, glancing with keen interest from shelf to shelf. Some of the works were massive tomes bound in brass. Verdigris shone bright green from their hinges, and cobwebs stretched between the raised edges of the covers across the dusty top of the leaves. He judged that many of the books had not been opened for years, perhaps not for generations, and wondered if any of them treated alchemy. Perhaps the secret of the stone he had so long sought in vain lay locked between their worm-eaten pages.

As he passed the window he glanced out, then stopped in midstep for a longer stare. He should be gazing across the steep rooftops of the ghetto. Through the clouded, rippled gray of the ancient glass, a lawn stretched into the distance and merged with a stand of mature oaks. Although there was nothing threatening about the pastoral scene, its very existence made him nervous. He wondered what would happen if he opened the window and climbed outside—not that he had any intention of trying so mad a trick.

He cast a quick glance at Loew. The Jew continued to talk to Dee about inconsequential matters, paying him no attention. Was there a glimmer of mild amusement in the corner of his wrinkled gray eye?

Loew gestured for Dee and Kelley to sit at the round table. He went to a low shelf and with considerable effort pulled out a huge book. The weight was almost more than he could manage. Kelley started forward to help him, but Loew shook his head.

"Better if you don't touch it until it has been unlocked."

He dropped it with a thud onto the table and brushed some of the dust off its heavy cover. The corners and hinges of the book were protected by tarnished black iron. A broad hasp spanned the pages and prevented the cover from opening. The Jew drew a ring with many small keys from his girdle and fumbled with it for several moments. At last he found what he searched after and fitted it into a slot in the center of the book's cover. The key turned with difficulty. There was a click. The hasp sprang loose and clanked open across the table.

Searching the edges of the leaves for some invisible place mark, Loew opened the great book from left to right. It groaned and creaked, complaining about this unaccustomed attention. Kelley saw that its vellum leaves were hand-lettered with Hebrew in black and red, with illuminated boxed capitals at the head of each page. Loew turned several leaves to reveal an illustration that occupied a full page.

"What beautiful work," Dee murmured, leaning forward to examine it.

"Arabic," Loew said. "This book was made in Baghdad in the ninth century of the Christian era by a secret Kabbalist sect."

Bright reds and greens leapt out from a background of gold leaf and a silvery material that appeared to Kelley's practiced alchemical eye to be some variety of fixed mercury. The illumination depicted the seated figure of a woman. The upper half of her body was humanoid; the lower half divided into two coiling serpent tails. It was highly stylized. Her hair showed an array of eleven vipers raised as though to strike. Her arms were curling arabesques that spiraled in opposite directions. Similar spirals defined her breasts.

Black ovals flecked with silver specks stood in place of her eyes. From her snarling mouth darted a forked tongue. The left half of her face was silver and the right half, gold. Above her right shoulder flamed the disk of the sun. Over her left shoulder shone the waning crescent of the moon. She seemed to beckon with her outstretched left hand and threaten to strike with her raised right. Her gaping sexual parts were inexpressibly obscene. Kelley, though no prude, blushed as he looked at them. The figure sat completely naked except for a circlet around her brow that reared up in the front into the form of a viper with a shining white stone between its jaws.

"The degenerate sect of Hebrew gnostics that made this book worshiped this creature as their supreme goddess," Loew said.

"Lilith," Dee murmured in a quiet voice, as though fearful of invoking the spirit.

He bent over the image and studied its details with an expression of distaste. A miasma of ancient evil breathed from the vellum leaf. The anonymous artist had captured far more than merely the appearance of the demon. Suddenly he snatched his face back and stared at Loew. The Jew nodded.

"If you look at it for more than a few moments, it moves," he said.

Kelley turned the heavy book on the table and examined the features of the image. He discovered that when he focused his attention upon the eyes of the figure, he could see its limbs and serpentine tresses slide and coil. Even the extended tongue appeared to flicker as though testing the air for prey. There was something infinitely soothing in the sinuous gestures of the figure, like the rhythmic sway and swirl of seaweed beneath the rolling waves.

Rabbi Loew turned the book back toward Dee, breaking the light trance into which Kelley had drifted.

"She has many names and titles," he told Dee. "Lilitu is what the Chaldeans named her. In the folklore of my nation she is known as the Old One and Grandmother Lilith and the Queen of Screeching. She comes in the night on the soft, silent wings of an owl and sucks the semen from men who sleep alone. She visits women in their travail and makes their babies stillborn. She comes to infants in their cribs at night and plays with them so that they gurgle and laugh in their sleep. God forbid that you should let a child that laughs in its sleep remain undisturbed. You must tap it on the side of the nose to wake it to drive Lilith away before she steals its breath."

"All these tales I know," Dee told him. "You wrote in your letter that you had learned the secret of the book. How is it to be used?"

Rabbi Loew raised a hand in admonishment.

"Patience, my friend. The sect that made this book had a secret teaching about the Old One which they set down in its pages. I first discovered it three weeks ago, when I wrote to you."

"Well, what is it?" Kelley demanded. He, too, was growing impatient with the Jew's circuitous way of conveying information.

"You want in two minutes the knowledge my people have gathered over millennia," Loew said with a frown. "Very well. I will give it to you."

He turned the leaves of the book with care until he located another full-page illumination. This showed a straight serpent with a golden crown on its head. It was tinted with the bright crimson of dragon's blood. Around it coiled a green serpent with small wings. A smaller silver crown rested upon its head. The open mouths of the two snakes pressed together. They might have been fighting or making love, it was difficult to tell which. Between their jaws they held a large white jewel. It looked to Kelley to be the same stone that was set in the circlet around the head of Lilith in the other picture. Encircling both these serpents was yet a third, larger serpent that was colored black, its scales defined with hair-like lines of silver. It made a large loop with its body and swallowed the tip of its own tail. It was horned, and had no eyes.

"This is Samael, whom you Christians call Satan and Lucifer," Loew said, pointing to the straight serpent with the crown of gold. "He is the Radiant One, the Light Bearer, the beautiful son of heaven, cast down into the Abyss of darkness for his sin of pride. Very few even among the adepts of magic know his true name, the name by which he is named by the angels of God. Among the host of heaven he is Coronzon, the Fallen One, the Death Dragon. We call him the slant or piercing serpent because he strikes through to the heart like the blade of a sword.

"There is a secret teaching among my tribe that Coronzon is all spirit and light, without a body, without even a form of his own. He has no power to directly influence events in this universe. In order to bring forth his will in our world, he must act through the creative womb of his consort in hell, she who is named Lilith. Coronzon impregnates his consort with ideas, his spiritual seed, which she nurtures within herself until they are mature, and then gives birth to them as actions in the world of Assiah, the world of forms. We call Lilith the convolute or tortuous serpent because she is subtle and full of guile, with many masks and shapes.

"The prophets say in their secret teachings that the children of Lilith would soon overwhelm the entire universe, were they not restrained by the merciful hand of the Lord, blessed be He. In order to generate offspring, Coronzon and his harlot must copulate upon the back of the Blindragon. There you can see him circling the other two. His lust is an endless ocean of fire that rings the universe and provides the heat that is necessary for all engenderings. Without this heat nothing can be created anew. Life is carried on from father to son, and mother to daughter, through the spark of fire from the Blindragon that lies within each living thing.

"There is no end to the number of births Lilith is capable of nurturing within her womb. If she were allowed to breed unchecked, her verminous brood would overwhelm the world. To prevent this disaster the Holy One, blessed be He, weakened the virility of the Blindragon by putting it to sleep. We symbolize this by saying that He put out its eyes and castrated it. Without the fire of the Blindragon to join their seeds, the couplings of Samael and Lilith are sterile."

Rabbi Loew paused and bent his hoary head closer to Dee and Kelley across the open book.

"There is a secret teaching that is whispered but never spoken openly, not even from master to disciple, that it was Lilith, not the Holy One, blessed by He, who first fashioned the body of Adam out of clay after the heavenly image of Adam Kadmon. Then she tricked Coronzon into breathing the spark of spirit he had received into himself from his mother, the Queen of Heaven, who is called Barbalon among the initiated, into the body of Adam. In this way the power of creation passed out of Coronzon and into Adam. Before creating Adam, Coronzon made many mighty angels to rule the heavenly spheres, but after breathing the fire of the Blindragon into the first man, he lost the power to create through the womb of his consort. That is why the Old Serpent hates the sons of man so passionately. We possess the power of creation that he has lost.

"All of Lilith's spirit children are born of seed that she steals from men who sleep alone. She gives them erotic dreams and when they ejaculate their semen she catches it and uses it to make a demon. Sometimes she comes in the form of a male and lies with women. The women bear children that my people call *lilin*. They are human children, outwardly, but grow with uncommon swiftness and possess more than natural strength and vitality. It is possible to recognize them because they always lose the hair on the crowns of their heads at a very young age.

"Neither the living children engendered by Lilith in mortal women when she assumes the shape of Samael and lies with them, nor the spirit children she makes in her own womb from the stolen seed of mortal men, have souls. Both classes are incomplete. They are only images of living beings, mere golems of clay."

Rabbi Loew paused in his narration, giving Dee and Kelley time to absorb all that he had revealed before continuing.

"Imagine for a moment what would happen if the virility of the Blindragon could be restored. Then Lilith and Coronzon could bear living children of their own, beings able to travel and function within our universe, creatures with unique material forms and individual souls. Their power would be beyond comprehension. They would be eternal and virtually indestructible. To such beings, we humans would be nothing more than playthings for their amusement. They would execute the will of their father Coronzon upon the earth, and bring about an age of chaos in which every living thing would be annihilated or enslaved."

Dee and Kelley stared at him across the table. The sheer cosmic scope of the disaster that loomed before them was almost beyond comprehension.

"What role does the Book of Lilith play in this nightmare?" Dee asked at last.

"The book is a cipher. Within its rituals lies concealed a certain sequence of letters with a precise numerical relationship. By isolating this mathematical formula and reciting the permutations of the letters with ritual concentration, the virility of the Blindragon shall be reawakened, and its sleeping purpose, which the old rabbis symbolized by its blinded vision, restored. That purpose is to bring forth the hellish spawn of the Slant Serpent and the Tortuous Serpent into our universe. To become potent once more, Coronzon must first incarnate in living flesh upon the earth, and rejoin his nature with the divine spark he gave to Adam. After he lies with Lilith in his human incarnation, the children that issue from her endlessly fertile womb will enslave and destroy all of hated mankind."

"If the Sons of Coronzon already possess the book, why hasn't this happened already?" Kelley asked.

"The formula of the permutations is extraordinarily complex. It cannot be held all at once in the mind, but must be built up on the astral level bit by bit. It will require weeks of ritual work to bring it to its consummation. However, there are clear signs that the Sons of Coronzon have already begun this labor. There is a gathering confusion on the astral plane. The spirits are frightened. They report a great vortex filled with lightning and thunder over the Abyss. With each passing day it grows larger. The astral world is not a safe place to travel alone. Demons can now find their way up from the Abyss. This turbulence has revealed itself to men in the form of frequent nightmares. You yourselves may have noticed that your sleep is more troubled than usual these last two weeks."

Dee nodded. Thinking about it, Kelley realized that his dreams had indeed been more disturbed since their arrival on the Continent. He had dismissed this as an effect of the unfamiliar food and constantly changing surroundings.

"The awakening of the Blindragon will show itself in other ways after the chanting of the permutations of the Lilith formula is consummated. There will arise madness among beasts and prolific breeding of insects and other creeping things. Storms, earthquakes, floods, and other disasters will occur as the soul of the world becomes more tormented. This will lead to plagues, famine, and warfare among men."

Kelley released an uneasy laugh.

"You're describing the apocalypse."

Rabbi Loew nodded, a solemn expression on his weathered face.

"The opened womb of Lilith is the gate of Gehenna," he said.

"Perhaps it is God's will that this happen," Dee suggested.

"No!" Loew slammed his palm down on the surface of the table. His face shone with righteous anger. "That a small band of madmen use a mathematical formula to bring about the end of the world? I cannot believe the

Holy One, blessed be He, would be so capricious. There is no destiny in this. But it may become our fate, unless we have the wisdom and courage to stop it."

"What can we do?" Kelley asked.

"For the present, only wait. My disciples are searching all of Bohemia for the location of the fortress of the Sons of Coronzon. I have other agents on the astral plane engaged in a similar search. It is only a matter of time before we learn its physical location."

"I have resources of my own," Dee said. "Tomorrow I will send letters instructing the brothers and sisters of Hermes to begin their own search."

"Good. It may be what is needed. Wherever the fortress is situated, it lies well-concealed. My disciples have turned over every leaf and stone for a radius of a hundred miles. Yet I am certain it must be somewhere near Prague."

"Why don't you search for it yourself on the astral plane?" Kelley asked.

Loew spread his hands with frustration.

"What do you think I've been doing every night for the past month? The astral world is a big place."

"We could attempt it together," Dee suggested. "Our combined strength may be enough to overcome the barriers erected against us."

"It's worth a try," Loew said with a shrug. He did not seem optimistic about the chance for success.

Locking the book, he returned it to its place on the shelf, then stood over the round table and inscribed on its surface with his right index finger the outline of a hexagram, at the same time muttering a series of Hebrew letters. To Kelley's spiritual sight, the lines of the six-pointed star continued to glow with shimmering white fire.

Loew sat down and extended his hands across the table to the men on either side of him.

"Link hands. We will make out bodies our circle of protection."

A shock ran up Kelley's right arm as he touched the fingers of the Jew. Vitality infused his body. Unable to turn away from the gray eyes of the rabbi, he fumbled blindly until he located Dee's slender fingers by touch.

"Transition from the material plane to the astral will not be difficult," Loew muttered. His eyelids fluttered shut. "As you have already observed, this house extends beyond the bounds of physical reality."

He began to rhythmically chant the permutations of the Tetragrammaton, the divine fourfold name of God. It was this ability to control the occult forces released by the different patterns of the letters that made him a Ba'al Shem, Kelley thought, a title Dee had once told him signified "Master of the Name."

"Yud, Hey, Vav, Hey; Yud, Hey, Hey, Vav; Yud, Vav, Hey, Hey; Hey, Vav, Hey, Yud; Hey, Vav, Yud, Hey; Hey, Hey, Yud, Vav; Vav, Hey, Yud, Hey; Vav, Hey, Hey, Yud, Vav, Yud, Hey, Hey; Hey, Yud, Hey, Vav; Hey, Yud, Vav, Hey; Hey, Hey, Vav, Yud...."

After each complete cycle of permutation he began again, using a different sequence. The meaningless sounds had a mesmerizing effect on Kelley. He felt his awareness become light and float upward. The only feeling that remained was the pressure of hands clasping his hands. While the chanting of the letters lifted him up and carried him away from the physical world, the touch of flesh against his palms reminded him of who he was.

In the past he had found it all too easy to forget his identity when no longer tied to his body. Kelley disliked astral travel intensely. Those few occasions when he had experimented with it, he had almost lost the desire to return to his flesh. The body seemed completely unimportant once it was left behind. Astral travel frightened him. He preferred to use the black mirror or the crystal in his communications with the Enochian angels.

He felt that he was rushing horizontally through the darkness with Dee on his left side and Loew on his right. When he looked, he was unable to see them. His own body was also invisible, no more than a point of consciousness soaring through a midnight void. Gradually, he began to distinguish stars in the heavens and buildings amid the fields that passed below. He flew over the land of Bohemia like some bodiless bird.

"I see nothing," Loew said. The voice of the Jew seemed to speak directly into Kelley's right ear.

"I'm also blind," Dee murmured.

"We're passing over fields," Kelley said. "It's night. I see mountains in the distance. I think we're flying east."

"Concentrate on the symbol of the Sons of Coronzon," Loew advised. "That will draw us toward their stronghold."

Upon the astral plane it was necessary to think of a place to go there. Since none of them know where the fortress of Coronzon was located or what it looked like, they could only attempt to approach it through its symbolic associations.

Kelley perceived movement in the darkness around him. The void that at first had appeared empty crowded with nebulous shapes and invisible points of awareness that he sensed rather than saw as they passed him on their individual errands. Most of the astral beings ignored him. Several snarled in his mind and threatened as they drew near, but the circle created by Rabbi Loew protected him. They fell behind, gnashing invisible teeth in frustration. Once he passed what looked like a scarf of diaphanous white silk undulating upon the astral breeze. A warm wave of love washed over his mind and left him breathless. The words "go with God" echoed softly in his thoughts.

The mountain range drew steadily closer. As he approached, its rounded peaks loomed over him and gave him the unpleasant impression that he was shrinking. To Kelley, accustomed only to the modest hills of Wales, the peaks seemed unimaginably huge.

"I see something," he spoke with excitement.

He strained his astral perception. A wall of stone reared above the pines on the steep slope of a mountain. It overlooked a high pass. He saw a road winding through the pass far below it. Upon the wall stood a tower with a conical roof of slate.

Without warning, an invisible hand seized him around the chest with an icy grasp and hurled him back the way he had come as easily as a man might throw a stone across a pond. Kelley felt his re-entry into his body as a palpable shock. Gasping a breath, he opened his dark eyes and stared wildly at Rabbi Loew. The tranquil expression on the face of the Jew calmed him. He glanced at Dee, and saw that his face was covered with a fine sheen of sweat.

"We were thrown back," Dee said.

Loew nodded. A smile played at the corners of his lips.

"Because we were getting close. You see the power of the forces we confront. They have potent sentinels." He turned to Kelley. "Quick, describe everything you sensed."

The alchemist gave a complete account of his impressions of the stone tower and the mountain pass. Loew nodded with satisfaction.

"The eastern mountains that lie on the border between Bohemia and Silesia. Now we know where to concentrate our search. I suspected the mountains but was never certain. The region is almost uninhabited and difficult to reach. There can't be many roads."

Kelley pressed his sides gingerly with his hands. He could still feel the icy impression of giant fingers across his ribs.

"There was something else," he muttered.

With hesitation, he tried to describe the diaphanous white spirit that had passed him. He found it impossible to put the sensation of love that had emanated from it into words, and ended up by trailing away into silence.

"An angel?" Dee inquired.

Loew nodded. He seemed to gather inner resolve. Kelley felt it across the table as clearly as he might feel the sun beaming against his face.

"We are not the only beings who oppose the awakening of the Blindragon. Therefore, remain steadfast. Gather your courage. Always remember that we have unknown allies in other worlds who work for the same goal. Even in the darkest despair of the soul, we are not alone."

TWENTY-FIVE

The Italian's awareness floated on darkness in a vast enclosure still in the process of defining itself. Its inhuman architecture melted and reformed in an endless dance of unearthly geometries. The vault of the ceiling, lost amid shadows, hung somewhere above eleven unshaped crystal pillars of irregular diameters and lengths that drifted chaotically on splintered stumps, yet managed somehow to give the vague impression of a circle. One moment the Italian sensed himself within the ring, then the next he seemed to look through the pillars from outside. Irregular polygons of polished obsidian floated like broken panes of ice upon the midnight surface of a frozen lake.

With keen interest he surveyed the cyclopean geometry. He had descended in his astral husk through the great Abyss that forms an impassable gulf around the physical universe, and discovered this ordered place where before had existed only a slime-coated island in the midst of a dead sea.

He felt little surprise. The astral plane underwent constant change. The emotions and unconscious thoughts of all intelligent beings molded it like wet clay on a potter's wheel. It was only to be expected that the

rituals now being conducted by the Sons of Coronzon to
open the gates of the Abyss should alter the astral land-
scape, even as they were transforming the world of matter in more subtle ways.

Lilith, the matrix of demons, was also greatly transformed. She sat in an onyx throne upon a large dais of
black stone that floated in the center of the chamber close
above the shifting shards of the floor, her shape that of a
woman of gigantic dimension. The Italian sensed that he
might easily stand upon her outstretched palm. Her body
curved voluptuously with an abundance of flesh. Naked
breasts distended with milk hung heavy upon her swollen,
pregnant belly. A long, flaring skirt of scarlet cloth concealed her lower parts.

Her vast countenance changed ceaselessly, one
moment lit with unearthly beauty, the next twisted by
grotesque passions, a mirror of madness. Sorrow turned
her skin the color of chalk. Anger ruddied it to copper.
Hatred darkened it to indigo. Her shoulder-length hair
lifted and swirled on invisible currents, passing from the
black of a raven's wing to the blazing rust of autumn to
the shimmer of spun gold, then back again in the span of
a heartbeat.

Only her eyes remained constant. Large supine man-
dorlas without pupil or iris, their midnight openings
sparkled with glittering pinpoints. With a shock of insight
the Italian realized these points of light were actual stars.
Her eyes were twin windows that opened upon the universe—whether this universe or some other, the Italian
did not dare to speculate.

Upon her head rested a delicate diadem of wrought
silver with a single white jewel set in it above her brow.
The stone pulsed with inner life, swelling in brightness or

dimming from moment to moment in harmony with her changing passions. Its radiant light became at times painful to look upon. He felt this discomfort, not in his physical eyes, which continued to reside within his entranced body in the mountain fortress in Bohemia, but in his very soul. It burned there, an incredibly cold fire. He fought a powerful impulse to fall down before the crown and worship the blazing stone, to torture and abase and degrade himself under its light. It was only with the greatest effort that he was able to suppress this urge.

She observed his inner struggle as though his astral body were a vessel of glass, and smiled with amusement.

"You may adore the Lord Coronzon."

She gestured with a sinuous hand. A weight of intense, selfless desire dragged his astral shell out of the air, down to its knees upon the dais before the hem of her scarlet skirt. He fell forward upon his face and writhed with his cheek pressed to the clammy, polished stone, moaning softly with delight.

"Mighty Coronzon, Lord of the Abyss, Great Dragon whose endless coils encircle the universe with three and one half turnings, I offer my soul in your service. I am your instrument. Use me to bring about the Day of Burning upon the face of the world. Infuse me with the power to blast and kill. My body is your stepping stone. I am nothing before your majesty...."

He was not even conscious of the words he babbled. They were broken fragments of memory snatched from countless rituals of invocation before the altar of the Fallen One.

"Where is the Sacred Scribe?" she demanded at last.

"In Prague," he gasped. "At the house of the Jew."

"What of his vessel?"

"She is safe. She is with her husband."

"You will bring her to me."

He forced himself up to his hands and knees and sought to clear his head. To remain so near to her, under the radiance of his Lord, was almost beyond his mental endurance.

"That will be difficult. We cannot enter Loew's house. It is too well-guarded."

"You will bring her to me," she repeated.

The Italian felt his desire swell. She carried him to the very brink of release and held him there, balanced like a piece of straw on the edge of a razor. The agony of unfulfilled need ripped a cry of anguish from his thundering heart.

"She is an innocent. The soulless receptacle she carries is pure, and has the power of the Sacred Scribe woven into its elemental matrix. Our Lord needs the fruit of her womb to clothe the limbs of my children."

Slowly she drew apart the two sides of her scarlet skirt. The Italian gazed in a mingled torment of desire and horror. In place of legs, the thick tails of scaled black serpents writhed. Amid their coils newborn infants, filthy with excrements, their eyes blind, their limbs and faces twisted into grotesque parodies of the human shape, crawled and fought and clung. Their near resemblance to human infants only rendered them more repulsive.

As the Italian watched, unable to turn his awareness away, the thick lips of her vulva opened to reveal a distorted face, and another monster birth twisted and fell from her endlessly fecund womb to lie on top of the squirming mass. He heard it mew.

"I don't know how," he grated between clenched teeth.

His desire was so tormenting that, had he been able at that instant, he would gladly have hurled his physical body from a high place rather than endure it a moment more.

"I will tell you how."

The jewel in her silver crown blazed. He felt at a great distance his tenantless physical shell climax with racking force. He collapsed in his astral form onto the stone dais before her throne, shivering with relief.

"Fool," she said with contempt. "You make me regret ever having created your pathetic race."

"We are your adoring children, your slaves," he gasped in an abject tone.

She regarded him with emotionless black eyes that were filled with stars. He heard her silent laughter within his mind.

"Then worship me."

The Italian crawled forward.

TWENTY-SIX

John Dee found the experience of passing with his friend Kelley out through the gates of the ghetto to the old city of Prague curiously unreal. Narrow streets broadened. Leaning houses became upright. The filth and squalor vanished. Even the sky appeared bluer on the other side of the wall. It was like waking up from a bad dream, or stepping from one century to another. So Dante must have felt upon finding his way out of hell, Dee mused. He wondered how the Jewish traders who left the ghetto every morning to conduct business in the Jew's Market could bear to return at night. Perhaps it was only because they had nowhere else to go.

"What a relief to breath fresh air again," Kelley said.

He scowled at a soldier leaning on his pike near the gate, who gave him a hard stare when he passed. Dee noticed that they seemed to be attracting an unusual number of hostile looks from the folk of the city, but put it down to Kelley's surly expression and dismissed it from his mind. He had more important matters with which to concern himself. They were on their way to meet with the Queen's agent in Prague, a sea captain named Peter Gwyn who posed as a trader.

"I've never seen such sour faces in my life," Kelley said with a snarl.

Dee glanced at his friend's swarthy, threatening features, but held his tongue.

They crossed the market place and made their way westward toward the river. Gwyn had arranged to meet with them in an inn by the docks. There were many such places that sold cheap ale to bargemen and porters. They were convenient dens in which to gamble, get drunk, and pick up women. Understandably, they were quite popular, not only with working men but with rich merchants' sons and young noblemen out for an illicit thrill.

"We're being followed," Kelley said as they walked.

Dee was not particularly surprised.

"Who is it?"

"Tall man with a pock-marked face and a beak of a nose."

Dee stopped and pretended to scrap a bit of horse manure from the bottom of his boot. The two continued down the cobbled street.

"Who does he work for, do you think?"

"Not the Sons," Dee muttered. "They'd hardly use a human spy, not when their Watcher is so much more reliable. The Inquisition, perhaps."

"How did they learn we were in Prague?"

"They may have spotted me getting off the barge. Or Normand may have told them. He knew our destination."

"You're convinced Normand is an agent of the Inquisition?"

"I've always suspected it. This makes it seem more probable."

"You should have told me before. I would have taken pleasure in killing him."

"You still may get your chance. It's not unlikely that he followed us here from the Low Countries."

"I hope you're right," Kelley murmured darkly.

Dee glanced back as they rounded a corner and saw that the reedy, pock-faced man still hung on their heels.

"He mustn't witness my meeting with Peter Gwyn."

"Don't worry, I'll handle it."

When they turned down another street, Kelley told Dee to keep going. He stopped and waited at the corner with his back against a brick building, listening to the approaching footfalls for a dozen heartbeats. Abruptly, he stepped away from the wall and rounded the corner. The man following walked directly into his arms.

Kelley lifted him and threw him back against the building. He pinned him there with a forearm across the throat. The slender spy squawked and struggled, but he was no match for the bull strength of the alchemist. His eyes rolled like those of a trapped animal. Up close, his face was a patchwork of scars and pus-filled pimples.

"Why are you following me?" Kelley yelled in Bohemian. "Do you think you can steal my purse when my back is turned? I thought Prague was an honest city. You're nothing but a common footpad!"

Listening to Kelley's enraged bellow diminish behind him, Dee smiled to himself. The alchemist was a man of many talents.

He quickened his step, turned several corners and doubled back to make sure that no other spy still followed him. When he was satisfied that he attracted no special attention, he worked his way swiftly through the crowded and disordered dock-side streets to the sign of the Green Falcon.

As promised in his note, Peter Gwyn sat by himself at a table in a dark back corner of the room. There were few patrons at this early morning hour. A scattering of men with tar-stained clothes stood drinking silently at the bar, or bent over the small round tables in serious muttered conversations. Nobody looked up when Dee entered, but he sensed their suspicion as he made his way across the floor to Gwyn.

The Queen's agent was a wiry, rugged Devonshire man shaped by the hard life of the sea. Several scars crossed his deeply tanned face. One half of his spade beard was snowy white. A similar streak of white ran over the right side of his head from his forehead to his collar. His doublet and hose were a conservative indigo, travel-worn but well cut. A saber in its scabbard lay across the middle of the table, where Gwyn had evidently placed it to allow him to sit with comfort. On top of it rested a brace of snaphance pistols. It was a notice to those loitering in the ale house that he was a fighting man.

Dee sat without ceremony at the table. He had met Gwyn twice before, once in the company of the Queen in London, and another time while traveling through Cracow. This last encounter had occurred three years ago.

Gwyn gestured for the girl tending the bar to bring a tankard of ale. She set it down before Dee and flashed him a saucy smile. A young pretty thing with yellow braids, she reminded Dee of his daughter Katherine, and for a moment he felt a pang of homesickness for England.

"Little Nana would be delighted to take you to her bed," Gwyn murmured to him with a smile. Despite his heavy Devon accent, his voice was surprisingly cultured and mellow.

"You and she are on a first name basis, I take it?"

"We met last night. I suppose I know her as well as everyone else."

The ale was cool and bitter on Dee's dry lips, surprisingly good. He drank deeply.

"I thought there would be two of you," Gwyn said, glancing at the open door.

"My friend was delayed. He'll be along shortly."

Gwyn drank from his pewter tankard and stared at Dee over the rim, his lips concealed behind the vessel.

"I've had word from Niebuhr. He wants to meet you outside the city."

"Where?"

He picked up a small piece of paper that Gwyn laid on the table, and unfolded it. A rough but workmanlike map showed a road and landmarks leading to a house in the forest northeast of Prague.

"It's about half a day's ride," Gwyn told him. "Can you get there?"

Dee nodded. He folded the map and put it into his cloak pocket.

"Tell Niebuhr I'll meet him there tomorrow at noon."

"One other matter. Niebuhr wants you to come alone. He says he doesn't trust the English. He's afraid you'll try to murder him to ensure his silence."

A shadow slid over the table. Gwyn set his hand without haste upon the butt of one of his pistols.

"This is my friend, Edward Kelley," Dee told him.

Gwyn relaxed marginally and nodded. Kelley sat between the two men. He glanced at Dee with a sardonic lift of one eyebrow.

"I persuaded our late acquaintance to swear before thirty-odd good townspeople of Prague that he had no intention of cutting my purse strings. I doubt if they believed him."

Dee told Kelley about the rendezvous with Niebuhr and showed him Gwyn's map.

"If you go alone you're a fool," Kelley advised. "You have no reason to trust this traitor."

"I trust his motives. He's a traitor for money. So long as he's well paid he should be satisfied."

"He risks discovery. It would be safer for him to take your money and silence you to ensure there could be no future blackmail," Gwyn pointed out.

"That risk I will have to take." Dee put his hand on Kelley's sleeve. "Edward, I'm worried about the security of Jane and Joanna. Will you watch over them while I'm away on this political business and see that they come to no harm?"

Kelley saw the concern in his friend's eyes. His features softened into a more gentle mask.

"Rely on me."

"Don't let them wander away from Judah's house without your escort. Stay with them, even inside the ghetto."

"The women should be safe enough during the day," Gwyn said. "All the murders have happened at night."

Both men looked at him curiously.

"Have there been murders in Prague?" Dee asked.

"Didn't you know? I must have misunderstood your meaning. I thought you were concerned about your wives' safety because of the killing last night. It was the second this month, and the fourth since the snow melted."

"Who was killed last night?" Kelley asked.

"A member of the city council. He was found in his bed with his neck broken. There were finger marks on his throat. He was one of the fanatical faction in Prague agitating for the expulsion of the Jews. So were the other three killed. The belief is growing that the murderer is an assassin from the ghetto."

"That's explains the dark looks I've been getting," Kelley said.

"You have the arms for the job," Gwyn agreed. "Whoever it is, he must be strong as an ox. All the murdered men had their necks snapped like twigs."

"You say they were all agitators against the Jews?"

"That's right," Gwyn said. "Does that mean something to you?"

Dee shook his head, a thoughtful expression on his face.

Kelley reached out with a long arm and grasped the blond-haired serving maid around the waist as she passed. With a squeal of delight she landed on his knee.

"What's wrong with you, girl?" he said in Bohemian. "Don't you serve thirsty customers?"

Giggling, she twisted away from his embrace as he tried to kiss her and avoided his swatting hand with a practiced wriggle of her backside. With a lingering backward glance she went behind the bar to draw a tankard of ale.

"Chart a straight course, friend," Gwyn told him with a wink of his hazel eye. "You'll find favorable winds and a safe harbor."

"And a dose of the French disease, like as not," Kelley said, watching Nana draw ale from one of the recumbent kegs.

"Jesu, I hope not," Gwyn said with alarm.

He looked at Kelley. The two men broke forth in loud laughter that drew the momentary attention of everyone in the Green Falcon. A pale smile touched Dee's thin, ascetic lips. It lingered there for a moment before fading like a ghost. He was pleased that Kelley and Gwyn had found some common understanding between them. They might need to rely on the resourcefulness of the Queen's agent if events took an unexpected turn. It troubled him to see the alchemist behave so rakishly, but this was not the time or place to admonish him.

As little Nana returned with Kelley's ale, her skirt swirled up around her thighs. With a cry of dismay she tried to hold it down with her free hand. Dust from the dirty floor filled the air and blinded them. A man cursed drunkenly.

"Shut the door," Gwyn shouted.

Someone staggered to his feet and kicked the door shut, then held it with his shoulder while he latched it. The dust settled. A faint keening sounded through the door.

"Freak wind," Gwyn muttered before washing the dust from his throat with ale.

Dee caught Kelley's eye. There was no need to express their shared thought in words. They might have momentarily escaped the scrutiny of the Inquisition, but the Watcher was a different matter.

TWENTY-SEVEN

Edward Kelley moved down the darkened hallway. His feet made no sound, nor could he feel them against the floor. He floated like a feather on a current of breath. It was late at night. The house of Rabbi Loew lay shrouded in sleep. He was searching for something—precisely what, he would not know until he found it. The need for stealth possessed his heart. It was imperative he not be discovered until he accomplished his task. There was something he must do. When he tried to focus his thoughts upon his purpose it slipped from his mind like an elusive, chattering beast.

He paused before a door and swung it back on silent hinges. The air in the room beyond glowed with pale luminescence. John and Jane Dee lay asleep in a canopy bed. The curtains were drawn back to allow some hint of a breeze to reach them from the open window. Jane lay on her back with one leg drawn up under the sheet, her lips parted. Dee lay on his right side facing away from his wife. A light mist of sweat covered his face. His features appeared more youthful in sleep. Kelley realized that the perpetual lines of concentration were absent. He stared at Jane Dee for several seconds, then shut the door.

He moved on to the bedroom of Rabbi Loew and his wife. Miriam Loew lay on her side with one arm draped across her husband. The entire body of the Kabbalist glowed with a soft pearl radiance that was like the luster of moonstone. Loew groaned in his sleep as though sensing an intrusion. Something stirred to life in the corner of the bedroom. An amorphous shape began to form upon the air. Before it could take on a definite outline, Kelley withdrew.

In the next room Esther Katz lay with her head on the shoulder of her husband. There was something angelic in the sleeping innocence of their youthful faces that made Kelley ache with inexpressible longing. It would be so easy to kill all the inhabitants of the house while they slept. He shuddered, wondering what had put such a thought into his head, and went on to the next door.

The iron padlock on the outside defeated him for several seconds. He stood motionless and waited for inspiration. Abruptly he pressed his forehead against the planks. His face penetrated the oak with the sensation of lowering it into warm water. When he eyes reached the other side of the planks, he blinked and looked around. The room contained a narrow wooden cot with a mattress but no sheets or blankets. The dark outline of a man lay on the mattress.

The man stirred as though sensing that he was being watched. With ponderous strength he swung his heavy legs off the bed and stood facing the door. Although it was no darker in this room than it had been in the others, Kelley found it impossible to distinguish more than the outline of his body. He stood impassively, his naked black silhouette lined with flickering electric fire that danced just off the surface of his skin. He was massively muscled, bigger even than Kelley himself. Slowly, he raised his hands and held them out with the palms up in a gesture of mute supplication. His crooked fingers dripped with blood.

This was not the thing Kelley sought. Disappointed, he withdrew his face and went down the main staircase to the second level of the house. As he approached the padded leather door of the library, the guardian angels who stood on either side stirred uneasily. They were more sharply defined than they had been during the day. Within the twisting columns of smoke he distinguished vigilant eyes that burned like rubies and the silver gleam of swords. He hesitated before them, then smiled as he realized he was invisible to the spirits. With casual ease he walked through the closed door as effortlessly as he might pass his finger into a soap bubble.

The need grew stronger. It guided him to the spiral staircase. He saw that the stair led down through the floor of the library and accepted this as something preordained, even though he distinctly remembered stepping onto the bottom tread of the stair when he had followed Loew and Dee to the chamber of magical books. He looked down into its dark circular aperture. The stairs below were carved from green stone that glistened with moisture. A foul breeze blew from the depths against his cheek like the exhalation of some vast subterranean dragon, carrying with it the distant rhythmic pulse of many voices.

Kelley hesitated. What was he doing here? The question fluttered away from his awareness. Deep inside, a part of his mind screamed a warning, but it was far away and concerned the fate of someone whose name he could not remember. He stepped onto the stair and descended widdershins, turning in a direction opposite to the course of the sun. The stair seemed to wind down to the very center of the world. He made no attempt to count its revolutions.

Grotesque faces leered at him from the darkness beyond the rail of the staircase. Their lips twisted to form obscenities, but no sound reached him except the remote primal chant. Beyond the spiteful faces larger shapes floated upon the darkness, vast amorphous forms in continual transformation, immense sculptured balloons that were possessed of a malign sentience and a fathomless vitality. In a vague way Kelley became aware that their shapes changed with their thoughts, and he realized they were dreaming.

He found himself standing in Normand's room at the farmhouse outside of Leerdam. Jane Dee stood before him, dressed in a thin nightgown. Kelley realized with a twinge of embarrassment that he was naked.

"How did you get here?" he muttered in confusion.

"I had to talk with you, Edward," she said in her gentle, familiar tone.

"Talk?" He struggled with the word. "About what? Where is this place?"

She came to him. He felt the warmth radiate from her body against his bare skin, and smelled her feminine scent. With a shock he became aware of the rumpled, unmade bed beside them. Throbs of blood began to swell his yard in spite of his effort to deny his growing desire.

"I know you and Joanna are unhappy," Jane said, staring up into his eyes.

He felt the flutter of her breath on his lips.

"Aye, that's true enough," he muttered. "She wants a child and I can't give her one."

"You can give her a child, Edward," Jane said. "A strong, healthy son to carry your name. You only need the book."

She touched the strings that closed the front of her gown. It fell apart to reveal the hollow between her breasts. She drew her fingernail along his left arm and smiled tenderly, her soft brown eyes filled with loving concern.

"Can't get the book," he gasped. "The Sons have it."

"You must go to the Sons and ask them to help you. They will do so if you join them. They have great power, Edward, power you've never even dreamed about. They can make Joanna fertile."

"Join the Sons?" he repeated. His mind spun with confusion. The Sons of Coronzon were his enemies. He could never join them.

The supple body of Jane Dee pressed against his nakedness. He groaned and felt his desire surge upward.

"Join me, Edward," she said in a voice strangely changed. "Become one of my children. We will make love each night with a passion you cannot yet imagine. I will make you virile and tireless. I will initiate you with a thousand delightful perversions so exotic, they have never before been named. Join me, my dear, dear child."

Her lips intoxicated his senses. Driven by the agony of his desire, his member swelled to an immense size and took on the hardness of iron. He felt that he could impale her upon it and lift her into the air with no other support. He returned her kiss passionately while her long fingernails dug and clutched at his body.

A whisper of conscience intruded itself upon his raging lust. He turned his mind from it, but it pursued his awareness doggedly, and at last compelled his attention. This is wrong, he thought. His seductress clutched him tighter, as though sensing his qualms.

"No!" he cried.

With a supreme effort he forced her lips away from his mouth. He recoiled in revulsion from what he saw. It was not Jane's face before him, but that of a succubus demon. Its eyes were catlike, its teeth pointed.

"Fool," it spat. "This was your only chance. You will die with all the others, along with your barren bitch."

The face twisted and roiled as he watched, descending through levels of genera so swiftly he could not follow the transformations. It stabilized in the shape of a great serpent. Its long tongue flicked out to lick his lips.

Gagging with nausea, he locked his powerful hands around the neck of the snake and squeezed. Blows rained upon his arms and face. He minded them no more than he would a spring shower. The serpentine features before his eyes wavered and grew dim. He felt himself rise swiftly as though from a great depth. In the distance a voice called his name. Then, very distinctly, he heard three words.

"Edward, wake up."

Kelley blinked in confusion. He peered through the dim light of early morning into the terrified eyes of his wife, and realized that his hands were around her neck. She struck at him over and over with her clenched fists, each blow weaker than the last. Her lips were already turning blue. With a strangled cry of anguish he released her and examined his trembling hands as though seeing them for the first time.

She rolled away from him, gasping and rubbing her throat. When she regained a measure of strength, she pushed herself into a sitting position on the bed and stared at him as though at a dangerous animal.

"I was asleep," he said. "I had a nightmare. I thought you were a great snake."

Her still, pale face might have been carved of marble.

Kelley tried to remember the details of his dream, but already it had faded from his consciousness. Vainly, he sought to capture and assemble the fleeting fragments. It was no use. Not a single trace of the dream remained except the battle with the serpent.

He reached out to comfort her.

"Joanna, you know I would never harm you...."

She cringed away from his touch and scrambled out of the bed. Silently, she dressed and left the room. Kelley realized the futility of following her or trying to explain before she calmed down. It would only bring on an ugly shouting match. He lay on his back, naked to the waist, the sheet down at the level of his knees, and stared at the canopy over the bed.

Whose voice had called out to awaken him? It could not have been Joanna. The memory of the ethereal being of diaphanous silk he had glimpsed on his astral flight arose in his mind. Was it his guardian angel? Or was there a simpler explanation? Mayhap his many years of dealing with spirits had at last driven him mad.

TWENTY-EIGHT

Dee forded a gurgling brook that crossed the country road and dismounted to stretch his legs while his horse drank. It was blissfully cool in the hollow beneath the over-sweeping oaks. The shade of the leaves was almost as refreshing as a breeze.

He wiped his forehead with a handkerchief. A mixture of sweat and dust stained the white linen. All morning he had ridden northeast from Prague on his rented gray mare, setting as brisk a pace as he dared. Lather flecked the neck and flanks of his mount. If possible, he intended to arrive at the meeting place before Friedrich Niebuhr did and position himself against treachery, but he had no wish to kill the animal.

He touched the ball end of one of the German dueling pistols Kelley had insisted on giving him before his departure from the city. It was a wickedly efficient killing device, the ten-inch octagonal barrel of finest Italian manufacture and the snaphance firing mechanism of the latest German design. In the unlikely event of a misfire, the heavy walnut stock served as a mace.

The weight of the pistol and its twin brother in the opposite side of the leather girdle he had worn over his scholar's robe felt unnatural. Dee thought that he must look like an old fool. He considered putting the pistols safely away in his saddlebag. He was no duelist. It was more than likely if he tried to use the pistols that he would only shoot himself in the leg.

As he had done many times in the course of the morning, he patted the saddlebag to reassure himself that the sack of one hundred Spanish gold pieces was still in its place. He had carried the coins in his trunk all the way from Hampton Court. They were to be Niebuhr's payment for allowing him to view the cipher document.

Dee hoped the traitor would be content with the gold and not seek the additional surcharge of his life. He did not regard himself as a courageous man, although he had often done things that might be called heroic. Over the course of his career he had played many strange parts, and these had thrust him into danger on numerous occasions, but he derived no pleasure from putting his life in jeopardy and sometimes wished that the Queen would allow him to retire in peace to Mortlake to pursue his studies.

Unfolding Gwyn's map, he traced the course of the road, which was really more of a footpath, as it wound through the hills. He located what he thought to be the brook, and saw that he was quite close to the meeting place. Gwyn had described it as a deserted farmhouse. He put the map back into his pocket and began to unstrap his water bottle, then thought better of it. The water in the bottle would be warm from the sweating side of the mare. Instead, he went upstream from where the horse drank and knelt to dip his cupped hand into the crystal cool water of the brook. It trickled down his parched throat like nectar.

The biblical story of the vigilant soldiers of Gideon, who proved their worthiness by lapping from one hand while their more thoughtless companions knelt face down to drink, came to mind. Dee smiled at the comparison as he studied his reflection. No one was likely to mistake his silver beard and lined gray eyes for those of a warrior.

A breeze stirred the leaves in the trees above the brook. Dee stood up and took off his skullcap to enjoy its cooling touch on his head. Pleasure quickly turned to alarm when he realized the rising wind was not natural. It swirled in a great circle over the center of the brook, turning the overhanging leaves backward and tearing them loose from their stems. In moments this circular wind contracted into a funnel of black sparks that danced and dazzled Dee's sight like dust motes caught in a sunbeam. The mare neighed uneasily and took a step back from the water, her eyes rolling.

Dee drew the pistols from his girdle and cocked them alternately by bracing the barrels between his forearm and thigh as he pulled back the stiff hammers with his thumbs. A lead ball would be no use against a spiritual foe, but if the spirit assumed material form the ball would drill a hole just as certainly as it would through a body of more wholesome flesh.

The restlessness of the mare increased. When the whirlwind of midnight sparks turned itself onto its side and became a vortex with a large red lidless eye, the animal bolted in terror. Too late Dee remembered the gold in the saddlebag. He cursed above the roaring of the wind but did not dare take his gaze away from the red eye that regarded him without emotion. There was no threat in its flickering, swirling depths, but no mercy either.

"What are you?" Dee demanded. He considered the effect of a ball through the center of the vortex, but decided to hold his fire until it was needed.

There was a pause. The spinning wheel of air seemed to consider.

An observer. The words whispered inside Dee's head.

"Did the Sons of Coronzon send you?"

Yes.

"To kill me?"

Not yet.

Relief washed through Dee's body. He took a deep breath.

"You are the Watcher that followed me from Mortlake in England?"

Yes.

"Why have you chosen to reveal yourself?"

Another pause. Dee detected a thought too complex to be expressed in a few words. The vortex struggled to cast its meaning into human speech.

You are an adept in the art of magic.

It was more of an observation than a question.

"I have some skill," Dee admitted.

Fashion for me a body in which to dwell.

Dee considered this bizarre statement. Was it a request or a command? A memory surfaced, a day decades ago in his youth in Paris when he had sat reading in the library of the university. Had it been one of the books of Albertus, or of Robertus Anglicus? He did not remember. But the words in the ancient text remained clear. The book had stated that some aerial spirits who were bound with desire to the earthly plane longed for bodies of flesh in which they could find a degree of stability and permanency. These creatures were so changeable that every thought or emotion transformed them, robbing them of a true identity or soul.

"Why should I help you?"

Again, the vortex seemed to consider his words.

Help me, and I will help you.

"You would turn against your masters if I give you a body of living flesh?"

Yes.

A great sadness filled Dee's heart. The longing of the creature was so intense, he felt it palpably. How many ages had it searched in vain for a stable identity, a sense of self? Elementals were extremely long of life. This one might well be older than the human race. He regarded its red eye with regret.

"I'm sorry. It is not within my power to fashion a living being. This type of magic exceeds my skills. I am sorry for you."

The creature revolved slowly upon the air as though digesting his words. No hint of emotion disturbed its pattern. There was nothing outwardly to show that its most deeply cherished hope had been dashed.

Then you will die.

The vortex condensed and whirled more rapidly as it descended toward Dee. He took careful aim and fired the pistol in his right hand. In the split second between the flash of the flint and the ignition of the powder, the eye vanished and the center of the vortex expanded. The ball passed harmlessly through the opening.

You are a fool.

The jagged stump of a dead branch detached itself from a tree with a sharp crack. Too swiftly for Dee's eyes to follow, it flew in a circular arc and knocked the smoking pistol from his hand with a clatter. His fingers stung from the force of the impact.

Before Dee could level the other pistol, the vortex tilted onto its side and became once more a black funnel. As it expanded, the swirling wind grew weaker until, in a few moments, its sparkling inverted cone dissolved into the air, leaving only a widening ring of ripples on the surface of the brook.

Dee picked up the pistol and examined it. The mechanism did not appear to be damaged. He looked at the heavy stump of wood that had knocked the pistol from his hand, and reflected that the Watcher might just as easily have driven it through his heart. Was it possible the Sons of Coronzon wanted him alive for some reason? There was no comfort in the thought.

TWENTY-NINE

Jane and Esther were making small talk in the little rose bower in the corner of the walled back garden when Joanna joined them.

"There you are," she called from the step. "I thought you'd gone out. I searched all over the house for you."

It was her first appearance. Throughout the morning she had remained behind the closed door of her room. Twice Jane had called through the door to ask if she needed anything but had received no answer. She had begun to wonder whether she should induce Kelley to inquire about his wife's health. It relieved her fears to see Joanna on her feet.

Joanna approached the bower along the brick path between the flower beds, swaying slightly as she walked. With a sinking heart Jane realized that she was drunk. She had on the same mint green dress with the farthingale and wide ruff that she had worn yesterday, which was unusual for her during the summer. Joanna suffered in the heat and commonly wore an open-necked country dress without a ruff whenever decorum permitted. She took pleasure in displaying the flaming cascade of her hair against the creamy whiteness of her throat and shoulders. It was one of her few vanities.

"Where is everyone?" she asked brightly, an unnatural luster in her eyes. "The house is almost deserted."

"My father and my husband were called away to attend a special meeting of the Jewish council," Esther told her. "My mother is resting in her room with a headache."

"Edward's reading in the library," Jane added.

Joanna frowned at the sound of her husband's name. She sat down on a bench opposite the other women. Her face looked unnaturally flushed, an effect of the alcohol. Jane wondered if Esther noticed. Probably not, she decided. Both her father and husband were holy men. It was unlikely she had gained much experience with drunkenness.

"What was the meeting about?" Joanna asked, idly plucking leaves from the rose stems on the trellis over her head.

"It was called to discuss the murders," Esther told her, lowering her voice in a conspiratorial manner. Her dark eyes sparkled with excitement. Away from the oppressive influence of her mother, the inherent volatility of her emotional nature expressed itself.

"Have there been murders?" Jane asked.

"Four. The last was two nights ago. All of them were found with their necks broken and finger marks on their throats."

Jane shivered. Joanna put her hand to the ruff of her dress, her face suddenly pale. She stared at the two women like a startled fawn.

"I'm sorry," Esther said, taking her hand. "I didn't mean to frighten you. We've been talking about the murders so much in the ghetto, I've forgotten how horrible they are when first you hear about them."

"The first murder," Joanna whispered. "When was it?"

"Let me think. It was an instructor at the College of Jesuits. About two months ago."

Joanna relaxed slightly and allowed her shoulders to sag.

"We Jews don't know whether to be frightened or to celebrate," Esther went on. "All four of the murdered men were outspoken against our race. Along with that devil of a Jesuit, Thaddeus, they were trying to incite public hatred against us with a campaign of slanders and libels. We're not sorry they are dead, but the murders have focused suspicion on the ghetto. Some madmen are even saying it should be burned to the ground. My father and the rest of the council are meeting to decide how to defuse this growing hostility before it becomes violent."

"But if everyone in the ghetto is locked in at night, how can the murderer be a Jew?" Joanna asked.

Esther smiled a secret smile.

"I have never done it myself, but I have been told it's not difficult to get over the wall, if there is compelling need."

"I hope John is not in danger," Jane said.

"As long as he gets back inside the gates before sunset he should be safe," Esther told her.

They listened to the soft hum of bees in the open roses over their heads.

"How many disciples does your father have?" Joanna asked.

"I've never counted them," Esther said with a shrug. "Many dozens. Perhaps hundreds."

"Will they defend this house if the ghetto is attacked?"

"They will defend it with their lives, I'm sure of it. You must understand, to them my father is not an ordinary man. He is the Maharal. He is filled with the Shekhinah, the radiance of holiness." Esther glanced at the back door of the house. "I'm not supposed to know these things. I'm merely a woman. We're not allowed to study the Torah, or sit at the feet of the *ba'alei shem* and receive the secret teachings. But my husband tells me things about the Torah. He says it's not right to expect a woman to be holy without knowing holy matters."

"What is the Shekhinah?" Jane asked curiously.

"It's a very sacred subject. Nobody talks about it. Yitzhaq told me once that it's a goddess who has conjugal relations with holy men, but he wouldn't say anything more about it when I asked him. I think he was sorry he had told me anything."

"I thought you said it was a kind of light?" Joanna reminded her.

"It's that also. How can I describe it?" She thought for a moment. "It's like your own Holy Ghost and Virgin Mary combined into one."

Jane was relieved that Joanna's tipsiness had not made her vulgar and abusive. This sometimes happened when she drank a great deal. From bitter experience gained over the last six months, Jane knew there was no point in trying to counsel her friend while she was still intoxicated. Alcohol transformed Joanna into a different person, someone who would not listen to reason.

The marriage between Edward and Joanna had always been stormy, but until the past winter their arguments had run their course like sudden thunder showers. Seemingly overnight, Joanna began to suffer from periods of melancholia. Her consumption of wine rose dramatically. On a number of occasions Jane had gently questioned her friend. Joanna always spoke of her inability to give Edward a son, but privately Jane felt convinced there was something more to the drinking.

She excused herself on the pretext of fetching her sun-bonnet and left Joanna chatting with Esther about meta-physical questions, thinking how surprised the men would be to overhear the conversation. Men thought women had no interest in anything but fashion and gossip. Her John was the rare exception to this rule, and even he did not confide all the details of his occult studies. Once he had told her that the less she knew, the less danger there was of her being tried as a heretic.

The stairs and upper hall were deserted. She went directly to Joanna's room. It was not locked. With guilty haste she began to search her friend's travel cases for bottles. As much as she hated to interfere, she could not allow Joanna to alienate Miriam Loew or her husband by insult-ing them or their race. She was not certain of all the details of Dee's search for the stolen book, but Jane knew he regarded Loew as vital in helping him locate it. For this reason she went against her own better nature and forced herself to carefully examine her friend's belongings.

She found what she searched for where she least expected it, hidden at the bottom of one of Kelley's trunks. Joanna was far from a stupid woman. Kelley would never have thought of searching his own trunks. Jane twisted off the cork and smelled. The bottle of forti-fied port was potent enough to light a lamp. About a third of its contents remained.

"So you've found her secret store. Good. I knew she had something but never thought to look there."

Jane turned like a housebreaker caught in the act. Kel-ley's smile reassured her. She returned it timidly.

"I couldn't allow her to become worse," she said.

"No need to explain," he said in a strangely gentle tone. "You don't think for a moment that I would suspect you of any but the noblest motives? Jesu, you're the most honest woman I've ever met."

He helped her search through the rest of the luggage without speaking. They found nothing.

"There must have been just the one bottle," he grunted.

"Unless she's hidden others elsewhere in the house." She took up the partly filled bottle of port and turned to leave. "I'd better dispose of this before she misses me."

Kelley caught her hand as she passed and drew her to the side of the bed. He sat facing her, still holding her slender fingers. She regarded him with surprise but did not attempt to pull away. They were a strange study in contrast. Her ivory complexion and fine features might have been painted on porcelain, whereas his heavy head appeared to be hammered from tarnished bronze.

"Jane, will you help me?"

"Of course, Edward. You have only to ask."

"I'm worried about Joanna. She thinks I tried to kill her last night."

He explained about his forgotten nightmare, how he had awakened with his fingers around his wife's throat.

Jane felt the latent power in the dark hand that clasped hers and shuddered inwardly. No wonder Joanna had been upset.

"She became completely irrational. I tried to talk to her this morning but she refused to listen. She must have started to drink as soon as I left the bedroom."

"What is it you want me to do, Edward?"

"Talk to her. Explain what happened. Convince the silly little fool that I wasn't trying to murder her."

"I'll try. As soon as she's sober I'll tell her what you've told me."

"Good." He seemed satisfied. "She'll listen to you."

"She would listen to you, Edward, if you spoke to her gently."

"I try, Jane. It's no use. The woman maddens me. She sneers at every word. Whenever I attempt to correct her for her own good, she has some effrontery on the tip of her tongue. For the past few months it's been like trying to stroke a wildcat. I'm at the end of my wits. I don't know how to talk to her anymore."

"You might start by telling her that you love her."

He laughed with bitterness.

"If I didn't love her, would I tolerate this madness day after day? The poison lies deeper. Joanna has come to hate me because I can't sire a child on her. That's the nut of the affair. We've been married these five years and still without issue. She wants a child, and I can't give her a child."

Jane regarded his tortured face with pity.

"Edward, she wants a son for your sake, not her own. She thinks you're unhappy because you have no male offspring to carry on your name. She blames herself for being barren, not you."

He stared into her gentle brown eyes as he struggled to absorb her words.

"Who put that fool idea into her head?"

"Didn't you ever mention to Joanna that you wanted a son?"

"I may have done, years ago. I don't remember."

"Joanna remembers, and she's blamed herself ever since."

"Why should she think it's her fault? She's a healthy young woman."

"It's in a woman's nature to blame herself," Jane said. "But why should you think the fault was yours?"

He shrugged his massive shoulders and looked away from her sympathetic gaze.

"In my youth I led a dissolute life. Many's the night I spent gambling and whoring with no regard for my health. I feared I'd weakened my manhood from some foul disease."

"Have you seen a physician about these fears?"

He made a sound of disgust.

"What do physicians know? They're all fools. So my father, who was an apothecary, always said, and so I believe also. They prod your dung, taste your urine, smell your breath, listen to your heart, and peer into your eyes. They talk a lot of nonsense about black bile and adust choler and white phlegm. Then they prescribe a potion or powder they've had for a penny from an apothecary and forget about you, until they hear from a friend that you've died during the night."

"But surely they know something, if only from their frequent contact with the same diseases over the years?" Jane said gently.

"Perhaps," Kelley conceded. "Anyway, I went to consult with a famous authority named Binge in London. He told me to drink the whites of eggs in milk, and to look at the portrait of our Lord, Jesu Christ, while making love. He could find nothing wrong with me."

"Did you follow his advice?" Jane asked. She felt her cheeks warm with embarrassment.

"I drank the egg whites for a month," Kelley conceded. "I saw no reason to inflict the sight of my backside on the Lord, who has surely suffered enough for our sins."

"If you told Joanna what you've done, how you blame yourself for her lack of issue, I'm sure she would listen."

"Listen? I can't even say good morning to the hellcat without having an insult cast into my face. No, Jane, she's come to hate me, why I don't know. She's no longer sane and reasonable, as you are. I can talk to you as if you were a man. Joanna's always sifting for hidden meanings and slights behind my words. She twists the simplest remark into an attack against her. It's reached such a pass that I don't have the heart to talk with her anymore."

Jane considered the tragedy of a complete breakdown of trust within a marriage. No matter what the circumstances, she had always been able to bare her innermost heart to her husband when the need arose, and was equally certain he confided his true feelings to her with candor. Those secrets he kept from her concerning his work were withheld out of regard for her safety. She knew that if she asked him a direct question about any matter, he would answer honestly, even if it involved the security of the realm, and knowing this, she had never asked. She kept her own, more personal secrets that concerned her life at court before meeting John, but her husband had been discrete enough never to seek to learn them.

She squeezed Kelley's hand in sympathy, and felt his response against her fingers.

"I'll talk to her this afternoon, I promise, and tell her all that you've told me."

"Thank you, Jane. I knew I could rely upon you."

He looked at her with dark, serious eyes as he struggled inwardly to find words that would accurately express his feelings.

"How long have we known each other? Five years? In all those years I've never found a way to tell you what I think of you, but I've wanted to many a time. I'm no courtier, as you know well enough, so I'll just say plain that John is the luckiest man in England. There's no better woman than you on this earth. It gladdens my heart just to see your face and hear your voice each day. I never thought I'd speak such words to the wife of my best friend, but they need to be said. If it weren't for Joanna...."

As he spoke, he leaned forward imperceptibly until only a few inches separated their lips. Jane did not draw her face away. This revelation of feeling stunned her. She did not know how to react or what to think. She had always felt a strong liking mingled with an animal attraction for this rough man with his dangerous moods and smoldering slate blue eyes. She did not want to injure his feelings when he was so vulnerably exposed. Contrary emotions raged within her own heart.

He started to lean forward. She pressed her fingers to his lips.

"Edward, no...."

"I came to help you search for your bonnet."

The words fell with the hollow echo of stones dropped into the ocean. Jane and Kelley turned to the door at the same moment. Joanna stood limply, shoulders drooped, head at a slight angle, a rag doll held up on a wire. Her face was pallid, her eyes empty wells of emotion.

Jane realized how compromising her own position must appear to her friend. She leapt up and stepped backward from the bed.

Joanna surged into the room. Her glance took in every detail, the flush on Jane's cheek, the guilty glare of her husband, the bottle of port upon the coverlet of the bed, the open lid of her travel case.

"How can you be such a monster?" she demanded of Kelley.

"Joanna, you don't understand," Jane said.

Joanna whirled and slapped her across the cheek. Jane cringed back until her shoulder pressed against the wall paneling. It was the first time she had been struck since childhood.

"Slut! You spy on me, search through my belongings, and laugh at me behind my back while whoring with my husband. I want no words from you."

The blow galvanized Kelley. He seized his wife by the elbows and shook her.

"Keep your hands off her. She's twice the woman you are. You're not fit to kiss her boots."

"That's your job, is it?" Joanna hissed. "How could I be so blind? All these years you've been fawning after her and praising her virtue. How long have you been bedding her?"

"You're drunk. You don't know what you're saying."

"I know you never wanted to marry me. I know you were forced into it by those foul demons you consort with in your damned crystal."

He held her frozen, staring into her eyes.

"Yes," she said with vindictive triumph. "Don't even try to deny it. I heard you and John talking in the back room at the inn in Amsterdam last year. You thought I was asleep, didn't you? I heard what you said, that you regretted our union, that you never would have wed me had not the angels commanded it."

Kelley's face softened.

"Joanna, it's true, I said those things, but I was in a rage against John at the time. I hardly knew what words passed my lips."

She began to struggle wildly in Kelley's vise-like grasp. Like a snared leopard she twisted and clawed at his arms, spat at his face and tried to bite him, kicked his legs, all the while cursing him in profanity Jane had never heard before. Jane edged around her toward the open door, in a state of shock. Her dearest friend had transformed into a maddened beast before her eyes. Accustomed all her life to civility and the veneer of manners, she did not know how to deal with such a naked display of fury.

Kelley endured the scratching and blows for a while, but when Joanna began to bite at his wrists in an effort to compel him to release her, he lost whatever measure of self-control he possessed. Grasping her around the neck with one massive hand, he shook her.

"Edward, let her go," Jane cried in terror. "You'll kill her."

A spark of reason crept back into his blazing eyes. He seemed to realize what he was doing for the first time. As easily as a child casts aside a discarded doll, he threw his wife across the bed. She choked and coughed, then stared at him with a look of vindictive triumph.

"Why don't you kill me?" she rasped. "That's what you want. Kill me and put me out of your life forever."

Kelley stared at her triumphant face with mute anguish, then looked down at his hands. Abruptly, he turned from the bed and stalked out of the room. Jane ran after him and caught him by the arm in the hall.

"Where are you going?" she demanded.

"I have to get out of this house," he said. "If I stay here I will kill her, or she'll kill me."

The bedroom door slammed shut behind them. They heard the latch of the lock fall into place.

"Where will you go?" Jane asked.

Kelley shook his head as though in a daze.

"I don't know. Some lodging house. I'll send a note with the address when I'm settled."

"Edward, don't leave us," Jane pleaded. "We need you. It's only the strong drink that's driven her mad.

After she sleeps I'll talk to her and tell her what really happened. She'll listen when she's sober."

Jane's gentle appeal and the imploring expression in her eyes had a calming effect on the big man. He patted her hand to reassure her.

"Perhaps you're right. I need to get out to clear my head. I'll return later this evening. John should be back from his errand by then."

Nothing Jane could think of to say changed his mind. He passed Esther Katz on the stair with only a curt nod. Jane heard the front door bang. Esther met Jane descending the stair.

"I heard arguing," she murmured. "Is everything well with Joanna?"

The two made their way to the parlor that overlooked the garden. While they sat together on the settee holding hands, Jane explained to Esther the cause of the argument. None of the servants intruded with questions, although they must have heard the raised voices of Joanna and Kelley earlier. Jane was thankful for their discretion. Neither did Miriam Loew come forth, which surprised Jane.

"Please apologize to your mother for this deplorable behavior," Jane told her. "It's inexcusable."

"I doubt if she even heard it," Esther said. "When she gets a headache she takes laudanum. She's probably deep asleep."

Jane received this news with relief. It was a small mercy that both Rabbi Loew and his wife had been spared the histrionics of their guests. She did not want the behavior of the Kelleys to injure the relationship between Rabbi Loew and her husband. John had often told her how highly he valued the friendship of the Jew.

"I wouldn't blame your father if he threw the lot of us out of his house," Jane admitted with a blush of embarrassment.

"I'm sure it won't come to that," Esther told her. "My father is a tolerant man. He's seen a great deal of human nature."

"Strange that everything happened at once," Jane said. "First my husband was called away, then your father and your husband, and now Edward has left us. We're alone."

"Only for a few hours," Esther reminded her. "Yitzhaq and the Maharal will return tonight, and your husband should be back before sunset."

"So he told me," Jane murmured, glancing at the blue sky through the window.

Esther was right, she thought. It could only be coincidence that the men had been drawn from the house at the same time. There was no danger. The house was protected by occult wards that no hostile being, spirit or flesh, could penetrate. Yet if all this was true, why did she feel such a sense of foreboding?

THIRTY

Dee wasted an hour in a futile search for his horse. Lacking any familiarity with her rider, the terrified mare had felt no compulsion to remain near the fording place. After lacerating his face and hands pressing through tangled underbrush and testing the durability of his slender ankles on moss-covered stones and rotting tree roots, Dee gave up in disgust and continued along the narrow forest track on foot.

His nimble mind raced to formulate a plan that would allow him to gain access to the cipher document without payment. The truth would never serve. Niebuhr was certain to assume Dee intended to rob him. Force was a risky option. Dee had only a single charge in one pistol, and no way to recharge the other, since the powder and shot were on the saddle of his wayward mare along with his food, water, and Spanish gold.

Whoever found the animal would reap a considerable windfall, he reflected. With philosophical fatalism he put the matter from his mind. The gold was gone, therefore it was of no further concern.

He still carried Gwyn's map. When he drew near the meeting place, he took the map out and studied it with care. Although it showed no topographical features, he was able to deduce from the course of the brook that the land to the north of the farmhouse was higher than the land on the opposite side of the road. He worked his way through the woods parallel to the road on the left side until he judged he was behind the house, then carefully pressed down the slope.

It was fortunate that the meadow in back of the farm-house had not been abandoned long enough to com-pletely return to forest. Dee was able to look down over the tops of low shrubs and poplars upon the roof of the rough little building. Its walls were split planks, its roof shingles of slab wood, some of them two inches in thick-ness, all weathered to a uniform silver gray. A chimney of wattle and clay projected through the peak at one end, its top worn to a ragged crown of twigs. Neither window nor door broke the north face of the sagging structure.

A gray horse in saddle and bridle stood patiently behind the house, hugging the shade as it clipped the long wild grasses. For an instant Dee thought it was his own runaway mare. It shifted its stance, and he realized it was the wrong sex. Niebuhr had arrived ahead of him. Dee glanced at the sun and judged it an hour past noon. The Bavarian count must be growing impatient.

He scanned the brush and trees around the aban-doned cottage. None of the undergrowth appeared thick enough to hide a man, but it was impossible to be certain from such a distance. Dee took a deep breath and closed his eyes in an attempt to slow his pounding heart. His mouth felt dry and his face unnaturally cool. At another time he might have suspected the onset of some illness, but he knew the present reason for his discomfort was simple anxiety. Wiping his palm against his cloak, he pulled the unfired pistol from his girdle and hefted it. The weight of the steel reassured him.

He forced his unwilling legs to carry him down the slope of the meadow. Pausing at the rear of the cottage, he listened. No sound came from inside. The gray stallion tossed its head at him. Dee crept cautiously around the corner of the dilapidated structure. The two windows in the south wall were shuttered, but the front door stood open. He approached it with the enthusiasm of a man going to his own execution.

"You must be John Dee," said a cultured voice in English with only the faintest trace of accent. "Please come in. I've been waiting for you."

Dee abruptly realized the old house had so many cracks and chinks in its walls, its occupant had been able to follow his progress down the hill as though watching him through a latticework screen. At least the man did not intend to shoot him at once, or he would already have done so.

Dee paused a moment in the doorway, blinking in an effort to adjust his eyes to the dimness of the interior. Broken furniture and a pile of empty burlap sacks littered one corner of the floor. A man sat in a chair before a small table of rough-hewn planks. Both his hands lay flat on its surface. Dee saw no weapon, but assumed the other man carried a pistol at his waist, and probably a sword as well. Not to have done so would have been a sign of foolishness.

"You are Count Friedrich Niebuhr, advisor to His Majesty Rudolph II?"

The man stood slowly and bowed.

"At your service, Doctor Dee. You may put away your pistol. As you see, I am unarmed."

"You are very trusting," Dee murmured, easing the hammer down and putting his pistol back into his girdle.

"Not at all. You are known to be an honorable man. Please, sit down."

Dee sat in the chair on the opposite side of the little table. The sunlight from the open door fell across his face and lit his silver beard and hair where it showed beneath his skullcap with golden filaments. He realized Niebuhr had positioned the table for this result, and wondered how many times he had moved it while waiting. At least once, to judge by the drag marks in the dusty floor.

"Your horse was very quiet. I didn't hear you approach," Niebuhr said in a conversational tone.

"I left it tied among the trees a little way down the road," Dee lied.

He began to make out Niebuhr's distinctive features as his eyes adjusted to the gloom. There was no mistaking his thin, deeply lined cheeks, dark eyes, high forehead and black spade beard cut in the Spanish fashion. In the poor light the face of the count wavered and softened when Dee stared directly at it, but it was undoubtedly the face in the miniature the Queen had given him an eternity ago in Hampton Court.

"Show me the cipher document," he demanded, deliberately injecting a note of impatience into his voice. "We haven't much time."

Niebuhr made an exaggerated effort to look at either side of Dee's body.

"I see no gold. Where are the hundred Spanish doubloons promised to me by Gwyn?"

Dee laughed, determined to beat the nobleman at his own game.

"You don't really think I would be such a fool as to bring the gold with me to this house?"

"That is exactly what I did think," Niebuhr admitted, smiling as a cat smiles at a bird. "You have the gold nearby, I assume?"

"With my horse," Dee told him truthfully.

Niebuhr spread his hands in a gesture of surrender.

"Evidently I am a more trusting man than you, Doctor Dee. I did not leave the letter with my horse. Here it is."

Opening the left side of his cloak, he drew a leather folio from an interior pocket and untied it, then took from the folder a folded piece of parchment with a broken wax seal. A second seal had been impressed beside the first. It was intact. Niebuhr indicated the second seal with his finger.

"This is the reason I cannot obtain this document again, or at least, not for several months. The Emperor ordered this royal seal placed upon it to prevent it being copied. Once I break it, I will have to remake it with great care."

"How do you plan to obtain the royal seal?" Dee asked.

"My sister, as perhaps you know, is a close friend of Emperor Rudolph," the nobleman said with a thin smile. "She arranged to enliven his bed tonight. When the Emperor is asleep she will borrow the seal and return it before he wakes. We have only this one chance. The Emperor's passions are, shall we say, sophisticated, and he becomes easily bored with his lovers. He never sleeps with the same woman two nights together, usually not twice in the same month."

"Were the letter not returned before morning, I assume suspicion would fall upon you?"

"My guilt would be certain. So you see how great a risk I take for the security of your island nation."

"And one hundred pieces of Spanish gold," Dee reminded him.

"An additional incentive, nothing more," Niebuhr said. "The Spaniards threaten to dominate all of Europe. They must be stopped. Only Elizabeth with her English navy can cut off the wealth flowing to Philip from the New World that is the source of all his power."

This assessment of the political status of Europe surprised Dee. He had heard a similar argument spoken by Elizabeth herself, and by her triumvirate of adventurous explorers, the captains Drake, Hawkins, and Frobisher. He had not expected to hear it from a Bavarian count in Bohemia. Niebuhr possessed unexpected complexities in his character. Dee would greatly have preferred the nobleman to be motivated solely by greed, a predictable emotion.

Breaking the royal seal of Bohemia neatly into two pieces, Niebuhr passed the letter to Dee.

"None of the scholars consulted by the Emperor was able to decode it, if indeed it is a code. What do you make of it?"

Dee held the letter where the sunlight would illuminate it and read it through once. It was in Latin, a conventional request on behalf of a Spanish priest for an audience with Pope Sixtus V. A single page of banality, nothing more. He began to run it through his mind, applying one after another the more obvious ciphers that were likely to be used by the Spanish court. No matter how difficult or abstruse a cipher, it invariably possessed its own pattern. By its nature a code must convey meaning. This was its inherit weakness. The meaning one man could disguise, another man could unveil, given enough time. Time, however, was something Dee did not possess.

Exhausting the more common Italian and French codes, Dee began to apply the far more numerous and difficult German ciphers to the letter. A glimmer of understanding began to dawn. The cipher was original, completely unknown, yet based upon a structure with which he was familiar. Vainly, Dee longed for his lost library at Mortlake. With access to his books he was certain he could solve the puzzle in an hour. Without them, it would take longer.

"Well?" Niebuhr demanded with impatience, watching Dee's lips form silent letters. "Can you solve it or not?"

"I can solve it," Dee admitted. "It may take several hours. The code is based upon a variation of the Seraphim Cipher used by the Abbot Trithemius in his *Polygraphia*, as modified by Giovanni della Porta. Significant words are arranged in a repetitive pattern from back to front, and there are a considerable number of null letters, which makes decoding more difficult. The coded message is in Latin, of course...."

Dee stopped talking. He stared at the small pistol with a short, thick barrel that had appeared as if by magic in Niebuhr's left hand.

"Thank you, Doctor Dee, that's all I need to know at this juncture. Please do nothing foolish. It would be such a pity to shoot you on so slight an acquaintance."

"If you do, you will never get the gold," Dee assured him.

"The gold is a minor consideration," Niebuhr said with a smile. "You are the prize, Doctor. Have you not realized that yet?"

He placed a slender tin whistle to his lips and blew a piercing note. They waited in silence. Dee considered what chance he had of jerking the dueling pistol from his girdle, cocking it, and firing before the count sent the ball from his own piece through his head. None at all, he reflected. Even if he could free the weapon in time, he did not possess enough strength in his thumb to cock the hammer with one hand without bracing the barrel. The dueling pistol had not been designed for rapid firing, but for reliability.

The rustle of footsteps through the dry grass announced the arrival of three men. The leader of the group stood framed in the open doorway for several seconds regarding Dee, who could not distinguish his features because of the bright light behind him. Yet there was something familiar about his carriage.

"Has he given us what we needed?" The man spoke Bohemian with a cultured French accent.

"Not yet, but he will soon enough. Take him."

"Normand." Dee spat the name like a curse. "Kelley told me he would relish killing you. I should have allowed him to do it earlier."

"You came without your trained ape," Normand said, shaking his golden head in mock regret. "I am sorry. I was looking forward to cutting his throat."

His two companions started forward with purposeful expressions. Dee noted with passing surprise their youthfulness. The taller, dark-haired man could not have reached his mid-twenties, while the other blond stripling might easily have posed for Normand's younger brother, so similar were they in appearance and manner. Both projected an indefinable military bearing, although they wore common attire.

Dee held up the letter between his hands.

"Stay back, all of you. I'll rip this letter into fragments."

Niebuhr laughed in hearty, ringing tones.

"Go ahead. How many times do you think you can tear it before I put a ball between your eyes?"

"Only once. That should be enough to ensure that it can't be returned to the royal archives."

"You credulous Englanders," Niebuhr said, shaking his head with amusement. "You believe everything anyone tells you."

He nodded for Normand and his confederates to seize Dee. Casting the letter into the face of Niebuhr, Dee pushed Normand against the dark men behind him and pretended to fall to the floor beside the pile of discarded burlap sacks. He drew out one of his pistols and scored the floorboards with the sharp corner of its lock. In the dim light there was a chance the mark would not be noticed.

"Slide the gun away from your body," Normand ordered, setting his boot in the small of Dee's back. "That's good. Now take out the other and do the same. Excellent."

He grabbed Dee by the arm and roughly pulled him to his feet. As he did so, Dee's toe caught against one of the sacks in the pile and knocked it across the scratch mark.

"Where are you taking me?" Dee asked Niebuhr.

He felt a strange calm. With the likelihood of imminent death looming before him, he no longer suffered anxiety over the need to make the right decisions. He had done what was possible. For the moment at least, the future was out of his hands.

"A sanctuary," the Bavarian count told him. "A place where you can be questioned without fear of interruption."

They wasted no more time, but dragged him toward a small clump of trees where they had hidden their horses. Dee saw with a bitter taste that they had brought an extra mount. His abduction had been planned from the beginning. More and more the cipher letter was assuming the appearance of bait for a trap. Yet surely all these machinations were not for his benefit. Dee knew he was not so important. There must be complications at play that he had not begun to imagine. He wondered if they could have any connection with the Book of Lilith.

About one thing, at least, Dee was absolutely certain. Whoever might be this thin-faced man with the dark eyes and spade beard presently giving orders to Normand and his two silent confederates, he was not Friedrich Niebuhr, even though he looked enough like Niebuhr to be his doppelganger. Dee had only obtained a single glance, but it had been enough. Niebuhr lay beneath the rumpled pile of dusty burlap bags, his throat cut from ear to ear.

THIRTY-ONE

For two hours after the fight with Jane and Kelley, Joanna brooded behind the bolted door of her bedroom. Several times Jane tapped on the boards without gaining a response. The sound of purposeful movement within the room alerted Jane to her friend's intention. When Joanna emerged into the hall wearing her cloak and French bonnet, and carrying her small travel case in her left hand, Jane stood ready to confront her.

"Joanna, you can't leave the house. Not this afternoon. At least wait until Edward returns and talk to him."

She might as well have been invisible for all the notice Joanna took of her. The redhead continued along the hall, her shoulders tilted beneath the weight of the travel case. Her resolute eyes, puffy from recent tears, were dry now, her pale mouth drawn into a determined line.

"Where would you stay?" Jane argued, following close at her heels. "You have no friends in Prague and almost no money. The streets are dangerous at night. You heard what Esther said, there's a murderer at large. Please, Joanna, for the sake of our friendship."

She put her hand on Joanna's arm. Joanna shook it off and whirled on her in fury.

"I'm not your servant. Just because John gives Edward a yearly wage doesn't mean you've got the right to order me about."

Their raised voices drew Esther Katz from her sewing room. She stood at the top of the stair and spread her arms imploringly.

"Jane is right, Joanna, it's too dangerous. You're angry. Why don't you wait for a few hours, just a few hours, until your husband comes home."

"When he gets back I won't be here," Joanna told her in a blunt tone. "Get out of my way."

Esther inclined her head with determination.

"No. I won't let you pass. You are being foolish. You don't realize the risks."

Joanna swept the Jewish woman aside. Esther stumbled and cried out in pain when her shoulder struck the paneled wall. Joanna started down the stair.

"Joanna, how could you?" Jane said in shock. "She's only trying to help."

"Mind your own cursed business, the both of you," Joanna said without turning.

Silver shadows swirled over the stair, flowing up and down in confusion. They were agitated by the inflamed emotions of the women but did not perceive a clear course of action. Joanna walked through them and onto the second floor landing. If she noticed their clinging touch, she gave no sign.

Jane rushed back into her room. She emerged with her hat and cloak.

"I can't let her leave alone," she explained breathlessly to Esther. "Tell my husband I've gone to watch over her and see that she comes to no harm."

Esther trailed after Jane in a fluttering state of anxiety.

"You shouldn't go out. Wait until the men return. They will know what to do. They can look for her."

"They might not find her before she hurts herself. I must go."

They reached the second level. Joanna was already at the front door. They heard it open and bang shut.

"Esther, what's going on? Why is there banging?"

The voice of Miriam Loew drifted from one of the rooms in the rear of the house.

"You've awakened Mother," Esther said, staring with nervous accusation at Jane.

Miriam had evidently impressed upon her daughter the severity of such a crime from an early age. Jane paused to take Esther by the shoulders and gazed seriously into the dark eyes of the other woman.

"Please tell your mother how sorry I am that we bothered her. Our behavior has been inexcusable." She hurried down the stairs.

"Wait, I'm coming with you," Esther called after her. She ran into the parlor to grab up a linen kerchief for her hair and an embroidered shawl, which she threw around her shoulders.

"Esther, where are you going?" The querulous voice of her mother floated after her on the air. "Come here. I want to talk to you."

Jane held the heavy front door open while Esther rushed through, then closed it behind them.

"You mother will be unhappy that you came with me," Jane murmured.

"She's always unhappy about something," Esther told her with a timid smile.

Joanna had already disappeared.

"She must be headed for the gates," Jane observed as they set out in that direction. "She wouldn't stay overnight in the ghetto alone."

They caught sight of her russet cloak and flaming red hair as she hurried past the vendors' carts lining the busy street that ran through the open gates. Jane called out to her above the clatter of wagon traffic and the babble of Yiddish. Joanna glanced back at them but did not stop. She ducked behind an enclosed coach parked across the narrow mouth of an alley.

Jane and Esther ran breathlessly behind the coach and stood staring around in confusion. Joanna had vanished.

"She must have gone down the alley to get away from us," Jane decided.

They started in that direction. A faint cry from behind made them stop and turn. The coach rocked on its wheels. Something thudded inside. Jane saw with growing alarm that the leather window shades were lashed down.

"Joanna?" she called loudly. "Are you in there?"

She approached the coach nervously and heard the mutter of male voices.

"Quick, Esther, run home," Jane said. She tried to push the bewildered girl away.

Before Esther could take a step, the door of the coach burst open and two men leapt out. Jane only had time to note their rough clothes and sallow, bitter faces before one of the men grabbed her from behind and covered her mouth and nose with his dirty hand.

"What should we do with them?" he asked in Bohemian.

A ferret of a man with seeping abscesses on his cheeks stuck his head out the door of the couch. He cast a pale eye over the women as though looking upon his evening supper and grinned, displaying crooked yellow teeth blackened in the cracks from advanced decay.

"Put them with the other one. We'll take them all."

"We weren't told to take this Jewess," the man who held Esther objected.

She stared at Jane in terror, her dark eyes wide as she struggled feebly against her captor like a butterfly caught in a spider web. Even in the midst of her own terror, Jane's heart went out to her. She tried to project courage into Esther through her gaze, but saw no sign that she was successful. Esther appeared on the point of fainting.

The pimple-faced man examined Esther for several moments in a predatory fashion.

"Bring her anyway," he leered. "We'll find a use for her."

THIRTY-TWO

"Untie his hands."

Dee sensed rather than felt the manipulations of the leather thong that bound his wrists together behind his back. He had lost all sensation in his fingers many hours ago on the long, excruciating ride from the farmhouse. His arms fell loosely to his sides. Rough hands forced him back into a chair. The black canvas hood that had blinded him since his capture was jerked off his head. A door closed behind him.

He drew cool draughts of air that tasted like wine after the stifling mustiness of the hood. The lamp light made his eyes water when he tried to open them. Blinking away the tears, he saw that he was in a well-furnished room that had the appearance of a gentleman's study. Full darkness lay outside the window. The man who wore the face of Friedrich Niebuhr sat behind an ornately carved desk and regarded Dee with a faint smile. The cipher letter lay open on the surface of the desk.

Dee studied his numb hands. The flesh beneath his nails was blue, but a flush of pink had returned to his palms. He pressed his lifeless fingers together to bend them, and was relieved to feel a tingle of pain like a thousand needles. His hands began to swell. This was a good sign. He had worried he might lose his fingers to gangrene.

"Where have you brought me?"

"Where is unimportant. This is the country estate of a Bohemian nobleman sympathetic to the needs of our Mother Church in the battle she is waging against the forces of heresy."

"Who are you?"

The man behind the desk blinked in feigned surprise.

"What an odd question. Surely you know your own confederate?"

Dee's gaze lingered on the left palm of his captor. The thin line of a scar in the shape of a jagged cross stood out redly against the pallid skin. It was the symbol described to Kelley by Thomas Beecher, who had seen it on the hand of his murderer. With sickness in the pit of his stomach Dee realized he was looking at a Son of Coronzon. He knew how a hare must feel when it falls into the pit of a viper.

"Your mask is skillfully fashioned but unnecessary. You may as well remove it."

This time the surprise of the other man was genuine. Dee saw it flicker in his eyes before it was suppressed behind a shield of cynicism.

"What nonsense you are speaking. The long ride has disturbed the humors in your brain."

"Your deception is wasted," Dee said. "I saw Niebuhr's corpse."

The other man relaxed. He shrugged and smiled.

"Of course. I should have guessed. The simplest explanation is usually correct. For a moment I was amazed by your powers of discernment."

His thin, deeply-lined features wavered as though viewed through rippling water. They reformed into a face that was broader, with a naked square jaw and a brutal Roman nose. The large, round head was hairless, the lips thick and sensual. Dee noted that the prominent ears lacked lobes. Fine, dark eyebrows framed the palest gray eyes he had ever seen. They projected an other-worldly quality, as though able to pierce through material facades to reach the spiritual inner heart. If ever a man possessed the power of the evil eye, it was this man.

He was a curious mixture of sensuality and intellect. The bright awareness in his startling eyes seemed to war with the twitching corners of his mouth, by turns quirked into a faint sneer or a sardonic smile as inner demons passed through his soul and left their shadows on his face. His hands were long and graceful, those of a surgeon or a musician, but they were attached to the shoulders and arms of a wrestler.

"Again, who are you?"

"You may call me Victor Azoth."

Dee snorted with contempt.

"You must take me for a complete fool. Azoth is an alchemical acronym for the philosopher's stone."

"So it is. It also happens to be one of the names I employ in my worldly dealings. I'm rather fond of it."

Dee wondered if this strange visage represented the true features of the man who called himself Azoth. An adept with such command of the art of glamoury could mold his face into any shape he wished. Dee could detect none of the faint shimmer he had noticed when the man wore the mask of the late Count Niebuhr, so perhaps these were Azoth's actual features. He might never know for certain, unless he had the good fortune to view the man's corpse.

"Why do you smile?" Azoth asked with mild curiosity.

"A happy thought occurred to me."

"I'm glad you retain your good humor. It will make our work together easier."

"We share no common purpose."

"Are you so sure?" Azoth shrugged. "Personally, I would like to see you live. True, it must be within the walls of an Italian prison, but even in bondage life is sweet."

"Are you of the Inquisition?" Dee demanded in an effort to draw out his foe.

Azoth frowned slightly.

"I'm growing a little weary of your idle questions, Englander."

"I merely wish to know with whom I'm dealing," Dee said in a reasonable tone. "After all, I'm completely in your power. What have you to fear?"

"Very well. I have served the Inquisition from time to time, when it suited my purpose."

"You're a Jesuit, or pretend to be." Dee's blunt tone challenged Azoth to deny it. "So is Paul Normand. I should have realized it at once when he claimed to be a Huguenot. It's an old trick of spies to identify themselves with their enemies."

The expression on Azoth's face did not change, but Dee sensed that he was inwardly laughing.

"We prefer to call ourselves clerks regular of the Society of Jesus."

Dee wondered why this Son of Coronzon chose to adopt the guise of a Jesuit. Was he merely using the army of Loyola for his own dark purposes, or did he have some closer and more personal link with the Society? Dee decided to pretend ignorance about his true identity.

"I know your kind," Dee said with a scowl. "We captured one of your missionaries in London several years ago and put him to the question. He admitted that he had been sent from Rome by your damned Black Pope,

Claude Aquaviva, to promote the Spanish cause and to incite English Catholics to assassinate our blessed sovereign Elizabeth."

At the name of the general of the Jesuits an expression of pure hatred passed over Azoth's face. It was gone in an instant, replaced by an urbane smile, but it left Dee puzzled. Why should the revered name of Aquaviva, leader of the Jesuits and second in power only to the Pope, move this Son of Coronzon with such malice?

"It's common knowledge that most English hate your queen and wish to return to the true Church," Azoth said. "Our Society merely desires to spare your nation unnecessary grief. You cannot possibly stand against the military might of Spain. It would be so much easier for all your people if you put a Catholic on the English throne and swore obedience to Philip. Our Pope would receive you back into the bosom of the Church with open arms."

"You're wrong," Dee told him. "You don't know my race. They will never submit to Philip or Sixtus. The days of our slavery to continental potentates are ended."

Azoth seemed to listen with only half an ear, his mind elsewhere.

"Your Society is overconfident," Dee went on, hoping to anger Azoth into committing an error he could turn to advantage. "Because your priests are organized into an army with military discipline under your general, and move throughout the world wearing the clothes and speaking the vernacular of the common people, you believe yourselves invincible. Don't you realize that you are universally hated and despised? The people know you by your false words and traitorous actions. You went too far in France when you allied yourselves with the Catholic League against Henry of Navarre. It is certain to lead to some bloody act of fanaticism that will rebound against you."

"You must remember your argument for Monsieur Normand, who may wish to debate with you," Azoth said in a bored fashion. "Presently we have more pressing matters to discuss."

"I wondered why you chose to preserve my life," Dee said, glancing at the cipher document.

"When you were recognized entering the port of Antwerp, assassins were sent against you," Azoth admitted. "Since then I have convinced my brothers that your unique knowledge of political matters may be of use to us. Provided you cooperate fully, your life will be preserved. Who knows? At some distant time you may even obtain your freedom. Where there is life, there is hope. Please, Doctor, don't compel me to kill you."

"What exactly do you want me to do?" Dee asked. In his own heart he had already decided to give the Jesuits and this masquerading Son of Coronzon nothing. He would prevaricate and lead them on as long as he could. As Azoth had said, where there was life, there was hope.

"I wish a demonstration of your cipher skills. Personally I believe them to be vastly overrated, but if they are as extensive as rumor would have us believe, they may be of advantage to the Society."

He opened the cipher letter and slid it to the front of the desk where Dee could reach it. Dee made no attempt to pick it up.

"We happen to have an excellent test document with us, thanks to the foolish greed of Count Niebuhr. At the farmhouse you boasted that you could solve it. Very well, do so. I will compare your solution with the actual cipher message to determine your skill. If you do well, the Society may have other ciphers for you to decode."

As much as Dee longed to seize the letter and study it, he allowed it to lie face down on the desk. What he did not know, no torturer could extract from his mind regardless of his methods.

"I think you're a liar, like all the rest of your kind," Dee told Azoth. "You want me to decode the letter because you don't know the solution and can't solve the cipher yourself."

"You're a fool," Azoth snapped in irritation, his white eyes blazing like stars. "The Society knows everything that happens in the Church."

"Do they?" Dee asked. "I wonder. My guess is that Philip of Spain entrusted his letter to a Jesuit courier, but not the message concealed within the letter. Your own Black Pope, Aquaviva, wants that knowledge."

Again, the mention of Aquaviva's name sent a shiver of rage through the athletic frame of Azoth.

"What you believe is immaterial," he snarled. "You will do as I say because I wish it. Other motives scarcely enter into the matter."

"If you kill me, you'll never learn the contents of the letter," Dee pointed out.

"If you resist, there will come a stage when death will be your supreme desire, and you will bless me for granting it to you."

He rapped three times sharply with his knuckles against the desk. Dee heard the door swing open behind him. Before he could turn his face, the same canvas hood he had already endured for so many hours was again thrust over his head.

ThiRTy-ThREE

Strong hands seized Dee by the arms from each side. Resistance was impossible. They lifted him bodily from his chair and forced him to march blindly across the level floor and down a long flight of stone steps to a place where the air felt much cooler against his skin.

The drawstring was loosened and the hood snatched away from his head. Dee recoiled in involuntary horror. Demonic faces floated before his sight, their twisted, bestial mouths leering at him. The two silent Jesuits on either side thrust him forward by the arms. With a shiver of relief Dee realized the faces were carved on spherical stones the size of cabbages, which dangled on chains from brackets in the vaulted roof of the chamber.

"Release him."

Paul Normand sat upon the edge of a low wooden frame upon the flagstone floor, his forearm resting on one knee that was drawn up close under his shaven chin. His clear blue eyes regarded Dee with an enthusiasm that was almost boyish.

Dee's captors let go of his arms and stepped back. They would do whatever Normand told them, Dee realized. Jesuits were sworn from the age of fourteen to obey without question any orders delivered by a superior of their Society, even commands leading to their own death.

"Where is Azoth?"

Normand looked at him without comprehension for a moment.

"If you mean Father Giovanni, he has more important work than giving you a guided tour of the cellars."

Another name, Dee thought. Did it also mean another face?

"Has it occurred to you that your Father Giovanni may not be the person you believe him to be?"

Normand laughed lightly.

"I expected you to argue for your freedom, but I confess that this strange approach interests me. Why should Father Giovanni not be Father Giovanni?"

"You saw him change his face at the farmhouse. How do you know he hasn't done it earlier?"

"Why are you talking like a madman?" Normand asked. "It won't serve your interests, I assure you."

Dee stared at him in surprise.

"Didn't you see this Giovanni's face alter at the farmhouse?"

"This conversation is absurd, and growing tiresome. I advise you to end it before you try my temper."

Normand was not aware that Azoth had changed his features, Dee realized. That meant Azoth could present different aspects to different individuals at the same time and place. It was an astounding display of glamoury, the magic of deception and false appearance. It meant that Azoth was an adept of considerable attainment. He did not bother to press the point further with Normand. The young French Jesuit would never believe it, and would only think Dee was trying to confuse and deceive him.

Normand stood easily and made a broad gesture at the bizarre furnishings that filled the barrel-vaulted cellar.

"Our host has a passion for collecting mechanical devices. Father Giovanni thought they might amuse you, and help you pass the time while you are deciding whether or not to accede to his wishes."

He went to Dee and wrapped his arm in a familiar way around the slender shoulders of the older man, then drew him toward the wooden frame upon which he had been sitting.

"I believe in your language this instrument is called a rack. It's operation is very simple—perhaps you've seen it? No? Let me explain it to you. A man is stretched upon his back within the frame, his arms extended above his head. Ropes are tied to his ankles and passed around that wooden cylinder at the base of the frame. Other ropes secure his wrists to the cylinder opposite. Two operators are required, you understand. They put long levers into those slots on the drums and turn them in opposite directions. The ropes tighten, and the poor man is stretched apart until his knee and shoulder joints separate."

He drew Dee past the rack to a small wooden barrel with iron spikes projecting some four inches from its sides. A rope ran through a hole that was bored through the axis of the barrel. The spikes were stained with brown rust.

"Sometimes men on the rack fall asleep. Perhaps they grow bored, who knows? To wake them up this charming tool, which is known as the hare, is rolled repeatedly up and down their bodies from their necks to their feet. They are naked, of course. I'm told that after a few passes of the hare, a man's body cannot be distinguished from raw liver."

In spite of his resolve, Dee felt a chill sweat break out on his forehead. He inwardly cursed his own weakness, knowing that Normand had detected the reaction. The Frenchman patted him affectionately on the shoulder.

"This iron rack attached to the stones of the wall is called the spider. Why, I can't guess. Its use is mainly confined to women. You see these numerous projecting hooks over its surface? Like fish hooks, aren't they? The women are drawn naked from one side of the spider to the other until their breasts are shredded from their bodies. I suppose it could be used on men as well. After all, men have their own protruding organs. It might be interesting to test its effect."

He picked up a wooden paddle from a table and showed Dee that one side was studded with nails.

"Personally, if I were to chastise a woman I would use this battoir. It's just as effective and so much more intimate. Can you imagine the result if I were to employ it on the buttocks of the charming Joanna Kelley? Just the thing to calm her rebellious nature."

"Were you trained by the Inquisition?" Dee asked.

"Regrettably, no, I am self-taught. An enthusiastic amateur, nothing more."

"You are familiar with the three degrees."

Normand laughed.

"The extent of your knowledge is amazing. Yes, I know about the three degrees used by the Inquisition to extract the truth from heretics. The first is the interrogation. The second degree involves showing the instruments of torture. The third, or course, is the actual torture itself. You would be surprised how seldom it is necessary to proceed to the third degree."

He drew Dee past the table in a brotherly way. Dee saw that he intended to make a complete circle of the vault.

"These little things are called thumbscrews," he said off-handedly. "No need to explain their use. It is enough to say that once they are applied you lose all ambition to play the guitar."

Stopping before a large iron brazier filled with unlit charcoal, Normand released Dee. He pointed to a set of iron instruments that hung from hooks on the wall.

"The uses of fire are innumerable. In my opinion, no other methods of persuasion are needed. You see these pokers of different diameters? They are heated until they are red and then drawn along the skin, or inserted into the orifices of the body. The pincers are used to tear away small pieces of flesh. Usually the torturer begins with the nipples—I don't know why. Sometimes gunpowder is piled upon the pubes of witches and set alight. The hair on their heads is soaked in oil and burned. These little stones are heated until they are white and then inserted into the armpits with the arms strapped tight to the sides. I am told they take a long time to cool. The Spanish like to dip the hand repeatedly into hot tallow, then light the tips of the fingers like candles. The flesh acts as a wick, you see. Even the simplest methods can be effective. Bits of glowing charcoal are scattered over the body while the prisoner is tied down, then allowed to burn themselves out where they fall."

Normand's face glowed with a strange animation. Dee realized with a sick feeling in the pit of his belly that the Frenchman was arousing himself with his lurid descriptions. He had heard it said that some torturers became sexually excited even to the point of climax by their work, but had never credited such a perverse tale. He knew now that it must be true. Naturally men with Normand's sickness would seek employment in the Inquisition and among the Jesuits, where their fantasies could find complete realization.

"Our host is a traditionalist, like all true collectors," Normand said. "As you probably know, the Inquisition relies exclusively on three methods of persuasion. You see them here before you. The frame attached to the ceiling supports prisoners undergoing the garrote. This operation consists of wrapping cords around the limbs and tightening them with a stick until the cords cut through to the bone.

"The second traditional method of the Inquisition is called the strappado. You see that pulley attached to the ceiling? The hands are tied behind the back, then drawn up by a rope until the prisoner is suspended from his toes, or even dangles completely in the air. Sometimes to make the agony more intense these spherical stone weights, which are called cherubim, are tied to his ankles. Each weighs about thirty English pounds. I believe you noticed their carved faces when you first came in.

"The third traditional technique is what you would call the water torture. A prisoner is bound upside down to this inclined ladder, which the Spanish call an escalera, and forced to swallow a long strip of linen. If he won't open his mouth, his jaw is pried open with that iron prong you see on the table. It is known as the bostezo, which translates into English as the yawn. Isn't that droll? Then water is poured slowly down his throat. He must swallow, you see, to avoid choking on the cloth. The belly becomes hugely distended, and the water pours out through all the orifices."

The litany of horror had carried them completely around the perimeter of the vault and back to the door, where the two lay brothers, as Dee assumed them to be, stood waiting impassively.

"A most impressive collection, wouldn't you say, Doctor?" Normand asked Dee. "And not merely an academic interest, I assure you. Each of these devices has been put to practical use many times."

"The playthings of a madman," Dee said.

"We are not playing," Normand told him seriously. "We will get what we want in the end. In your own heart you already know this to be true. Why subject yourself to needless suffering? What can you possibly accomplish by the slow mutilation of your body? Be reasonable, Doctor Dee. Help us and help yourself at the same time. Obey Father Giovanni. You may not believe this in the depths of your poor heretical ignorance, but we are all fighting for the salvation of your soul."

Dee stared at him impassively. Words were useless. It was impossible to persuade a religious fanatic to forgo his mania.

"I see you need time to think the matter over," Normand said. He glanced at the two lay brothers. "Escort the prisoner to his cell. We will talk again tomorrow."

They took Dee by the arms as before and turned him toward the doorway.

"Pause a moment," Normand said.

He approached Dee with a gentle smile, a large wooden collar in his hands that was hinged to open. Iron spikes studded its inner rim.

"It would hardly be polite to show you this interesting collection of mechanical devices without giving you a practical demonstration. This little object is a sachentage, or Spanish collar."

Removing Dee's conservative ruff, he fitted the wheel around Dee's neck and clicked shut its padlock. Dee was surprised by its heaviness. It must contain lead weights, he decided. The needle points of the rusty iron spikes tickled against the back of his neck. He raised his hand quickly to balance the collar on his slender shoulders.

"You perceive the purpose," Normand said. "It requires constant attention to prevent the spikes from biting into your flesh. Sleep is impossible, of course."

Once more the hated hood shut out the light.

thirty-four

Kelley returned around midnight to find the stuffy, respectable house of the Maharal in an uproar. Lights burned in every window. The front door stood open. Men with serious expressions came and went in a stream. Others kept guard with watchful eyes. They prevented Kelley from entering until his angry protests drew the attention of a harried Rabbi Katz.

"Let him in, he's one of the men who was missing," he told the suspicious guards.

"What the devil's going on?" Kelley demanded.

Katz studied his face as though searching for some sign. Kelley saw dark circles under the rabbi's eyes, and worry lines between his eyebrows.

"Follow me," he said.

He led Kelley along the back hall of the lower level of the house into the large, brightly-lit kitchen. Rabbi Loew stood with a group of Jewish men both old and young. They were clustered in conference around the bare table. All wore the same expression of concern.

Loew said something to the other men in Yiddish. They stared at Kelley with interest. Kelley experienced a stab of apprehension.

"What's wrong?" he demanded. "Has John been killed?"

"Not so far as we know," Loew told him.

Kelley exhaled with relief.

"Hasn't he returned yet? He said he'd be back by sunset."

"No one has returned," Rabbi Katz told him with a note of hysteria in his voice. "We've been searching the ghetto for you all night."

"I don't understand," Kelley said to Loew. "Who else is missing?"

"When Rabbi Katz and I came back to the house earlier this evening I thought it had fallen under attack," Loew told him. "You were gone. Your wife was gone. So was John's wife and my daughter. John had not returned."

Kelley stared at him in shock.

"How can this be?"

"We thought perhaps you could explain it," Katz said. "The wife of the Maharal heard your wife arguing with Jane Dee. She had just awakened from sleep and was unclear over the cause of the argument. She thinks your wife left the house, and that Jane Dee and my wife Esther followed after her. Can you explain why they would do such a foolish thing?"

Although his voice was cultured and reasonable, Kelley detected the accusation hidden beneath his words. He realized at once what must have occurred after his departure from the house and cursed himself for his thoughtlessness. He should have guessed Joanna would not remain under the same roof as Jane Dee after jumping to the false conclusion that Jane had deceived her.

With a flush of embarrassment he related the tempestuous events of the afternoon to Loew and Katz, and gave them his assessment of what had probably taken place after he left the house.

"Joanna is an impetuous fool. When she gets angry she has no fear of anything. She probably left the ghetto to stay at one of the inns on the river. It seems likely that Jane and Esther followed her to keep her from falling into mischief, and got locked out of the ghetto at sunset."

"Perhaps," Loew said in a doubtful tone. "I hope you are right. I have caused inquiries to be made at all the respectable inns and no one has seen any of the ladies. It may be that they are staying at some rooming house or private residence. My daughter has several friends in the old city."

"Would any of them shelter a Jewess under their own roof overnight?"

"Probably not," Loew conceded. "Still, it is a place to look in the morning."

"Shouldn't we open the gates of the ghetto and raise a hue and cry throughout the city?"

Rabbi Katz smiled bitterly, and Loew shook his gray head.

"You don't understand the way things are done in Prague. The women were sheltered under my roof. That makes it a Jewish problem. The authorities outside the gates will expect us to deal with it ourselves."

"As we should," Rabbi Katz said. "If we start allowing the Christians to handle our affairs we'll have no freedom at all."

There were murmurs of assent from the men around the table who understood English. Loew stilled their voices with a gesture of his hand.

"My friend, can you ever forgive me?" he said to Kelley. "I should not have left the house without assigning one of my disciples to guard it. I knew it was safe from intruders from outside. It never occurred to me that anyone would voluntarily leave its security."

"You're not at fault," Kelley said with a shake of his head. "I am. The reason you didn't post a guard is because I was here. I never should have left the house. My anger overcame my judgement."

Loew patted him gently on the shoulder.

"Let's wait until we find the women before we worry about who was at fault."

Kelley sat at the table drinking cup after cup of potent Turkish coffee while the reports came in from those searching the ghetto and the old city. His suppressed concern gradually increased to alarm, then became a tight sickness in his lower belly. All reports were negative. No one had seen the women leave through the gates. It was possible they were still within the ghetto, but a thorough search could not be conducted until daybreak.

"Isn't it dangerous for your people to be walking the streets of Prague since the last murder?" he asked Rabbi Katz.

Katz shrugged philosophically.

"It's a risk they are willing to take for the sake of the Maharal. Everyone knows it's his daughter who is missing."

When dawn reluctantly revealed itself through the windows, Rabbi Loew's wife appeared at the kitchen door wrapped in a robe, her face haggard. It was evident she had not slept. Loew went over to comfort her. She stared at Kelley with undisguised hostility and whispered anxiously to her husband, who shook his head. She laid her cheek against Loew's shoulder and began to weep with silent sobs that racked her body. It was painful to witness such uncontrolled emotion from this proud, stern woman. Kelley turned his gaze away.

There was little he could do to aid the search, he realized. Loew had mobilized several hundred Jews both inside the ghetto and beyond its walls. If the women remained in Prague, sooner or later they would be located. Since Dee had still not returned, Kelley decided it would be more useful to make inquiries about his friend, whom Rabbi Loew had all but forgotten in his concern for his daughter. He conveyed his intention to Loew, who received the news absently, and set out for the livery stable where Dee had rented his horse the morning before.

This modest establishment stood not far beyond the northern wall of the ghetto. It consisted of a small barn with stalls for horses, a blacksmith's forge, and a fenced yard of churned black mud. Kelley was alarmed to see the mare rented by Dee standing quietly in the yard nibbling the corner of a bail of hay.

He sought out the proprietor, a short man near his own age with a freckled face and brick red hair. The stabler's bare arms had an inflated look from long years of throwing sacks of feed and shaping horseshoes on the anvil. He listened to Kelley with a frank expression on his flattened face, staring up into the smoldering dark eyes of the taller man.

"The horse came back just after dark," he told the alchemist in Bohemian. "That's all I know."

"Do you think she threw her rider?"

The stabler scratched his left ear.

"Doubt it. She's a good horse. More likely she stumbled. Or maybe your friend rode into a tree branch. That happens sometimes to those not used to riding."

"My friend could ride," Kelley assured him. "What about his belongings?"

"Inside the stable. I'll show you."

The stabler led him into the dim interior. Dust motes danced in slanting beams of morning sunlight. From the stalls came the restless rustle of several horses. Dee's belongings were heaped upon a rough work bench. They consisted of saddle bags with some food, small pouches of black powder and lead shot, along with a water bottle and a compact portable writing desk. Kelley opened it. Nothing appeared to be missing. There was no message. He turned his dark gaze on the stabler.

"Was there nothing else?"

The freckled man started to shake his head, hesitated, then dropped his eyes. He went to a corner of the stable and unlocked a heavy box with a key that hung at his belt. He took a swollen leather purse out and dropped in on the bench in front of Kelley. It clinked as it struck the wood.

"I put it in the box to keep it safe," the stabler said, staring at Kelley with defiance.

Kelley counted out the gold coins in the purse. They totaled one hundred. He extended his hand to the stabler.

"It's not often I meet an honest man," he said.

The stabler grinned and shook his hand.

"I need the best horse you've got right away," Kelley told him.

"That would be the black. I'll have him saddled."

He whistled for a boy and ordered him to saddle the coal black gelding he led out of its stall. Kelley counted out five Spanish gold pieces and laid them on the bench.

"I may have to ride him hard. I should have him back by the afternoon. This will pay you for your trouble."

"More than generous, my lord," the man murmured as he pocketed the coins. "Many thanks."

"One doubloon is for the horse. The other four are for your honest nature."

Kelley alternated between a canter and a walk all along the road that led northeast from the outer gates of Prague. The map given to Dee by Peter Gwyn remained sharp in his mind, even though he had obtained only a single look at it. He suspected that Dee had shown it to him so that Kelley could find his way to the meeting place should the need arise. By the time he reached the ford across the brook, the gelding's midnight sides were streaked with white foam. He paused to allow the horse to drink, then pressed on to the farmhouse.

The gray stallion behind the house tugged restlessly on its tether when it saw Kelley. He dismounted slowly, looking all around at the wooded hills, and secured his own mount to the worn post in front of the house. As he approached the open door, his nose alerted him that something was terribly wrong. Putting his hand over his mouth, he peered into the dim interior of the single-room structure. Flies circled a heap of burlap sacks in the corner of the floor.

Filled with foreboding, he forced himself to enter the deserted house and flipped off several of the sacks with the toe of his boot. When he saw that the corpse was not Dee, a wave of relief washed through his body and left him shaking.

He drew a deep breath and held it while he bent close over the bloody corpse and rifled its pockets. The dry, sightless eyes of the dead man stared up at him with mute accusation. His mouth was frozen in a death grin. Kelley found a silk handkerchief with a lace border and a silver snuffbox inlaid with tortoise shell. The inner lid of the snuffbox was engraved with the initials "F. N." This confirmed the identity of the dead man in Kelley's mind.

Disquieted by the staring eyes of Niebuhr's flyblown corpse, he picked up a loose sack and laid it across the ghastly face. By this time his eyes had adapted to the dim light. He noticed fresh scratches in the dusty floorboards, and traced them with his fingertips. They formed a lopsided "J." He searched the rest of the room for other signs but found nothing.

The sound of an approaching rider made him reach reflexively for his pistols before he remembered that he had given both weapons to Dee. With a silent curse, he drew his rapier and waited with his back against the wall on one side of the open doorway. He heard the rider dismount and approach through the dry grass. His shadow was framed in the rectangle of sunlight that fell across the floor.

"I mean no harm, friend. I'm just a traveler."

Kelley recognized the voice and stepped into the light. Peter Gwyn regarded the alchemist in silence for several seconds. He removed his right hand from behind his thigh, eased off the hammer of the pistol it carried, and slid the weapon into his broad belt. Kelley sheathed his rapier.

"Who is the dead man?" Gwyn asked.

Kelley stepped aside.

"See for yourself."

Gwyn entered the farmhouse and uncovered the corpse.

"Count Friedrich Niebuhr. I feared as much. The fool was supposed to meet with me this morning. When he didn't appear I decided to look for him. Did John Dee kill him?"

"I doubt it."

Kelley told Gwyn about the return of the riderless mare with the Queen's gold still in its saddlebag, and the failure of Dee to appear at the house of Rabbi Loew. He showed the sea captain the enigmatic scratches in the floor.

"Niebuhr couldn't have done it," Gwyn grunted. "There's nothing in his hands to make such a mark."

"What do you think it means?"

"Maybe the initial of a name, or a town."

"It can't stand for my wife, Joanna, or Dee's wife, Jane. When John left the ghetto yesterday, both were safe at the house of Judah Loew."

"You don't suppose it stands for Judah? Or Jew?"

Kelley shook his head.

"Judah Loew is above suspicion. If John drew it, he intended it to convey something important, something we don't already know."

"Unless...." Gwyn hesitated.

"What?"

"If Dee knew he was about to be killed, he might have made this letter as a form of prayer. Perhaps it stands for Jesus."

"That's not like him. If he knew he was about to be taken prisoner, he was thinking of ways to escape, or a sign that would lead me to him, not the name of our Lord."

He lapsed into brooding silence as he stared down at the crude letter. A thought tickled in his mind. Patiently he waited for it to grow stronger. It flashed upon him.

"Not Jesus, but the Society of Jesus," he said, staring hard at Gwyn.

The eyes of the seaman narrowed. He nodded meditatively.

"Jesuits. There's a notion. Their meddling hands are in every intrigue across Europe."

They left the house and examined the ground around it. Gwyn's quick eyes picked up a faint track through the tall wild grasses. They followed it to a clump of trees.

"There were horses tethered here," Gwyn said as he examined the ground. "See the holes left by the pegs?"

"They must have taken John with them."

"Unless they left his body in the forest."

Kelley shook his head.

"Why take him into the forest to murder him, when they killed Niebuhr inside the house? Anyway, in this heat we'd smell him if he lay within a hundred yards."

"You're right. They must have taken him to a safe house to interrogate him at their leisure. Poor bastard."

They returned to the deserted house. Kelley watched while Gwyn made a careful search of Niebuhr's corpse, then went outside to examine the contents of the saddle-bags on the horse. These contained scant provisions. Clearly Niebuhr had not intended to be outside the walls of Prague for more than a few hours.

"No letter," Gwyn said. "Either he never brought it in the first place, or whoever killed him took it."

Kelley began to untie the reins of the stallion from its tether peg.

"What are you doing?" Gwyn asked.

"We can't leave the animal here. He needs food and water. I'm going to take him back to the city. I know a stabler who will take him in without asking questions."

"A bad idea," Gwyn told him. "Sooner or later some-one is going to recognize this horse. That will link you to Niebuhr's death. You can imagine the excitement when the King realizes one of his closest advisors is missing, especially in light of the recent murders. The King's soldiers are likely to turn over the entire city looking for Niebuhr. Do you really want to try explaining to Rudolph how you happened to come into possession of Niebuhr's horse?"

"I see your point," Kelley murmured.

He went to his own horse and got his water bottle, then returned to the back of the house and poured water into his cupped hand for the gray stallion a drink. He took off its saddle and bridle. A swat on its rump sent it dancing skittishly up the slope of the overgrown meadow. It stood staring nervously back at Kelley and Gwyn from the corner of its rolling eye.

"He'll find his way to water," Kelley said. "He's a fine horse. Someone will take him in."

"We'd better get out of here ourselves, before a trav-eler happens along the road."

They mounted their horses and started back in the direction of Prague.

"I have to try to find John before those papist devils murder him," Kelley told Gwyn. "Do you have any notion where they might have taken him?"

"It would have to be somewhere close. They couldn't risk taking a prisoner on a long journey. It would be too likely to attract attention. The Jesuits, if it was the Jesuits, have many wealthy patrons willing to lend money and resources to their cause. My guess is, they took him to a remote house in the countryside."

"Not back to their college?"

Gwyn shook his head.

"How would they get him through the outer gate of the city? Unless he were tied inside a wagon. But there are no fresh wagon tracks. No, I think he was taken by horse to the house of a sympathizer."

"How can I find this house?"

Gwyn studied his companion.

"You mean to go after Dee yourself, alone?"

"I do."

"Let me think a while."

They rode in silence.

"It must be a house by itself," Gwyn said at last. "That eliminates villages or other populated regions. It must be the house of someone with considerable authority who can control the tongues of his servants. It probably lies within a day's ride. Most important, it must be the house of a fanatical advocate of the Jesuit cause."

"Can you give me a list of the most likely sympathizers with houses in the country?"

Gwyn grinned savagely. His lips pulled back from his barred teeth like those of a snarling wolf.

"I'll do better than that. I'll come with you."

Kelley reached across his saddle and grasped Gwyn's sinewy forearm. He was too overcome with emotion to speak.

"Let me make a few inquiries when we enter the city to narrow the possibilities. We don't want to set out on a fool's errand."

Both men had the same thought but neither voiced it. They might waste days riding around Bohemia from estate to estate before they stumbled upon the house in which Dee was imprisoned. By then it would probably be too late.

"We'll get Dee out of there," Gwyn said with forced bravado. "The Queen would never forgive me if I left him rotting in the hands of the Jesuits. She places a high value on his hide."

"As do I," Kelley said.

THIRTY-FIVE

I hope you slept well last night," Normand said in a solicitous tone.

Dee rolled his head to look at the Jesuit. His slender neck was marked with a ring of a dozen or more scabs where the spikes of the Spanish collar had bitten into his pale flesh.

"Well enough," he muttered through cracked lips. "I could wish for a change of bedding."

He stood naked in the vault, his wrists bound together behind his back with his elbows locked straight. A rope ran from his wrists to a pulley in the ceiling, then back down to a wooden winch with a locking ratchet. The older of the two Jesuit lay brothers was in the process of winding the rope tight. The tension forced Dee to bend forward at the waist to relieve the growing strain on his shoulders. His white skin was covered with red welts from the bites of fleas and other vermin that made his unfurnished cell their home.

Normand laughed.

"I'll speak to the chambermaid about it."

Dee glanced at the bucket of water beside the boot of the Frenchman. He cleared his throat.

"Would you mind giving me a drink? I haven't had any water since yesterday morning."

"Perhaps. If I thought it would help you to speak."

"I'll talk about any subject you wish," Dee said, wincing as the rope drew tighter. Each clink of the ratchet increased the strain. "What do you want to discuss? Physics? Astronomy? Cartography?"

"Before we hold our conversation, there is one little thing that Father Giovanni wishes you to do. I'm sure you won't want to injure his feelings by refusing."

"What would that be?"

Normand drew the folded cipher letter from the girdle of his black silk doublet and let it fall open before Dee's bending head.

"The good Father wants you to study this document. Nothing more. You need say not a single word about it today. Merely agree to read it over and we will allow you to dress and provide you with a comfortable desk and pens and paper. And water, of course. And food as well."

Dee closed his eyes and shook his head.

"I'm so glad," Normand told him. "I was looking forward to demonstrating the strappado."

Another clink of the ratchet. Dee gritted his teeth. He found himself forced to stand upon his toes to relieve the excruciating strain on his shoulder joints.

"The sensation is always most intense in the beginning, before the shoulders become stretched," Normand said in a conversational tone. "At first it is quite easy to balance on the toes, but after an hour the muscles in the feet and calves become exhausted. I'm sure you can appreciate how intense the pain would be were I to have you lifted completely away from the floor, to say nothing of attaching the cherubim to your ankles."

Dee stared up at the smug, smooth-faced Frenchman. Seldom in his life had he felt such complete loathing and contempt for a human being. He suppressed these emotions. There was nothing to be gained by expressing his hatred, which in any case ill became a true Christian.

"The whole exercise is one of obedience," Normand said. "If you do as I require, I will loosen the rope one notch. If your response displeases me, I will tighten it. How is it feeling now? Is it beginning to tighten?"

He slapped Dee lightly on the shoulder. Dee trembled and cried out as red flames of agony lanced from his shoulders throughout his straining body.

"You must be getting tired," Normand said with concern. "Would you like me to loosen the rope a little so that you can stand on your heels?"

He bent his head close to Dee and cocked his ear.

"I'm sorry, I didn't hear that. What did you say?"

"Yes," Dee gasped. "Loosen the rope."

"Very well. There is just one thing you can do for me first. Do you happen to know the Miserere?"

Dee blinked the sweat from his eyes and shook his head to clear his thoughts. He looked up at Normand's smirking, hateful face.

"The fifty-first psalm?"

"The fiftieth of the Vulgate. I'd like you to recite it for me, please, in Latin."

"I don't think I can remember the exact text...."

"Think nothing of it. If you make a mistake, you can start over again from the beginning. That's fair enough, isn't it?"

Dee's whole consciousness was concentrated upon the burning pain of his shoulders. Philosophy meant nothing. Intellect meant nothing. Even courage meant nothing. With absolute clarity he realized that a simple length of rope had reduced him to the level of a fox with its leg caught in the steel jaws of a trap. He had no other wish or desire or ambition beyond escape from his present predicament.

"Have mercy upon me, O God, according unto the multitude of thy tender mercies...."

"No, that's wrong," Normand said with the tone of a school master. "Again, please."

"Have mercy upon me, O God, according to thy loving-kindness; according unto the multitude of thy tender mercies blot out my transgressions. Cleanse me thoroughly...."

"Wrong. Again, if you please."

Dee felt the calf muscles in his legs begin to cramp. His knees and ankles trembled uncontrollably. Yet he did not dare ease the strain even for a second. He was certain that if he relaxed his legs, he would dislocate his shoulders. Then he would know what true agony was all about.

"Have mercy upon me, O God, according to thy loving-kindness; according unto the multitude of thy tender mercies blot out my transgressions. Wash me thoroughly from mine iniquities...."

"Wrong."

"Mine iniquity," Dee gasped. "I meant mine iniquity. Wash me thoroughly from mine iniquity, and cleanse me from my sin."

Normand made a curt gesture to the lay brother at the winch. He was the dark-haired one with the villainous face. The stoic Jesuit tightened the rope a notch. When Dee heard the metallic clink of the ratchet, he thought he would faint, and fought desperately to shake the shadows from his vision. He did not dare lose consciousness.

"Begin again," Normand ordered.

Somehow Dee managed to recite the psalm from start to finish. He did not know if he had done it accurately, but Normand did not correct him.

"Very good, Doctor. I'm proud of you."

The release of tension was almost more agonizing than its increase. The rope slacked just enough to allow Dee to stand flat upon his bare feet on the stone flags. Never before in his long, complex life had the scholar felt such gratitude toward another human being, mingled with such hatred.

"Thank you," he muttered.

"You did very well," Norman said in a soothing tone. "So well, in fact, I have decided to give you a little water. Would you like a drink?"

"Yes. Jesu, yes."

Normand filled a tin ladle from the water bucket and held it to Dee's swollen lips while he eagerly gulped it down.

"More," he said hoarsely.

"Perhaps later," Normand told him. "Are you rested now? Do your legs feel better? Good. Let's try it again."

The click of the ratchet as the rope tightened almost drove Dee to complete despair. He clung to sanity by filling his imagination with the image of his beloved Jane smiling sweetly upon him. His legs began to tremble with fatigue the moment he was forced onto his toes.

"You can imagine how intense the sensation would be were I to have you raised several feet into the air, and suddenly dropped to dangle like a fish on a line. But I hope it won't come to that. Let's see if you remember your lesson. Recite the Miserere, please, slowly so that I can correct your mistakes."

"Have mercy upon me, O God...."

Dee lost count of the number of times he was raised and lowered. When Normand finally released him, his arms were completely useless and he discovered that he lacked the strength in his legs to take a step. Normand called the blond lay brother into the vault. He thrust the hood over Dee's head, then supported him by the shoulder as he led Dee, still naked, back to his windowless cell.

Dee realized that he had lost all track of time. He did not know if hours or days had passed since his interview with Azoth. He had not glimpsed the light of the sun since his abduction at the farmhouse.

The lay brother removed his hood and lowered Dee gently to the bare stone floor of his cell. In the lamplight that entered the cell through the open door from the corridor beyond, his youthful features appeared almost kindly. Dee judged that he could not be older than eighteen.

The Jesuit pressed something into his numb hand. Dee had to use both arms to raise it to his face, he was so weak. With wonder he saw that it was a piece of black bread. The lay brother stepped from the cell and returned in several minutes with a leather-covered bottle. He raised it to Dee's lips.

"Drink," he murmured.

Dee sucked like a starving infant at the cool water. He protested when it was drawn away.

"Not too much," the Jesuit said. "You'll get sick. Here, try to eat."

He helped Dee raise the bread to his mouth. It was dry and hard. Dee chewed a small morsel. The saliva gushed from the insides of his cheeks in painful spurts. He forced the rest of the bread down his throat. It was the most wonderful food he had ever tasted.

"I swept the vermin to one corner of your cell," the Jesuit murmured, glancing nervously out the open door. "It was the best I could do, I'm afraid. They watch all the time."

Dee grasped his arm weakly.

"Who are you?" he whispered.

For answer, the young man straightened out Dee's left palm and used the nail of his index finger to trace a symbol. Dee recognized his own hieroglyphic monad.

"You are of the Order of Hermes?"

"I managed to send a note by messenger to Prague," the Jesuit murmured. "Understand my position. If it fails to reach its destination, I can't help you. My own life would be forfeit."

"I understand," Dee said. He reached up and gripped the blond youth's shoulder. "Thank you."

The heavy ironbound door closed Dee into a sea of darkness. He felt as Jonah must have felt within the belly of the whale. Not even his own hand was visible in front of his face. Still, he was thankful for small mercies. He no longer lay upon verminous filth. The Spanish collar had not been reattached around his neck. Presumably Azoth wished him to sleep. He regretted his failure to ask the blond brother how many hours had elapsed since his capture.

At least he would go to sleep with hope. In his position hope was more comforting that any material possession. He lay his weary head upon his naked arm and closed his eyes.

A serpent of doubt glided through his mind. Was the Jesuit truly a member of the Order of Hermes? Or was his kindness a deception designed to disappoint Dee and plunge him into despair? The more he thought about it, the more likely it seemed that it was a ruse of Azoth's to wear down his resistance. The fragile ghost of optimism that had stirred momentarily in his heart faded away like a shadow. For a long while he lay awake, staring into the darkness, afraid to sleep because he dreaded what new horror the morrow might bring.

PART FOUR

THE BLACK MOUNTAIN

ThIRTY-SIX

Joanna awoke upon a narrow cot in the corner of a
bare chamber with unfinished stone walls and a low
beamed ceiling. She rolled onto her shoulder and peered
around from under puffy eyelids. Other than her bed,
the room contained a small table and a single chair. She
tried to rise from the cot and almost fell onto her face
with dizziness. Sitting up on the side of the felt mattress,
her bare feet pressed against rough floorboards, she
forced herself to wait for her head to stop spinning and
her stomach to settle.

When she felt strong enough, she swayed across the
room and tested the iron latch of the door. Locked.
Someone had taken her clothes and dressed her in a loose
shift of unbleached linen similar to the kind worn by novi-
tiate nuns. Her long flaming hair fanned over her shoulders. Under the shift she was completely naked.

On the table by the bed she discovered a pewter plate
with half a loaf of black bread and a large bottle of forti-
fied wine. Even though she was parched from want of
water, she resisted drinking more than a few mouthfuls of
the wine. She wanted her wits about her. Why she had
been taken, or where, she could not guess. One thing she
understood plainly enough—she was in mortal danger.

307

She went to the tall, narrow window of her cheerless prison room and gazed morosely through the iron bars at the mountain valley far below. The casement opened outward, but the bars set into the inner edge of the window frame were too close to permit her to pass her head between them. Strain as she might, she managed to see only a section of the pitched slate roof of a long barracks below, a cobbled courtyard with an entrance gate, and the top of an outer fortification wall.

She judged she was being kept in the tower of a mountain fortress. A narrow road climbed over the shoulder of a pass at the extreme left edge of her field of view. She could not follow it where it ran close under the wall, but it was visible on the floor of the valley to her right as a winding gray ribbon interrupted frequently by stands of evergreen trees. A cataract spilled off the mountain slope opposite her window and crossed the road far below on the valley floor.

Pulling the wooden chair in front of the window, she sat heavily and stared with a bleak expression at the cascading fall of white foam. Under other circumstances, the breathtaking view might have entranced her with its primordial grandeur, but now she barely noticed it. A muddy torrent of guilt, shame, and dread of the unknown raged through her thoughts and defiled her sense of wonder.

She remembered slapping Jane Dee and accusing her of adultery with Edward, then leaving the house of Rabbi Loew in a fury and striding toward the gates of the ghetto. Even though the events were sharp in her memory, she found it hard to believe she had been such a fool. Wine always fuddled her wits, but this was the first time it had made her think ill of her best friend. Jane would never betray her own husband. Even drunk, how could she have imagined it for an instant? Unless more than wine was the cause of her temporary madness. All of the events from Edward's dream until her capture had a distorted quality of unreality.

She recalled blurting out to Edward her knowledge that he had married her against his will at the command of the Enochian angels. It was the sole action of that horrible afternoon she did not regret. The truth had been a poison in her heart for months, filling her with constant worry that if Edward had never loved her, and if she remained unable to give him a child, one day he would abandon her. Despite her resentment against him, she could not help loving her husband. Her warring emotions had driven her to seek forgetfulness in wine. With the secret revealed at last, she felt a curious sense of freedom.

How much time had passed since her abduction? She remembered walking past an inconspicuous coach, a confused struggle, and something forced over her head. A strange scent lingered in the back of her throat. It was similar to rotting rose petals, both sweet and revolting. She guessed that some potent unguent had been smeared inside the hood to render her unconscious. She had probably slept for many hours, perhaps days.

The rattle of a bolt on the outside of her door startled Joanna from her seat. She searched desperately around the room for a weapon, then picked up the chair by its back. Its light frame and wicker seat was better than nothing. She stood against the wall with the chair raised overhead to strike.

Jane Dee slipped into the room and shut the door. Someone on the outside shot the bolt, locking her in. She saw Joanna in her threatening posture and laughed lightly at her expression.

Joanna dropped the chair and embraced the other woman. Tears of relief welled into her eyes.

"Jane, thank Jesu you're here. I thought I was alone."

"Poor Joanna," Jane said with emotion. "You're safe now. Mamma's come to comfort you."

Joanna studied her friend's face. There was something strange about the light in Jane's lustrous eyes. Jane had on the same drab, unbleached linen shift that she herself wore. Her glossy sable hair hung straight down her slender back, one of the few times Joanna had ever seen it unbound.

"Where are we? Who brought us to this place?"

Jane spun away from her touch and danced across the floor to stare out the window with a dreamy expression.

"Have you ever heard of the Sons of Coronzon?"

"I don't think so," Joanna said. "Who are they?"

"They're the people who took the book."

"You mean the book that was stolen from John's library?" Joanna asked.

Jane giggled and glanced at Joanna slyly from the corner of her eye.

"They took us, too. This is their stronghold. It's called the Black Mountain. Isn't it lovely?"

A rush of shame overcame Joanna. She put her hand on her friend's shoulder.

"Jane, I've been so wrong. This is all my fault. If I hadn't run out of the house we'd still be safe. I've been thinking about you and Edward, and I realize what a fool I was to accuse you of infidelity. Jane, can you ever forgive me?"

Jane turned to face her. They stood with their bodies nearly touching before the window. A shadow seemed to pass across the eyes of the smaller woman. For a moment they filled with anguish. Beneath the pain, Joanna recognized the familiar awareness of her friend. Jane's features twitched as though from some inner struggle. The strange brightness returned.

"Dear Joanna, of course I forgive you. Let's kiss and make up."

She put her arms around the neck of the taller woman and drew her down. Joanna felt the soft touch of her lips, gentle at first, then more insistent. The probing tip of Jane's tongue parted her teeth. She pulled away and stared in shock at Jane.

"What did they do to you?" she whispered.

Jane spun in a lazy circle on her bare toes so that the hem of her shift spiraled out from her legs, then allowed herself to fall back across the cot with her bare legs exposed up to the lower part of her thighs, her oval face framed in a soft halo of dark hair. She laced her fingers through her hair over her head and lay regarding Joanna with amusement.

"John and Edward are wrong about the Sons. They only want to be our friends. If we join them, they'll give us everything we've ever wanted. Gold. Jewels. Costly clothes and stately houses. They'll make us richer than princes."

"When did you ever care about money?" Joanna said, backing away. "They've bewitched you."

"Don't be silly. Come here and lie beside me."

"You're possessed," Joanna told her.

Jane spread her legs under her loose shift and undulated her hips. The dome of her pregnant belly lifted the gray fabric.

"I've always loved your hair. Come, let me run my fingers through it."

"Who are you?" Joanna demanded.

Jane threw back her head and laughed richly. It was a harlot's laughter, brazen and unrestrained.

"You're the Whore of Babylon," Joanna breathed. Her heart pounded with terror.

"You honor me," Jane said. "The time of the Ancient One is not yet come upon the earth. I'm only her poor handmaiden."

She uncoiled herself from the cot and began to rise to her feet. Joanna felt the cool stones of the wall against her back.

"Stay away. I'm warning you."

"I thought you liked me," Jane said with an injured expression. "Won't you kiss me again?"

"It's unnatural."

"I thought you'd be glad of a little tenderness. Edward told me you were a cold fish in bed but I didn't believe him."

"He told you?" Joanna said, staring at her.

"We talk about you all them time while we're making love," Jane said with a lazy smile. "He thinks you're barren."

"You and Edward have made love?" Joanna did not believe it, but something compelled her to speak the words.

"Of course," Jane laughed. "We could scarcely avoid it, living under the same roof these last five years and traveling together. Poor Edward gets so frustrated, and my husband's no good to me. I'm a young woman and John is an old man."

"But you're pregnant," Joanna objected.

"Whose child do you think it is? Really, Joanna, I'm surprised you're such an innocent. Whose child could it be? John is nearly sixty. There's nothing in his seed but sour water."

She put the red tip of her tongue against her upper front teeth.

"Stay away from me," Joanna said.

She stepped quickly behind the chair. It was a frail defense. Defense against what, she wondered. The thing that possessed her friend made no threatening gesture, yet she felt its deadliness hidden within like the envenomed fangs of a viper. It was toying with her.

Jane went to the table and poured some of the port into the pewter goblet that stood beside it. She drank deeply, then extended the remainder of the wine to Joanna.

"You must be thirsty. Why don't you drink? We can have a party. There are lots of wonderful men about this place."

"I'm not thirsty," Joanna said.

"No?" Jane drained the goblet and set it upside down on the table. "You're not much fun anymore, Joanna. You disappoint me."

"Jane, this isn't like you. What did they do? Try to remember? Did they torture you?"

Jane pouted in thought. She rolled her eyes heavenward. She appeared to be intoxicated with something other than wine. Joanna wondered what strange potions and extracts the Sons of Coronzon possessed. Did they have a drug that could take away reason?

"They opened my mind," Jane said. "I was blind and they let me see. You wouldn't believe the beauty of our Scarlet Lady, Joanna. She's made all of precious jewels and shimmering fire. Her voice is music. Her touch is joy. She promised me wonderful things if I worshiped her. I would have been a fool to refuse. No one could refuse her sweet seductions. You'll see. When she comes to you as she came to me, you'll worship her also, and forget all about the foolish, petty ways of men."

"Poor Jane, you don't even know what you're saying," Joanna murmured. "They drugged you and possessed your soul."

"My soul?" Jane laughed hysterically. "What makes you think I have a soul?"

All this while Jane crept closer and Joanna shrank away, drawing the chair in front of her like a shield, until her back pressed into the corner of the room and she found herself with no retreat.

"Stay away from me, demon."

"Don't you want a baby, Joanna?" Jane cooed. She rubbed the dome of her belly. "Don't you want one of these inside you? My Mother is the goddess of birth and death. She'll give you a child. All you need to do is ask her. Many virile young men serve her. You can take your pick of them. Only swear to love and obey her, as I have done."

Joanna raised the chair and threatened to strike.

"I'm warning you. Don't come a step closer. Don't touch me."

"Do you want to hit me?" Jane said with a strange smile. "Go ahead, I don't mind. In fact, I like it."

She struck herself repeatedly on the cheek with the flat of her right hand. The sharp crack of each slap turned her head. After a few blows the side of her face became bright red.

Joanna dropped the chair in horror.

"Stop it, Jane. You'll injure yourself."

She grabbed Jane's slender wrists and held them apart over her head. To her amazement Jane threw her off as easily as an adult shakes off the grasp of an infant. Joanna fell backward across the floor and landed on her hip. Jane stared down at her with an unreadable expression, a mixture of amusement, contempt, and compassion.

"I'll leave you now. Think about what I've said. It's no use fighting. Our Mother is too powerful and wise for you to deny her will. She's older than the roots of the mountains. Eventually you will accept her into your heart. I wanted to give you the chance to do so voluntarily, but if you are stubborn she will take you by force. You have no choice in this matter, foolish woman. No choice at all."

She rapped three times with her fist on the door. It opened at once. Joanna saw a man dressed in black with a black hood over his head, and realized he must have been waiting just outside the whole time Jane was in the room. He moved silently to allow Jane to pass, like an animated shadow.

"It's up to you, Joanna. It's so much easier if you give in to our Mother. I made the mistake of fighting, and look at my reward."

She bent and grasped the hem of her shift, then lifted it over her head so that her naked body was exposed from her bare feet to above the level of her breasts. Joanna cried out in horror. Her entire body was a mass of red scratches and ugly purple bruises. The shift dropped like a curtain. Joanna stared into Jane's celestially tranquil eyes.

"It's so much easier if you don't fight. You'll grow to like it. I did."

THIRTY-SEVEN

John? John? Where are you?" It was Jane's voice. Dee stood up and walked toward it, letting the sound lead him through the darkness.

"I'm coming, Jane."

"John? I'm frightened."

"I can't see you. Keep talking."

She called his name. He pursued her voice blindly with his arms stretched in front of him. The murk was impenetrable. He could not even see his own hands. Her voice grew stronger. In the far distance he perceived a tiny point of light and moved toward it. The point expanded into a miniature human figure.

"I see you," he shouted. "I'm coming."

"Where are you?"

She stood forlornly with her arms at her sides, staring all around like a frightened fawn. Dee hurried toward her. She wore a plain linen shift, with her glossy black hair loose at her back. Her feet were bare. The surface she stood upon, like a frozen lake of ink, reflected an inverted duplicate of her image.

He stopped in front of her. Jane stared blankly through him as though blind.

"I'm here, Jane. Can't you see me?"

His voice made her start. She narrowed her eyes and peered into the far distance. A smile illuminated her pale features.

"I see you now, John. Why are you standing so far away? Come closer."

Dee took a step forward to embrace his wife. Instead of drawing closer, she receded away from him. He stared at her in astonishment.

"Why did you step back?" she called. "I can barely see you."

"I'm sorry, dearest. Something is keeping us apart. I don't think I can come any closer."

"I'll come to you, then."

He watched her walk toward him and counted her paces. After more than a hundred steps she stopped in frustration. She stood no nearer than when she had started. It was almost impossible to gauge distance on this featureless black lake.

"How far away am I?" he asked.

"I don't know—perhaps a score of yards."

"You seem much nearer to me."

"What is this place?" she asked in confusion. "How did I get here?"

"What do you last recall?"

"I remember walking along the street. A man jumped out from a coach and pulled me inside. He put a sweet-smelling hood over my head. Then I was here."

"What were you doing in the street? Was anyone else with you?"

Jane's frowned in puzzlement.

"I don't remember. Isn't that strange? John, what am I doing here?"

Dee reflected that he would be better able to answer her question if only he knew where they were. He noticed that their voices lacked an echo. They sounded as they might in the middle of a vast windless plain. But if they stood in a plain, where were the stars?

A fragment of poetry from an ancient Greek papyrus ran through his memory:

We wake in sleep and flee to meet in solitude;
Our eyes embrace black tears upon a sea of glass.

"I'm frightened, John. Please help me."

"Jane, you must be brave. It may be a long time before I'm able to free you from this place."

"I'll try. It's just so, so...." She turned away from him to face the darkness behind her, searching for the right word. "It's so empty here."

In spite of the futility, Dee took a step toward her. The inverted reflection of his wife's long hair and slender back rippled. Dee felt the mirror surface rise and fall beneath his bare feet. In the limitless depths of the frozen lake a shadow stirred. Dee stared downward far into the glassy floor. It was like trying to pierce a dark abyss. Something moved down there. Something immense.

A scaled head larger than an ox cart erupted noiselessly from the black mirror upon a serpentine neck that extruded upward seemingly without end. Dee cried out and stumbled, his arms raised in an instinctive gesture of defense. He lost sight of Jane behind the body of the dragon. Its wedge-shaped head reared over him, forked tongue flickering in and out as if searching the air. Dee saw that its eye sockets gaped raw and empty.

A sharp word of command sounded behind it. At once the dragon arched over backward, its pale, scaled belly continuing to spew from the black lake as its coils became denser and more convolute. Dee shouted his wife's name in an agony of apprehension. She had stood in the same place where the body of the dragon now seethed and slid upon itself.

He saw her then, rising upon the flat head of the great beast. She was strangely changed. Henna reddened her lips and elongated fingernails, as well as the toenails of her bare feet. Egyptian black lined her eyes. Rouge gave her cheeks and throat a fever flush. In her long dark hair jewels and pearls of immense size hung braided. In place of her simple linen shift she wore a gown the color of blood with a slit up the front that revealed her thigh. A silver diadem circled her brow, plain except for a single large, white stone that glittered like a living thing with its own internal fire. The tightness of the dress accentuated the dome of her pregnant belly.

She gazed down at Dee as though upon an insect she was about to crush beneath her heel.

"I feel her love for you inside me."

It was Jane's voice, but chillingly altered.

Dee gathered the slivers of his courage.

"Where have you taken her?"

Lilith smiled with his wife's lips.

"The bitch is here. She's sleeping. I doubt if she'll ever wake up."

"Release her!"

Her laughter was as pitiless as shards of rock crystal cast down a dry well.

"I have a use for your seed, Scribe. Don't worry—I'll take loving care of this husk."

The head of the blind dragon descended. Dee felt its fetid breath against his lips. Its tongue flicked out and brushed his cheek. He leapt back in horror. Deep in his groin he felt his desire stir and begin to rise.

"Do you want to touch her?" the thing inside his wife taunted. "You can embrace her now. My dragon can bring you together if you lie within its coils. Go ahead, make love to her. I see that you want to."

Lilith laughed with Jane's mouth. Dee realized shamefully that he stood naked before her. He hid his erect yard behind his hands.

"Release her, whore, or I'll destroy you."

He felt a sharp pain on the tip of the big toe of his left foot. Lilith began to recede into the darkness.

"Remember, Scribe. Any night you wish, you can lie with her. Call upon my name and I will come to you. I'll bring this carcass with me. You can use it any way you desire, ways you never dared use it while she was awake."

Her voice became faint with distance.

"Remember, Scribe, call upon my name and I will come."

Dee ran to pursue the shrinking image of the dragon. In moments it was so distant, he could distinguish only the shining white stone in the circlet upon the head of his wife. It seemed to pulse and glitter in the forehead of the blind dragon itself. He cursed and stumbled. The pain in his left toe grew too sharp to ignore. It felt as though a hot needle were being thrust under his toenail.

With a start Dee awoke, covered in chill sweat. He felt something nip at his left foot and lashed out in the darkness. His instep struck a soft, furred body. It squeaked its frustration and scurried away to the corner of his cell.

A rat. The pain of its bite had awakened him from his strange dream. Perhaps he should be grateful. He reviewed the dream in his mind and realized it had been more than natural. In some way he had communicated with his wife. How far could he trust her words? If Jane had told the truth, she must be in the hands of the Sons of Coronzon. Or had the Jesuits taken her? Surely Normand would have made use of Jane to exact his obedience if the Society of Jesus held her prisoner.

If Azoth was one of the Sons, as Dee suspected from the crooked scar upon his left palm, and the Sons of Coronzon held Jane, why had Azoth not used this lever to force him to translate the cipher? He must be playing some complex double game with the Society of Jesus for his own twisted purposes. Perhaps it had something to do with the hatred the hairless adept exhibited at each mention of the name Aquaviva.

In some foul way Jane had fallen under the control of Lilith. Dee shivered and clenched his hands so tightly that his nails sank into his palms. Jane was in mortal danger, and here he lay rotting in this vermin-infested prison. Tears of frustration welled from the corners of his eyes and ran down his cheeks in the darkness. He heard the scurry of the rat and hissed. The sound stopped, at least for the moment. He would get little sleep in his cell, Spanish collar or not. It was common for rats to completely gnaw away the fingers and toes of prisoners too weak from torture and disease to resist. Thank Jesu he had yet to reach that stage.

He kicked out with his bare foot in the direction of the rat's rustling progress. At least he had something physical to hate.

Thirty-Eight

"I knew we should have turned east," Kelley said in disgust.

Gwyn twisted in his saddle and cast a bland look back at the alchemist.

"Aren't we riding east now?"

"Don't tell me you're both lost," Yitzhaq Katz moaned behind Kelley. He slapped his hand against his sweating neck to kill a hungry mosquito.

"I'm a mariner, not a damned woodsman. If you think you can do better, you lead."

"My people aren't exactly renowned for their wood-craft," Katz pointed out.

"I don't know why we didn't just keep to the road," Kelley grumbled.

"Because it's certain to be watched. I told you that already."

The three men had spent the last hour battling the heat and flies in the dense, wooded hills that lay to the northeast of the city of Prague. In places it was nearly impossible to find an opening through the underbrush wide enough for their horses to walk one after the other. Slanting afternoon sunlight had given way to purple twilight, and even that was rapidly fading to darkness. There would be no assistance from the waning moon, which had set unseen an hour ago.

No darkness was quite so black, Kelley reflected sourly, as the darkness of a forest on a moonless night. If they did not stumble across the estate of the Jesuit sympathizer in the next few minutes, they would be forced to make camp where they stood and wait for the dawn.

Luck had been with Gwyn and Kelley on their return to Prague. The hue and cry had yet to begin for the absent Count Niebuhr. Kelley accompanied Gwyn to his rented chambers over the Green Falcon. There the Queen's agent discovered a letter left in his name earlier that morning. He broke the seal with the point of his dagger and read it over while the elf-faced serving maid Nana deposited foaming tankards of cool, bitter ale on the table in Gwyn's sitting room. Kelley threw one booted foot up on an empty chair and fell upon his drink with gusto. His throat was caked with dust from the long ride back from the deserted farmhouse.

"Nana, did you see who delivered this note?" Gwyn asked the serving wench in her native Bohemian.

"It was a boy, sir," she said, flashing Kelley a smile of encouragement. "Country lad, by the look of him."

Kelley dropped his dark gaze to the foam in his tankard and dourly swirled his ale. Concern over the fate of his wife had left him with little inclination to flirt. Gwyn thanked the girl and waited until she closed the door.

"A paid messenger," he said to Kelley. "Probably doesn't know how to read, which is just as well."

He passed the letter to Kelley, who wiped his lips on the back of his hand before accepting it. The letter was in English. Kelley read it aloud.

The Jesuits have taken the Doctor to the country estate of Count Igor Kozminsky. I am alone and can do nothing to safeguard him. Send men who are resolute and know the use of the sword. A friend in Christ.

In place of a signature stood the hastily drawn symbol of the hieroglyphic monad.

"Do you know the meaning of this sign?" Gwyn asked Kelley.

"It signifies fraternity," Kelley told him evasively. "The man who made this mark can be trusted."

Gwyn drank deeply from his tankard.

"I hope so. We may need to rely on his help. I have no agents in Prague I can take on a fighting expedition. We'll have to risk it alone, unless you know someone willing to hazard his neck for John Dee."

"The Jew who owns the house where we're staying is his good friend," Kelley murmured. "He's an old man, but others of his race look upon him as their leader."

Gwyn laughed.

"You think a Jew is going to pick up a sword to fight for a Christian? Don't be foolish."

Kelley drained the dregs of his ale and grimaced at the bitter flavor. He banged the empty tankard down decisively on the table.

"You're probably right. Even so, I'd better get back to the house to see if the women have been found."

Gwyn nodded.

"I'll find out the safest approach to Kozminsky's estate. If memory serves me right, it's nearly a full day's ride from here. We'll need fresh horses."

"I know a stabler who should be able to provide us. By the way, do you have any idea where I can buy a brace of pistols? I gave my own set to John."

Gwyn looked at him and laughed.

"In this inn? Let's go downstairs. If you've enough gold I warrant you'll find a dozen men eager to sell you their arms."

"Gold is one thing I do have," Kelley said.

With Gwyn's help he negotiated to buy a brace of worn but well maintained German snaphance pistols with Italian barrels. They were not of the same quality as his own pair, but Kelley was reasonably certain they would not blow up in his face when he fired them. After agreeing to meet Gwyn at the stabler's in an hour, he rode there himself and arranged for the proprietor to have two fresh mounts saddled and waiting, then walked back to Loew's house.

The frantic anxiety of the previous night had given way to a strained expectation. A worried Rabbi Katz let him in.

"Any news?" Kelley asked, even though he guessed the answer from the rabbi's face.

"Nothing," Katz said with a discouraged shake of his curling side locks. "The Maharal's disciples have searched the entire ghetto. They are not within these walls. We have also made discrete inquiries at the hostelries on both banks of the river. Thus far no one has seen them. It's as if the earth opened and swallowed them up."

Kelley detected the frustration in his tone. Some shared emotion impelled him to put his hand on Katz's arm. He tried to keep the shadow of apprehension that darkened his own heart from his voice.

"We'll find them sooner or later. After all, where can they go? Unless...." A frown cut his forehead into angular planes.

"Unless what?"

"Is it possible the one responsible for the murders might have taken them?"

Rabbi Katz allowed the tension to fall from his shoulders. He shook his head with a slight smile.

"Put such a thought out of your mind. Whatever has happened to them, they are not with the assassin. I guarantee it."

Kelley wondered how he could be so certain, but before he could ask, Katz turned and ascended the stair. Kelley followed silently. At the first landing Miriam Loew met the rabbi with a troubled expression. Dark crescents beneath her eyes lent her regal face a haunted look.

"I heard the door. Has there been any word?"

"I'm sorry, Miriam, no, nothing yet," Katz told her.

She glanced at Kelley but did not speak. When the alchemist walked past her, she turned her face away. He saw that Loew's wife had chosen to blame him for the disappearance of her daughter, and in his heart Kelley could not find reason to resent her judgement. He blamed himself.

Loew sat in his library working at his desk, or at least pretending to work. He stood quickly when Katz ushered Kelley into the room and removed his ivory spectacles. Katz started to withdraw but Loew motioned for him to remain.

"This concerns you as much as it does me, Yitzhaq. Esther is my daughter, but she is your wife."

He turned to Kelley with such a look of anticipation that Kelley found it difficult to speak.

"I've heard nothing about the women. I'm here to ask for your help on another matter."

The old man maintained his composure. If he felt disappointment, he did not allow it to show on his deeply lined face. He invited Kelley with a gesture to walk with him to the sitting area in front of the fireplace. They sat together on the settee while Katz took a chair opposite.

"What may I do to help you, my friend?" Loew asked.

Kelley related the finding of Niebuhr's corpse at the meeting place and described the letter "J" that had been scratched into the floor by the body. He repeated Gwyn's surmise that Dee was being held at the house of a Jesuit sympathizer and recited from memory the contents of the mysterious note.

"We don't know what kind of force we may be up against, or even if the note is genuine," he concluded. "Gwyn has no confederates in Prague he can rely on in a fight."

A troubled expression clouded Loew's solemn gray eyes.

"So you want me to send you Jewish warriors who will fight beside you for the life of John Dee. Is that it? I am very sorry, Edward, but my disciples are scholars of the Torah. They can't stain their hands with human blood. Anyway, none of them would know one end of a sword from the other."

"You must have some followers who know how to fight," Kelley persisted.

Loew nodded reluctantly.

"We have trained men for the defense of the ghetto in the terrible event, may the Holy One, blessed be He, forbid it, that we should ever be attacked from outside. However, I can't ask them to offer up their lives for a stranger they don't even know."

"Would they do it if you asked them?"

"Undoubtedly. But don't you see, my friend, I have no right to abuse their trust in such a way. Even if I called them together and explained John's predicament, many of them would offer to fight beside you merely because they would believe I wished it. They would do this even if I told them to decide freely, to please me. I cannot place them in such a situation. Most men of the militia have wives and children."

"I understand," Kelley said bitterly.

"I would gladly go with you myself, but I must remain here to coordinate the search for Esther. And of course the other ladies," he added as an afterthought.

"Maybe it's just as well," Kelley told him. "A small force will have the advantage of surprise. Gwyn and I both know how to fight. A clumsy band of Torah scholars would likely be more of a hindrance than an aid."

Loew stood up on stiff, arthritic knees to signal the end of the interview. Rabbi Katz escorted Kelley from the library.

Kelley could not find it in his heart to feel angry at the old man. He understood Loew's position. His prime concern was the safety of his daughter, and the recovery of the Book of Lilith. He did not wish to embroil his disciples in what was essentially a dispute between Christians. The last thing the Jews of Prague needed was another reason for the Jesuits to persecute them. Even so, disappointment left a sour taste in his mouth.

"I'm going with you," Katz said after closing the padded red leather door behind them.

"You?"

A bark of harsh laughter escaped from Kelley's throat before he could suppress it. He looked at the slender shoulders and the soft, unmarked face of the young rabbi. Determination gleamed in Katz's solemn brown eyes.

"Forgive me, Rabbi, I didn't mean to laugh, but you caught me by surprise. Why should you want to fight?"

Katz shrugged.

"You need help, don't you?"

"Forgive me again, but have you ever fired a pistol?"

"No."

"Have you ever used a sword? A knife? Have you ever killed a man?"

Katz shook his head.

"Well then, what can you possibly do to help us?"

"I can try."

Kelley resisted the impulse to tell the Jew it took more than good intentions to go up against a skilled swordsman. At the very least it required years of training, coupled with a considerable fund of practical experience. He reflected that the pistol was a less difficult, albeit a less artistic, weapon. It might be just possible to teach Katz enough so that he would not shoot himself in the foot, or more importantly, shoot Kelley in the back of the head, by accident.

"Do you own a snaphance pistol?"

"I know where I can get a wheel-lock pistol."

"A heavy weapon to carry, but dependable. What about a horse?"

"I can borrow one."

Kelley met his gaze and grasped him by the forearm. He shook the arm of the young Jew vigorously and slapped him on the shoulder.

"You've got heart, anyway. That's worth fifty pounds in any fight," he lied. "I only hope I'm not making your wife a widow."

He regretted the last words as soon as they passed his lips. Mention of his missing wife brought an expression of tortured concern onto the face of the Jew. It passed in a moment. Katz forced a smile.

"I'll do my best not to slow you down."

As good as his word, Katz had managed to keep up with Gwyn and Kelley during the long, torturous ride

into the hills. His lack of riding skill was painfully evident
to the other men, but they made no comment. Nor did
the rabbi complain, even when he tumbled off into the
ditch. He merely brushed the dust from his broad black
hat in silence and remounted his bewildered mare.

They pressed their weary mounts as hard as they dared
on the open highway. About a mile before meeting the
private road that led across the Kozminsky estate, Gwyn
turned into the dense forest on the northern side, intend-
ing to approach the house in a wide crescent to avoid
detection. They wasted more than an hour of precious
daylight beating their way through the undergrowth, only
to find their progress blocked repeatedly by small pocket
bogs and steep ravines. Now they were truly lost.

The overhanging boughs became so dense, the three
dismounted and led their horses by hand through the
shadowed undergrowth.

"If only I could see the damned stars, I might be able
to get a bearing," Gwyn muttered.

"If we keep walking north, we're bound to come
upon the lake," Kelley pointed out. "We can follow its
margin to the house."

"You're sure we're moving north?" Gwyn said doubtfully.

"No, I'm not sure," Kelley snapped. "Why didn't you
think to bring a compass?"

"What the devil would I be doing with a compass,
when I'm more than a hundred leagues from the sea?"

"Gentlemen, I don't like to interrupt your conversation," Katz said mildly. "But I think you should know
that someone is watching us."

They turned to see a young woman emerge into the
small clearing. She stood regarding them, as naked as Eve,
a smile playing about the corners of her red lips. In the

deep gloom her pale, slender body glowed with its own luminescence against the somber evergreens. Berry bushes concealed her legs up to the knees, so that she appeared almost to float upon the twilight. Her long blond hair, more white than yellow, lifted and played around her large green eyes.

Gwyn let the reins of his horse drop and pressed through the bushes toward the apparition.

"What are you doing here, girl?" he asked in Bohemian. "Don't you know you can get lost in the woods at night?"

The woman did not answer. She raised her arms and held out her hands to Gwyn.

"The girl's probably simple in the head," Kelley said uneasily in English.

"If she lives around here she must know the way to Kozminsky's estate," Gwyn answered in the same language. He smiled and extended a welcoming hand toward her. "Where does Kozminsky live? You know, Count Kozminsky?"

"Don't touch her," Katz told him.

Gwyn drew back his hand just as his fingers were about to brush those of the girl.

"I won't hurt her," Gwyn said with amusement. "Though by the look of her, she wouldn't mind a pat or two on the bottom."

"Look at her hair."

"What about it?" Kelley asked.

He watched the fine white strands drift off the girl's ivory shoulders and rise to screen her parted lips with their gossamer veil.

"There's no wind," Katz said. "Would you tell me, please, what's moving her hair?"

Gwyn's eyes widened. He stepped back. Kelley cursed and drew his rapier. The metallic hiss of the long ribbon of steel as it cleared the brass guard of its scabbard sang a death song in the wilderness hush. Gwyn fumbled and drew his pistols.

"Don't fire," Kelley warned him. "You'll alert the house."

The mocking expression on the face of the girl did not change. Slowly she rose into the air. With a shiver of horror Kelley saw that she had no feet. Her luminous white legs ended at the knees. Below the stumps there was only a kind of swirling black smoke.

"It's a lamia," Kelley cried. "Don't let it touch you."

The apparition drifted toward Gwyn with its arms outstretched. He quickly moved to put himself behind the body of his horse, but the animal reared and pranced at the end of its reins until its body pressed into the stiff evergreen boughs at the margin of the clearing. Gwyn cursed and fell backward over his own feet in his haste to get out of reach of the inexorably approaching spirit.

Rabbi Katz began to chant in Hebrew. The head of the creature snapped around on its slender neck with inhuman force. It glared and snarled at the Jew. Slowly, under the impact of the chanted letters, the left side of its face melted and began to slide downward like wax exposed to the flame of a candle. Kelley leapt forward and swung the curved tip of his blade at the creature's neck. The steel passed through with light resistance, as if cutting water. Where the blade penetrated, the flesh healed itself while he watched.

He remembered the flying thing on the mast of the Bridget during the stormy Channel crossing. The body of this fell shade was of a similar nebulous substance, half matter and half mist. It might even be the same watchful spirit that had followed them from England.

"Cut at it, Gwyn," he cried. "It can't slay us until it takes on a solid body."

The two men slashed and hacked repeatedly at the shimmering form of the spirit while Katz continued his monotonous, rolling chant. The combination of holy words and cold steel proved too much for the creature. With a shriek of frustration it expanded into a whirling disk of black sparks and dissolved into the gathering darkness.

They stood staring at each other, swords raised to strike. In the distance echoed the shriek of something that might have been a owl. After a few moments Kelley sheathed his rapier. As though in a dream, Gwyn imitated his action with his shorter saber.

"What was that you chanted?" Kelley asked Katz.

"A sacred text," Katz shrugged. "We call it the Kedushah."

"How is it said in English?"

The rabbi paused to consider.

"'Holy, holy, holy is the Lord of Hosts: the whole earth is filled with His glory.'"

"Isaiah," Gwyn said. He seemed to shake himself from a nightmare and flashed white teeth at Kelley. "The pastor of our local parish was always assigning us children verses to memorize. That's one of the things that drove me to sea."

Kelley could make out the white blaze that ran through Gwyn's hair and beard, but little else. In a few minutes it would be black as pitch.

"We'd better press on," he muttered.

"Which way?" Katz asked.

The three men cast blank looks at each other. None of them had the faintest notion.

Kelley took a breath and closed his eyes. He extended his mind through his inner darkness. It was difficult without the aid of the crystal. He felt nothing.

"Madimi," he muttered. "It's Edward. I need you. Come to me, Madimi. Come, damn you. John's in trouble. John needs your help."

After five futile minutes, Kelley gave up. The spirit Madimi had never liked him, he reflected. He was not surprised that it would choose to let him rot in the forest, but he had hoped it would respond to him for Dee's sake. Dee and Madimi were so close, Kelley often thought their relationship unnatural. Dee treated the quick-witted little spirit almost as if she were his own child. Kelley had always been a bit afraid of her, and even more so of her unseen Mother.

"We may as well try to get some sleep here," he said with disgust. "We don't dare move a step in this ink."

"Look there," Gwyn cried. "A light."

"A will-o'-the-wisp," Kelley said, watching the shimmering ball of green fire dance and dart between the boughs of the trees.

"Maybe it's the lamia," Katz suggested.

The motions of the globe had a playful appearance, like those of a ball thrown by a child. Something about the fiery sphere was strangely familiar. Kelley cursed under his breath and laughed as he realized the truth. The green sphere was exactly the shade of Madimi's dress.

"It's no lamia," he told them. "It our guide. Come on, we have to follow it."

THIRTY-NINE

Joanna jerked awake from her nightmare with a silent scream on her lips. She felt a hand upon her shoulder and instinctively rolled off the opposite side of her narrow cot. The crystal tinkle of Jane's pitiless laughter brought her to her bare feet with her fists clenched.

"I wanted you to know how vulnerable you are," Jane told her.

A glowing oil lamp on the table showed the open door of her tower prison. Darkness crouched on the other side of the narrow window. The hour must be late. No hooded sentinel stood guard outside the door. Jane had come alone to taunt her. Was it possible that in her madness Jane had acted without the knowledge or authority of the Sons of Coronzon? Joanna licked dry, cracked lips and wondered how to make the best of her opportunity.

"You look thirsty," Jane said with concern. "Why don't you have something to drink?"

"I need water," Joanna told her.

"That's not possible. But you can have all the wine you want. See, the bottle is still half full."

"I'm not thirsty," Joanna said firmly. If she was ever to escape from this nightmare, she must remain sober.

"Well, when you want a drink it's right here for you," Jane told her.

She gestured toward the table. Joanna saw a spatter of blood on her sleeve and put her hand over her mouth.

"Jane, there's blood on your shift."

Jane looked down at her sleeve, smiling strangely.

"I helped at a sacrifice. You should have been there, Joanna. It was so beautiful."

"Will you take me next time?" Joanna asked. She slid her foot sideward toward the open door. "I'd love to see it."

"First you must accept our Mother into your mind and heart," Jane said. Her pale face shone with fanatical enthusiasm.

"I'm trying, Jane, but all this is so strange to me."

"That's why I'm here, my love. To help you. The children of our Mother wanted to kill you, but I convinced them that you could serve them."

"Is that what happened to Esther? Did they kill her?"

"Esther is much too valuable to kill. When I told them she was the daughter of Judah Loew they were ecstatic." Her eyes darkened with jealousy. "I thought I was their great prize, but sometimes I think they value her more than they do me."

She rubbed her swollen belly and smiled.

"I have something Esther doesn't, something they need. It makes me more important than Esther. That's the only reason I haven't killed it."

Joanna slid another sidestep toward the beckoning doorway. Jane did not appear to notice.

"What do they want with your baby?"

"It's to be the earthly vehicle, silly. Our Lord Coronzon needs an uncontaminated host." Jane giggled. "They think it's so funny that it should be the seed of their pious enemy John Dee."

"You told me Edward was the father of your child." Another step.

"Did I? You shouldn't believe everything I say, Joanna. Coronzon is the father of all lies."

Joanna darted through the black rectangle and grabbed the heavy oak door as she passed. The last thing she saw before it banged shut was Jane's ironic smile. She shot home the iron bolt. In the night stillness it boomed like thunder.

"What do you think you're doing?" Jane asked through the door. "There's no escape from this place."

"We'll see about that," Joanna muttered.

By the lamplight that gleamed through the crack under the door she found the stone steps of the open stairwell and realized the spiral stair had no railing. Hugging the wall with her right hand, she felt her way downward. The tower seemed completely deserted; that, or everyone in it lay asleep. She heard no sound. Why didn't the fiend possessing Jane scream or hammer on the door? In the silence she was bound to be noticed.

Joanna counted nine landings before she lost track of their number. The tower could not possibly be so high. The conviction grew that she must be descending under the ground. This was a disquieting notion. Somewhere in the inky darkness she had passed an exit that led from the tower into the courtyard. But on which level? She considered retracing her steps, then decided to go on. There was no guarantee she could find the door out, and if she did it would probably be locked. She wanted to put distance between herself and her prison room before her escape was discovered.

A sound came to her ears, at first so faint it was lost under the thud of her own heartbeat. As she continued down, it grew louder. Male voices chanted in monotonous unison in a language unfamiliar to her. The sonorous sound possessed the rolling thunder and timeless rhythm of ocean waves breaking against the rocks. It echoed up from the depths as if from some vast subterranean chamber. As she listened, she detected its subtle music. It was not mere repetition of the same phrase, but a progression of some kind. After each cycle a new word was added to the chant and an old word dropped—if the barbaric sounds were words.

Fascinated in spite of her better judgement, she continued down. The rhythm of the chant drew her in a kind of trance. She caught herself breathing unconsciously in the same cadence as the chant and forced a slow, deep breath into her lungs. This cleared her head. She felt for the edge of the step she stood upon with her toe and bent forward to peer into the open well. Not far below she detected a faint red glow. She hastened toward it, anxious to get off the stair, which more and more appeared to be the stairway to hell itself.

The fiery light shone through an open doorway onto a landing. Joanna paused and cast a last glance down the stairwell. It yawned like a hungry throat. She shivered, wondering how far into the bowels of the earth it extended. Cautiously, she put her head around the edge of the door. A long corridor cut into raw stone stretched in either direction, lit by a single smoking oil lamp that dangled on iron chains from the ceiling.

The mesmerizing chant emanated from the dark extremity of the corridor on her left. It was much louder, even more compelling. It took all her strength of will not to run in its direction, voicing the guttural syllables in her own throat. She glanced up the opposite side of the corridor and wondered what secrets lay concealed in its shadows. Reason battled emotion in her heart. She felt compelled to follow the dark music of voices to its source and discover its meaning, yet she knew it would be foolhardy to run toward her captors when the other direction might lead to a way of escape.

A faint scream shattered her indecision. She recognized the voice of Esther Katz. Without pausing to consider, she hurried along the passage to her right, away from the siren song of the chant. The light of the lamp faded behind her. She caught herself on her extended hands against a stone wall, and realized the corridor had made a turning. In the distance she saw a pale rectangle that shone through an open side door. She hurried to the opening.

A second muffled cry impelled her through the doorway, careless of the consequences. The room beyond was empty. The light came through a narrow vertical slot set in a deep niche in the wall. Through the slot Joanna heard faint sounds of struggle, the slap of an open hand on bare flesh, the grunt of a male voice. With mounting horror, she forced herself toward the light. The nearer her face drew to the slot in the stone wall, the greater grew her reluctance to see what lay on the other side. The bar of light fell across the side of her face and illuminated her wide green eye.

The chamber on the far side of the wall was at a lower level, enabling Joanna to take in its occupants with a single glance. Esther Katz lay naked upon the bare stone floor, her arms and legs chained apart to iron rings. A blood-stained white cloth gagged her mouth. Fresh blood trickled onto her cheeks from her swollen nose. One of her eyes was purple and inflamed. Dark bruises and bleeding scratches covered her entire body. She stared blindly at the ceiling, a dull glaze of horror clouding her eyes, as her body jerked to the thrusts of the naked hooded man who raped her. Around her in a circle stood five other men, nude except for black hoods that somehow magnified the obscenity of their erect members.

The rapist drove himself brutally into Esther, shuddered in his climax, and lay still for a moment. In the silence Joanna heard the quick sobbing gasps of the tortured woman. He pushed himself off her trembling body without gentleness. Joanna saw with sick horror that her thighs were streaked with blood. Another hooded figure took the place of the first and began the same mindless, animal motion with his knotted buttocks.

A scream rose in Joanna's throat. Before she could contain it she found herself shouting Esther's name over and over, her voice strained to such unnatural thinness that she failed to recognize it as her own. She saw Esther's body jerk taunt against its chains. Several of the hooded men turned to gaze in the direction of her cries.

Joanna had no clear idea what she intended. Rage flamed in her heart. She knew only that she must reach the other woman and defend her against this unholy degradation, with her own life if necessary. The chamber she occupied had no second door. Joanna ran into the corridor to search for a way down to the lower chamber on the other side of the wall.

She noticed with one part of her awareness that the passage appeared strangely altered. Whereas she was certain it had bent to the right, it now bent to the left. Too maddened with fury to care, she hurried along it, feeling her way through the darkness that lay between the infrequent lamps. It twisted and angled back on itself in a bewildering maze as though the very stones were conscious of her purpose and determined to frustrate its realization. All the while the same monotonous cyclic chant progressed with the inexorable force of time itself. It taunted and maddened her. She could no longer determine its source. The sound seemed to be everywhere equally as it echoed through the corridors of her mind.

She found steps leading down and descended them. At the bottom a closed door beckoned. Her frustrated search had allowed her anger time to cool slightly. She approached the door with caution. Light from the other side of the door shone beneath it. With trembling fingers Joanna eased open the iron bolt and pressed the door inward. She looked through the widening crack into her own familiar tower room.

"I told you there was no escape," Jane said.

Joanna fainted.

When she awoke, she found herself lying on her cot. Jane stood at the foot of the bed, watching her with an enigmatic smile. Beside her stood one of the hooded sentinels. Mercifully, he was dressed in a long black robe and made no move toward her. Joanna pushed herself up to a sitting position. The room tilted and spun. She took a deep breath and closed her eyes for a moment until it stabilized. With grim determination she forced her body onto its feet and held herself upright with one hand on the head-rail of the cot.

"Stop torturing Esther. I'll do whatever you wish."

"Of course you will, silly thing," Jane said. "There was never any question of that."

With a trembling hand Joanna opened the bottle of wine and filled the pewter goblet. She drained it at a single breath and set it down empty. The warmth of the wine spread through all her muscles and nerves like a poison.

"There, I've done what you want. Now will you let Esther go?"

"I'm afraid that's not possible," Jane said.

She reached over and stroked the muscular arm of the silent hooded male beside her. He might as well have been carved from the same black granite that composed the walls.

"Why are you tormenting her?" Joanna demanded.

"A certain degree of moral degradation is necessary before the soul can give itself wholeheartedly to the Fallen One in the manifesting aspect of his consort, our Mother of Screeching," Jane explained in a light tone, as though describing the weather. "First it must be made to hate its own existence and long for death. In the place of death we give it oblivion from pain and remorse. Its acceptance of this soothing balm is a tacit obedience to our Mother and her Dark Lord."

"Who were the men I saw raping Esther?" Joanna's head swam with the sudden assault of the wine. She took a firmer grip on the wooden head-rail. "Were they Sons of Coronzon?"

"They are the Sons of the Inner Circle, who have dedicated themselves as living instruments of Coronzon through the vessel of Lilith, his queen. She takes each of them as lovers and makes them indefatigable in their lust. In return they perform a certain sacrifice to her as a bond of their fidelity."

"Sacrifice?" Joanna blinked the haze from her eyes and tried to focus upon Jane's mocking face.

"Tonight was a good start," Jane told her. "We'll talk again tomorrow."

She turned to leave the room. The pent-up fury in Joanna's heart, which had not previously found an outlet, burst forth. She hurled herself at the back of the other woman.

"You bitch! I'll kill you."

The silent hooded sentinel intercepted her with inhuman swiftness and caught her clawed hands by the wrists before they could sink themselves into Jane's slender back. Joanna fought like a mad woman. She managed to free one hand and clutched at the eyes of her captor. He ducked and struck her arm away. With it went his hood.

The sight of his face drained her strength. She sagged against his grasp, staring with a numb expression. The multiple shocks of the night had stolen from her any capacity to feel horror. She could only gaze mutely at his hairless head, which lacked even eyebrows and eyelashes. Ragged scars stood out with startling whiteness where his ears should have been. They circled the tiny holes of his ear canals. His nose had also been amputated. Joanna found her eyes drawn to the gaping black opening in the center of his face. The sunken, ascetic cheeks and worm-white complexion of this Son of the Inner Circle lent his head an uncanny resemblance to a skull with eyes.

Without haste he took his hood from her hand and put it back on.

"Beautiful, isn't he?" Jane said from the doorway. "If you're obedient I may reward you and send him to your bed. Would you like that, Joanna?"

FORTY

"Come closer. What have you to tell me?" The Italian crawled forward on his hands and knees, his head bowed. No matter how many times he approached the goddess, he always experienced the same craven terror.

"The formula nears its fulfillment. I estimate your priests will vibrate the final sequence in three days."

She raised an imperious hand. Her frown sent a shiver down his spine.

"Don't insult me with your foolish human concept of time. You know it signifies nothing with me. Will you be ready on the night of the new moon?"

"Yes, Mother."

"That is sufficient."

As the ritual formula of evocation neared its completion, Lilith became more human. She sat upon her throne of banded onyx, no greater in stature than an ordinary woman. The Italian observed the painted toes of her bare foot peep from beneath the hem of her scarlet gown and felt a heady wave of lust wash through him. Her beauty moved him so intensely, the sensation was almost painful. The top of her gown lay folded open to reveal her full breasts. The swell of her belly was scarcely apparent.

From her diadem shone the blazing splendor of Him-Who-Is-Fallen. The pale white fire of the great jewel scintillated over the surface of her limbs and empowered her. He felt the energy of the stone beat against his face like the rays of the summer sun at noon, yet it gave off no heat, only a certain electrical potency that charged the atmosphere and made his astral body tingle.

Even her throne room was more substantial than it had appeared during his last audience. It possessed mirrored walls and a gilded, ornate ceiling. Carved figures from some opium nightmare adorned its eleven angles. They distorted strangely and shifted their forms as he looked at them. Tall windows over their heads let in the same pale brightness that radiated from the jewel. He wondered if she would cause her astral palace to be duplicated in glass and stone when at last the Sons succeeded in bringing the Dark Lord forth into living flesh.

The dawn of the Aeon of Coronzon would not occur overnight. After his manifestation there would come a period of chaos as Lilith gathered her power and bred her children. This would be characterized by political strife, famine, plague, and warfare. How long it would endure, the Italian did not pretend to know. It might be months or years. She had promised that he would live to witness the shadow of her dark consort extend itself over the nations of the earth. With that he must content himself. Not for the first time, he speculated about his own role in the new order.

"You will be taken care of," she said, perceiving his thought. "Are you not my favorite?"

She regarded the Italian as a woman of substance might look upon her pampered lapdog, with amusement and detached affection.

"Has the Sacred Scribe been killed yet?"

He bowed his head.

"Not yet, Ancient One. The Jesuits seek to break his will and mold him to their purposes. I have allowed them to continue. His knowledge may prove useful during the coming political turmoil."

"Fool," she said with withering contempt. "The Scribe is dangerous. Now that I have his vessel in thrall, we no longer need him."

"Shall I have him executed?"

"Yes, immediately." She smiled. "But first, have him informed that you possess his wife and child. I want him to know that his seed serves our purpose before he dies."

He bowed again in acknowledgment. The urge to crawl away was strong, but he forced himself to remain at the foot of her throne. He sensed her mild interest.

"Is there something else?"

"Forgive me, Ancient One," he murmured. "Some months ago you promised to slay my half-brother. At last report he enjoys perfect health."

She stood. The crystal windows of the throne room darkened. Outside, thunder rolled. He felt her glare of anger as a palpable force pressing down upon his head. He did not dare meet her eyes.

"Do you question my power?"

"No, Mother. You are all-powerful."

"I will kill Aquaviva at my convenience, not yours. At present he fulfills my purposes upon the earth. The zealous priest acts on my behalf, yet goes on believing he serves his own craven Lord of Suffering."

The Italian gathered the tatters of his courage.

"You promised to kill him."

"In my own good time," she said, speaking each word separately.

He touched his forehead to the cool marble floor and awaited his death blow. When it failed to fall, he raised his trembling head. The goddess had reseated herself. She smiled at him with indulgence.

"Poor slave. Your hatred is so strong. I feel the killing lust in your black heart and sympathize with it. What you must understand is that my needs, no matter how trivial they may seem to you, are infinitely more important than your private desires. Have I made myself plain?"

"Perfectly, Ancient One."

"Then go and kill my enemy the Sacred Scribe, who in this incarnation calls himself John Dee. When you have done this little thing, we will talk again about the Black Pope, your hated half-brother."

FORTY-ONE

Kelley pursued the dancing green sphere for what seemed an eternity, through dense undergrowth in darkness so thick he could barely distinguish the outline of the black gelding he led at the end of its reins. Gwyn and Katz stayed close behind, each with one hand on the flank of the mount in front. Riding was out of the question. It was a challenge merely to find an opening in the evergreen scrub wide enough to walk through.

To Kelley's hypersensitive awareness they sounded like a herd of oxen lumbering through a hayfield. No one spoke, but each creak of a saddle harness, every snapping twig, even the periodic slaps against the marauding mosquitoes, echoed through the night stillness. He expected at any moment to be ambushed by Jesuits alerted a mile in advance to their approach by the noise they were making.

Abruptly, he stopped and cursed under his breath. A horse snorted behind him in the darkness.

"Why have we stopped here?" Gwyn whispered at his shoulder.

"The will-o'-the-wisp. It vanished. Damn that spirit, I knew she couldn't be trusted."

"Listen," Rabbi Katz hissed. "Do you hear something?"

They held their breath and strained their ears. Faintly from the distance in front of them came the peeping of frogs.

"We must be close to the lake," Gwyn said.

Kelley pressed forward, stopping every hundred feet to take his bearing from the song of the frogs. It grew steadily stronger. In the space of a few steps they passed out of the dense forest onto a level lawn. Before them stretched the surface of a small lake, its water revealed by the reflection of starlight. To the right they saw the outline of a large manor house with lamps burning in several windows on the ground level. It was surrounded by substantial out-buildings.

They tied their horses at the edge of the trees and made their way toward the main house. Peter Gwyn automatically took the lead. Kelley did not argue. During his years at sea Gwyn had served in numerous nighttime raiding parties on hostile shores. No training could be better suited for their present needs.

They reached the corner of the house without incident. Kelley peered through a window. A bald, beardless man sat at a desk, reading. His face was indistinct through the wavy leaded panes. From somewhere else in the house a dog began to bark. The bald man raised his head and said something through the open study door. He turned to look at the window.

Kelley ducked down. Gwyn touched his arm and motioned him around the corner. They waited with their backs pressed to the brick. A door rattled open in the rear of the house. Footfalls crunched on the gravel walk. They saw the dancing yellow glow of a lantern. Gwyn put his hand on Kelley's shoulder and squeezed. Kelley nodded, not certain whether Gwyn could see him in the blackness. He drew one of his pistols and cocked the hammer back with the lock pressed into his sleeve to muffle the click. Even so, it sounded loud in his ears.

A single figure with a lantern in his left hand and a pistol in his right paced slowly past the corner of the house and stopped. He raised his light and peered into the darkness across the lawn at the distant trees. Large white moths flashed around his head, attracted to the glow of the candle, which was magnified by the bullseye glass in the lantern window. He stood this way for several minutes. At last he lowered the light and started to walk around the angle of the house.

Gwyn touched Kelley sharply on the arm. Kelley heard Katz draw in a ragged breath and prayed the Jew would not shoot him in the back through sheer nervousness. He ran lightly forward across the grass, the rustle of his footsteps swallowed up in the louder crush of the gravel. He threw his left arm around the throat of the watchman and pressed the cold barrel of his pistol against his temple.

"One sound and I'll blow your brains out," he hissed in Bohemian.

The man struggled for an instant before he realized his situation. Gwyn wrapped his palm over the hammer of the sentry's pistol to prevent it being cocked and tore the weapon from his grasp. The lantern fell to the gravel walk and landed on its side. Kelley dragged the man back into the shadow close to the house while Katz picked up the lantern. Its flame ceased to flutter and strengthened when he turned it upright.

"Bring the light close," Gwyn told him.

The Rabbi raised it to the face of their captive. It revealed a young man with clear gray eyes, noble features, and straight, sandy hair.

"He's hardly more than a boy," Katz whispered.

Gwyn returned his pistol to his belt and passed the captured gun to the rabbi. He drew out his dirk and held up the long blade so that it gleamed in the glow from the lantern.

"How many men are in the house? Quick, lad, or I'll cut you from ear to ear."

"Six men," he said in a hoarse voice. His rolling eyes focused on Gwyn. "Are you Peter Gwyn the Englishman?"

"How do you know me?" Gwyn demanded. He pressed the point of his dirk into the youth's throat. "Were you warned of our coming?"

"No, I swear. I'm a friend. I wrote to tell you that John Dee was being taken to this house."

Gwyn glanced at Kelley, then studied the honest face of the youth. It signified nothing, Kelley thought. Jesuits were consummate liars.

"How do we know you're telling the truth?" Kelley demanded.

"Hold up your hand. I'll show you."

Kelley raised his hand. The young man took it and traced a symbol upon the palm with his index finger. Kelley felt the familiar outline of Dee's hieroglyphic monad.

"He wrote the letter," Kelley acknowledged to Gwyn.

"That doesn't mean he's on our side," Gwyn said.

"I am, I swear it by holy Christ."

"Are you a Jesuit?" Kelley asked.

The young man met his gaze without flinching.

"Yes. I joined the Society of Jesus when the Jesuits killed my father and stole his estates. I changed my name and entered their ranks to work against them from within."

"What is your true name?" Rabbi Katz asked.

"Jacques Bourinot. My father was Jean Bourinot, a Huguenot who served in the court of Henry of Navarre."

Gwyn grunted in surprise.

"I've heard of him. Your father was a brave man."

"There's no time for talk," Bourinot whispered urgently. "John Dee is being held in the vaults under the house. He is being put to the question even as we speak by a monster named Paul Normand."

Kelley grabbed him by the front of his jerkin and whirled him around. Bourinot blinked at the savage gleam in the dark man's eyes.

"Normand is here, in this house?"

"He is, along with two servants, another Jesuit lay brother, and an agent from Italy named Michael Giovanni. It was Father Giovanni who ordered Normand to capture Dee alive. Before that we had orders to kill him on sight."

"I don't know any Giovanni," Gwyn murmured. "Did he come with papal authority?"

"No, but his seal was that of Aquaviva himself."

"He must be a man of power," Gwyn said to Kelley. "I'd give my eyeteeth to question him."

"How can we get into the house without being seen?" Kelley asked the young Huguenot.

"This way. I'll show you."

They followed him down the dark side of the house. He stopped before an open casement, its sill four feet above the level of the gravel walk.

"The room beyond is empty. I left this window open because of the heat."

Kelley vaulted easily up to the sill and stepped down into the room. He helped Bourinot through the window, then stood back watchfully while Bourinot lent his arm to assist Gwyn and Katz.

"How do we reach the vaults?" Gwyn whispered.

"There's a concealed door in the study. Giovanni is in there reading."

They entered the study through a side door. Azoth threw his arms across his face in surprise when he saw them. After a moment he composed himself and allowed his hands to fall gently on either side of the parchment on the desk before him, his frosty gray eyes fixed on the muzzle of the pistol in Kelley's hand. It was pointed at a spot between his finely sculptured eyebrows.

"I know this man," Kelley murmured to Gwyn. "He tried to stiletto me at the Rose Theater in London. He's no more a Jesuit than I am."

Gwyn crossed the room and softly closed the door that led out to the front hallway. He tilted the back of a chair beneath its latch and wedged its legs firmly in place.

"So you are a traitor," Azoth said to Bourinot in a moderate tone with only the slightest trace of an Italian accent. "I suspected it the first day I met you."

"If you cry out there will be no need for silence," Gwyn told him. "I'll put a bullet in your guts."

For a man facing imminent death, Azoth was strangely at ease. He stood slowly from his seat and spread his arms as he backed away from the desk to show that he carried no weapon.

"Edward Kelley, I presume. And you must be Peter Gwyn. I confess I do not recognize the third member of your party."

"Tell him nothing," Gwyn said quickly.

A rough male voice spoke outside the barricaded door. Azoth tilted his head and looked inquiringly at Gwyn but made no attempt to speak. They heard the latch rattle.

"Father, is all well?" the voice called through the panels in Bohemian. "We heard voices."

"Help me!" Azoth bellowed loud enough to rattle the ceiling beams.

Gwyn leveled his pistol. A flash as bright as summer lightning filled the room and blinded all of them. Blinking through blue spots, Kelley saw Azoth raise something small in his left hand. A jet of fire cracked from it. Bourinot, who stood on Kelley's left side, groaned and fell clutching his breast. Azoth streaked across the room and vanished through the open side door. Both Kelley and Gwyn fired almost simultaneously. The lead balls from their pistols chipped the woodwork of the jamb.

With a curse Kelley jerked his other pistol from his belt and dashed after the adept. The room beyond lay empty. Reluctantly, he drew back and bolted the door from the inside. Thunderous blows began to rain upon the panels of the other door. Kelley thought quickly.

"That chair won't keep them out for long. You three stay here. Fire on them when they break in. I'm going down to the vaults to get John."

The blade of an ax crashed through one of the panels and sent a two foot splinter of oak flying across the room.

"All right," Gwyn said. "Watch yourself."

Kelley went to Bourinot and raised him to his feet.

Blood streamed between the fingers of the young Huguenot. The wound lay dangerously close to his heart.

"Can you open the door to the vaults?"

"I can work it," Bourinot gritted between his teeth. "Just get me over there."

Kelley supported him to an innocuous-looking section of bookcase. Bourinot reached under one of the shelves and pulled a concealed lever. He drew open the bookcase to show a stone stair leading down into darkness. Kelley accepted the lantern from Katz.

A pistol cracked outside the window. Glass fell like scattered diamonds across the desk.

"Put out the lamp," Gwyn shouted at Katz. "That bastard Giovanni is firing on us."

The rabbi ran to the desk and blew out the flame of the reading lamp that sat on one corner. Kelley concealed the lantern beneath a fold of his cloak.

"Close the door over behind me so this light won't betray you," he told the white-faced Bourinot, who nodded weakly.

He stepped onto the stair. The bookcase swung silently shut being him. Drawing his charged pistol, he uncloaked the lantern and descended. No sound emanated from the chambers below. He proceeded cautiously along a vaulted corridor toward a flickering light at the far end. It was scarcely to be believed that those in the vault had not heard the sound of gunfire above.

When he emerged into the lamplit vault he saw Dee naked and bound head down to an inclined wooden rack. His thin body was covered with filth and blood. Kelley took several involuntary steps forward, blinded to the danger by his concern for his friend.

"Courage, John. I'll get you out of here."

Dee rolled his eyes at Kelley and made an effort to focus. He blinked in recognition. An expression of urgency hardened his features.

"Edward," he gasped. "Behind you...."

Kelley whirled and fired in the same motion. The dark- haired Jesuit fell like a stone with a lead ball through his forehead. Normand froze with his rapier drawn, a snarl on his handsome, aristocratic face. Kelley let the pistol drop from his fingers and pulled his rapier. Watching

Normand, he set the lantern aside. The Frenchman realized then that Kelly's other pistol had already been fired. He smiled and drew himself up to his full height.

"I will give you a lesson in the sword, Englisher."

Kelley stepped into the open area between the circle of devilish torture machines, his gaze fixed on the smug blue eyes of the Jesuit.

"Did you know that I studied under Henry of Lorraine's private fencing instructor?" Normand asked conversationally. "I've killed seven men in duels. You can't imagine how I've looked forward to this moment. Christ himself must have led you to me."

Their blades clashed experimentally. Kelley felt surprise at the uncommon strength in the Frenchman's wrist but did not allow it to show in his eyes. Forsaking finesse, he used the power of his arm to beat down the blade of his foe and force him to step back. Once he had Normand pinned against the wall it would be harder for the Frenchman to avoid his thrusts. Normand read Kelley's mind and with a nimble sidestep freed himself from the wall and found the open floor. Kelley circled around the frame of the rack in frustration. Normand could not match his power, but held his own in the fight with the precision of his parries. Sparks rang from the striking steel.

Kelley felt the air against his left cheek and knew it had been a near miss. No, not a miss, he corrected himself. He tasted the salt of his own blood on his lip. He forced a smile. A scratch was nothing. The tip had spared his eye. He redoubled his overhead cuts and experienced the satisfaction of feeling the blade droop in Normand's grip. For all the skill of the Frenchman, his arm was growing tired. Not many men were strong enough to wield the long blade of a rapier for more than a few minutes. Kelley with his bull vitality was one of them.

Normand glanced down at Dee stretched out beside him while he parried and thrust under Kelley's hacking attack. The alchemist read what was in his mind. Normand longed to take an instant to slice through Dee's slender exposed throat. He did not do so only because he knew the least break in his concentration would bring his own death. Kelley hoped he would try it anyway. He was fairly certain he could kill Normand before Normand killed Dee.

Two muffled shots sounded down the stair and through the open doorway into the vault. Kelley turned his head an instant to see if any fresh attack threatened from this quarter. Normand caught him off guard and launched a furious assault that sent the alchemist stumbling back. With a cry of triumph the Jesuit beat the blade from Kelley's hand.

"Now I will kill you. I only wish I could rape your cow of a wife also, but then, deferred pleasures are always the sweetest."

Kelley felt a slender chain against his right hand and realized it was attached to one of the carved stone balls that hung from the vaulted ceiling. When Normand lunged for his killing stroke, Kelley twisted his body to avoid the thrusting steel and jerked the ring of the chain off its iron bracket. Standing to his full height, he swung the stone cherub like a mace with both hands. The heavy stone ball caught Normand on the crown. His skull make an audible noise as it crushed inward. He fell like a poleaxed bull, his brain spilling out through the jagged gap.

Kelley gasped deep lungfuls of the cool cellar air. He had come close to death many times in his colorful life, but never closer than tonight. He looked at Dee. The older man met his gaze solemnly, his face inverted and his long, dirty beard hanging down on one side almost to the stone floor.

"A cherub has carried our friend to heaven," he murmured.

Kelley ignored the enigmatic words, thinking they sprang from a fevered brain. He hurried to Dee and cut his bonds, then helped his off the escalera. So stiff were Dee's joints, he could not stand under his own power.

"Hold me up," he gasped. "I'll be better in a minute once the blood begins to flow."

"From the look of you it's been flowing freely," Kelley said, gazing over the burns and scabs on Dee's naked limbs.

"You saved me from the water torture," Dee said, indicating a clay jug on the floor. "Which reminds me, do you think you can upend that vessel? My throat's as dry as a harlot's cheek."

Kelley laughed at this uncharacteristic language. He hefted the clay jug and tilted it so that Dee could drink from its mouth. Water ran down either side of his beard as he gulped at the flow.

"Enough," he gasped, pushing the jug away. "Let's get out of here. I assume you have confederates above?"

"I did when I left them," Kelley said.

He gathered up his rapier and sheathed it, then found his spent pistol. He stripped off his cloak and wrapped it around Dee's shoulders. It would provide at least some shield for the natural modesty of the philosopher, he thought. Prying Normand's blade from the fingers of the corpse, he handed it to Dee. The older man hefted it in a way that revealed he knew something of swordsmanship.

Kelley's momentary surprise gave way to admiration. Years ago he had discovered that John Dee knew something about everything. There was not a man in England, perhaps not in the entire world, with a wider span of learning.

Taking up the lantern, Kelley led Dee up the stone stairway. No light shone through the crack around the bookcase. He listened. Silence.

"Gwyn? Katz? Are you there?"

The bookcase swung open on darkness. Kelley put his hand on the hilt of his dagger, then relaxed when he recognized the solemn face of Rabbi Katz in the lantern's glow. Gwyn stood behind him, supporting the wounded Jacques Bourinot on his shoulder.

"I think Kozminsky's house servants have fled," Gwyn told him. "We heard horses on the gravel."

"They shattered the door with an ax," Katz said. His limpid dark eyes danced with excitement. "We were ready for them. Captain Gwyn put a ball in the first man's shoulder. I think I hit him in the thigh. They had no stomach for a real fight and ran away."

He took the lantern from Kelley and used its flame to relight the reading lamp on the desk while Kelley helped Dee into the padded chair.

"What about Giovanni?" Kelley asked.

"Giovanni?" Dee murmured. "You mean Azoth."

"Who is this Azoth?" Katz wanted to know.

Dee explained the ability of the Jesuit impostor to assume different faces, and told how he had imitated the features of the murdered Count Niebuhr.

"He carried the scar of the man who stabbed Beecher the actor at the Rose in London," Dee told Kelley.

"He's the same man. I recognized him."

"It's my guess that he also killed the real Michael Giovanni and assumed his place in order to manipulate the Jesuits for his own purposes."

"Did you ever see Giovanni alter his face?" Gwyn asked the pale-cheeked Bourinot.

The Huguenot shook his head.

"To me he always looked the same. A thin man with a high forehead, long black hair, and a spade beard."

Kelley glanced at Gwyn. This was not a description of the man they had encountered earlier.

Bourinot groaned and fell to one knee. For the first time Dee noticed his injury. He pushed himself weakly to his feet.

"Bring the boy into the chair," he ordered.

He opened the young Huguenot's doublet and undershirt and examined his wound with a worried expression while Kelley held the reading lamp close.

"The ball broke a rib," he murmured. "It's not deep. I can see it. Edward, lend me your knife."

Kelley handed over his dagger. Dee passed its slender blade through the flame of the lamp, then applied its point to the gaping wound in the chest of the Frenchman. Bourinot gritted his teeth but made no outcry. The sharp point of the dagger proved an ideal instrument for the surgery. Dee pried out the bloody lead ball, which had flattened upon impact with the youth's rib. He tore a section from the hem of Bourinot's undershirt and folded it against the wound to stop it bleeding.

"A souvenir," he said, handing the ball to the sweat-drenched Huguenot. "Thank you for what you did. I owe you my life."

"And I owe you mine," Bourinot said with a smile.

"Rest now," Dee said, patting him on the shoulder.

The troubled expression did not leave his face. The Sons of Coronzon were known to poison their weapons. Only time would reveal whether he had saved the life of the brave Huguenot or merely increased his suffering.

He noticed the parchment on the desk and picked it up to examine it.

"Well, well, what have we here?"

"Not the cipher letter," Kelley said. "We couldn't be so lucky."

"We are, though. I wonder what it's doing here?"

"Giovanni, or Azoth as you call him, was studying it when we broke in," Gwyn told him.

"Probably trying to decode it himself," Dee murmured. He spent several minutes looking it over, then folded it and put it into a pocket on the inside of Kelley's cloak. "I only wish I had the Queen's gold to go with it."

"You have that also," Kelley told him. "Most of it, anyway."

"What do you mean, most of it?"

Kelley explained that he had used some of the gold to rent horses and buy pistols. Dee was shocked.

"That gold belongs to Elizabeth. It wasn't ours to spend."

"The Queen has the cipher and most of her gold as well," Kelley said. "I don't think she'll complain."

"You don't know the Queen," Dee said. He grasped Kelley by the forearm. "Let that pass for the moment and tell me, Edward, is Jane well? I had a terrible dream that she has come into some danger."

Kelley glanced at Rabbi Katz. There was no easy way to speak of the disappearance.

"Joanna Kelley and your wife, along with my wife, Esther, left the house of the Maharal two days ago. They

did not return and no one has been able to find them,"
Katz explained.

"The Sons have them," Dee said with conviction.

He described his strange dream encounter with Jane,
and her transformation into Lilith. The others silently
digested this information.

"Still, it may only have been a nightmare," Gwyn
pointed out.

"The Sons have them," Dee repeated. "I know it."

"I wonder if this disappearance has anything to do
with what Father Giovanni said in the college at Prague?"
Bourinot murmured, his eyes half-closed. His aristocratic
face had begun to flush with the first glow of fever.

"What did he say?" Kelley demanded.

"I was standing outside the door. He didn't know I
was there." The youth winced, waiting for his pain to sub-
side. "He spoke to someone about conveying the captives
to the Black Mountain. The words held no meaning for
me at the time they were spoken, so I forgot about them."

"I know the Black Mountain," Gwyn told them. "It
lies on the border between Bohemia and Silesia. There's a
high pass that runs over its shoulder, with a ruined
fortress. The road through the pass is closed by snows in
the winter and is little used."

Rabbi Katz said something in Yiddish and stared at
Kelley with excitement.

"For months the Maharal has been searching for the
fortress of the Sons of Coronzon, and all the time it's
been right under our noses."

"I saw a stronghold in the mountains," Kelley said to
Dee, his own excitement rising in spite of his better judgement. "When we scried with Rabbi Loew. Remember?"

Dee nodded.

"It's a place to start, in any case. We'd better leave this house. The men who fled will return with reinforcements. I hate to move you, Jacques, but you can't stay here."

"I understand. Put me on a horse. I can ride."

"He must be taken back to Prague, where he can receive the care of a physician," Dee told Kelley.

"I, too, must return at once," Katz said. "The Maharal will want to know what we have discovered tonight."

"You go back," Kelley told Dee. "I'll ride ahead to sound out the fortress."

"You can't go alone," Dee said firmly. "It's too dangerous. If this truly is the fortress of Coronzon, it will be guarded by dreadful sentinels. You wouldn't stand a chance."

"I'm going," Kelley said with a scowl, daring Dee to contradict him.

"But not alone."

Gwyn grinned at Kelley, displaying his even white teeth against the shocking white blaze of his beard. There was a wild, reckless light in his hazel eyes. Too overcome by emotion to speak, Kelley locked his forearm with that of the mariner.

Dee looked at the two men and shook his head.

"You're either the bravest fools I've ever met, or the most foolhardy heroes."

They retrieved their horses from the edge of the lawn and led them to the house. Two additional mounts were taken from the stable and saddled for Dee and Bourinot. Rabbi Katz managed to find Dee's clothes in a pile in the corner of the kitchen. Dee was grateful to dress in his familiar scholar's garb. He returned the cloak to Kelley.

The five mounted and rode together to the end of the private road that led across Kozminsky's estate. When they reached the stone gate that opened on the public highway, they paused.

"Jesu protect you," Dee told Kelley. "I'll come after you as soon as I can. Don't do anything rash. Wait for me."

Kelley made no answer. Deep in his dark eyes a fire glowed. Dee knew it to be an evil portent for any man who blocked the path of the alchemist. Dee grasped Kelley's hand.

"God speed you, my friend."

"And you," Kelley told him.

The riders parted, three to follow the road back to Prague and the other two to enter the unknown.

FORTY-TWO

J oanna, I have a present for you," Jane said cheerily
from the doorway.

Joanna smelled the water before she saw it. She had
not had a drink of wine for over a day, and had not drunk
water since her abduction. Forcing open dry eyelids to let
in the morning light from the window, she rolled to the
side of her narrow cot and raised her head against her
shoulder on her elbow.

"Why don't you leave me alone?"

Jane entered the tower room with a glass pitcher. One
of the faceless guardians came in behind her and stood
beside the doorway. Joanna stared at his featureless black
hood and wondered if it was the same man she had
exposed on the night of her attempt to escape. Her stomach rolled with nausea.

"The guards tell me you haven't been drinking your
wine," Jane said. "I thought you might like some water
instead."

She filled the pewter goblet from the clear contents of
the decanter and set the decanter on the table beside
Joanna's cot. With a smile, she extended the goblet.
Joanna licked her cracked lips. She made no attempt to
take the vessel.

"What's wrong?" Jane asked in an injured tone. "Don't you trust me? It's just water. Look, I'll show you."

Jane drank deeply from the brimming goblet. Watching her throat work, Joanna found herself trying to swallow. She pushed herself into a sitting posture and pressed her bare feet flat on the floor. Her head spun. Never in her life had she wanted anything so much as the water that remained in the goblet. Her hand trembled when she extended it. Jane drew the goblet out of reach.

"There is just one little thing you can do for me. Agree, and I'll give you all the water you want."

Joanna let her arm drop to her knee and stared with hate at the demon-thing that possessed the body of her friend. She tried to speak, found that she had to clear her throat, and licked her broken lips with her dry, swollen tongue.

"Go to hell."

Jane shook her head in sadness.

"I've seen to it that you've been treated well. Why do you still have such a poor attitude? At least you might listen to what I wish you to do."

"If you're going to tell me, you'll tell me. I can't stop you."

"It's Esther," Jane said, ignoring her last remark. "She won't eat. Isn't that silly? We want you to convince her that she has nothing to gain by starving herself to death. Of course, we could force the food down her throat, but it would be so much easier if she'd listen to common sense."

Joanna began to understand why Jane was here. Esther Katz was a valuable hostage. Obviously her violent rape had failed to break her spirit. The Sons of Coronzon were afraid she would succeed in starving herself, and worried they might kill her themselves if they tried to force-feed her. She felt an impulse to smile, but the pain from her cracked lips extinguished it.

"Is that all you want from me?" she croaked. "To convince her to eat?"

"That's all, for the moment. Really, Joanna, it's such a small service. I'm surprised you aren't eager to help your little Jewish friend."

"All right, I'll do it."

"That's better. I knew you'd be sensible."

Joanna clutched at the goblet. She cried out when some of the water slopped over the rim onto the floor and drank the remainder greedily. It tasted sweet, like nectar.

"More," she gasped.

Smiling, Jane filled the goblet to the brim from the decanter. Joanna drank two more glasses before she was able to force herself to pause. She feared if she drank more she might vomit the water up. It was too precious to lose in such a way. She could almost feel it entering her veins and flesh, cooling her fever, giving her strength. At that moment she would gladly have traded a hundred barrels of port for a single bottle of water.

Jane seemed to lose interest in Joanna. She walked to the door.

"Follow me," she said without looking back.

Joanna discovered that her trembling knees supported her just well enough for her to take small, careful steps. She kept her balance with one hand on the wall as she trailed after Jane, who walked with her back straight and head held up like a woman in a dream. The hooded guard took a position a pace behind Joanna. They descended three levels and exited the stairwell through an archway to traverse a vaulted corridor. Narrow windows along one side overlooked the paved courtyard of the fortress.

Another Son of Coronzon moved aside to allow Jane to unbolt a door at the end of the passage. Esther's room was larger and more richly furnished than her own,

Joanna observed. Tapestries hung from the walls. A rug took the bareness from the floor. Esther's bed was twice as wide as her own narrow cot.

Esther sat in a wooden chair beside the solitary window, staring out through the iron bars at the clouds that drifted on the wind over the battlement wall of the courtyard. She wore the same kind of unbleached linen shift that Joanna had on. She did not turn or speak when they entered. Her face lacked expression. Her eyes were like polished brown stones. Joanna noticed a bandage around her left wrist.

"What happened to her wrist?"

"We had to take her dinner knife away," Jane said with a shrug. "The little fool slashed herself."

Joanna approached the seated woman silently and laid a gentle hand on her shoulder.

"Esther?"

Esther flinched but made no other response.

"Make her eat," Jane said. "As you see, there's plenty of food whenever she wants it."

A table against the wall contained a plate with sliced brown bread and cheese. Beside it a silver bowl overflowed with dates, dried figs, and green grapes. The Sons had also thoughtfully provided wine and milk.

"Leave us," Joanna snapped. "I can't talk with you in the room."

Jane withdrew with the two guards. The bolt rattled home in the door.

Joanna walked around Esther's chair and stood in front of the window so that her body blocked its light and cast a shadow over the seated woman. Esther blinked and shivered but made no other response. Fighting back tears, Joanna took the limp hand of her friend and held it. Esther's skin felt cold, like the flesh of a corpse.

"I know what they did to you," Joanna said. "I saw."

She rubbed Esther's fingers, trying to infuse life back into them from the warmth of her own body.

"You beat them. They don't control your mind. You won, Esther."

No response. Joanna decided to try a different tack.

"You can't kill yourself. It's a sin against God. How can you even think of shaming your husband by taking your own life?"

Esther blinked several times in succession.

"Yitzhaq loves you. So do your father and mother. They would want you to be strong. Yitzhaq would expect you to obey the Torah. Suicide is a sin, Esther. You must eat something."

A tear formed in the corner of Esther's dark brown eye and slowly trickled down her cheek. Another followed on the other side of her face. She drew a shaking breath.

"Eat something for my sake. You mustn't die in this place. Now that we're together we'll find some way to escape. Talk to me. My husband will come looking for me, and so will John Dee. They won't give up, Esther. We have to hold on until they reach us. We'll fight, the two of us."

Esther leaned forward and put her arms around Joanna's waist, her slender shoulders racked with sobs and her cheek pressed against the taller woman's belly. Joanna stroked her long black hair.

"What they did, what they did," she sobbed. "They did terrible things to me. I can't face Yitzhaq. I'm not clean anymore. How can I let Yitzhaq touch me?"

"He'll understand," Joanna murmured. "He's a good man. He loves you. What happened wasn't your fault. But if you kill yourself the sin will be upon your head. He won't be able to forgive you for that."

She drew the sobbing woman to her feet and led her over to the table.

"Eat something," she said. "If we're going to escape from this place you must keep up your strength."

"Do you really think there's a chance of escape?" Esther asked, looking up at her.

"Of course," Joanna lied. "We'll find a way now that we're together."

Feeling like a traitor, she pressed a fig into the hand of the other woman. Esther bit into it without enthusiasm. When she began to chew her body realized its hunger. She ate the rest of the sweet fruit greedily. Joanna poured a glass of milk and drank it.

"We don't accomplish anything by punishing ourselves," she said. "That's what these bastards want us to do. We have to stay strong so we can fight them."

"I thought you were like Jane," Esther murmured. She picked up a second fig and began to gnaw at it. "I thought I was alone."

"They haven't tried to break me yet. I guess I'm not important enough."

She thought of the wine but decided not to mention it. At least the Sons had not abused her physically. Perhaps they believed the compulsion of the wine strong enough to break her will by itself. They had almost been correct.

"Eat some bread. You need your strength."

She left Esther at the table and pounded on the door with her fist. It opened. The hooded guard stared at her silently.

"Get Jane," she snapped. "I need to talk with her."

She was not certain whether the man understood her English. In any case, he bolted the door. She waited, fuming with impatience. In ten minutes Jane appeared.

"She's eating," Jane said with delight when she saw Esther at the table.

Joanna drew her into the corridor and closed the door behind them.

"This is wonderful, Joanna," Jane gushed. "I'll make sure you're rewarded for this."

"I want you to let Esther outside this prison. She needs fresh air and sunlight. No wonder she tried to kill herself."

"You mean let her outside this room?" Jane asked. "I suppose it might be possible...."

"No, outside the wall. She needs to walk under the trees."

Jane laughed at her audacity.

"You must know that's completely out of the question. Really, Joanna, I'm surprised you would even ask for such a thing."

"Do you want her to kill herself?" Joanna demanded in a low voice. "Because if that's want you want, you'll soon get your wish. You'd better be prepared to watch her twenty-four hours a day. She'll find some way to do it."

Jane pouted with her perfect little mouth while she considered.

"I suppose I could arrange for you two to walk around the courtyard."

"That's not good enough," Joanna snapped. "She needs to see open spaces. At least let us walk on the battlements where she can look at the mountains."

"Very well. You understand I must have her guarded. The poor girl might take it into her head to throw herself down upon the rocks."

Joanna realized this was as much of a concession as she was going get from the demon that possessed Jane. She pretended to consider the offer, then nodded reluctantly.

"All right. If he stays behind us, out of sight."

"I'll tell him to walk three paces behind, but only if you keep the Jewess away from the edge."

"Agreed."

The afternoon of the same day, two women paced the battlements of the ancient fortress, a hooded guard close behind. The wind and sun uplifted Joanna's heart. She realized she probably needed the exercise more than Esther, although the other woman seemed stronger. They talked about their situation and their prospects for escape in low voices, each with an arm around her companion's waist. Once Joanna veered toward the outer parapet and glanced downward before the watchful guard could overtake them. Large boulders formed a steep slope from the base of the fortification.

"It's too far to jump," she murmured to Esther. "We might be able to climb down on the cracks between the stones, but it would be dangerous."

"I can't climb. I'm afraid of high places."

"We need a rope, then, or some way out through the gate. Unless there's another exit from this place."

She told Esther about the endless catacombs under the fortress, where the real work of the Sons of Coronzon was carried out.

"We would never find our way," Esther said with despair.

"Not by ourselves," Joanna agreed. "If only we had someone to guide us."

A commotion drew their attention down to the courtyard. Two hooded Sons of Coronzon dragged a man naked to the waist across the open space. Red whip-welts crossed his broad back. He cursed and struggled against the men holding his wrists wide apart.

Joanna felt her heart stumble.

"It's your husband," Esther gasped. "He's been captured."

He looked up and saw Joanna. His dark face twisted in anguish.

"Joanna, help me," he cried. "I need you, Joanna. Please. Help me."

She stared into his familiar slate blue eyes. Her blood chilled in her veins. She shook her head.

"That's not Edward."

"It is, Joanna," the other woman told her. "Don't you recognize him? It's your husband."

"He may look like my husband, but he's not Edward," she repeated with conviction.

As though able to read her mind, the man in the courtyard ceased to struggle. The hooded guards on either side released his wrists. He stared up at Joanna. His face wavered and changed into that of a beardless bald man with piercing, pale gray eyes that were framed by dark eyebrows. He put his heels together and bowed ironically. His frosty gaze never left the women. Without uttering a word, he turned and entered the door from which he had been dragged with such theatrics.

Joanna realized she had unconsciously held her breath. She released it slowly.

"But it was his face, his eyes. Even his voice was the same," Esther said wonderingly. "How could you be so sure he wasn't your husband?"

Joanna smiled a bitter smile.

"Edward would never ask me to help him."

FORTY-THREE

Kelley did not discover the cipher letter until near sunset, while rummaging in the pockets of his cloak for a handkerchief to wipe his sweating face. Instead he touched the parchment and cursed under his breath. He should have remembered Dee placing it there. It was not Dee's fault. After what he had suffered at the house of the Jesuits, he could be forgiven a momentary oversight.

There was nowhere on the road to hide the letter, no friend with whom to entrust it. Kelley resolved to keep it with him and say nothing to Peter Gwyn, who needed no additional worries to plague his mind. The letter would share his fate, however it might fall out.

At first sight of their objective, Kelley's heart sank with despair. The ancient castle on the shoulder of Black Mountain was no more than a ruin. They sat upon their horses and studied it through a gap in the trees.

"That's not the condition of the fortress I saw in my vision," he told Gwyn. "We may as well turn back."

"We're here," Gwyn pointed out. "Let's take a closer look. The Sons may have a haven built inside the walls."

To avoid detection by sentinels, they left the road and picked their way beneath the scattered, windblown pines that grew in the rocky soil. As they climbed higher up the slope, a curious change took place in the appearance of the ruin. It began to shimmer and dance as if seen through heated air, even though the sun had already set behind the western hills. They rounded the shoulder of a huge boulder. Kelley cried out in astonishment and grabbed Gwyn by the arm. In haste they backed their horses into the lee of the rock and dismounted, then crawled up on it for a better look.

No longer a ruin, the tower of the mighty fortress reared over the trees like the obscene organ of some dark god. Ravens circles its conical roof. The massive blocks of its rampart walls, quarried from the mountain itself, grew tumorously from the sooty stone. A man-made archway spanned the deep gorge between the winding mountain road and the huge bifold gate of ironbound oak that was the only entrance to the keep. On the intact battlements sentries paced with pikes in their hands and muskets slung over their backs.

"What sorcery is this?" Gwyn said hoarsely, his cheek pressed against the boulder.

"A spell of invisibility," Kelley murmured, impressed in spite of himself. "When we left the road we escaped its influence."

"Do you think they saw us coming?"

"I doubt it. The pines overhang the road."

They watched tensely for ten minutes. No outcry sounded from the wall of the fortress. The great gates remained shut. Kelley and Gwyn slid lower on the rock and lay on their backs, side by side.

"What do you want to do?" Gwyn asked.

"It's too late to accomplish much tonight. Let's find a safe place to make camp. Tomorrow we can climb the face of the mountain and try to get a look down inside the walls."

Deep among the trees they discovered a small ravine with a spring bubbling up from a fissure. The water was good. Since they found no signs of human passage near the spring, they made camp beneath a rock overhang.

After sunset the mountain air grew cool, but a fire could not be risked. Hardtack and dried beef furnished a rough, filling meal. Gwyn even produced a flask of port. Kelley took a single drink but declined the second. He wanted his wits in case he startled awake during the night. Gwyn seemed much more at ease. His early life as an English raider had accustomed the mariner to sleep under the shadow of his enemies with the ever-present threat of discovery.

Strange shrieks and a distant murmur that mingled with the bubbling of the spring kept Kelley awake in his blanket long after Gwyn began to snore. The cries might be those of some animal, he reflected uneasily, but they sounded almost human. The murmur rose and fell on the breeze. It reminded him of the monotonous chant of male voices, but was too faint for him to distinguish any words. Even when he finally drifted into a troubled sleep, the murmured chant haunted his dreams.

Before the sun rose, they began the arduous climb up the slope of the mountain. In places the wind-shaped trees helped, but in other places hindered their progress. Some sections were nearly vertical. Kelley found himself climbing angled trunks like a crazy ladder and prayed the roots of the pines were securely anchored. He watched in envy as Gwyn mounted the slope above him with the nimbleness of a monkey. His slender body and the uncommon strength of his arms, developed from many years at sea before the mast, made him a natural climber.

It was past noon before they attained a vantage that overlooked the fortress. They sat in the boughs of a large pine and studied the stronghold grimly, without speaking. The back of the castle pressed into a vertical face of rock that no man could descend without ropes. Were anyone foolish enough to try, he would become an easy prey to arrows shot across the courtyard from the outer battlements or from the windows of the tower. The roofs under the mountain were heavily reinforced against falling stones. On the outer side, the black fortification wall dropped for a hundred feet before merging with the dizzying incline of the mountain itself, almost as steep. The stone arch that lead from the road to the gate was just wide enough for two horsemen to ride abreast.

"A pleasant place," Gwyn muttered. "Give me a force of a thousand English seamen, a hundred cannon, and a year, and I might just be able to take it."

"I'll give you my good right hand," Kelley said, grinning in spite of himself. "Will that serve?"

"I suppose it must."

All afternoon they observed the movements of the sentries on the walls. Once a group of four riders came over the mountain pass and entered the keep. The clatter of their horses' hooves, delayed several seconds by the intervening distance, reached Kelley's ears as they rode across the arch and through the opened gate.

"A patrol. We were lucky to come so far along the road without being seen," he observed to Gwyn.

One other incident broke the monotony of their watch. A solitary figure left the fortress through a small door set in one corner of the gate, crossed the stone arch and descended several hundred feet along the road. He clambered down over the steep, broken boulders that dropped away from the edge of the road and worked his way toward the base of the fortress beneath the shadow of the tower. Although little larger than an ant to the unseen watchers, Kelley perceived that he carried a black staff with a hook in the end. He appeared to be a Moor. It was only when he drew closer that Kelley realized the man wore a black hood and gloves.

The strange figure picked a path over the angled stones to a cleft in the rock from which a stream foamed and fell in leaping cataracts. He reached to his waist and put something into the mouth of the stream, then with difficulty lifted up a large iron grate set on hinges within the gap. Propping it open with a rod, he proceeded to dig and poke around in the dark vent with his crook. At last he found what he searched after and dragged it forth.

"Jesu Christ," Kelley murmured.

A naked human corpse, swollen and made white by the action of the water, dangled at the end of his iron hook. The man was evidently familiar with his task. A few deft motions served to tumble the body down the face of the cataract. It fell and lodged in a small pool amid the rocks. The circling ravens descended with greedy caws. Following their flight with his gaze, Kelley made out bleached bones scattered over the entire expanse of the water-washed slope.

The black-hooded man poked hopefully in the cleft with his iron crook but failed to discover any additional fodder for the scavengers. He shut the grate and retraced his path across the rocky slope to the road. Gwyn and Kelley watched him climb the road and enter the fortress.

"At least we know there's a way out," Gwyn said. "Though I for one find scant comfort in it."

"Where there's a way out, there's a way in," Kelley observed.

Gwyn stared at him.

"Are you mad?"

"Perhaps. How else can we breech those walls?"

"We'll drown. And in such water—fagh!"

Kelley allowed the matter to lie. He had already resolved to attempt the entry that night. He would not blame Gwyn if the mariner remained outside. Kelley's study of necromancy had given him a tolerance of corpses in various states of decay. They no longer horrified him. At a certain level of awareness the open grave became just another hole in the ground.

He started to climb down from the pine. Gwyn drew his attention to movement on the battlement. He stared in wonder, scarcely able to believe his eyes. Even at this distance her flaming red hair was unmistakable.

"Joanna," he breathed. "I think that's Esther Katz with her."

"At least we know they're alive."

They watched the pair pace the battlements, a hooded guard behind them. Something drew the attention of the women into the open courtyard, but whatever it was lay below the wall. Kelley could not see it. He stared with inner hunger at his wife. Tears welled in his eyes. He blinked them away in fury. This was not a time to feel but to act. Silently he framed a prayer of thanks to God for sparing her life, and vowed that what a single man could accomplish, he would do to rescue her.

FORTY-FOUR

Jacques Bourinot managed to stay on his horse during the ride back to Prague, but the strain of so many hours in the saddle showed on his pinched, bloodless face. His sandy hair lay limp with sweat across his forehead. His eyelids drooped with fatigue.

"Do you have friends or family in the city?" Dee asked him as they passed through the outer gate.

"No. I stayed at the college with Paul Normand."

"You can't go back there. I know a house where you'll be safe."

They rode through the old city directly to the ghetto. Two royal guardsmen stopped them at the gate. The elder of the two, a grizzled veteran whose nose had been broken several times and whose hair was flecked with gray, studied Dee's face suspiciously.

"What happened to you?" he demanded gruffly.

Dee touched his hand lightly to the cuts and bruises on his left cheek and forehead.

"These?" he said in perfect Bohemian. "A fox darted across the path of my horse. I fell upon some stones."

He feigned a weak smile and allowed his gaze to slide away from the searching eyes of the guard, as though embarrassed by the admission.

"I fear I'm not as skilled a rider as I was in my youth."

The bent-nosed guardsman shifted his attention to Bourinot's sweating, pallid face.

"What's his story?"

"I ate some mushrooms when we stopped on the road," the young Huguenot muttered. He forced his attention to focus on the guard. "They were bad."

"What is the meaning of this interrogation?" Rabbi Katz asked in a reasonable tone. "Are you looking for someone?"

"An Englishman," the younger of the soldiers told him. "He killed Count Friedrich Niebuhr. We also have reason to believe that he was involved in the most recent murder within the walls of the old city."

"Shocking," Katz said. "Do you know the name of this monster?"

"Edward Kelley. He's with a party of English staying somewhere inside the ghetto."

"I don't suppose you know what he looks like?"

"Just what we've been told. He's a big man with dark eyes and a swarthy face."

"We'll certainly keep an eye open for this man," Katz assured him with a bland smile.

They entered the gate. Bourinot, who had held himself erect during the conversation, sagged forward and put his hand over his chest. Dee supported him under the elbow.

"Only a little farther. Then you can rest."

When they reached Loew's house, Rabbi Katz leapt down from his horse and ran inside. In seconds the Maharal's servants were whirling about making a sick-room ready for the young Huguenot on the third level next to Dee's room. Katz ordered a boy to put away their luggage and return the rented horses to the stabler.

Rabbi Loew entered the room as Dee and Katz were helping the naked Bourinot into bed. He nodded to the Frenchman and smiled encouragement.

"I've sent for my own physician, Ezra Solomon, to examine the young man," he murmured to Dee when they stood in the corridor outside the sickroom. "He's the best healer in Prague."

"I'm afraid the weapon used against him was poisoned," Dee said. "I picked the wadding from his wound when I removed the ball, but he still came down with fever. He's getting weaker by the minute."

Rabbi Loew gripped Dee by the hands and gazed solemnly at his battered face.

"My friend, I am glad to see you alive. I was very worried about you."

"We almost didn't get through the gate. The Jesuits have accused Edward of murder. The King's soldiers are searching for him—and his companions, presumably."

"Edward told me how he found Niebuhr's corpse when he went to look for you at the farmhouse. A terrible thing."

"They also accused him of a murder within the walls of the old city. Do you know anything about the circumstances, Judah?"

"How should I know anything about a murder?" Loew said, spreading his hands.

Dee studied his friend curiously. There was something Judah was not telling him, of that he was certain. He decided not to press the matter.

"Thanks to this young Huguenot, we may have discovered where the Sons of Coronzon have taken Jane, Joanna, and your daughter."

Miriam Loew approached along the hall while the two men were speaking. She overhead Dee's last remark as she looked into the sickroom. She went pale and clutched Dee by the hand.

"You know where my dear Esther is? Tell me, please, is she hurt?"

"Miriam," Loew said sharply. "Remember yourself."

She blinked and released Dee's hand as through it were a hot coal. Glancing at her husband, she blushed and drew herself up into a more regal posture.

"Forgive me," she said to Dee. "I am very concerned about the welfare of my daughter. She is my only child."

"I understand," Dee said kindly. "I don't know if Esther is well, but I may know where she has been taken. I'm going to discuss with your husband what we should do to get her back. If I learn anything more, I'll tell you, I promise."

She nodded and, with another glance at her husband, withdrew.

"My wife is very emotional," Loew said. "She forgets herself."

"In times like these, we all forget ourselves."

The physician arrived out of breath and red in the face. A fat little man with a bulbous nose and watery blue eyes, he went immediately to Bourinot and took off the bandage to examine his wound. He poked and probed it with his fingers until at last Bourinot cried out with pain. Dee could not resist stepping into the room.

"I took out the ball. The wound is clean, but the ball may have been poisoned."

The little Jew looked Dee up and down. He did not appear to be greatly impressed.

"I suppose you don't mind if I look for myself," he said, cocking a fuzzy brown eyebrow at Loew.

"The wound is closed. Surely there's no need to open it again," Dee persisted.

"Are you a physician?"

"I've studied the books of Hippocrates and Galen."

"Studied?" The little man nodded and smiled. "Study is fine for the university. Do you make your living healing the sick?"

"No," Dee admitted.

The doctor put his fat hands on Dee's shoulders and gently but firmly pushed him backward into the hallway.

"Well, I do. Kindly let me pursue my profession. Out, please, out, out."

He shooed Rabbi Katz out and closed the bedroom door in Dee's face. Dee looked at Loew, who wore a faint smile. Dee laughed.

"I suppose I asked for that. Your physician has a poor bedside manner."

"I don't pay him for his manners," Loew said. "Come, let's go down to the library where we can talk this matter over in private. The Huguenot is in good hands, I promise you."

Rabbi Katz and Dee took turns relating the events that had transpired since Dee's departure from the city. Loew sat and sipped a glass of steaming black tea while he listened. From time to time he nodded and glanced keenly at Dee. When Dee repeated the words Bourinot had overhead spoken by Azoth in the college of Jesuits, he banged his glass onto its saucer and set it down on the table.

"The Black Mountain. Of course, where else? All this time I've been looking in the south. I should have guessed the Sons would locate their stronghold on the border, in case it ever became necessary for them to flee Bohemia."

"We don't know that's where the women were taken," Dee reminded him. "It just seems the most likely place."

"It must be. It fits with Kelley's vision of a black fortress in a high mountain pass."

"I couldn't dissuade him from riding there directly. At least he has Peter Gwyn with him. Gwyn is a good man. Extremely resourceful. I only hope he can keep Edward out of trouble."

"Yitzhaq, I want you to send word to the council. Have our strongest force of fighting men assembled and ready to ride at first light tomorrow. Tell them I will lead the expedition myself."

"Is that wise, Maharal?" Katz asked hesitantly.

"No, it is not wise, but it is what's going to happen," Loew said with a smile. "I've been looking forward to this chance for years. I only pray we're not too late. The Lilith formula is almost complete. If we don't stop the Sons of Coronzon now, we never will."

Rabbi Katz bowed and left the library to deliver the message. At the same moment the doctor appeared with his brown leather case of instruments and potions. He looked harried and distraught.

"The youth is dead, Maharal," he said in Yiddish. "He took a fit and his heart stopped. There was nothing I could do." The doctor glanced at Dee. "This Englishman performed a skilled extraction of the ball. The wound was not that serious. The youth should not have died."

Loew considered the doctor's words in silence, shaking his head.

"Thank you, Ezra. I appreciate you treating a gentile. I know you don't do it as a rule."

"For you, Maharal, anything," the little man said.

"Please let me express my thanks also," Dee told the little man in Yiddish.

The doctor regarded Dee with surprise. He seemed to reassess the Englishman in his mind. He touched his index finger gently to Dee's left cheek.

"I should treat your wounds," he said in Yiddish.

"They're nothing," Dee assured him.

The doctor nodded.

"I'm sorry for your loss."

Without another word he left the library. They heard his slow, heavy footsteps on the stairs and the shutting of the front door.

Dee looked at Loew. The abrupt death of the young Huguenot had banished their fragile optimism. Dee sipped experimentally at his glass of tea. It was too bitter for his taste.

"You must know something I don't, Judah," he said.

"Very probably. What are you getting at?"

"How do you expect a small force of Jews to capture a mountain fortress that was designed to resist the prolonged attack of an entire army?"

Loew seemed to consider with himself.

"So you want to know my secret weapon?"

Dee shrugged his shoulders.

"You don't think I have one? But I do. What's more, I will show it to you."

He led Dee up to the third level of the house and stopped before the padlocked door. He fumbled with the ring of keys at his waist.

Dee took several moments to gaze in sorrow at the body of the Huguenot, whose death room was adjacent the locked chamber. Loew's physician had closed the eyes of the corpse and arranged its limbs so that the young Frenchman seemed to lie fast in the arms of sleep, save that his lips were blue. So handsome and so young, Dee thought as he bent his head in silent prayer. He returned to Loew just as Loew got the door to the mysterious room open.

A strange blend of emotions crossed the deeply lined face of the Jew. Pride mingled with childlike glee beneath a veil of solemnity. His gray eyes sparkled like those of a boy bent on mischief.

Whatever Dee expected, it was not what greeted his eyes when he entered the locked room. A man dressed in the plain dark robe of a law clerk stood beside the solitary window passively regarding them without expression. He was neither old nor young, neither handsome nor ugly. Straight black hair contrasted sharply with skin the color of raw dough from lack of sunlight. He was the type of man who could pass a dozen times in the street and never be noticed, unless the observer happened to meet his shadowy gaze. Then a shiver might run up the spine. His were dead eyes. Soulless.

Rabbi Loew closed the door behind them and turned to Dee inquiringly.

"How do you like him? I call him Yosef after Yosef Sheda, a man remembered in the Talmud."

"I know the legend. Sheda was a creature half-demon and half-man who defended the sages and served them."

"That's right. I'm impressed. You know your Talmud."

Dee studied the motionless figure as he might examine a new species of plant or a strange beast.

"Remarkable," he murmured. "What is it?"

Rabbi Loew laughed with delight. The man called Yosef did not so much as blink.

"I should have realized you are too clever to fool. You observed the absence of wrinkles. Of course you are right. He is not a man. We made him, myself and Rabbi Katz and my disciple Rabbi Sason, who is presently undergoing a spiritual retreat. He is formed from the elements fire, water, and air, in imitation of the way the Holy One, blessed be He, created Adam."

"A golem," Dee said. He felt an inner shiver of revulsion.

"Yes, a golem. I created him to defend the ghetto in case those mad Jesuits succeed in inciting a mob to storm its gates."

Dee walked around the golem cautiously. He watched its chest rise and fall. He laid his ear to its breast, and heard the slow thud of its heart.

"Can you understand me?" he asked, peering into the golem's midnight eyes.

"He hears you but he cannot speak," Loew explained. "He is a mute. Yosef, shake Doctor Dee's hand."

Dee flinched at the chill touch of the golem. Its long fingers felt like a mass of dry sticks. When the golem gripped his hand, Dee had to suppress a cry of pain.

"Not so hard, Yosef. Release him."

The golem followed the direction of Rabbi Loew like an automaton. Dee bent over the palm of the creature and studied it.

"No fingerprints," he noted to Loew. He looked more closely at its face. "And no earlobes."

"Signs of his imperfection. After all, I am not the Holy One, may He be blessed. However, he has several advantages over a common man. His strength is that of ten porters. He cannot be burned by fire. He cannot be drowned. He cannot be killed by a knife or sword. Here, I will show you. Open your shirt, Yosef. Bare your chest."

The golem silently parted its robe and opened its shirt. Loew took a small penknife from his pocket and made a cut diagonally across the white, hairless skin of the golem's breast. Red blood welled into the cut, but did not flow down its belly. Instead, the cut began to heal itself even as Dee watched in amazement. In a dozen seconds there was no sign of an injury, not even a scar.

"This thing is unholy," Dee said with disgust. He stared at Loew. "Judah, why did you make such a monster?"

"Do you think I wanted to?" Loew demanded in indignation. "Do you think I would make such a thing if I had any other choice? These are desperate times, my friend. I made it for the defense of Israel. It may be an unholy thing, but I made it for a holy purpose."

A thought struck Dee. He looked at the large hands of the creature and remembered their inhuman power.

"You have already used it, haven't you?" he accused Loew. "The four murders in the old city. All enemies of the Jews. All found with their necks broken. Judah, look me in the eye and tell me you didn't order the golem to commit those murders."

Loew turned his face away in anger.

"What if I did? You know our situation here in Prague. My people have lived here in peace for centuries, yet at any moment we may be expelled from Bohemia by a group of rabble rousers and hate mongers who hide their evil under the cloak of religion. If you were in my place, what would you have done? Wait for those fool Jesuits to come with torches to burn the ghetto to the ground? Or would you fight back, as I have, with the only weapon available to you? I ask you, John, to look me in the eye and tell me you would not have done the same thing."

Dee regarded his old friend sadly. Loew wanted approval for his unholy creation, and Dee could not find it in his heart to give it. But neither could he condemn the motives of Loew in defending his people.

"I can't condone murder, Judah. Not under any provocation."

"I should have known better than to expect a gentile to understand," Loew said angrily. "You don't know what our people have suffered. You don't know what it's like to be homeless even within the walls of your own home."

Dee thought of the wreck of his library at Mortlake, which had consumed the greater bulk of his personal fortune over a span of forty years. His books had been a living part of his soul.

"Perhaps I can guess. I'm not questioning your motives, Judah, only your choice of methods."

He stared into the soulless eyes of the golem. Those eyes had looked upon the horror of brutal murder not once but four times. Did this creature even remember its deeds, he wondered? Did it ever feel regret in the quiet hours of the night when the rest of the house lay asleep?

"Would you really unleash this terrible weapon against the old city?"

"If the Jesuits incite an attack I will have no choice. I hope it will never come to that. There is still time for the Emperor Rudolph to regain his senses and change the laws of blood libel. That will stop the Jesuits from arousing the population of Prague against us."

"When I return to England I will speak to the Queen," Dee promised. "I may be able to persuade her to write to Rudolph and express your concerns."

"That might be helpful," Loew agreed. "Rudolph is headstrong. It's difficult to know how best to influence him."

Dee returned his gaze to the golem. In spite of the repulsion he felt, the creature fascinated him. He could not help admiring the esoteric genius that had gone into its creation. Only a Ba'al Shem could harness the raw power to clothe a spirit with a fully developed living body. Dee doubted he could duplicate the creation of the golem. Not that he had any intention of attempting such an unholy act of hubris.

"How do you intend to use this thing against the Sons of Coronzon?"

Rabbi Loew looked at the golem the way a proud father regards his firstborn son.

"Let me keep one or two secrets from you for a little while. You will see yourself what Yosef can accomplish when we reach the Black Mountain."

FORTY-FIVE

Gwyn and Kelley crawled as near as they could to the outlet of the stream without being seen from the battlements above. They lay in dense bushes about a hundred yards from where the cascade of water danced down the rocky slope, in considerable discomfort from the attacks of flies and ants. The shade of the bushes provided no relief from the hot breeze that blew up the exposed flank of the mountain.

When full dark fell they picked their way across the boulders in the direction of the roaring water. It was the night of the new moon. A canopy of stars defined the outline of the fortress above them and gave them just enough illumination to see the ground. White human bones stood out with startling clarity against the black rocks.

It was a perilous traverse. Many of the smaller stones were loose, their rounded surfaces made slick by the windblown spray from the cascade. Gwyn picked a route across the treacherous slope with sure-footed ease. Kelley did his best to mimic Gwyn's movements. Had it not been for the uncanny skill of the mariner in finding secure footholds, he doubted he could have made the crossing at all. Fortunately, the roar of the water concealed the rattle of loose pebbles.

Midway on the traverse a stone turned under Kelley's left boot. He barely managed to save himself by throwing his body onto the steep slope and clinging with his fingertips to a boulder above him. His boots flailed in the loose rocks but failed to secure a toehold. A shout rose in his throat. He swallowed it and hung on to the rounded sides of the spray-slick boulder like death itself. Gwyn happened to glance over his shoulder. When he perceived Kelley's predicament, he hurried back and extended an arm to the alchemist. Kelley pulled himself to safety. Without a word, he grimly followed in the steps of the seaman as though nothing had occurred.

At last Kelley was able to pull himself up to the vent beside Gwyn. The flow of water was greater than it appeared from the trees, almost a small river. He fingered the ancient square lock that secured a flat iron bolt across the grate to the stones on either side. He found himself able to insert his finger into the keyhole. The key must be massive. He tested the grate with the strength of his arm. It rattled against its bolt but betrayed no weakness. The bars were set about six inches apart—too narrow even for a child to squeeze through.

"Now that we're here, how do we get in?" Kelley spoke loudly into Gwyn's ear. The roar of the waterfall was deafening.

"Leave that to me."

Gwyn took from his belt a leather pouch and laid it open on the flat surface of a rock. In the dim glow of the night sky Kelley observed that it was stuffed with files, small pry bars, and numerous lock picks of every imaginable size and shape. Gwyn selected one of the larger picks. His teeth flashed white in the starlight.

"It's always wise to have a second profession to fall back on," Gwyn said over the thunderous water.

He set to work on the lock. After ten minutes of futile fiddling he began to curse in a steady stream under his breath.

"What's wrong?" Kelley asked.

Gwyn banged his fist against the flat face of the lock in frustration.

"The mechanism's simple enough," he said. "But the damned thing's rusted from the action of the water. I don't have enough leverage in the picks to turn it."

"Let me try," Kelley suggested.

Leaning close against him, Gwyn showed him how to fit the pick at an angle into the large keyhole so that its point would engage between the wards. Kelley himself was not completely ignorant of the art. He twisted the pick experimentally. Something gave, whether the pick or the lock he was not certain. Gritting his teeth, he exerted his considerable strength against the pick. It snapped. He skinned his knuckles against the rough iron and cursed.

Gwyn bent anxiously to examine the lock. He probed it with another pick, then added his curses to Kelley's.

"The end is jammed in the mechanism. We'll never open it now."

Kelley stood and cast his eyes around until he located what he needed. With a grunt of effort he picked up a shard of stone that tapered to a triangular point. Raising it high over his head, he brought it down against the iron bolt. The grill rang out like a bell.

"Do you think the noise carries above the roar of the water?" he asked Gwyn doubtfully.

"We might as well shout our names and fire our pistols into the air."

"Anyway, it can't be helped. We have to get in somehow."

Again Kelley hefted the massive stone and dropped it against the flat bar. The bar snapped with a large red spark close to the lock. Kelley set the stone aside and worked the long end of the bolt out of its anchor in the rock. This allowed the other side to slide free. He raised the grate.

"Quick, get in before someone above lowers a light."

Gwyn gathered up the hem of his cloak and ducked under the grate. Kelley followed and gently lowered it back into place. It was possible that anyone looking down from the battlements the next morning would fail to notice the damage. He wondered how often the hooded man came to clear the vent.

The cave was larger than he had expected. He ran his hand over the curved ceiling and felt the impression of iron tools. In some earlier century, when the fortress had exacted tolls from travelers crossing the mountain pass, the passage had been widened. Perhaps it was intended as an emergency escape route. The headroom made their progress easier. They were able to walk in a crouched position with the water no higher than their knees.

A foul breeze blew an unimaginable stench into their faces. After a few paces Kelley wrapped his cloak over his mouth and breathed through the cloth. Gwyn hacked and spat repeatedly. It was a pointless exercise. As quickly as he spat the stench out of his mouth, the breeze blew it in again.

"This must be the sewer for the entire fortress," Kelley said through his cloak.

Gwyn said nothing.

The passage twisted and bent back on itself, at times ascending gently. After the first step they were forced to feel their way along the slime-caked walls through total darkness. The foul breeze in their faces kept them from becoming turned around, along with the flow of the stream against their legs.

Kelley cried out and danced to the side, banging his head against the slope of the stone roof.

"What's wrong?" Gwyn demanded from the darkness in front of him.

"Something touched my leg. Did you feel it?"

"I felt nothing."

Uneasily, Kelley continued after the splashes of the mariner's boots. His attention remained focused on the water at his feet. Perhaps this is why he noticed the gentle second caress. Flinching aside, his foot turned on something round and hard. He fell into the water on his arms. His left hand closed on something vaguely familiar. After a moment he realized the object was a human skull. He felt the eye-sockets with his fingers before releasing it with a reflexive shudder of revulsion. The bed of the stream was filled with bones.

There was no mistaking the next brush against his leg through the leather of his knee-high boots. Gwyn cursed at almost the same instant.

"I felt that," he said. "What the devil was it?"

"An eel, I think," Kelley told him.

The water was alive with the creatures. They pressed around the legs of the men with familiar affection but made no attempt to attack. Their natural aggression had been dulled by the plentiful supply of food. Only once did one of the beasts fasten its teeth into the leather of Kelley's boot. He felt it twist and vibrate against his calf and slashed down in the darkness with his knife. The water thrashed with its death throes. The severed head of the eel continued to cling to his boot, until at last he was forced to pry its teeth loose with the point of his dagger.

"Here's an opening in the wall," Gwyn said. "Should we take it?"

"Jesu, yes," Kelley muttered. "Anything to get out of this putrid stream."

The floor of the passage was level with their waists. They climbed out of the water and found themselves in a square tunnel with a roof high enough to allow them to walk upright. There was still no trace of light, but the breeze that had blown down the stream issued from the far reaches of the passage.

"This must be where they drop off the corpses," Kelley observed.

The air was enough improved to allow him to remove his cloak from his face. He spat the bitterness from his mouth and wrinkled his nose against the revolting taste.

"Here, clear your throat with this," Gwyn said.

Kelley heard the sound of a cork pulled from the neck of a bottle. He reached into the darkness and waved his hand around blindly until he struck Gwyn's hand. He accepted the flat flask and drank. Brandy. The strong fire of the alcohol settled his stomach. He passed the bottle back to Gwyn and heard him drink.

They continued along the passage until they came to a branching tunnel. No air stirred in its depths. It smelled of must and fungus.

"I say we keep our bowsprit to the wind," Gwyn murmured. "There must be an opening ahead to let the air blow through."

"Agreed."

They proceeded in silence, the sure-footed Gwyn taking the lead. The sensation grew steadily in Kelley's keen intuition that someone or something followed them. Gwyn must have felt the same thing. Several times he stopped and held his breath. Kelley imitated him. From behind they heard a faint rustle along the stone floor, as though something dry were being dragged. The sound always stopped after a few seconds. Though they held their breath to the bursting point and strained for the slightest noise, it was never repeated while they stood listening.

Unconsciously they found themselves increasing their pace. Several times they pursued the elusive breeze down side corridors. It was difficult to determine in the absolute darkness whether the floor sloped up or down. However, the flights of steps they encountered all led downward.

The rustle behind grew steadily louder, until at last it became audible even while they were walking. Kelley found it impossible to attach an image to the maddening noise. It reminded him of something dragged through dry grass on the end of a rope, or the scratching of countless mice behind a wainscot—except there were no squeaks. For some reason the dry hiss gave him an impression of blowing sand and burning sun.

Suddenly, the rustle swelled all around them in the darkness. Kelley stopped and stood like a statue. Cold sweat trickled down the back of his collar.

"What the devil is it?" Gwyn whispered.

They listened together to the unearthly hiss, which now came almost as loudly from in front as from behind.

"I don't know. Stay still. Maybe it will pass us by."

The alchemist felt something run over the toe of his boot and lashed out. It felt and sounded like kicking a pile of dead leaves. He took an involuntary step backward. Something crunched under his heel. In the darkness in front of him, Gwyn screamed in pain.

"What the devil's wrong?" Kelley demanded. He struggled to hold his frayed nerves together.

"Something stabbed my foot," Gwyn said. "Christ, it hurts."

With an oath Kelley whirled around and drew out his rapier. He shuffled backward until he felt Gwyn's crouching body with his hand.

"The pain," Gwyn groaned. "I have to sit down."

"No. If you value your life, stay on your feet."

He swung the sword in sweeping arcs, aiming the blade close to the floor. It cut through the unseen menace like a scythe through standing wheat. The tip caught the stone and sparked. In the flash Kelley saw what he was fighting.

"Jesu, we're done for," Gwyn cried. He drew his saber and hacked downward.

The entire expanse of the passage seethed with a living carpet of white scorpions, each as long as a man's hand. They clambered over one another with their venomous tails raised to strike, their claws snapping open and shut. The walls crawled with the albino insects. Some even clung to the rough stone ceiling. All this Kelley and Gwyn saw in the instantaneous flash of the steel.

Terror and revulsion doubled the force of Kelley's blows. As he struck with the rapier, he jumped and danced a macabre jig and crushed the scuttling scorpions under his boots. Intermittent sparks from the flashing steel showed them that they had succeeded in sweeping the circle around their feet clear of the plague for the moment. They fought their way down the corridor, slashing and cursing, until the greater mass of the insects lay behind them.

"Quick, give me your brandy," Kelley shouted.

He felt Gwyn's fumbling hands against his back. The brandy flask slapped into his palm as he reached out blindly for it. Holding the bottle by its neck between his teeth, Kelley took the cipher letter from the pocket of his cloak and tore a strip from one side. He got out his tinder box and began to strike its flint, inwardly cursing the tremble of his fingers. Gwyn continued to hack down against the floor with his saber.

The tinder in the box flickered to life. Holding it high in one hand, Kelley uncorked the brandy bottle with his teeth and clumsily stuffed one end of the parchment strip into its neck. He touched the parchment to the sputtering tinder and cast the bottle into the midst of the seething white mass that surged and pulsed at his feet like the foaming waves of the sea.

The brandy exploded into blue flame with an audible whoosh that blinded Kelley. He put up his arm to shield his face from the heat and blinked the spots from his eyes. The carapaces of the insects crackled like a burning thorn bush. For several moments they skittered madly over each other and spread the destruction. Then, without warning, they surged toward the two men in a blazing tide.

FORTY-SIX

Dee stood beside Rabbi Loew under the sheltering boughs of a stand of windswept pines. They studied the grim ruin of the black fortress that crouched like some sleeping stone giant on the opposite side of the steep mountain road, its battlements crumbling, its tower fallen, its bridge collapsed. It gave scant promise of habitation, but both men knew this appearance was deceptive.

An incantation murmured by Loew swept off the glamoury the way a rising wind blows away a mist. Even though he anticipated the transformation, Dee found it hard to suppress an exclamation of wonder.

It had been wise to approach through the trees, Dee thought, even if it had taken most of the night. The lack of a moon had helped them avoid detection. The cloak of magic that disguised the true nature of the keep only extended a short distance on either side of the road. They had glimpsed the torchlight on the walls from amid the pines, and so had not been deceived when the lights vanished as they neared the road.

"It's fortifications are formidable," Dee whispered.

"We have no time to search for a weakness," Loew told him. "We will go in through the gate."

Dee gazed at the ominous mouth of shadow.

"How can we breach the gate? It would take a battering ram, or a cannon."

For answer Loew called to Rabbi Katz, who stood hidden under the trees with the rest of the force of over a hundred young Jewish men.

"Bring Yosef to me," Loew murmured in Katz's ear.

The golem shambled forward. In the starlight its pale complexion glowed like the waxen mask of a corpse. Its unblinking black eyes reminded Dee of buttons on the face of a rag doll. He stepped back with intense revulsion to allow the golem to pass. It did not even glance at him. Its entire awareness centered on its master.

Loew addressed the creature as he might talk to a simple-minded son.

"Yosef, do you see that gate across the road? I want you to open it. Will you do that for me, Yosef?"

The golem stared at him and nodded.

"Good boy," Loew said, patting it on the shoulder.

Walking like a man in a trance, the golem left the pines and crossed the road. Its shoes echoed on the stone bridge as it approached the gate of the black fortress.

"Who goes there?" demanded a harsh male voice in Bohemian from the wall.

The golem continued its measured steps to the gate. It felt the ironbound planks with its fingertips. Clenching a fist, it pounded three times on the barrier. The echoes of the blows boomed off the stony hillside. An alarm bell clanged inside the fortress.

"Are you a madman?" the sentry demanded. "Get back from the gate or we'll kill you."

Again the golem raised its fist and demanded entry. The small access door set in one corner of the gate flew open. Three men in black hoods armed with swords leapt out and attacked the golem. Moving with astonishing swiftness, it knocked the swords from the hands of two soldiers and grasped them by their throats. Dee heard the snap of their necks. The third soldier cursed and slashed at the golem with his short double-edged sword. It cut deeply into the golem's shoulder. The golem swayed for a moment, then took a step forward and reached for the man. The guard screamed and fled back through the small door, which slammed shut behind him.

Again the golem pounded three measured strokes against the gate, mutely demanding entry. It stood waiting. A trap door creaked open above it in the overhanging stone arch.

"You've had your warning," someone cried.

Flames flared brightly on the battlements. A stream of liquid fire gushed down and drenched the golem from head to toe, transforming it into a human torch. Some of the flaming oil splashed on the gate itself. The curtain of fire lit the ghastly scene for the watchers across the road.

"They've killed him," Dee said. He did not know whether to feel regret or relief.

"Watch," Loew told him. "Now you will witness the true power of the holy Name."

The firelight reflected strangely in the eyes of the old Jew. Dee turned to the gate, expecting to see only a blackened corpse. He swore in amazement.

The golem stood with its arms at its sides, clothed in flame. From the stones at its feet the flames licked as high as its waist and swirled in the breeze around its legs. While Dee watched, its suit of clothes burned completely away and left its white body naked. Not even the hair on its head ignited. It noticed the fire no more than it noticed the night air.

The terrified guards within the fortress began to shoot arrows into the golem's naked body. These penetrated deeply. Flame ran up their shafts to their feathered ends. The arrows hung in the golem's flesh for a few seconds, then dropped out. They left no trace of a wound.

Musket shots echoed amid a growing confusion of excited voices. The balls chipped the stone around the golem's naked feet as it walked through the dying flames and laid its hands upon the burning planks of the gate. If any of the balls struck its body, the monster gave no sign. It set its feet firmly into the stone pavement and bent its back, then thrust against the massive barrier. Dee saw the muscles of its back articulate themselves as though carved from white marble. The gate flexed and groaned on its iron hinges.

"Help Yosef," Loew called to the armed host under the trees.

Rhythmically, he began to chant a series of Hebrew letters. His disciples took up the chant. It swelled and surged across the road like a living creature. The body of the golem began to glow. It turned dull red, then orange, then yellow. At last it blazed white with the intensity of lightning. Dee could not bear to look upon it. He shielded his eyes with his hand and tried to peer around the blazing outline of the golem.

Above the chanting a splintering crack rang out. The sides of the gate flew inward. When they struck against the black stone walls of the fortress, they shattered into fragments of molten iron and smoking oak. The golem straightened and walked with its measured pace into the fortress through a rain of arrows and a hail of gunfire.

"Follow Yosef," Loew cried. "Attack!"

The Jewish militia was poorly armed and badly trained, but their hearts burned with religious fervor.

They ran with eager joy through the open gates as though into the embrace of a lover. Once inside the courtyard, they fought to defend the life of their Maharal with fanatical zeal. Flesh wounds did not slow them. Only a lead ball or an arrow in a vital spot halted their advance.

Striving to keep his head amid the chaos that reigned in the courtyard, Dee noticed that the number of defenders was less than he had expected. He wondered if the Sons were holding a force of men in reserve for a counter strike. A bellowing, hooded foe ran at him with a pike and tried to skewer him. Dee stepped aside and thrust the point of Normand's rapier between the man's ribs and through his heart. He pulled the blade out with distaste. Killing was not an occupation he enjoyed.

In this respect he differed from the golem. The soulless creature moved in swift darts from one terrified defender to another, slaying them as quickly and as easily as a farmer wrings the necks of his poultry on market day. Dee heard the bones of men crack between the deft fingers of the monster. The only incident in his memory he could compare with the slaughter was the time when, as a young boy, he had watched a weasel systematically kill an entire colony of black rats by biting through the neck of each in turn. The weasel had displayed the same mindless homicidal joy Dee saw in the emotionless eyes of the golem.

In spite of their confusion, the hooded Sons of Coronzon fought with courage. They would easily have prevailed against the Jewish militia alone, but the relentless, elemental force of the monster broke their ranks and scattered them into the barracks and tower. The Jews hunted them down and put them to the sword.

Dee wondered where Azoth had hidden himself. Surely he would not allow his sworn brothers to go to their deaths without aiding them? Yet there was no focus of command in the ranks of the defenders. Each individual fought for himself where he found himself cornered, and died alone.

The fight momentarily shifted elsewhere. Dee entered the open doors at the base of the tower and moved along a corridor with his rapier drawn. A human voice drew him to a bolted door. He laid his ear against the planks.

Silence.

"Is anyone there?" he called through the door.

"Yes, help me, please. Let me out." A woman's voice.

The door was not locked. Dee drew the bolt. The door opened inward and Esther Katz threw herself into his arms, laughing and weeping at the same time.

"Calm yourself, Esther." Dee stroked her sable hair. "Yitzhaq's here. So is your father."

"Yitzhaq?" Her back stiffened. She stared at Dee in alarm. He saw the bruises on her face. "Keep him away. I can't let him look at me. I'm not clean."

Dee attempted to reason with her, but she continued to protest that she would not meet with her husband. Rabbi Katz entered the corridor with Rabbi Loew and the golem. The hands of the naked monster were red with blood up to its elbows.

"Esther, you're alive," Katz called to her in joy.

He ran to embrace his wife. She cowered behind Dee and avoided his touch. She refused to meet his gaze and tried to hide her face from his sight.

"What's wrong with her?" Katz asked Dee. "What have they done to her?"

"She's been beaten," Dee told him. "Give her a moment to calm herself."

Katz stepped away in confusion and looked for help from Loew.

"Esther," Loew said, approaching his daughter. "Look at me."

She continued to hide her face in Dee's cloak and shook her head. Loew laid his hand tenderly on her shoulder. She shook it off violently and glared at him, tears streaming from her dark brown eyes.

"Don't touch me, father. I'm dirty. I've sinned with men. Please go away, both of you. I can't bear to look at you."

Loew looked at Dee with a baffled expression.

"Let me talk to her," Dee said. "Alone."

Rabbi Katz glanced at Loew, then nodded to Dee. From distant parts of the fortress the report of pistols and the clash of swords still sounded. Dee put his arm around the young woman and led her back into her prison room. He used his tinder box to ignite a candle in a brass holder on the table, then closed the door. Sitting Esther on the side of the bed, he drew up a wooden chair opposite her and took her hand between his own.

"Did they violate your virtue?"

She turned her face away. Silent sobs racked her shoulders.

"It's no reason to be ashamed. The sin falls upon the head of the sinner, not upon she who is sinned against."

"I'm so embarrassed," she whispered. "Yitzhaq will never want to touch me again."

"Your husband loves your more than you realize. It's wrong to shun him."

"I should have killed myself. I tried, but they took away my knife. When I refused to eat, they sent Joanna to me. I didn't want to die."

"Joanna is here?" Dee tried to keep the anxiety out of his voice. "What about Jane?"

Esther looked at him with a strange expression.

"She's here also, but they did something to her mind. She does their bidding."

Dee fought a wave of despair that threatened to engulf him. It was as he feared.

"Where are they held, do you know?"

"They were keeping Joanna in the tower. I think Jane took her down to the catacombs."

"Can you show us the way?"

She nodded and stood up. Dee escorted her out of the room. Her mouth remained a thin line, her face expressionless, as though he led her to her execution. Rabbi Katz embraced her and laughed with joy into her hair.

"Dear Esther, may the Holy One be praised."

"Blessed be He," Loew added. "Be brave, daughter. No one can hurt you. See, I've brought Yosef to protect you."

Esther blinked away her tears and looked at the golem. She smiled gently.

"Yosef, what are you doing here? Why are your hands all bloody?"

The golem stared at her solemnly with the vacant expression of an idiot.

"Esther thinks Yosef is a poor half-wit her father took in off the street out of charity," Katz whispered aside to Dee. "It would be better if she never learned the truth."

"I understand."

A Jew ran in with a blood-stained sword in his hand and announced to Rabbi Loew that the defenders of the fortress had all either been slain or driven into hiding. Loew gave orders for his force to gather themselves in the courtyard.

Dee and Katz ascended the tower to ensure that the remaining women were not being held in its chambers. All the doors stood open. The rooms were empty. They came down the spiral stair in disappointment and returned to Rabbi Loew.

"How do we get into the catacombs?" Dee asked Esther.

She pointed through the arch behind them to where the stairwell continued downward into the floor.

"I think they went that way."

Dee and Loew stood on the landing and peered into the black gulf of the open stair. The sound of battle had died. Dee cocked his ear.

"Listen. Do you hear anything?"

Loew bent his head in concentration. The murmured chant drifted up like the forgotten memory of a dream.

"The Lilith formula," Loew told Dee with alarm. "We have to get down there at once. We may already be too late."

"What will happen if the formula is completed?" Dee asked.

"We will become slaves of the Fallen One, all of us," Loew told him solemnly. "It would be hell on earth."

fORTY-SEVEN

Gwyn, this way!" Kelley swept aside the burning carpet of vermin with his sword point and ran toward a doorway in the wall revealed by the flickering flames. Gwyn limped after him, cursing with the unique intensity of an English seaman. They fled down the slope of the unexplored passage. A few of the flaming scorpions ran after them, but these were easily crushed under the heels of their boots. After several turnings, Kelley deemed it safe enough for them to pause and catch their breath.

"Hold this."

He passed Gwyn his flickering tinder box, which was almost too hot to hold. It had never been intended for use as a lamp. From the side of his cloak he tore a dry strip of linen. This he wrapped many times around the point of his sword and tied tightly. He lit the makeshift torch from the tinder and shut the overheated silver box. The cloth burned poorly, but gave promise of sustaining its flame for many minutes.

"We must be in hell," Gwyn said weakly.

Kelley examined his leg. It was swollen to twice its normal size. Gwyn could no longer bend his knee. His teeth chattered and his face dripped with cold sweat. Kelley saw that the pupils in the hazel eyes of the mariner had shrunk to the size of pinheads.

"It stung me right through my boot. What kind of insect can sting through leather? Did you ever see anything so big? The damn things are like lobsters. They must be works of the Devil. They're white. That's the color of death."

Kelley took him by the shoulders and shook him. Gwyn stopped babbling and tried to focus his eyes on the alchemist.

"I can't see you. It's so dark. Did the torch go out?"

"No, the torch is alight."

Kelley moved it in front of Gwyn's face. The mariner smiled.

"I feel it on my cheeks. I still can't see the damn thing. The venom blinded me."

"It'll wear off," Kelley said roughly. He kept the doubt he felt in his own heart out of his voice. "Here, put your arm around my shoulder. I'll guide you."

"You might as well leave me," Gwyn said. "I'm going to die anyway."

"The hell you are."

Kelley grabbed Gwyn's arm and wrapped it around his broad shoulders. He had to practically carry the other man in one arm while holding his flaming sword in the opposite hand. Gwyn's head lolled on his neck. He began to mutter deliriously.

How long he staggered through the labyrinth of passages Kelley could not have told. The guiding breeze had been lost when they dashed into the side passage to escape the scorpions. The only measure of time was the consuming flame of the torch. Kelley had used up his own cloak and more than half of Gwyn's when he heard the murmur of male voices chanting in the distant darkness. So desperate was he for some guide through the endless nightmare world beneath the ground that he nearly cried out with joy.

"Gwyn, do you hear that? Gwyn?"

He shook the mariner, and noticed the gland beneath his armpit was swollen to the size of an orange. Gwyn forced his eyes partway open.

"I hear," he mumbled. "Voices."

Kelley knew he rushed to his own destruction. The chanting voices could only belong to the Sons of Coronzon, who were unlikely to look with favor upon intruders at the best of times. Even so, he hurried his steps, terrified that the chanting would cease and leave him forever lost in this maze of tunnels and blind passages that seemed to shift and change with its own perverse life. He could not bear the thought of silence. Even his purpose for entering the fortress, the rescue of Joanna and the other women, was submerged by his overmastering need to escape from the labyrinth, which twisted like the black gullet of some vast, writhing dragon. Had it not been for the weight of Gwyn on his arm, he would have run heedlessly toward the chanters to slay as many as he could before they cut him down.

The sound grew stronger. Kelley felt it vibrate in his chest and in the stones under his feet. He stopped before a closed door. The chant came from somewhere on the other side. Cautiously, he opened it. The sonorous music of many voices rolled over him. Light flooded through the opening along with the sound. Kelley peered through the door and saw that the corridor on the other side was illuminated at intervals by oil lamps that hung on chains from its roof. After the dim, flickering glow of his crude torch the light blinded him.

He smothered the rag on the tip of his rapier beneath his boot and slid it off the blackened blade. In the clear light from the lamps he was able to assess the condition of Peter Gwyn. The mariner's lean face appeared puffy. His lips were cracked and dry. His left leg looked like the black barrel of a cannon beneath his hose. Somehow Gwyn managed to balance on his feet even though his head hung on his chest.

"Leave me," Gwyn whispered huskily. "Going to die anyway. Save yourself."

"You're not dead yet," Kelley said as he helped Gwyn limp along the lighted corridor. "I'll leave you when you stop breathing, not before."

The chant possessed a mesmerizing quality. It vibrated throughout Kelley's body as though his chest were a hollow drum. He found his lips echoing the chant automatically and had to force himself to remain silent. Even so, it continued to voice itself within his mind. He recognized the language as Enochian, but could distinguish no actual words. The chant sounded as if it were composed of random Enochian letters grouped into pronounceable sets. These were repeated in cycles that evolved as new sets of letters were added to the chant and old sets dropped.

Kelley wished Dee could hear it. Dee might be able to analyze the chant and make sense out of its structure. To Kelley it remained only a kind of savage music that spurred his heart and sent his blood racing. He noted with surprise the stiff ache of his erection and wondered how his body could choose so ill-opportune a moment to become aroused.

The air in the midst of the corridor before him shimmered like the aurora borealis. He hesitated before the glowing curtain, but the lure of the chant was too strong to resist. Kelley pressed through the insubstantial barrier and felt a tingle on his skin. It reminded him of the occult barrier on the lower stair of Rabbi Loew's house, but the sensation was completely different. Beyond it the corridor glowed with golden light reflected off sculptured panels of gold leaf set into the ceiling. The walls and floor were lined with pink marble. Costly tapestries adorned the walls and rugs covered the floor. Lamps of the finest leaded crystal replaced those of brass. It was a hallway such as might be expected in the palace of a Byzantine potentate.

The chant reverberated all around them as they neared the open double doors at the end of the gilded corridor. Still there was no sight of any of the keepers of the fortress. Kelley knew this luck would never last. He paused at the door before passing through, thinking himself ready for any sight he might see in the lofty chamber that lay beyond. His body mocked his expectations. He found himself paralyzed with horror at the bizarre tableau that spread itself before his eyes.

He stood on a circular balcony that wrapped completely around a vast domed amphitheater a hundred feet across and twice that in height. Light shone through crystal panes in the dome and illuminated the colorful tiled floor with the brightness of day. It could not have been natural, since the dome was scores of fathoms beneath the mountain. Nearly a hundred hooded men who wore the long black robes of monks and carried thick black candles alight in their clasped hands chanted the monotonous but compelling Enochian mantra.

As they vibrated the syllables deep in their chests they walked in a complex, interweaving circular pattern, some moving sunwise while others paced widdershins, pivoting on their heels and spinning in opposite directions as they passed each other, their rhythmic breaths fluttering the flames of their candles. Kelley observed that they moved in three human chains, which were interwoven like the braided strands of a rope around the ring of black stone pillars that supported the balcony.

He remembered a story he had heard once from a traveling Turk concerning the strange cult of the spinning dervishes, whose complex ritual dance imitated the interlocked motion of the planets in their heavenly spheres. The dance of the dervishes must resemble what he saw below, Kelley thought, except that the dance of the Sons of Coronzon had a repellent, reptilian aspect.

"Music, I hear music," Gwyn muttered into Kelley's ear.

Kelley shook the mariner. His head rolled on his neck. He had lapsed into merciful unconsciousness and spoke from his fevered dreams. Reluctant to release him, Kelley held him up by the waist and edged forward, closer to the gilt marble rail of the balcony, so that he could see down into the center of the floor.

Joanna lay on her back, naked, upon a mandorla-shaped slab of black stone. A gag stifled her cries. Chains stretched wide her arms and legs. Jane Dee sat straddling Joanna's hips with her knees spread away from the swollen dome of her own belly. She was also naked. She leaned forward and stared down into Joanna's terror-stricken green eyes with maniacal intensity. A strange smile played over her scarlet-painted lips. Between her hands she held a large silver dagger with a broad blade and a jewel-encrusted hilt. The needle point of the dagger hung poised above Joanna's panting breast.

Thirteen hooded priests of Coronzon stood in a circle around the altar with their hands linked, facing inward. Their robes stood open in front to reveal their erect sexual members. At the head of the lens-shaped altar, outside the circle of priests, another man in a scarlet robe contemplated the interlocked bodies of the two women as if studying a work of art. Before him, a large book lay open atop a pedestal of black stone, its leaves inscribed with silver letters. It glowed like the sun with its own light. As Kelley looked on, the scarlet priest turned a golden page.

With a feeling of hopelessness Kelley recognized the bald head and finely-drawn black eyebrows of Giovanni, whom Dee had called Azoth. As though able to sense his name in Kelley's mind, the bald man turned his frosty gaze upward directly at Kelley and beckoned him.

Kelley turned to escape. The doorway behind him welled forth hooded men armed with daggers. He let the unconscious Peter Gwyn sag to the floor of the balcony and raised his rapier. For a dozen seconds the air filled with singing steel and spattered blood. He killed three and wounded four others before the rest overpowered him and tore the rapier from his grasp.

The silent, hooded Sons stripped Gwyn and Kelley of their weapons and searched them. Kelley cursed himself inwardly when they removed the cipher letter from the girdle of his doublet. He had an instant to wish that he had hidden it outside the keep, or burned the entire letter rather than merely a strip from it.

He was dragged with Gwyn through dark corridors and out onto the open floor of the amphitheater. The dancing priests remained oblivious to their passage through the sinuous, chanting ring of their bodies. With absent attention Kelley noted that they danced around eleven pillars. He remembered Dee telling him that eleven was the number of Lilith, just as thirteen was the number of Coronzon.

Two Sons held Kelley's wrists wide apart. Two more supported Gwyn, who had regained enough of his senses to stand upright. Azoth left the book on its pedestal and approached them. Kelley stared past him at the altar and met the terrified gaze of his wife. When she saw him, she struggled to throw Jane off her hips. The chains that bound her limbs were too tight. Jane rode her undulating body with ease.

Azoth studied Gwyn for a moment with an expression of contempt. The mariner's poisoned leg seemed to amuse him. He prodded the swollen thigh lightly. Gwyn shrieked in a thin voice and fainted. The hooded men on either side continued to hold him up under the shoulders. Azoth moved on to Kelley. His powerful, naked face bore an expression of supreme happiness.

One of the Sons handed him the cipher letter. He examined it briefly.

"We seem to keep bumping into each other," he told Kelley. "First at the Rose Theater in London. Then at Kozminsky's country estate. And now you come to visit me at my home. I'm flattered."

Kelly glanced at the left palm of the other man and saw a scar in the shape of a bent solar cross, just as Thomas Beecher had described.

Azoth turned the letter in his hands and held it up to Kelley. "Tell me, where is the rest of it? Some of the text is missing."

Kelley grinned, showing Azoth his barred teeth.

"Where you'll never find it."

Azoth regarded him for several moments. He folded the letter and put it into a pocket of his scarlet robe.

"Once our business here is concluded, I'll ask you that question again. You will be eager to answer, I assure you."

Kelley glared at him. He longed to gouge out those mocking, frosty gray eyes with his thumbnails.

"It is a matter of small importance," continued Azoth. "Still, it will infuriate Aquaviva to learn that his hated illegitimate brother, whom he cast out of the Society of Jesus for necromancy, has obtained the information he so desperately sought for himself."

"The Black Pope is your brother?" Kelley struggled to comprehend this revelation. It explained Azoth's interest in the cipher document.

"When our father died, he took my place as head of our family, even though I was the elder son. I let him do so because I loved him. For years I tried to please him. I even joined the Society to be near him. But he always thought himself my superior due to the taint of my birth. When I was accused of necromancy, he seized the opportunity to utterly disown me. I vowed that I would destroy him."

The gaze of the bald man drifted upward over Kelley's head. He stared at some infinitely distant vista that was invisible to the rest of mankind. Kelley held his tongue. He recognized madness when he saw it.

"Strange, isn't it?" Azoth told him. "That the half-brother of the second most powerful man in Christendom is fated to be the agent for its final downfall. I'm sure my dear brother will appreciate the irony—before he dies."

The hatred in Azoth's voice as he spoke of Aquaviva was almost palpable. He blinked and appeared to recollect himself with difficulty.

"I'm glad you could be here to witness the fulfillment of my vow," Azoth said. "It will be a sight such as no man has seen since Adam. When the Lilith formula is complete, Jane Dee will cut open the belly of your wife and give birth to a male child upon her steaming entrails. The life force in your wife's blood will provide the nourishing energy needed if the child is to survive its premature issue. Then Lilith will manifest and prepare the child to become the physical vessel for her dark lord, Coronzon, the Antichrist foretold by ancient prophecy. It is a great honor.

If John Dee were not such a fool he would welcome it, but he clings to the craven Christian faith like an intellectual coward. Once Mother Lilith has mated with her consort Coronzon upon the spine of the earth, a new aeon will dawn. Those who dwell in shadow will rule those who dwell in light. Old debts will be paid, I promise you."

The chant rose to a fever pitch. The very air shimmered with sexual excitement. Its odor hung thick as musk. Even Kelley was not immune from the charged atmosphere that signaled the approach of Lilith, the goddess of all lust. His yard stood stiff as an iron rod. He cursed the blind compliance of his flesh but had no more control over his arousal than a rutting stag. He watched the last golden leaf of the transfigured Book of Lilith turn of its own accord as if by some unfelt breeze.

The space under the glowing crystal dome darkened. A shadow began to form high over the altar. It twisted and squirmed like a nest of serpents, with each passing moment denser and more visible. Its obscene outline defied comprehension, but Kelley sensed the concentrated wickedness and ancient awareness of the thing.

Abruptly, with the mental force of a thunderclap, the chant ceased. The revolving dancers turned inward as though moved by a single mind and waited in the breathless hush. At the same time the thirteen priests around the altar surged inward and raised their linked hands high overhead. They cried out as their seed spurted across the naked bodies of the joined women. Kelley felt his own climax shake him to the bone and cursed his weakness. Azoth observed the thought in his eyes and pointed toward the altar.

"Your wife's destiny is fulfilled, as it was ordained from the beginning of time. Watch."

The possessed Jane Dee raised the great dagger between both her hands for the killing stroke. Hot tears of frustration blurred Kelley's eyes.

"Joanna, forgive me," he cried. "I love you."

Azoth struck him across the mouth as though he had spoken blasphemy. Joanna struggled against the taut chains that held her spread-eagled on the stone. Her rolling green eyes met his tortured gaze. Then they turned upward, to fix upon the point of the poised dagger.

"Now," Azoth roared. "Strike now!"

FORTY-EIGHT

Dee stared in horror as his wife raised the knife. Heedless of his own safety, he ran into the vast domed chamber.

"Jane!"

Her head snapped around at the sound of his voice. Elemental lust flashed from her brown eyes. Dee's heart grew cold. It was not the face of the woman he loved.

Behind him the Jewish militia surged into the amphitheater. The Sons of Coronzon fell back in confusion, their daggers drawn. For a moment nothing stirred except the writhing mass that continued to coalesce in the air high over the altar.

Kelley lashed out with his heel at the ribs of the man who held his left arm. The blow doubled his captor into a heap on the floor. The alchemist sent his fist crashing into the side of the head of the man on his right. Without a glance at Azoth, he leapt onto the altar and twisted the dagger out of Jane's hand. She fought him with her teeth and nails, but even possessed was no match for his strength.

"Kill them!" Azoth shrieked.

He fell back as his disciples surged forward against the Jews. The hooded Sons were more numerous but possessed only daggers for weapons, whereas the militia attacked them with pistols, bows, and swords. The golem waded into the fury and lashed out this way and that with machine-like precision. Every blow it struck broke bone and ruptured flesh.

The one-sided battle would soon have ended in the Jews' favor had not the pullulating monstrosity in the air over the altar sent down a cascade of barbed tentacles. Like the stinging filaments of the hydra, the deadly poison in their barbs paralyzed whoever they touched and made them easy prey for the blood-drenched daggers of the Sons. The tentacles avoided the hooded men with uncanny deftness. The swords and knives of the Jews made no impression upon them. Only the golem was impervious to their insidious caresses. It want on killing.

His curses inaudible amid the clashing din, Kelley slashed at the sinuous serpent arms with the ritual silver dagger while he pinned down the writhing Jane Dee across the naked body of his terrified wife. The unholy weapon cut through the venomous tentacles. As the tips fell away, they dissolved into mist before striking the floor. The black ichor that spattered from the bleeding ends burned like fire against his bare skin but did no other harm.

A screaming priest ran at him with dagger raised. Kelley thrust the point of his silver blade into the man's open mouth and through the back of his throat. He dropped dead, his spinal cord severed.

Avoiding the battle, John Dee worked his way toward the mandorla altar. One of the Sons, already dying from a gaping slash that had exposed his bleeding bowels, grabbed Dee around the knees and tried to gnaw at Dee's genitals. In the fight his hood had been torn away. Cringing with disgust, Dee forced himself to put his hand against the hideous skull-face and force it back until he could cut his attacker's throat with his rapier.

He caught Kelley's rolling eye, red with bloodlust, but it was impossible to speak in the bedlam. Trusting that the alchemist would guard his back, Dee bent over the chain that held Joanna's left arm and tried to open it. The shackles were not locked into place, but the mechanism was a cunning design.

Azoth worked himself around the battle toward the black pedestal on which the book rested. Perceiving his plan, Rabbi Loew approached the pedestal from the other side while Rabbi Katz fought to open a path for his master. The Jew was a step too late. Azoth snatched up the book and held it like a shield across his breast.

"I see that you brought your slave with you," he shouted in exultation. "I also have my instrument. Let us see which is stronger."

He murmured an evocation. The air over the head of the golem began to swirl with black sparks. It thickened into a vortex and rotated itself through space to form a tight whirlwind of shadow. The golem sensed the attack. It struck futile blows at the yielding body of the Watcher. It was the same as fighting smoke. The Watcher came together again a moment after the golem's flailing arms pierced it.

The Watcher extended itself into a tight, spinning axle and abruptly drove itself into the top of the golem's skull. It disappeared into the body of the golem. The creature bellowed, its bull-like cry rising above the clash of blades and the clamor of voices. It shuddered, and stood motionless for several heartbeats. Those near the golem shrank back as it turned and approached Rabbi Loew with slow steps.

Its eyes were no longer soulless. A terrible, exultant intelligence stared out of them. A smile of delight twisted its lips. It spread its arms before Azoth and bowed with irony.

"At last I have a physical vessel," it said in a deep, ringing voice. "No thanks to you, my human master."

Azoth realized then the significance of what had occurred. He laughed at Loew.

"Your creation had no soul. It was an empty vessel for my slave to fill. Now my airy elemental controls it."

"Yosef, stop. I command you," Loew said to the creature.

It merely laughed and stepped between the two men.

"Kill him," Azoth cried. "Kill the Jew."

"You cannot command me. No man can ever command me again."

With lightning quickness it reached out and grabbed Azoth by the throat in its left hand. His frosted gray eyes widened in surprise. A gurgling noise escaped from his gaping mouth. The golem lifted him slowly into the air until the toes of his leather sandals hung twitching above the marble floor. The book dropped from his limp arms.

"How I hate you, my master," the golem said with contempt. "For years I have hated you. All your promises were lies."

"Ancient Mother, help me," Azoth gurgled.

"She doesn't care about you," the golem told him, laughing at the credulity of the man. "You have served your purpose. Look above. She's come forth. You are no more than a speck of dust under her foot. And mine."

Azoth struck and clawed at the fingers and arms of the creature. It noticed the blows no more than a stone feels the fall of a leaf. Raising the man higher, it tightened its grasp with infinite slowness, savoring every moment. Azoth's eyes bulged from his head. Blood spurted from his ears and nose. His face shimmered and dissolved. In its place was the hairless, skull-like visage of a disciple of

Coronzon. The bones in Azoth's neck began to crack one after another. Blood streamed between the golem's relentless fingers. Azoth's body shivered once in its death throes, and hung limp.

When Azoth died, the glamour he had cast over the amphitheater ceased. The dome became dark save for the dim light from the lamps and the lurid glow emanating from the formless, pulsating mass. The gold leaf vanished from the walls. The lamps changed from crystal to tarnished brass, and the floor and columns from marble to common black stone. Even the Book of Lilith reverted to its plain, unimpressive former appearance.

The golem reached up with its other hand and sank its fingers deep into Azoth's blind, dead eyes. It gripped his face and with a twisting motion tore his head away from his neck. Releasing his decapitated corpse, it extended the bloody head to Loew.

"A last gift from your faithful servant," it said to the Jew.

The head fell to the floor and rolled against Loew's leg.

"You have no right to the body of Yosef," Loew told the spirit. "I command you to leave it at once."

One of the questing tentacles of the bloated Mother-thing in the air overhead lashed down toward the rabbi's unprotected neck. The golem reached out and caught it with a deft hand. It held the barbed tip before Loew's grim face.

"Don't you understand yet? You can't command me. I am free to go wherever and do whatever I desire." It rolled its black eyes in delight. "I think I will walk the earth for a time. You humans amuse me."

With casual ease it crushed the tentacle and broke it off. The end turned to a gray mist. Rabbi Katz ran forward and fired his wheel-lock pistol directly into the face of the creature. The ball entered its cheek under its eye. After a moment it popped out and the entry wound healed itself. The golem knocked the pistol from Katz's hand and picked him up to dash him against the stone dais.

Rabbi Loew pointed at the golem and spoke a single word of command in Hebrew. The golem shuddered and dropped Katz. It stared at Loew with incomprehension.

"Why?" it said. "I would not have hurt you."

"You have no right," Loew repeated. "Yosef was a servant of the Holy One."

The skin of the golem began to darken. It body stiffened and ceased to move. In moments it reverted to the red clay from which it had been formed. Slowly it tipped forward onto its face and shattered into a dozen large pieces. Black smoke boiled up from the fragments in an expanding cloud and vanished.

At the altar Dee unfastened the last of Joanna's chains and set about untying the gag from her mouth while Kelley defended his back from the seeking tentacles of the floating pink mass. During the few brief minutes of battle it had become a completely solid blob of flesh that rippled and pulsed with unnatural vitality. Eyes formed all over its irregular surface and stared down at the struggling humans in fury.

The Jews and Sons of Coronzon no longer warred against each other. Both sides fought shoulder to shoulder to avoid the lashing barbs of the tentacles, which had ceased to discriminate between them. The monster in the dome guarded the entrances to the amphitheater jealously and refused to let them escape. It might easily have destroyed them all in a matter of moments, but seemed to take pleasure in slaying them one by one while the others scrambled like mice in a trap.

Kelley caught Jane's wrists and wrenched her hands behind her back to prevent her from striking her pregnant belly with her fists. Spittle foamed from her writhing lips. She cursed him with an endless stream of obscenities and spat at his face.

"Here, hold her," Kelley barked at Dee.

He thrust Jane into Dee's arms and helped the sobbing Joanna to her feet. They embraced in the midst of the chaos.

"Thank Jesu you're safe," he murmured into her ear. "I feared I'd lost you forever."

"I'm not hurt," she said, struggling to control her sobs. "But poor Jane is mad."

Dee found it taxed his strength to the limit to restrain his wife. He caught the eye of Rabbi Katz, who came to help him.

"Don't let her injure herself," Dee told him. "She's possessed."

"Jesu, what now?" Kelley cried.

The grotesque, pulsating ball of pink flesh floating in the vault of the dome split down its side with a ripe sound. From the gaping lips of the slot began to issue creatures of nightmare with translucent, watery bodies. Its fecundity appeared endless. In moments the entire air filled with its obscene offspring. They pulled and clawed at the terrified humans but did not yet possess enough solidity to injure them. With each passing second they grew more opaque as they drew substance from the will of Lilith.

"Edward, help me," Dee cried.

Kelley passed the silver dagger to Joanna so that she could defend herself and went to Dee.

"I need to evoke the Enochian angels," Dee told him. "Nothing else will stop these creatures."

Kelley nodded. They locked forearms and stared at each other. Dee began to chant words he had never before dared utter, not even in the guarded chambers of his own mind. They vibrated deeply in his chest. Kelley took up the chant. The rhythmic words cut through the babble of frightened voices. Countless eyes turned in the pink mass and glared down at them. The watery horrors swirled around them and tried to distract their minds.

Loew saw what was happening and called for the attention of his disciples.

"Protect them," he cried, pointing at Dee and Kelley.

The Jews regained a measure of courage and formed a defensive ring, their backs to the joined pair. Joanna stood at the center next to her husband. The Jews fended off the concentrated attack from the tentacles of the Mother-thing with their swords. They could not sever them, but were able to beat them back, at the cost of many lives. With the charged silver dagger, Joanna cut through the venomous ropes that came too close. The Maharal began to chant silently to himself in an effort to add to the potency of Dee's evocation.

Staring into Dee's entranced face, Kelley was the first to see his gray eyes begin to glow with light. Blinding radiance shone from his open mouth, his nostrils, and even his ears. It was as though a living star had ignited within his skull. Kelley felt heat beat against his face. Dee's clothes began to smoke. In moments his arms were hot under the alchemist's touch.

A flame danced above the crown of Dee's skullcap. From it issued a ball of light that shone with the ever-changing iridescence of the rainbow. This drifted toward one of the bloated, watery monsters and entered its body.

The nightmare creature exploded.

Other glowing spheres rose from the dancing flame. They sought out the offspring of Lilith and destroyed them. In minutes all had been erased. The space under the dome danced with a thousand bright spheres. They ringed the pink mass.

"Those are angels?" Rabbi Katz asked in Yiddish.

"They must be," Rabbi Loew said. "Judge them not by how they look, but by what they do."

Lilith had one final transformation. The pink mass split completely apart and spread itself like an opening flower. Upon it sat a woman with her arms wrapped around one knee, her head bowed and hidden beneath her long black hair. She lifted her head and slowly stood upon the fleshy disk that supported her in the air. Her naked body was perfect but five times human stature. With a tranquil expression in her green eyes, she gazed down at the humans beneath her feet.

Dee completed the evocation. The flame flickered out over the crown of his skull, and the light streaming from the orifices of his head dimmed and vanished. Kelley released his arms. They had done all they could. Now they must wait for the judgement of Lilith. He saw that all the Sons of Coronzon lay dead, along with many of the Jews. Only those still clustered around them in a defensive ring had survived the final onslaught of the tentacles.

An expression of scorn twisted the perfect features of the goddess. With a disdainful finality she raised her right hand. The white stone in her diadem blazed forth with terrifying brilliance. Kelley felt his heart quake with a fear so primal he could not even begin to control it. The same terror had gripped the hearts of humans a hundred thousand years before when they had cowered in caves and stared at the shapes in the outer darkness.

The sparkling ring of rainbow spheres suddenly drew
together and took on the outline of a human form. In
moments they coalesced into a goddess clothed in white
who was the same stature as Lilith in her incarnation.
Where Lilith was dark, this goddess was golden. Where
Lilith frowned, the other smiled. Yet in every detail they
were the mirror image of one another.

"Jesu, where did this one come from?" Kelley murmured in the sudden hush.

"This must be Madimi's Mother," Dee whispered.

Lilith stared at her double in wonder. She raised a
curious hand to explore the cheek of the other spirit.
Simultaneously, the golden-haired goddess touched the
cheek of her dark sister. Smiling, Lilith reached out to
embrace the other. Instead she fastened her hands around
the throat of the golden spirit. The Enochian goddess
gripped the throat of the Ancient One. They struggled,
equally matched. The ground beneath them rumbled and
shook. Joanna screamed in terror.

"Neither can prevail," Dee shouted to Kelley over the
rumble. "They are the light and dark faces of the moon."

Kelley understood. Dodging a stone from the crumbling dome, he leaped to Joanna and took the silver dagger
out of her hand, then ran to the low black pedestal. It had
to be around here somewhere, he thought. For several seconds he searched the trembling floor with mounting
despair. Then he began to turn the fallen bodies. Under the
headless corpse of Azoth he found the book, once more
returned to its modest, unimpressive earthly appearance.

A small piece of stone struck him a glancing blow on
the shoulder and knocked him off his feet. He blinked
and looked upward. The two mirror-goddesses appeared
to be waltzing in a mutual embrace. It might be true that

neither could prevail over the other, but together they could destroy the catacombs and anything that lived within their passages.

None of the Jews could keep his feet. They rolled and crawled over the shaking floor. Kelley saw with relief that Rabbi Katz had maintained a grim hold on the struggling Jane Dee. He pushed himself upright against the black pedestal and set the book on its rounded cap. With both hands he drove the point of the silver dagger through the book and into the stone beneath.

The book ignited with a single blinding flash and burned to ashes in seconds. Kelley raised his eyes to the dome in time to see the black goddess and the white goddess dissolve together into a mutual embrace. The ground stilled. After the screams and the grinding rumble and crack of stone, the silence deafened him.

"We'd better get out of here before the whole place falls in on us," Kelley said to Dee.

Dee picked himself off the floor and nodded with a dazed expression. He gazed around at the carnage of corpses, the fallen stones and cracked columns, the fragments of the golem. It was difficult to comprehend the events of the night. Their significance overwhelmed him and left him numb. His gaze fell on Rabbi Katz, who sat on the floor cradling Jane Dee's head in his lap.

The naked thighs of his wife were stained with streaks of blood. A scarlet pool spread over the stones of the floor between her legs. In it lay the pathetic body of a premature foetus, quite dead.

"Jane!"

Dee ran over and took the face of his wife between his hands. Her cheeks felt cold to the touch. With his thumb and forefinger he parted her eyelids in turn. Her eyes rolled vacantly upward. She barely breathed.

"What happened?" Dee demanded.

"She kept striking her belly with her fist," Katz said, his face a mask of tragedy as he stared at Dee. "I tried to stop her, but she was too strong."

"When the ground stopped shaking, she just collapsed," Loew told him.

Kelley pulled the cloak from a dead Jew and wrapped it around Joanna's shaking shoulders. They approached behind the kneeling Dee.

"Will she be all right?" Joanna asked.

Dee looked up at her with anguish. He shook his head.

"The spirit of Lilith that possessed her is gone, but it left her empty. She has no soul."

FORTY-NINE

The library at Loew's house held the breathless hush of a mortuary. John Dee sat at a writing desk beneath the tall windows, a parchment sheet, goose-quill pen, and silver inkwell in front of him. His chin cupped on his left hand, he stared through the rippled glass at the blue sky. From time to time he dipped the pen into the ink and scratched a few words.

Edward Kelley lay on the upholstered settee by the unlit fireplace at the other end of the long room. He read from a fat little worm-eaten volume in Latin. Other books lay piled on the nearby table, along with a cold glass of black coffee and a half-eaten currant bun. The scratch of Dee's pen made him grit his teeth.

He snapped the book shut and sat up.

"All this inaction is driving me mad."

Dee glanced at him absently.

"I thought you intended to discover the secret of the red powder."

"I won't learn it from these," Kelley complained bitterly of the pile of books. "All the really valuable texts are in the Rabbi's private library, under lock and key."

"Give up this notion of making gold, Edward," Dee advised. "If you succeed it will bring nothing but trouble."

"That's a risk I'm willing to run."

They had carried on this same conversation numerous times during their five years together. Both knew it had no satisfactory conclusion.

A week had passed since their clandestine return to Prague. The Jewish militia had been able to smuggle their weapons and the gentiles through the gates under the noses of Rudolph's soldiers. Although the search for the English murderer of Count Niebuhr was losing its urgency as day after day passed with no discovery, it would still be madness for Kelley to show his distinctive face outside the ghetto, or even outside Loew's house. Safe arrangements to depart from Bohemia could not be made for at least another week, perhaps longer. Kelley knew this well enough, but the need to hide chaffed at his dignity.

"How's Peter doing?"

"The last time I looked into his room, he was joking while Esther fed him soup," Dee murmured as he scratched another word. "Why don't you sit with him for a while and cheer him up?" And leave me to work in peace, he added in his own mind.

"I'm glad he won't lose the leg. Gwyn's too good a man to be a cripple for the rest of his life."

"Loss of a limb is not uncommon for English seamen. It doesn't turn a good man into a bad one."

"You know my meaning," Kelley grumbled. "What the devil are you scratching over?"

"I'm drafting my report to the Queen about the cipher document."

"Damn Azoth," Kelley said. "If I had only left that cursed letter with the horses you would still have it to decipher."

"I've already deciphered it," Dee murmured. "What do you think I've been working on for the past seven days?"

"A report to the Queen, you said. How can you decipher a letter that was torn into two pieces, and one of them burned?"

Dee held up the bloodstained fragment he had rescued from Azoth's corpse.

"My memory may not be as keen as it once was, but it's sharp enough to preserve the text of a brief letter twice read. I gathered its meaning when I scanned it over the first time in the abandoned farmhouse. When I read it at Kozminsky's estate I was able to memorize it. I've included the full text of the letter, along with the deciphered message from Philip of Spain to Pope Sixtus, in my report to Elizabeth."

"What does the cipher message say?" Kelley asked.

Dee leafed through a pile of parchment sheets and drew one out. Interested in spite of himself, Kelley went over and stood behind Dee's shoulder where he could examine the transcript while Dee read its contents aloud.

Philip II of Spain sends greetings to Pope Sixtus V at Rome. Holy Father, you will by this time have received word concerning the lawless and unprovoked attack launched against our Armada by the English Dragon. Many ships were lost. Our shipbuilders inform us that it will require at least a full year to replace the tonnage burned on that evil day. It is not our intention to strike against the foe with a dull sword, but rather with one decisive stroke to decapitate her. Therefore I write to inform you that our holy expedition will not depart from Spanish waters until middle May of next year. This additional period will enable our forces in the Netherlands to consolidate themselves. Then we will light ample fires of our own, both on the sea and on the

*land, and roast the English Drake on a spit before
the gates of his bastard queen. Pray for us, Father,
for our cause is just. Farewell.*

"May," Kelley murmured, scanning the page. "Sooner
than I expected."

"Philip must wait the winter in any case," Dee said.
"It's clear he doesn't intend to waste the spring."

"The Queen will be delighted. She has her cipher
message and her gold."

"Most of her gold," Dee reminded him.

Loew came into the library with a smile creasing his
wrinkled face.

"Why are you so happy, my friend?" Dee asked.

"I just spoke to Yitzhaq," Loew said. "This morning
Esther let him hold her in his arms and kiss her. She
grows better every day. Time will heal her wounds, I'm
sure of it."

"I'm glad," Dee said softly.

The smile melted from Loew's face. He studied his
friend's distant gray eyes with sympathy.

"What of Jane?" he asked. "Has there been any
change?"

Dee shook his head.

"I'm going to go and sit with her for awhile, if you
will excuse me."

"Do you want me to come with you?" Kelley murmured, laying a gentle hand on his arm.

"No. I'd like to be alone with her."

Dee left the library and climbed with slow steps to the
third level of the house, where his wife lay entranced
behind the closed door of their bedroom.

Dread smothered his heart. Each time he looked at
Jane he prayed for some improvement in her condition,

however slight, but she was always the same. Since her miscarriage in the catacombs under the fortress of Coronzon, she had not opened her eyes. Dee could barely summon enough courage to gaze upon her bloodless face. Thank Jesu for Joanna. She hardly left Jane's bedside. She forced broth between her lips, gave her sips of water, and cleaned her bedpan without complaint.

Since returning from the Black Mountain, Joanna had scarcely drunk a glass of port. Edward found time to talk with her, now that she no longer mocked and baited him. His tone was mild, his touch gentle. For the first time in almost a year, an amorous light kindled in his dark eyes when his gaze met the glance of his wife. Dee had no knowledge of what passed between them in the privacy of their bedchamber, but at least domestic civility had been restored.

Edward's marriage had always been stormy, but Dee had never doubted his love for Joanna, nor her love for Edward. For both their sakes he hoped their passion had been rekindled. Only time would tell.

He passed Peter Gwyn's room. The mariner had been placed in the bed vacated by the dead Bourinot, whose corpse Loew had contrived to bury in the Jewish cemetery within the ghetto. Animated conversation filtered through the panels. Dee smiled weakly when he recognized Gwyn's rough laughter. The door opened. Esther Katz came out with an empty bowl of soup on a tray. She shut the door behind her.

"How is he?" Dee murmured.

"Stronger," she whispered. "The blackness has left his thigh and is fading from his calf. He can bend his knee again."

"I'm delighted for him." The words tasted bitter on Dee's tongue. Everyone, it seemed, was well except his beloved Jane.

He caught Esther's arm as she started to pass. She turned to him with surprise.

"Your husband loves you with a deep passion," he told her.

"I know. It has been difficult for me. I still feel so much shame."

"When he comes to you tonight, receive him," Dee said gruffly.

She blushed and dropped her eyes. These were not matters to discuss with a devout Jewess.

"I will try. It's very hard. When I close my eyes I still see those horrible masks."

"Do it. Time is too short to waste on hesitation and regret. Yitzhaq will understand, whatever happens. He's a good man."

She nodded and met his gaze with difficulty.

"I will do as you say. You are right. It is foolish to cling to the past, no matter whether it is good or bad. I will try to be strong."

Dee watched her walk away from him toward the stairs, and cursed himself for interfering. It was none of his business how soon Esther Katz received her husband. He had spoken out of frustration over his own situation. For all his pretense of philosophy, he could not bear even to think about losing Jane.

He knocked on her door and entered softly. Joanna sat in a wooden chair beside the bed. A pan of water and several damp cloths rested on the nearby table. Joanna nodded to Dee. She took a cloth from Jane's forehead and wrung it out over the bowl.

"How is she today?"

"Not good," Joanna said, biting her lower lip. "She spat up the broth I gave her. I'm afraid she's losing weight."

Dee noted Joanna's disordered red hair and the dark circles under her eyes. He doubted she had slept more than four hours a night while tending Jane. It was her self-imposed penance for leaving the house and causing Jane to be abducted. She would not allow anyone else to take her place, not even Dee.

"This wasn't your fault," he said. "The Sons of Coronzon manipulated your mind. They tricked you into leaving the house."

She shook her head.

"I left out of pride and jealousy. I was drunk and blinded by anger. This is God's punishment for my sins."

"Nonsense. You're punishing yourself."

Joanna used a damp cloth to pat away flecks of white froth from the corners of Jane's mouth. Dee looked at his wife's face and saw her eyes flutter from side to side beneath the lids. He wondered if she dreamed.

"Leave me with her for a few hours. You get some sleep."

"No, I'll stay. You may need my help."

"Leave us," Dee snapped.

His nerves were frayed to the breaking point. He realized it was grossly unfair to punish Joanna.

"Leave us," he said more softly. "I want to be alone with my wife."

Silently Joanna gathered up the cloths and carried the bowl out of the room. She closed the door behind her.

Dee sat in the chair looking at his wife's face, willing her eyes to open, her lips to speak. He knelt on the floor beside the bed and took her hand between his to pray. He

continued for many minutes, scarcely aware of what he
said in the depth of his grief. Tears fell from his cheeks
onto Jane's cool, lifeless fingers. He pressed her hand to
his lips and sobbed. All the emotion contained for days
within his heart spilled out in a torrent. He begged God
for mercy and pleaded and cursed His obstinacy all in a
single breath.

Utterly spent, at last he forced himself painfully to his
feet. His knees ached. In a kind of trance he went around
the bed and lay down on it beside his wife, his head close
to hers. He took her hand in his hand. Closing his eyes,
he fell into a troubled sleep.

Somewhere in the dark Jane called his name. Dee
stumbled blindly toward the voiceless sound. This place
felt familiar. Memory darted like a silver fish into the
depths of his unconscious when he tried to catch it. His
heart ached with mingled love and sorrow.

"Jane, where are you?"

He saw her lying in the far distance and ran toward
her with slow, gliding steps across the polished midnight
surface of an endless frozen lake. Jane lay on her back
upon a raised mandorla altar, her hands folded across her
breast as though in death. She was clothed in a simple
shift of unbleached linen. Her feet were bare. This, too,
was familiar in some strange way.

As he approached, he slowed his steps.

"Jane, what's wrong? Why don't you answer me?"

Her hands and face glowed with the whiteness of
newly fallen snow. No blush of color warmed her lips. No
sigh of breath caused her breasts to rise and fall. A terrible
suspicion gathered in Dee's heart.

He began to run toward her. The polished black ice
slid beneath his boots. The nearer he drew to his wife, the
slipperier it grew. It was as if he tried to ascend an icy

slope that grew steeper with each step. When at last he drew almost close enough to touch her reclining body, the ice seemed to rear up in some inexplicable way into an invisible wall that barred his passage. He threw his body against it and slid down with agonizing frustration. He tried crawling up it on his hands and knees. It was no use. Whatever he did, the unseen barrier resisted his efforts.

Jane's angelic face bore an expression of profound sorrow.

"I'll find a way to reach you, Jane. I won't give up."

He cursed and threw himself at the icy wall. As before, he slipped down to his knees with his cheek against the barrier. Tears of bitter frustration welled in his eyes. It seemed hopeless.

"No!" Dee leapt to his feet. "I won't lose you."

He struck the wall with his clenched fist. Deep beneath his feet he felt a distant echo.

A little golden-haired girl in a green dress appeared at his side.

"Take my hand," the girl said, smiling.

At first Dee stared at her without comprehension.

"Madimi?"

"Hurry, take my hand. She's slipping away from you."

He slid his tapered fingers into the small hand of the spirit. She led him in a direction opposite the altar where Jane lay. Dee struggled to detach his hand, but the grasp of the spirit was too strong.

"We're going the wrong way," he cried.

"No we're not, silly. She's over here. That was only her reflection you were chasing. No wonder you couldn't reach her."

He looked frantically back over his shoulder. Already Jane was out of sight. He allowed the spirit to lead him blindly forward, his heart empty of hope and expectation.

"There she is. I told you."

In the distance Dee made out a woman lying upon a lens-shaped slab of black stone. Her face was turned from him. Strands of her long black hair covered her cheek. He approached hesitantly, apprehensive of what he might see when she turned to face him. At last he stood within touching distance of the woman. She did not move.

"What should I do now?" Dee asked the spirit.

Madimi laughed at his ignorance.

"Kiss her, silly man."

Dee brushed the hair from the face of the woman on the stone and saw that it was Jane. Her eyes were closed. He leaned down and kissed her marble brow. As he did so, his anguished heart overflowed with love.

Dee opened his eyes and discovered they were wet with tears. Without haste he turned his face on the pillow toward his wife. He was not surprised to see Jane watching him. They both smiled at the same moment.

"I knew you'd find me," she murmured.

"Dearest Jane," he said as he kissed her again, this time upon her warm lips.

author's note

John Dee is arguably the most fascinating figure of the Elizabethan Age. A brilliant mathematician, cartographer, geographer, and astronomer, he also drew up astrological charts, studied alchemy, and practiced ritual magic. Along with a handful of other intellectual giants of the Renaissance, Dee cast his shadow across the entire face of Europe, standing with one foot upon the deep foundation of the occult philosophy of the past and the other upon the rising edifice of the new science of the future.

Dee played a significant role in encouraging the colonial expansionism of England during the reign of Elizabeth. Explorers such as Drake and Frobisher consulted his charts when seeking routes to the New World, and benefited from his improvements to the instruments of navigation. Dee wrote a learned treatise in which he sought to justify Elizabeth's legal claim to lands in the Americas in the face of Spain's prior foothold. He advocated the expansion of the English navy. It was Dee who coined the term "British Empire."

He also proposed a system to amend the calendar, which was rejected as too disruptive, and sought to found a national library for the purpose of preserving the precious manuscripts scattered far and wide by the destruction of the Catholic monasteries under Henry VIII. When the library was deemed too costly, Dee expended his own personal fortune of 3000 pounds (about one quarter of a million dollars in today's money) in acquiring books and manuscripts. Before its tragic destruction, his library was the greatest in England.

There is good reason to believe that, while on his many journeys to the Continent, Dee acted as an espionage agent for the English crown, gathering information of a strategic nature and passing on political secrets in the form of letter ciphers. He was proficient in many languages, including Greek, and an expert cryptographer. One of Dee's modern biographers, Richard Deacon, writes that in Germany during the seventeenth century it was widely accepted that Dee was an English secret agent who carried out his espionage work by means of magical communications.[1]

There is also reason to suspect that he belonged to a Rosicrucian society, or perhaps was the head of such a society, which probably had its genesis in Dee's university years. Although the term "Rosicrucian" did not come into use until around the time of Dee's death, there almost certainly existed at a much earlier date occult organizations under various names devoted, like the Rosicrucians, to the preservation and teaching of the Hermetic wisdom of the ancient world. After leaving Cambridge, he traveled to many universities in Europe as an itinerant lecturer, where he met with universal acclaim, and perhaps sowed the seeds of his occult fraternity.

It is possible that Elizabeth herself knew about and approved this society, making use of it in her political

---

1. Deacon, Richard. *John Dee: Scientist, Geographer, Astrologer and Secret Agent of Elizabeth I* (London: Frederick Muller, 1968), 64.

espionage. At her request, Dee gave her private instructions concerning the esoteric meaning of his enigmatic *Monas Hieroglyphica*. Concerning this episode, Dee later wrote that he had "disclosed some of my secretes to her...and the true purpose of my boke." The Queen often called Dee her "philosopher" with familiar affection, and said of the *Monas* to Dee, "Verilie, deare Doctor, you have contrived a moste economicall and ingeniouslie cunninge communication of your secretes." Deacon concludes from this statement that Dee's book contained a hidden system of cryptography veiled in the form of esoteric symbolism.[2]

For many years Dee pursued a secret communication with a hierarchy of spiritual beings who identified themselves as the same angels who had instructed Enoch in sacred wisdom. Dee employed several professional seers as mediums, through whom he was enabled to talk to these angels and to obtain from the angels their magical teachings. The most successful seer was the alchemist Edward Kelley, who scried the angels in Dee's mysterious crystal globe, which Dee always asserted had been given to him by the angels themselves.

Dee kept a meticulous written record of the years he spent in association with Kelley. Students of Enochian magic will notice that the incidents in Dee's diaries conflict with events recorded in the novel. This could hardly be avoided, so complete is Dee's chronology of his own life. However, it should be remembered that Dee was involved in spying expeditions during this period. Dee always carried these diaries with him on his travels through Europe. It is reasonable to speculate that some

---

2. Ibid., 63.

of the dates in his diaries are deliberate falsifications designed to mislead any investigators as to his true movements and actions.

Occult interests made an excellent blind for Dee's clandestine political doings. The Inquisition despised the sorcery Dee practiced, but did not see in his spirit communications any threat to the crowned heads of the Catholic empire. It is not beyond conjecture that a portion at least of Dee's extensive occult diaries, which record the complex system of Enochian magic, is in reality a system of ciphers devised by Dee for political espionage.

There is historical precedent for this subterfuge. That great German magician and scholar, the Abbot Johannes Trithemius, wrote a work titled *Steganographia* that concerned a system of cryptography that could be used for political espionage, but disguised this cipher manuscript as a system for evoking demonic spirits by ritual magic. John Dee esteemed the *Steganographia* highly. While staying at Antwerp in 1563 he obtained a manuscript of the work and recopied it by hand. Writing to Sir William Cecil in February, 1563, Dee says:

> *I have purchased one book, for which a thousand crowns have been by others offered, and yet it could not be obtained. A book for which many a learned man has long sought and daily yet does seek: whose use is greater than the fame spread about it; the name is not unknown to you. The title is* Steganographia *by John Trithemius, concerning which mention is made in both the editions of his* Polygraphia, *and in his epistles, and in sundry other men's books. A book for your Honour or a Prince, so fit, so needed and commodious in human knowledge that none can be fitter or more worthy.*

This is my own working hypothesis as the author of Dee's occult adventures. If nothing else, it permits the willing suspension of disbelief so necessary to the enjoyment of any piece of fiction. As someone once said, everything in this story is true except the facts. There was a John Dee. He did practice magic with Edward Kelley. These remarkable men did travel across Europe in the company of their wives visiting the homes of kings and sages. Dee acted as a spy for Queen Elizabeth during England's troubles with Spain, and probably did visit the famous Jewish Kabbalist Rabbi Judah Loew while staying in Prague. Very likely he was the head of a secret society similar to that of the Rosicrucians.

As is true of magic itself, this novel is a weave of truth and fantasy, myth and reality. It is not easy to tell where one begins and the other ends. Does it really matter? This is an adventure that Dee and Kelley should have had, and perhaps did have, if not in this reality then in some other. It is not intended to be a historical document, but an entertainment. If it meets with success, I will write other tales of these two remarkable explorers of the unknown.

STAY IN TOUCH...

Llewellyn publishes hundreds of books on your favorite subjects.

On the following pages you will find listed some books now available on related subjects. Your local bookstore stocks most of these and will stock new Llewellyn titles as they become available. We urge your patronage.

Order by Phone

Call toll-free within the U.S. and Canada, 1–800–THE MOON. In Minnesota call (612) 291–1970. We accept Visa, MasterCard, and American Express.

Order by Mail

Send the full price of your order (MN residents add 7% sales tax) in U.S. funds to:

> Llewellyn Worldwide
> P.O. Box 64383, Dept. K-743-9
> St. Paul, MN 55164–0383, U.S.A.

Postage and Handling

- $4.00 for orders $15.00 and under
- $5.00 for orders over $15.00
- No charge for orders over $100.00

We ship UPS in the continental United States. We cannot ship to P.O. boxes. Orders shipped to Alaska, Hawaii, Canada, Mexico, and Puerto Rico will be sent first-class mail.

International orders: Airmail—add freight equal to price of each book to the total price of order, plus $5.00 for each non-book item (audiotapes, etc.). Surface mail—Add $1.00 per item.

Allow 4–6 weeks delivery on all orders. Postage and handling rates subject to change.

Group Discounts

We offer a 20% quantity discount to group leaders or agents. You must order a minimum of 5 copies of the same book to get our special quantity price.

Free Catalog

Get a free copy of our color catalog, *New Worlds of Mind and Spirit*. Subscribe for just $10.00 in the United States and Canada ($20.00 overseas, first class mail). Many bookstores carry *New Worlds*—ask for it!

Lilith
A Novel

D. A. Heeley

The first book of the occult *Darkness and Light* trilogy weaves together authentic magical techniques and teachings of the Hebrew Qabalah with the suspenseful story of the spiritual evolution of Malak, an Adept of the White School of Magick.

Malak and his fellow magicians from the White, Yellow and Black Schools of Magick live on Enya, the lower astral plane of the Qabalistic Tree of Life. Malak's brother and arch-rival, Dethen, is an Adept of the Black School. Dethen plots a coup to destroy the White School completely and begin a reign of terror on Enya—with the hope of destroying the Tree of Life and the world—and a colossal battle between Good and Evil ensues. As the Black Adepts summon the Arch-demon Lilith into Enya, Malak is faced with a terrible choice: should he barter with the ultimate evil to free his wife's soul—even if freeing her condemns other innocent souls forever?

The second half of Lilith takes place 1,000 years later, in feudal Japan. Malak has been reincarnated as Shadrack, who struggles with an inner demon who will not be denied. He must conquer Lilith's evil or there will be a bloody rampage amid the Shogun's Royal Guard.

1-56718-355-7, 256 pp., 6 x 9, softcover $10.00

To order call 1–800–THE MOON
Prices subject to change without notice.